The
STRAWBERRY
FIELDS
of
HEAVEN

The STRAWBERRY FIELDS of HEAVEN

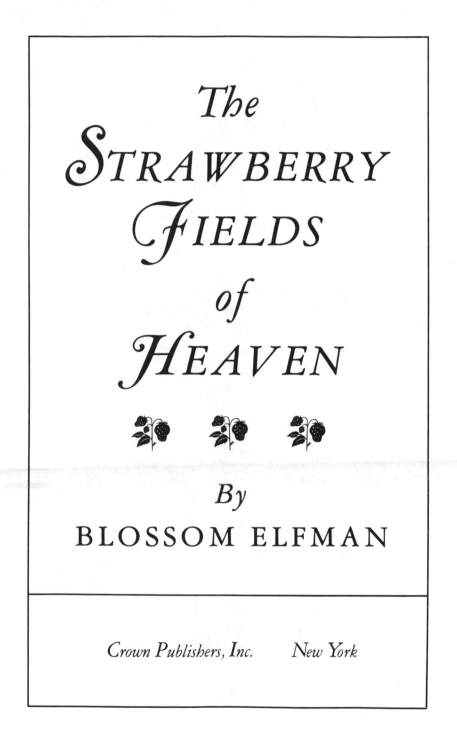

By

BLOSSOM ELFMAN

Crown Publishers, Inc.   New York

Copyright 1983 © by Blossom Elfman
All rights reserved. No part of this book may be reproduced
or utilized in any form or by any means,
electronic or mechanical, including photocopying, recording,
or by any information storage and retrieval system,
without permission in writing from the publisher.
Published by Crown Publishers, Inc.,
One Park Avenue, New York, New York 10016
and simultaneously in Canada
by General Publishing Company Limited
Manufactured in the United States of America
Library of Congress Cataloging in Publication Data
Elfman, Blossom.
The strawberry fields of heaven.
I. Title.
PS3555.L39S8 1983   813'.54   82-19869
ISBN: 0-517-54830-5
Book design by Camilla Filancia
10 9 8 7 6 5 4 3 2 1
First edition

To Milt: . . . for his love *is* better than wine . . .

ACKNOWLEDGMENTS

It was the late Guy Endore's own interest in Oneida which first sparked mine. My thanks to the good people who still live in the Mansion House for inviting me in as a casual visitor and asking me to their table; to the Los Angeles Downtown Public Library for its fine Oneida materials; to Daphne Abeel for invaluable editorial suggestions and finally to Pamela Thomas for pulling it all together.

CONTENTS

Contents

The
STRAWBERRY
FIELDS
of
HEAVEN

ONE

NEW YORK, MARCH 1, 1870

... they that have wives be as though they had none...
the fashion of this world passeth away.
                    I Corinthians 7:29, 31

... for they neither marry, nor are given
in marriage, but are as the angels
of God in heaven.
                    Matthew 22:30

It must have been very late but she hadn't slept at all, conscious of him beside her. The bed was their battlefield, the only evidence of the struggle between them.

Peter had always slept restively. He let out anguished sighs, he gave small child-cries, and he groped for her body as if she were his only salvation. Even when he fell into a deep-breathing sleep, he seemed to need her. If she curled away from him, he cupped her body with his own.

Now she felt his leg against her. Soon he'd be aroused and she didn't want that. She tried to take the far edge of the bed. He heaved and dropped an arm across her breast, his hand searching her out. She felt the weight of that arm like a millstone pinning her down.

All at once she couldn't bear it, not another night, not an hour more. Carefully she drew herself from under his arm and sat up at the edge of the bed. She rose quietly but the bedsprings, relieved of her weight, groaned. She prayed he wouldn't wake. What could she say to him? There was no explanation; she understood none of it: whether it was his fault or hers, or why she felt this way. The message came from her body; that was all.

If she hunted under the bed for her slippers, she might pull the bedcovers or move a table. She couldn't risk it. She walked on bare feet to the hall and opened the linen cupboard. She felt among the shelves, over the goosedown pillows and comforters and the heavy-smooth-ironed linen until she found the hand-pieced quilt that was all she had left of her mother. She took it out quietly, wrapped it around herself and walked toward the stairs.

It was more than this feeling about Peter's body. That was an ancient story, an unspoken but palpable issue between them. It was a profound sense of loss. Loss of what? she wondered, that she hadn't lost many years before. She thought, loss of configuration, of the familiar shape of things, the way a walker in the dark knows every corner, each turn of the stairway. This house, its movements and rhythms and necessities had held her together. Now she was losing the shape of it, floor by floor.

The rooms were closing up, like the chambers of a dying heart. The way she closed the carved doors of the great dining room that had been the center of the house. Those grand dinner parties when Peter was moving up in his career, around the oak table under the bright cut-glass. Not Bitsie's elegant French soirées, with the *selle d'agneau de Central Park,* and all the French sauces, but popular just the same. Everyone in the courts knew Peter Berger. He had that kind of regal bearing, that dark Berger intensity, especially in the eyes. She'd loved those eyes once; she couldn't deny it. And they'd played the modern couple in the best sense. They never quarreled in company like Moira and Edgar. They kept a stall at Wallach's Theatre and a box at the Academy of Music, a riding master for Deirdre and Rebecca's morning canters in the new park. Life had a pattern to it. Now for months they'd neither entertained nor gone out. They took their meals in a smaller room or Katherine had a tray sent up, because of the migraine. Behind the double doors was something she remembered, like a scene from a play or an old story.

And the second floor of the brownstone, the floor she shared with Peter, their intimate life. Each night in their sitting room, she brushing her hair, he with his last cigar, they'd discuss the day's events or go over the household problems, or laugh at some silly thing Rebecca had said at Miss Moffat's School. Or Deirdre's dream of being a singer. Poor sweet girl had not that much voice, but how could they tell her? And the awful misspelled letters from Paulie. And their dealing, or not dealing, with the problem of intimacy, or lack of it. All that had its shape and necessity. Now she moved out of their bedroom in body as well as in spirit.

She climbed the steps, holding the quilt around her, a woman walking a dark house without knowing why. She stopped on the third floor landing . . . the nursery floor. They still called it that. Deirdre was sixteen and dreamed of being Jenny Lind. Rebecca at ten had a mouth of her own already. And Paulie sent off to the Academy at fifteen. She didn't approve of all that military nonsense, but his friends had fallen in love with the romance of Bull Run and Shiloh, being boys, and they *would* go and Paulie begged not to be left behind. Peter indulged him, the only son. And so she let Paulie go. She didn't have the energy to fight anymore. So she'd moved up to the next floor, where she was silently climbing now.

To the little fourth floor parlor she'd made into her private morning room, her sanctuary in a shrinking house. She sat in her needlepoint chair in front of the cold grate in the cold moonlight that came between the open drapes, and she covered herself with the pieced quilt.

Her sanctuary. No, her escape. She painted here; it was her latest enthusiasm. She had to have the good morning light for her watercolors, and of course they all humored her. "Mother's little paintings"– as if it were a child's game. As soon as Peter took the girls off to school she came up here and closed the door and set herself a good fire in the grate. She loved the room, its graceful wainscot and the window seat where she could watch the horses pass and the trees change their coats of season. A decanter of wine, her chair, her fire, the blue and orange points of fire reflected in the purple claret. And she dreamed. In front of the fire, all through the winter, with her slippers on the warm grate.

A fantasy had come to her that winter, a sort of daydream that started . . . she couldn't remember when. It was just there, all the characters, and the events reeled out before her like thread off a spool. Moira was in it and Bitsie, and the man, the *wounded soldier*.

She was shamed by her fantasy; it embarrassed her, and she tried to let it go. She even prayed to God to release her from it. But He hadn't seen fit to do that. And so, day after day, she came up here and leaned back in her chair and closed her eyes and sipped her claret in guilty luxury and dreamed.

In this fantasy the wounded had just begun to return from the battlefields of the South: from *Lincoln's charnel house,* they called it. New York was hellish that year, all the awful anger against the war and the terrible riots. She and Moira and Bitsie had offered to wind bandages at the hospital. Sometimes they bathed the hands and foreheads of the suffering men, some of them mutilated in body and spirit.

In her fantasy, she was on the ward alone. It was an unexpectedly soft and golden autumn afternoon. Suddenly, one of the wounded men cried out, the sort of cry one hears in nightmares. She rushed to the bedside to comfort the dreamer. She knew from hospital gossip who he was. He'd suffered the worst wound a man could suffer. The manly part of him was gone. When she woke him from his dream, he begged to be allowed to die. She bathed his hands and face, tears of sympathy in her own eyes. He was sandy-haired, freckled from the sun, his eyes were pale and hurt, but his voice was so gentle. And whenever she came through the ward, she would set up a curtain and sit with him. She'd read him the news in the *Times* or sometimes they read a chapter of a story by Mr. Dickens and that would take him away from his reality for a little while. And then she found she looked forward to those visits as the best part of her day. He was a farmer from New Hampshire, and when she could turn his thoughts away from the awful thing that had happened to him, he told her about the land he farmed, the granite rocks and the great oaks; he loved that piece of land but he never wanted to go home. Not now, Not like this. He held onto her hand as if it were all that was left of the world. And her compassion grew to affection.

And she combed the city for things that might interest him: a marvelous book of botanical pictures, or Mr. Audubon's wonderful birds; she showed him the pictures of the great horned owl and the crested pileated woodpecker and the cedar waxwing. He was so grateful that she took the time to find it. And stories that might distract him. Since he was country-born, she found an amusing story about a jumping frog and tried to read it in the country accent. He turned his face away. She was upset. Was the language too coarse? Was he offended? He refused to explain it to her. She begged him to tell her what she'd done! What was wrong? If she offended him, it was without realizing it. Would he please forgive her! He turned to her with tortured eyes and confessed he loved her. And he could never love a woman again.

He was a freak, a eunuch. He might as well be dead. As soon as they let him out of the hospital, he was going to take his own life.

She couldn't bear to see him hurt, she was so fond of him. She'd never known a man with so soft a voice and manner, the way he looked at her face, hungrily, and yet wanting to please her. It broke her heart. She took him to her breast and told him that love was *not* the thing he'd lost, that love manifested itself in a thousand other ways. In fact she herself was only too happy to give *it* up; many women were, if he wanted the truth.

And in this fantasy he became dearer and dearer as days passed until he got the courage to kiss her. And she kissed him, on the mouth. When he asked her if she dared to go away with him, she said yes. And when he asked what of her husband, she said that she must have her children but that she no longer loved her husband and was happy to leave him.

So they began to plan their escape.

Then one morning, as she lay back dreaming, the orange points of the fire reflected in her glass, she suddenly remembered that it was only a dream and the loss was unbearable. This room, which had been her sanctuary and her escape, became a prison, full of shadows, a haunted place. She tried to paint again and nothing came.

She sat in that room now, in darkness, shivering in the thin quilt, wondering why the house had betrayed her. Her life had betrayed her. Even her body betrayed her. She felt trapped in her body, and she didn't know why.

Above her, at the top of the house, above the noisy plumbing and the hissing gas, was the rude attic where Else and Cook slept. She envied them that room with its hidden corners and its dovecotes; close and intimate and homely, their comfortable women's private laughter. She could hear the scraping of the chamber pot along the floor; even that. She wondered about the world of women without husbands. Like those places down on Greene Street; those women. That kind of woman. Peter may have been to Greene Street. She suspected he had, before he came to her bed. It was *that* she sensed on him, or thought so.

But what did it matter? Let him go to someone else. It simply didn't matter. And that was the worst loss of all.

She felt breathless; she wanted air. She got up and opened the window to the night sounds: the sad whine of the freight whistle on the tracks leading to the docks of the Hudson; the heavy clop-clop-clop-clop of the drays pulling the work wagons filled with brick and mortar for the morning's start. By night and day the city moved north. All those wonderful outcroppings of native stone which had seemed to her like pieces of sculptures blasted away bit by bit. All the lovely birches, the catalpas, cut down; this was not her city. This was not her life. The room was cold, but she had no other place to go. Her mind drifted from one disturbing question to another. Always she reached an impenetrable barrier, a wall, an opaque window. Was she an unnatural woman, to dislike her husband's body? She was only thirty-four. She wasn't old.

Outside she heard the rills and cries of the night birds on the bare branches of the ailanthus across the way in the park with the iron rail and the locked iron gate. The city was shifting from under them, the good old neighborhoods giving way to warehouses and factories. But Gramercy Park still meant money and security. So Peter said when he mortgaged his life and hers to buy the house. He put that little gold gate key in his waistcoat pocket and it was enough for him. But he'd locked her in with that key. She detested parks that were locked that way. The mockingbirds and the terns and the mourning doves—they were free to fly. She was trapped by that low gate. She thought of the women of Greene Street, some of those houses so elegant, Moira had said, they could have been private residences of anyone of their set. And the women, their gowns and jewels, all borrowed from the Madam, of course. You couldn't tell those women from society, the way they held themselves. The carriage trade demanded that. Peter would, she supposed. At the end of the day, how did they feel when they had to put aside the rich gowns, all that borrowed glory, and beg a ride from one of their gentlemen, up beyond the cobbled pavements to the mud lanes of Dutch Hill, to those shanty houses with their tin roofs, pigs sleeping in mud, rats eating at the carcasses of dead dogs. She'd been told this by Moira, who loved those stories. . . .

The heavy wheels of a cart on cobbles echoed through the tunneled night. Something was dreadfully wrong with her life. She was a spirit, disembodied, searching for a place that seemed familiar. She floated against the night sounds, down a hospital corridor; she opened a door. Her wounded soldier looked up with surprise and delight, with such happiness, her heart swelled . . . she was home . . . home. . . .

"Momma?"

Rebecca's voice shocked her. And the light, and the stiffness; she was cold to the bone. The door pushed open. "Poppa said you were up here painting. Why are you painting in your nightgown?"

Deirdre pushed past her. "She isn't painting, can't you see? She's been up since dawn worrying about me." Deirdre bent and kissed Katherine on both cheeks in the European style, thank Moira for that. "She's sick with worry because I told her that I was going to the theater with that boy Poppa hates."

"Poppa said you couldn't go," said Rebecca, kissing Katherine a still-childish sucking kiss on the cheek. "And that was that, he said."

"All I *asked,*" said Deirdre with dramatic passion, "was a chance to see Mr. Booth's *Hamlet!* It's not Mr. Fox's! It's an uplifting play. I know lots of girls my age who go without their parents to see it. It's historical because of Mr. Booth's terrible brother, and everyone is suppose to go to let him know he's forgiven."

Peter stepped into the room, dressed for the city. His eyes never met Katherine's. He signaled with his pocket watch to the girls that he was late. "It's Shakespeare, Peter. Can it hurt her, really?"

Peter checked his waistcoat in the cheval mirror. "You think she's interested in *Hamlet?* She wants to go with that boy, the bicycle fiend who roaches down his hair with bear grease."

"It's only because he's on the racing team! He goes to Harvard! *Please,* Momma!"

"I'd as soon trust her with a Bowery Boy. If she's so keen on going, she can go with the Bannermans. They have a box."

"Why are you all treating me like a child!" wailed Deirdre. "Hasn't anybody around here noticed I've grown up!"

"*I* haven't," said Rebecca. "When did you?"

Peter herded them out of the room after good-bye kisses and Deirdre's plea for her not to worry, that she intended to be an actress and that was simply that.

Peter waited until the girls' footsteps disappeared, he bent over her, gripped the arms of her chair so that she was surrounded by his presence. "I don't forgive you for this, Katie. You and I have accounts to settle."

Then he left her too.

When she heard the carriage leave, she ran down to the warm quilt of her own bed. She closed her eyes and drew the quilt up around her and begged for the wounded soldier to come and comfort her. But Else knocked and brought in a breakfast tray and opened the drapes and let in the sunlight and then opened the windows and let in the morning.

When she heard the horses on the cobbles she thought for a panicked moment that Peter had come back. To settle accounts. She could not face settling them. *Let it be someone else.* She went to the window and saw her sister's black landau with the matched black horses. She stood quickly back and away but it was too late. Berthe had seen her. Berthe's horses pulled at the reins, the breath from those flared nostrils in the chill morning like a stroke of pale color on a Japanese canvas. She didn't want to see Berthe this morning. If Berthe would leave she might paint . . . she *might*. But Berthe raised a hand to her in a sort of gesture. The imperial arch of Berthe's brow, the critical lines of that spare face. A gesture of what? Triumph. Oh, yes, triumph. So Berthe had come with news, finally. But it was news she didn't want to hear, not any longer. She didn't want news and she didn't want accounts settled. She only wanted . . . *what?* It was a loss of that also.

The room became close, her hands wet and clammy. Berthe's sharp little boot heels clicked up the stone steps. The pull of the bell. Berthe's strident voice arguing that surely she knew her way to her own sister's bedroom. Berthe in the hall, click-click, click-click, like a clock ticking too fast, or a heart. Up the steps. Katherine felt the nausea of apprehension. Berthe opened the door, shattering peace and silence, sniffing the way she always did to catch the scent, like some predatory animal assuring its own safety. "Have I got you in bed so late?" Berthe was breathless from the quick climb.

"Give me a few minutes to dress. Else will make you some coffee."

Berthe closed the door behind her. "What I have to say won't wait. Get back under the covers. Haven't we talked in bed enough times in our lives?"

Katherine pulled her quilt up around her, like a child wanting warmth and safety. Berthe saw that it was Momma's quilt. Berthe always saw everything. She unbuttoned her cape and dropped it on the bed. "The way carriages race up Broadway you take your life in your hands. They're so wild for speed. If they want to break their heads racing up in Harlem Lane then let them, but to race on Broadway is sheer madness. We hit a dog with a wheel. All that yelping. It depresses the morning."

"How terrible." Katherine wished Berthe would be silent and go away.

They still hadn't embraced. Berthe pulled off her gloves, held them in one hand and slapped the other, and then with a thin smile she said, "I've found him out."

Katherine pressed back against the pillow, away from Berthe's triumphant eyes. "I supposed you had, coming out this early. I only wish you didn't make it sound like some kind of victory." As soon as she'd said it, she was sorry. Time had betrayed her, not Berthe. Or was it her body that had betrayed her finally? She'd taken such pride in that body when she was young. The sin of pride. She thought herself quite beautiful, when she and Peter were young and Peter was courting her. Out in the country for a picnic, a linen cloth spread on the wild oats up in Brooklyn Heights overlooking the river. Clandestine. If Momma knew, and if Peter's father knew. Peter never cared much for convention, not then. And it was all so romantic. Life was so promising then. He read her verses from that sad Lord Byron and he looked down at where she lay, eyes partly closed against the light and he watched her with his hot dark eyes. That was the only reason he proposed marriage, because he wanted her, only she didn't know that then. Then it was all Lord Byron and dreams. At home, later, with her door locked, she took off her clothes and looked at herself naked. She had such fair skin, and her hair, down to her waist, was the color that Deirdre's was now, a sort of honey gold. She looked like one of those Greek statues that Momma shielded from her eyes at the museum, her hair down around her like a silk mantle. She looked at the roundness of her nipples . . . she dared to touch them . . . oh, the way it made her feel. She wondered, when he comes to me will he love me and touch me like this?

And then the wedding day came finally. Peter's father performed the ceremony. He was terrible, old Dr. Berger, full of hellfire and the temptation of Eve and the wages of sin and evil. Bitsie got the hiccups and Moira fed her so much wine she got tipsy and then they cut the cake and Bitsie caught the bouquet and finally it was over and they were alone and Peter kissed her and loosed her stays, and she waited for the gentle fingers and the passionate words of Lord Byron, and for him to touch her breasts . . . and he came at her like a goat . . . rutting . . .

"Victory?" Berthe frowned. "That's just like you, Katie. You send me on a very painful errand, and then you blame me for doing it."

What Berthe said was true. Now she leaned toward Berthe and

embraced her. They held onto each other in a confusion of feelings. They'd never liked each other, even as children. But Katherine had no other place to turn. Momma had said that, *Blood is thicker, remember!* She never said thicker than what. Where should she begin with Berthe? She never knew where to begin. "Would you like some tea and cakes? Ring for Else."

"I haven't got time for tea. I have too much to tell you."

Berthe rarely took tea or coffee. She never enjoyed the pleasures of the table. Food didn't nourish her. Other things she took with a kind of gloating pleasure, but not food. She kept slim, not out of fashion. She didn't need corsets, but she was corseted tightly. Her spirit also. Her body, unlike Katherine's, was thin and angular. From that spare fortress her eyes, very much alive, moved warily, taking in what was around her, anything that might catch her unaware if she wasn't vigilant. There was something behind her eyes that Berthe relished more than cakes. And that thing frightened Katherine. She wanted to run from it, back into the past, back to her father's farm in Virginia, onto one of Poppa's mares, and ride across the fields again until the buttons at the wrists and the throat of her nightdress would burst and fly away and let her breathe again.

"After what you said," Berthe confided, "I decided to have him followed."

Katherine felt the blood drain from her face. She thought she might faint. "You said . . . a few discreet questions . . . a few people who knew Peter. Oh, Berthe, what have you done?" But even as she said it, she knew she couldn't blame Berthe. What had been done was done and finished a long time ago. Even on that first morning more than seventeen yeas ago. At the breakfast table. Animal, even in the way he ate. Why hadn't she seen that before? His eyes full of lust, not love. She flushed with shame, the way he looked at her. The delicacy was gone, all the poetry. But he was a man and he had the right. It was her own body that had betrayed her. Unnatural woman, no desire. Other women came to enjoy it. No, not Bitsie, poor Bitsie who had gone all to fat so that her husband never bothered her anymore. Bitsie spent her days walking that silly beribboned Pekingese down Fifth Avenue looking at shop windows. The best part of her morning was eating rich pastries at John Taylor's ice cream saloon.

Moira, of course, always bragged of herself as being a modern woman. And she loved it; she said she did. Her husband had moved them into a Fifth Avenue hotel and spent most of his time with his horses, racing like a madman through the new Central Park, his long mustaches plastered against his face in the wind. And Moira had nothing to do but spend her days at A. T. Stewart's, buying china and laces. She always leaned toward the bohemian. She said that her husband taught her to make love like a prostitute. Moira spoke of love, but her eyes had gone so vacant. Katherine thought she talked too much of it. Once Moira dared them all to rent a cab and drive out to Five Points where the women were on streets. To look at the women. Then up Broadway and down Greene Street, past the Tin Lizzie and Forget-me-Not, and Sinbad's, which catered to sailors. To see the women's eyes. Some of them so brazen, hawking their bodies. Or some, Moira said, you could tell them even if they were dressed well by the way they turned and cast a glance, or lifted a skirt and showed an ankle. Thousands of them did it every night. Bitsie, sucking on her endless chocolates, asked if they enjoyed it. Katherine said they did it for money. They had to survive. Oh, they enjoyed it, said Moira, as if she knew it all. She was so daring. Once she even suggested that they should dress the part of whores and see how men acted when they weren't with their wives. Moira said that even children did it. Virgins claimed a higher price on the market. Edgar had told her that. Some of the whores played virgin, with a little bit of bloodied sponge or even a splinter of glass to make them bleed. Bitsie almost choked. How horrible! Were they sewed up after? Katherine thought about the eyes of the women even then. Did they lust, like men? Or simply do it to survive? Long after, when she had borne three children and lost two through miscarriages, when she looked at Peter's advances with disgust or disinterest, she thought of those women. Was she unnatural? she wondered then. Life was so many other things beside the bed. Peter had never betrayed her as a provider and a father. Her children were clothed, well kept, the house was hers, he said. The pattern of their lives was established . . . by day. By night . . . there was a cold edge. And later the cold edge crept into his eyes also. For what she kept from him, he never forgave her. And soon she found it hard to forgive herself. Unnatural. Now the children were growing and Else kept the house so well and Cook tended to the kitchen and she was shoved into her morning room painting her endless watercolors. Peter had his life in the city and she had a wounded soldier, a gentle wounded soldier. . . .

"How can you say I came in victory?" Berthe was truly hurt. "But never mind. You have to know the truth."

Katherine had no more energy to resist. She leaned forward and accepted Berthe's embrace. When she and Berthe were children, when they fought over some nonsense, Berthe always won. She had to win. Katherine knew that. And she always came to Berthe like this, leaning on her shoulder, as an act of submission. "I never should have told you," she said. "I wish now I hadn't."

"I'm surprised you did," said Berthe. "You were always such a secret one. But we're sisters. Where else should you go? I don't know why you always retreat into silence, Katie. Don't you think I've suffered as much as you, with Hector, who's a pig as well as a man? At least when Peter comes to you at night you can admire the cut of him. Picture my nights with Hector, if you have the stomach. That porker's belly, stuffed from the table, and his pitiful thing beneath, good for less and less than to disturb my sleep."

"If Hector's too fat," said Katherine, "blame yourself. You set a heavy table."

Berthe opened her beaded bag and took out a scented handkerchief, sniffed at it, and settled apart from Katherine. "Do you want me to tell you the truth? Since you've come to me with a somewhat opened heart? Yes, I set a heavy table. I stuff him with the sausage he loves, and the blood pudding, and the cream pies and do you know why? Because he'll die of apoplexy sooner or later. So why not sooner, while I still have a little life in me?" She put her handkerchief into her beaded purse. "Does that shock you? Well, I've told you my secret, now you tell me yours. It's too late to hide behind modesty. What's between me and Hector, I can bear it. I've turned it to my advantage. Mind you, I always thought you could do more with Peter. If you were clever. But you were never clever with men."

She was never clever. She and Berthe had both met Peter at the same time, when Poppa took them to New York with him on business and they went to see the great Crystal Palace, that huge mansion of glass, the marvel of the world, magnificent and indestructible. But it had caught fire from the inside and all the glass burst and shattered. Poppa took them to hear Dr. Berger, who was preaching at Trinity Church on how men seemed on the outside full of crystal purity, but the rotted heart ate away inside until the whole shattered.

And since Dr. Berger knew their own minister in Virginia where the Episcopals were having a great revival, they were invited to dinner at his oak-paneled house in St. John's Park. And Peter was there. Peter had always hated his father, that was eminently clear, not only in his little sarcasms, but in the soft Byronic collar he wore that made his father so angry. And Peter's eyes during dinner hadn't left her face. Peter fixed his passion on her then and she, poor lamb from the country, was never clever enough to look into the heart. She saw only the crystal surface. He was so handsome, even Berthe saw that, tall like Dr. Berger, the same ramrod bearing, thick black hair and hot dark eyes. But he *was* his father. Eyes fixed never on heaven, but always below. You could almost see hellfires reflected in the black pitch of the irises. Nothing of heaven, always the other way. Perhaps Dr. Berger could see through her own secret heart, into her thoughts, seeing her standing shameless and naked before the mirror, touching her breasts, feeling that there was some other Katherine, some strange wanton, inside her body, and seeing those thoughts he had sent her God's judgment. No, she'd never been clever with men. That first terrible night with Peter, it was all gone. That feeling. Vanished. Now she dressed in the dark.

"Before you married," Berthe confided, "I tried to talk with you. . . ."

"Oh, don't," begged Katherine. "What does it matter now?"

"Oh, yes, it does matter. There hasn't been much love between us but I'm still your sister. I've seen you bear two miscarriages since Rebecca was born. Well, you wouldn't talk with me about these things, I thought at least you talked with your friends. I've seen the way you act with Peter. Even Hector, who's as dense as fog, noticed it. I always wondered what Momma told you on that wedding night. *Katie, my child, please your husband even if it hurts, use half a reamed lemon for your protection and trust the rest to God?*"

"Please . . ."

"Katie, these are modern times! This is 1870, not the Middle Ages! If you don't want more children, there are ways! Everyone uses sponges. . . ."

"Don't . . . please . . ."

"Sophisticated women talk of these things. We're not Momma dying out of shame to let a man look at her naked, that terrible fat doctor trying to examine her under a sheet in a dark room. Doesn't Peter have the sense to use the *baudruche?* I mean, the man is civilized. . . ."

Katherine's face flamed. *"Please,* Berthe . . . I don't *want . . ."*

"I don't care what you *want!* Even Hector uses the *glove.* Although he detests it. I won't let him come near me unless he does. If that's what keeps you apart . . ."

"It's not that," said Katherine. "After Rebecca, I just couldn't bear to let him touch me, that's all. No . . . it was long before that. I never wanted him." The words slipped out. She wished them unsaid. Too late. She saw how Berthe reacted. The door to her inmost privacy had burst and all her secrets tumbled out as from an untidy closet.

Berthe fanned herself. "And being a man he took you guiltily and you closed your eyes and suffered."

"Yes."

"Or turned away until he couldn't bear the guilt any longer and then he stayed away more and more often."

"I was to blame," said Katherine. "I never enjoyed . . ."

"Enjoyed? Oh, my poor Katherine. So you sent him to brothels and risked disease . . . and now he comes home night after night, late, sweated in guilt, like a tomcat in heat."

"It isn't that. If it were just that . . . it's something else. I can see it in his eyes." Katherines throat tightened. "But I don't want to know. Not anymore. I'm sorry I spoke of it. I shouldn't have troubled you. Please, let's not speak of it ever again."

Berthe was astonished. "I told you I had found him out! You mean to say that you don't care where your husband goes night after night? You must be a saint!"

She wanted her glass of claret. She wanted a wounded soldier who would come for her in the night with a carriage and call to her with pebbles at the window. She would take a few clothes, things for the children, nothing she had got from Peter. And they would be gone before Peter woke, out of the fetid city, out into the country, up to New Hampshire with the great oaks and the granite rocks and the climbing roses against the back fence and the early crocuses which broke through the winter ice, her tender soldier had told her that; when you thought that winter still had a grip on things suddenly the little white star appeared bringing hope. No . . . that was a dream. He was a dream. He didn't exist except in her fantasy and she was lost. "I'm not a saint. I can be as hurt as any woman. But I read something the other day . . ." Her eyes were drowsy. She wanted to sleep. She wanted her fantasy. It was a drug, she knew that now. Pipe dreams, luring her into nothingness.

"Read? What? I don't understand you."

"In the *Times.* A woman, she was only twenty-two. She killed herself."

"Where was this?"

"In New Utrecht."

"What woman?"

"I don't know what woman."

"But you don't know anyone in New Utrecht."

"It doesn't matter." Yes, Katherine knew her, without knowing her. "They said she'd drowned herself in a pond."

"What are you talking about?"

"In a pond. She was wearing a black-and-white alpaca dress and white cotton stockings, and she drowned herself."

"Is it someone in Peter's family? The Bergers are all mad."

"It was no one I knew. It said she wore a white petticoat and a hoop and prunella gaiters."

"A whore, you mean? Some whore who drowned herself in a pond?"

"She wore jet earrings and a new corset. And a gold ring on her left forefinger and she had a locket with a child's picture in it."

"Why ever should you give a tinker's damn if some whore throws herself in somebody's pond?"

"She must have sat so long in front of her mirror," said Katherine, "so worried that when she was found she'd be proper, knowing there was no other place for her but the pond."

"Oh, I see it now," said Berthe. "I understand it. And you'll put on your best dress and your new corset and walk yourself into a pond because of Peter? It would be just like you, Katie. You always loved your little bit of drama. Well, if it were me, I would have enticed the man, the father of the child in the locket, down to the pond with great promises of favors and when his back was turned I would have pushed *him* in. I don't have any patience with women who drop into ponds over unrequited love. It's a great waste of corsets."

No, she didn't want the pond, she had to think of her children.

"I read the other day," said Berthe, "of a woman who had a quarrel with her husband, and she set the room on fire in her rage. They had her up for arson, and the mad thing is spending a year in prison. A year! They would have had her up for ten except that the judge took pity on her. And what had she done, after all? He was the culprit! She wasn't clever enough. She should have got him drunk and left his cigar on the bed and the whole lot would have burned and she would have been free."

What *did* she want? The house to herself and her children? Would it become alive again? Would she? There was something stifling in the picture she had of them all: Deirdre sitting beside her near the fire, arching her neck over some bright needlework like a princess about to prick her finger and sleep for a hundred years. Deirdre was sixteen. She herself had been just sixteen when she went on the picnic in the wild oats out in Brooklyn Heights. Did she want to keep Deirdre a child forever, in that long sleep, guarding her bed so that Deirdre couldn't know that princes came only in fantasy? And Rebecca back from her lessons sitting at Deirdre's feet, fussing over her best doll, her Mathilda-of-the painted-china-face. Is that what she wanted? The three of them fixed in time? Three women in a portrait, with the pale sun reflected in the mirror, and the blue and orange points of the fire? A canvas in watercolor, indistinct, like a dream, safe in a frame? *What was it she wanted?* "It doesn't matter anymore. Whoever she is, let Peter have her. You want a secret? I'm long past caring. I want to be left in peace now. Here in my house. Let him make a settlement on me, without a scandal." She hesitated. "Have you seen her? For Deirdre's sake I hope she's not young."

"You think he has another woman?" asked Berthe smugly.

"I know he has. Let him have what he wants. And let him leave me alone for once and all."

"What he wants? What he wants is to root with his porker's nose in every sweet garden, tearing up roots and flowers. Let me tell you it's no woman. Not one woman, at least. It's much worse."

Alarm swirled like fireworks in her stomach. "What could be worse?"

"He's gone quite mad. Like his father. Like all the Bergers."

"How? I don't understand what you're saying."

"How *could* you understand? Who taught us to understand men? Momma? Whose whole life was those pieced quilts of hers? No, Peter is mad. His father always had a heavy hand on him and it's got him at last. He's turned to the devil."

"Please say what you mean! What has he done?"

"He's joined the *free lovers.*"

Nothing was making sense. Free lovers? "Some political party, you mean? You mean he's joined the Socialists?"

"The free lovers, Katie! The Perfectionists! From Oneida! Those madmen who say that Christ has already come back. The Second Coming. God forgive me for repeating it, the ones who say that Christ has returned and that since He's here, it's heaven on earth and God is love and love is sleeping in everybody's bed! And they quote Scriptures for it!"

It didn't make sense to her. "Peter hasn't stepped inside a church since we've been married. He's an atheist. You know how he feels about his father." She tried to search her memory. What had she heard about the free lovers? Oneida. Moira had said something. Somebody wrote an article in the *Times.* Yes. Someplace upstate. They cast lots, Moira said, to see who would sleep with whom. And all in the same bed. But that was Moira. Moira read Walt Whitman's poetry. Who was to believe Moira?

"Don't you remember all that scandal years ago in the *Times?* Oneida, Katie. Where they trap men in their middle years with promises of free love and they lure them into the Community. And they bring their fortunes with them. *Fortunes,* Katie. That means your house and your money and your carriages. He'll sell the house right out from under you. Thank God I came in time. Are you listening, Katie?"

Listening? What was clear to hear? No, Peter would never bring harm to his children. That was unthinkable. His only quarrel with her was about the bed, his terrible lust. If only he had been in the war and had been wounded. No, he would never sell the house away from her and leave his children unprotected. Unthinkable. Berthe was lying. She didn't know why. It was just Berthe's way.

"The *Oneidans,* Katie! You know the ones! They were kicked out of Putney, up in Vermont. They would have been tarred and feathered but they stole away in the night. And they settled upstate near the Indians, shoving their bottoms in the face of God."

"And you're trying to tell me that Peter's mixed up with these . . . whatever they are? I don't believe you!"

"Then believe this. Your husband is growing older. And un-satisfied. And suddenly he's offered a kind of paradise. They sleep with each other, Katie. A sexual paradise. Why are you keeping your head in the sand like an ostrich? But you always were a little ostrich, with your poetry and your watercolors. Poppa loved to watch you paint. Poppa always loved you best. Quiet Katie. Pretty Katie." Katherine was as-tonished by the bitterness on Berthe's face, by the depth of her feelings. They both understood and they were both trapped, yoked together, sisters, blood was thicker in spite of both of them. "Don't be a fool," Berthe said. "Poppa isn't here anymore to watch out for you. You have to deal with this. You must, for the sake of your children."

Deal with what? Her mind was confused.

Berthe settled in like a tradesman striking a bargain. "Now, let's say for the sake of argument that Peter has gone out of his mind with passion. And that he's been seduced by this . . . monstrous hoax against God. And now you know the truth. Be smart for once. Use what you know."

"Use?"

"Turn it to your advantage. Accuse him. Let him know he's been found out. Remind him of the shame to his children. If not to you. Be hurt. Let him confess it. And once confessed, forgive."

She hadn't heard clearly. She couldn't have. Blood pounded in her head. Fragments . . . pictures . . . Poppa watching her at her canvas, bending to kiss her forehead. Berthe standing in the doorway, hurt and sullen. Her mind was exploding. "Forgive *him!*"

"Katherine, if he takes his whole estate and joins these . . . Socialists . . . what will you have? Where will you be? How will you feed your children? Take in mending? Teach French to your friends' children? Of course . . ." Now Berthe's face took on a different look. "Of course my house is always open to you." Triumphant to the end. "Or you'll be smart, you'll realize what Peter is looking for in these . . . Socialists . . . these antichrists, and you'll be clever and seduce your husband."

"Seduce . . ."

Berthe was annoyed. "Every woman is whore to her husband in one way or another. Oh, if she's working class and she does her own floors and slaves over cookpots, I'd say she's worked well enough for what she has. But a woman of our class with our houses, our servants. Else keeps your house, you have a coachman, you shop where you please. And what do you do to earn it all? You lie on your back and if you're clever, you moan and twist and tell him he's a magnificent stallion. That *is* marriage."

Katherine was hearing nothing that she hadn't thought about before. Realities. She was thirty-four, poised on change. She watched her face in the morning mirror, not lined but *lining,* her hair bright but not as bright. And behind that face she saw another face, another Katherine, older, her eyes growing vacant like Moira's, bitter and empty. And behind the shifting portrait of herself, another girl, a girl not twenty-two, ready to put on a black-and-white alpaca dress.

Berthe dabbed at her brow with her handkerchief. She drew on her gloves. "Think about what I've said. Think of yourself as an actress. And for heaven's sake, see some of your old friends. Moira is back from Europe. She's written to you countless times. She tells me she's worried that you haven't answered her. Don't shut yourself up like this. Open your eyes. You'll see a few things that might surprise you."

The girl, still in her shift, opened a package and took out a new corset. She pulled on white stockings, searched her box for the right earrings.

Berthe put on her cape. "You have two daughters. You're a woman without protection. He's put you in a perilous position." She kissed Katherine on the cheek. "What was between us . . . is past. The world has done some turns and tricks. We're acrobats, Katie. Poised on the wire. It's all such a joke, a joke on us both." She left Katherine without saying another word.

Katherine put a few coals in the grate. She was cold, cold to the bone. She sat at her dressing table and searched for truth. What reason would Berthe have to lie? Peter would never bring harm to his children . . . but to her? She'd left his bed last night. She was a fool to have done it. She searched the mirror. She saw a girl at her dressing table, putting on jet earrings and thinking, *I have only one place to go. All other places are closed to me. At least God has a place for me in His house.* Which God? Dr. Berger's raging God, with his hellfire and his temptation of Eve? Her mother's God, pallid and meek, who turned the other cheek when one cheek flamed? Somewhere an angry woman struck a match and set the drapes on fire because her husband screamed at her and she had no voice to answer with. A mouth opened and no sound came out. And she saw the flaming curtains and she was afraid and ran with a pitcher of water to put out the fire and now she was in prison because that was also a place . . . like the bottom of a pond. .

Where was she to go?

What did it mean, *free* love? Love was never free. Love between man and woman? She doubted if it existed. It was a fantasy. A woman in a black-and-white alpaca dress opened a locket and wept looking at the portrait of a child. And now she had only the pond. Katherine stood at the edge of the pond and saw the sky reflected in the water. Across the pond, in a field of wild oats, a horse came galloping. It stood snorting at her. Then it reared and pawed space with its great hooves and whinnied at her. She waited at the pond's edge, and she and the horse watched each other. Then the horse stood still and waited to see what she would do.

"Mathilda is frightened, so can I sleep with you, *please?*" Rebecca, with her hair in night braids, dragging her Mathilda-child by one arm, stood in the doorway.

Deirdre sat in her shift in front of her mirror, combing her hair and dreaming of standing center stage and being applauded by the audiences of Europe and America. On the wall was a portrait of the great Jenny Lind, whose life she knew by heart in all detail. "Why are you such a liar?" said Deirdre. "If you're having a nightmare, say so. Why do you have to blame it on the doll?"

"It *wasn't* me," said Rebecca, bouncing into Deirdre's bed and snuggling under the covers. "Anyhow it was my friend Emmeline's fault."

Deirdre was practicing how to hold her mouth when she hit the high notes. When Jenny Lind had first come to New York she sang *Norma* in the key of F, which was an impossible thing. Deirdre wasn't actually far enough in her music lessons to envision *Norma* in F, but it must have been a wonderful feat and then Miss Jenny Lind donated all of the profits, more than $12,000, to charity. Deirdre stood on center stage with the spotlight on her, having just accomplished astonishing vocal acrobatics, and the crowds roared their approval.

"Emmeline was telling me about the Fox sisters who could talk to spirits and dead people."

Deirdre stood up to better observe her figure. She practiced a deep curtsy to her cheering audiences.

"Emmeline said that the Fox sisters could hear rapping noises coming from the other world. And people tried to find out how they did it and they couldn't, so the Fox sisters were real clair–clair–somethings."

"Clairvoyant. That's just childish silliness. Somebody was making the knocking noises for them. Everyone knows that."

"No, they didn't! People tried to find out where they came from but they couldn't!"

Deirdre began to braid up her hair for the night. "I'm going on the stage, did I tell you that?"

"So I was lying in bed with Mathilda listening for the knocks from the other world."

"I detest when Momma treats me like a child," said Deirdre. "Especially in front of other people."

"I don't mind being treated like a child," said Rebecca. "In fact I *like* being a child."

Deirdre knelt at the side of the bed to say her prayers.

"I said mine already," said Rebecca. Then thinking about it, she jumped out of bed and knelt beside Deirdre. "I heard something, that's what frightened Mathilda. She heard it too."

The room was cold. They both climbed under the feather quilt. "Did you hear knocking?" said Deirdre.

"No, I heard Momma crying."

"Crying? Where?"

"It was funny. At first I thought it was voices from another world. It came from heaven. Then I heard it up the stairs and I went up and Momma was in her little painting room and she had the light out and she was crying."

"Was Poppa in his room?"

"Poppa went out. He went to his club. What does he do at his club every night anyhow?"

"Why was Momma crying? Why is everything so funny in this house? I suppose it's because I'm intending to go on the stage. Miss Moffat says it's coarse. No young ladies go on the stage."

"Maybe she was crying because Aunt Berthe was here today."

"When? I didn't see her."

"Neither did I. I could smell her though. She wears a scent like dead funeral flowers. I could smell her all over Momma's bedroom. Momma hates her."

"You shouldn't say things like that," said Deirdre. "Momma doesn't hate her own sister."

"Yes, she does. She said so once. When Aunt Berthe wouldn't give her Grandma's pieced quilts. When Grandma passed away to heaven. Do you think if I call Grandma, she'll come to me with knocks?" Rebecca curled close for protection.

"Why would Momma be crying? It makes me so nervous to think about it. Are you sure?"

Rebecca stuffed her doll, Mathilda, between them. "It's probably because she doesn't want to go live in the country."

Deirdre sat up in bed. *"Who's* going to live in the country?"

Rebecca put her hand to her mouth, and turned the other way around. "Good-night."

Deirdre pulled her back. "Where did you hear such a thing?"

"I promised I wouldn't say. I promised so don't ask me. I'll die and go to hell before I tell. Miss Moffat said this morning if I didn't tell who was chattering during the reading lesson, I'd be punished and I didn't tell. Anyhow, it was me."

"Who did you promise?"

"Poppa. I promised Poppa. And my lips are locked so good-night."

Deirdre shook her, but Rebecca had clutched her Mathilda and sealed her lips. Deirdre lay back and turned off the gas lamp. The gaslight from the square below made odd flickerings on the ceiling and cast ominous shadows on the familiar room. She reached a leg over and touched Rebecca's foot. Things had got all strange in this house. She listened to hear if Momma was crying. Rebecca was probably lying. She didn't want to go to the country, which was insufferably boring. She wanted to go to Paris, where Aunt Moira went, to see the great singers and actresses. Terrible wonderful things happened in Paris. And she was a woman. And she was ready for all these terrible wonderful things.

In the soft silence suddenly something knocked. Once. Twice. Rebecca put her head under the covers and moaned. She grasped for Deirdre's hand. The knocking persisted. Bang. Bang. "Did you *do* that?" said Rebecca, desperately frightened.

Bang. Bang.

"Deirdre, don't, if it's you! Is it you?"

Deirdre turned her back. "My lips are sealed."

Rebecca punched her on the back. "It was you! Wasn't it!"

Deirdre was sinking into sleep. Riding down the Champs Elysées in a black phaeton with two white horses, her scarves flying out behind her, and along the way men lifted their hats, and workmen on the streets stopped at their labors and waved and shouted, because she'd been so wonderful and donated all of the concert's profits to their charity. For a while she thought of Grandpa Berger and his stern face, what he would say if he heard she was going on the stage. And then she thought of Grandma Olsen and her lovely pieced quilts and Aunt Berthe's refusal to give them to Momma, and how Grandma Olsen used to invite them down to the farm in Virginia. Farms were chickens and pigs. And mud. Without music and lights. She drifted off on a high *F,* which came from her lips with the clarity of pale blue ice.

Peter Berger, in order to be redeemed, had been advised by his new brothers and sisters of the Oneida Community to confess Christ and pray. But his back was stiff against prayer and his knees wouldn't bend. Neither would his spirit. He would have liked to pray the way he prepared for a case in court: to lay out the facts, keeping the lawyer's edge, and trust to a merciful judge to acquit him.

He walked along streets without destination, his ungloved hands jammed into his greatcoat pockets, feeling a damn fool. It was bitter cold. And then he saw the flag on the passing omnibus which meant that the ball was up in the park! The lake north of the Mall and the pond at Fifty-ninth Street would be frozen over and the skaters would be out for a night on the ice!

Something of the boy in him rose with the flag. He hopped onto the bus. The horses, their great iron hooves galloping up toward Fifty-ninth, pulled the crowd of high-spirited skaters, and the lovers who were free to skate unchaperoned, and the fathers shepherding their flocks of bundled-to-the-eyes children, skates over shoulders. When he jumped off with the rest at the entrance to the park, he remembered another season, a late cold like this one. It must have been 1836 or '37. The park was still a swamp then, full of hard-eyed squatters and bands of angry abandoned children, the squalid street Arabs who threw rocks at passing carriages and ate trash and leavings, and peed against the walls and trees in disdain for the world that had betrayed them. And he, poor Peter, living in the dim-lighted dark oak of the stone house on St. John's Park with his monster of a father and his father's vengeful ever-watchful God, he would have borne the hunger and the homelessness happily if only to be free to pee against a tree or to run with the wind or do any single act in animal freedom without the eye of judgment on him. That hurt boy in him walked into Central Park which was the last shred of Eden in New York City to find a place to pray.

The night was windless but bone-cold and so clear that the moon lit the path and the stars hung low—the Dipper and Sirius, and the Belt of Orion, the Hunter. He felt close to the sky. He found himself an isolated bench on a rise where he could see the brilliantly calcium-lighted pond and watch the skaters and make his reacquaintance with God. He closed his eyes and began; but all that came to his mind was a litany of hate against his father:

Goddamn my father and give me the grace to forgive him. It was an anger that soured his life, that he carried with him like an albatross. He had to let out the anger first, like emptying a chamber pot . . . *give me the grace to forgive him. He nursed me in hell . . . he sealed me off from all sensual pleasure. He bound my life spirit the way he bound my hands to the sides of the bed against self-abuse. I married a virgin who stayed a virgin for seventeen years, who left me swimming in holy water and dying of thirst, who forced me into brothels to lie in the arms of girls no older than my daughter. I could have scourged myself for the shame of it. For my animal nature. All this I confess, Christ. And I bless Father Noyes who is the better father and is leading me to the new life. Would God have created hot fires in my blood if only to make me deny myself and in denying myself deny Him in whose image I'm created? God who makes all things flourish and multiply must understand the nature of desire. I make this confession in the manner taught me by my new family of the Community. Help me to be repentant and to accept criticism, and if my father burns in hell, it would be no less than he deserves. Amen.*

When he opened his eyes, the purity and innocence of the scene almost moved him to tears: the skaters on the ice, two by two, holding hands and swinging them like pendulums, or fathers supporting the wobbly skates of children, or a whole line of skaters holding hands and whipping around in perilous speed, but always together so that the chain was never broken. The laughter rose in the sweet cold air, the scraping of the skates and the rills of music, and above it all, looking down at the lighted pond and the skaters and the little hills and pathways of the park, the still-bare trees with their promise of spring and the arm-around lovers walking together . . . was the full moon. It *was* a sort of Eden. Or would have been except that he knew the park with its little sweet valleys and byways and graceful willows and streams was a magnificent scheme to keep real estate values up. Bitsie's Harry knew that gold would come crashing down on his head and had gone into real estate and tried to get him to invest. Leave it to Harry. So Eden was a hedge against gold. The city behind him, the grayish haze of the gaslights, the pollution of mind and spirit. To step into the park, one might feel purified of it all. Especially if one owned land adjacent.

So how was he to go about it? He'd be a fool to bend his knee and say *God help me* and expect his skeptic's mind to give over to the *true believer's* mindless faith. That was the climate of the thirties, when all the northeast was a "burnt-over" region, with conversions and hellfire preachers at every corner. These were more rational times. Darwin had put a damper on hell and heaven. It was the Community that interested him. Rationally it was the most logical system of life he'd ever seen. Noyes was a genius. But God was the condition he had to deal with, and he meant to go into it with good faith.

Now, laying himself bare to the soul, between himself and the all-seeing eye of the moon which could just as well have been the eye of God, he asked himself: *Are my motives pure?*

To uproot his family from at least a false security into an unknown life? Was he honest? Was it for them, or for pure self-interest?

And then he thought: *If a drowning man is handed a spar, does he have time for the luxury of truth?*

He could have left Katherine and the children for a year to try it alone. But Katherine was a child herself, fluttering in indecision and inconsistency. How could he trust Deirdre to Katherine's decision? She wasn't watchful. And who knew better than himself how men were?

Katherine's denial of her own sexual nature had destroyed them both; *and* he suspected she was taking too much wine in that blasted room of hers. No, she and the children wouldn't survive without him.

And if they knew that Katherine was set against it, he doubted the Community would take him. They'd been closed to new families for so long. It was only by special dispensation from Noyes himself, because of Peter's service to the Community, that they had taken him.

It was so mucked up. He wished hungrily he could go up to Josephine Woods's and lie in the gentle arms of one of Jo's compassionate girls, not to fornicate, just to lie there and be comforted. He wondered in fact if the Community's sexual ways were even physically possible. They claimed a man could lie inside a woman for more than an hour, sometimes an hour and a half hand-running, enjoying a kind of delight that made an art of love, and then with sheer power of mind let it all subside until the engorged member withdrew of its own accord. A woman could climax two or three times . . . and *that* pleasure Katherine could never imagine. The girls at Jo's, they did, or said they did. Probably *said* they did. Although he fancied that with him it was the truth. Just to lie inside a woman without guilt . . . sanctioned by God . . . and the Community. Not just one woman but many women . . . any woman . . . any who would accept the invitation. He was randy thinking about it. And why would they lie? Amos, his old friend in the Community, told him this long before he dreamed he might join the Perfectionists.

Noyes was so damned sensible about it all. Where did anyone see reflected in nature that man was contented with one wife all his life? The organ of procreation and pleasure was God's gift to man. Noyes contended that procreation and pleasure were two distinct offices. Why not simply stop the procreation, which left women wasted with unwanted children, and sometimes left men depleted and filled with self-disgust, and leave only the wonder of the joining together and the sensation of the moment? An hour and a half! No semen spent, so where was all the sin? And it was all kept within the family. Unwanted children, that was a sin. Masturbation, that was a sin. To use women only to bring on the climax, that was a kind of masturbation. But to give happiness to many women, sometimes two or three times in an evening, that was an act of loving kindness. Still, he had to be instructed. It was an embarrassment, to be instructed in something he'd done for twenty years. But Paulie was only fifteen, and he wouldn't have Paulie deprived as he was. Once Peter had found a clipping in his drawer. Paulie had ordered something from the *Times:* a *glove* to be sent in a plain white envelope. So pathetically covert. Noyes was the only sensible voice who understood the nature of boys, who believed boys when they started to get randy should be instructed and initiated.

If only he himself could have been spared all the anguish, beset by what his father called the *devil's temptations.* He wondered, could he be taught at all? He'd be a hard case. And Katherine had left his bed for good and all. No, it was never good. Not with Katherine, never. In any case it looked like a long drought. Salvation had its bleaker aspects.

"Peter, is that you?"

Bannerman, walking between the shrubs, that great girth bundled in a huge fur coat, those drooping mustaches so famous in the courtroom, looking like a woolly walrus, and leading his old pug Grace by the leash. Grace was one of the most graceless of animals, with bowed rickety legs and hanging folds of skin. She waddled, like Bannerman, scraping the cold ground with her belly. Bannerman had her swaddled, like himself, in a wool blanket to save her privates from freezing. Bannerman grunted and settled himself on the bench next to Peter.

"I wondered why she kept tugging in this direction. She must be part bird dog to have caught your scent." He bent with effort to pat the panting dog.

"Are you out for a night on the ice?" asked Peter. Bannerman was notoriously sedentary.

"In point of fact," said Bannerman, "I drove up to Harlem Lane to watch the racing. Flatbush Girl was working out and I have money on her, and since the skaters were on the ice, I decided to take my dinner at the Pavilion and then I had to consider that poor old Grace had kidneys no better than mine and I brought her up here for a walk and a sniff, and she ferreted you out. Surprised to see you. I would have thought you'd be on the town tonight celebrating your great victory."

"What victory is that?" asked Peter.

"Unless I'm mistaken you won a whopping big case today."

"If you see that as a victory. He was guilty as sin. Up to his ballocks in Tweed's filth. I didn't get him off, Tweed bought out the jury. I never should have taken the case."

"Nonsense," said Bannerman. "What has sin to do with the law? You get an ax murderer off scot-free and you earn yourself a medal."

"Sin wasn't what I meant. I meant what of justice?"

"Justice?" Bannerman drew his bushy gray brows together in a query. "You're in a singular mood tonight." He took a cigar out of his pocket and bit off the end, his eyes fixed on Peter. Familiar Bannerman behavior. He lit the end of it, the glow from the match reddening his bulbous nose. "In any case, justice is blind. You can do what you damn please in front of her face as well as behind her back."

"For the first time since I began to practice the law," said Peter, "I'm beginning to feel that the money is tainted."

Bannerman pulled at the cigar. "Tainted? What an old-fashioned word. The law is a fine game, Peter. When you get to my age you'll see what a game of chess it is. Win a piece, lose a piece, what does it matter in the long run. And money is money. The only thing tainted, my boy, is meat when you're starving for it and it can't be eaten. By the way, are you taking Lillienthal's brief? I heard he was after you to represent him."

Down at the pond one of the skaters was showing off his skill; the rest had ringed him and he skated backward, his hands clasped behind him, he took a master leap, spinning like a top and landing on his feet. The crowd cheered him wildly. What a choice moment of glory. "What's up with Lillienthal? I hope to God he isn't mixed up with Tweed, or dealing in gold."

Bannerman screwed up his fat cheeks and pulled at his mustaches. "You mean you haven't read today's *Times?*"

"What the hell would Lillienthal be doing in the *Times?*" asked Peter.

Bannerman settled his belly more comfortably on his knees. "It seems that our friend Lillienthal engaged a laundry maid for his wife. You know his wife, Peter. The woman with the great bosoms. Drag her forward when she walks. Well, he engaged this little laundry maid and, as the paper tells it, he would take a bottle of wine down to the laundry room and share a glass with her."

"How on earth would the *Times* get hold of a thing like that?" asked Peter. "Or want to?"

"You may well ask. It seems he made advances to this laundry creature, when his wife was out walking her bosom. Of course there's nothing new about that. I'd say it was a blessing to most of us that there are laundry maids to ease the morning. But as it happens he got her in a family way."

"Old Lillienthal? He must be sixty, at least."

"My dear Peter, Lillienthal is scarcely fifty-seven." Bannerman rubbed the tip of his nose to warm it. "Between us it gets worse. It doesn't lie down with age like an old dog. Pity of it. And so he gets this laundry girl in a family way and of course he does the honorable thing. He offers her money to go to Madame Restell, who performs expensive but discreet abortions, and he finds her a room somewhere and he makes her a good settlement. Even offers to pay for the funeral in case things go badly for her. And here is where he makes his mistake. He throws in three thousand to boot for her to open a little flower shop. And the damn fool puts it in writing."

"I find that generous, in the least," said Peter.

"Nothing of the sort. The girl was provocative. If the girl had been chaste, she would have had him over the head with the first bottle of wine. Those girls, they're out to better themselves. Can't blame them, I suppose. What other way have they got to get out of the laundry? So as the *Times* would have it, she gets rid of the child, she doesn't die, worst luck, and once it's blown over, Lillienthal reneges on the three thousand, offers her a couple of hundred, and she's got him in court for breach of contract!"

"What a farce," said Peter.

"Better than a novel," said Bannerman. "A sterling life ruined, a marriage in shards, his wife has him up for divorce. And for what? A few dusty moments on the laundry room floor. They have us, Peter. No doubt of it."

"Doesn't it strike you," said Peter, "that there ought to be better ways of loving? That something is terribly wrong between men and women?"

"Follies and indiscretions," said Bannerman. "The animals have the best of it. Watch the monkeys in the zoo. Get their fill of it and never rate a column in the *Times*. But it makes good press and lawyers have to live. One man's folly is another man's dinner." Bannerman rubbed his gloved hands together. "By the way, Peter, if you wouldn't mind a word of advice from an elder statesman . . ."

"Yes?"

"Have you yourself been doing anything indiscreet? Anything that would cause questions being asked about the court?"

Peter's heart skipped. "Questions by whom?"

"Exactly what I asked. Some unsatisfied client, I suppose, sniffing out some scandal, a nose into your privacies. I mean each of us has certain . . . shall I say . . . legal connections he's happy to let go when questions are asked. For instance, if I can share a fact that I'd wish you to keep in confidence, I handle the legal matters for both Josephine Woods and Madame Restell."

"I knew that."

"I thought you might. Now if my connections to those interesting ladies were to come to scrutiny, by my wife, for instance, I'd deny them both. I don't put such things on paper, like poor Lillienthal. So if you have business connections that anyone might want to make the subject of inquiries . . ."

"I handle business affairs for members of the Oneida Community. I've done so for ten years."

"By my soul," said Bannerman with interest. "Those Christian satyrs and their harlots?"

"Not harlots," said Peter. "Zealots. They're wizards at business. They trust in God, I watch their contracts."

"Business, my heart and liver!" said Bannerman. "I thought their business was monkey's business."

"Then you haven't read their case," said Peter surlily "They're most misunderstood. There isn't a hunter west of the Appalachian who hasn't relied on their traps for a living. You've heard of the Newhouse trap? He's with them. They make handsome silk and rustic furniture and bags for traveling men and the rest is fiction."

Bannerman sucked at his cigar. "Ten years you say."

"Yes, I've know them for years. Noyes, the Cragins, most of the men."

Bannerman beetled his brows. "And you've been upstate to visit with them?"

"Whenever I've had business in Syracuse or Utica, yes."

"And it's business only. You say business is what they're about?"

"Business in the Communist way. All for the Community. They call it Bible Communism. Communism in the fashion of St. Paul."

"Noble," said Bannerman, "and biblical. And Katherine knows about these trips? She goes with you to see the rustic furniture or to buy silk?"

Peter hesitated. "In fact, no. I had business in Utica and I went by chance . . ."

"No?" Bannerman's voice rose as it did when he was cross-examining a client.

"How could she understand?" said Peter in annoyance. "All anyone cares to see in them is the prurient."

"So there is prurience to see?"

"They practice Complex Marriage."

"It does sound very complex to me," said Bannerman.

"They're all married to each other. It's in the open for anyone to read. And people find that so scandalous. But they don't find scandalous people married one to one and having to take mistresses and lovers because the system has failed. Nobody bothers to talk about how they work in Oneida. With a happy heart, for love and not for profit. And come home tired and happy to eat at the common table, knowing that their food isn't bought with blood money. That they didn't have to set some scoundrel free to make their profit."

"The law preserve me," said Bannerman in astonishment. "I believe you've fallen under the spell of these paradoxes of Christian virtue. But you're a sworn atheist."

He prayed to God, if there were a God, to send him a sign. "I may have been." Prayed for a concrete sign that He existed. "I was."

Bannerman puffed on the cigar. "I've known a good many lawyers who have fallen from Grace, Peter, and it's made their fortunes. But to fall *to* grace, that could be deadly, especially to a man like you."

Bannerman's probing words cut at him. He didn't want this kind of cross-examination. He was at God's bar, not man's. He wasn't sure yet who would be the sterner judge.

"Men like you," Bannerman went on, "full of banked fires. Passionate men who can let out their passions in front of a packed court and sway jurors with their pleading. It's grand for juries. A good show. But passions in the realm of religion? Well, look at your father. Let God alone, Peter. He's one passion a good lawyer can't protect you from." Bannerman dragged himself up and beat the bushes for old Grace, who pulled herself up from a bed of leaves and licked his fingers whimpering to be taken home. "One last question, Peter." Bannerman always made ready to leave and then popped one last question. It was called in professional circles the Bannerman retreat. His famous "last words." "These wizards of the traps, these preservers of fruit and spinners of silk, it isn't true then that they sleep in each other's beds? Isn't that the Complex Marriage?"

Peter's face flamed. He was thankful it couldn't be seen. "It's not that which interests me. To work for the common good interests me. Perhaps after a career at the bar I have something to atone for. Do you know what I do when I visit Oneida? I work at the forge."

Bannerman took the cigar out of his mouth.

"I worked the forge with the smithy when I was a boy. I love to work with my hands, do you know that? I'd like to know what it is for once to come home after a good sweat at the forge and eat simple food and sleep with good conscience."

"Hmmm," said Bannerman.

He was a liar. That wasn't all he wanted.

Was he wrestling with God or with the devil?

"You're quite sure," said Bannerman sharply, "that they don't snare their victims with this promise of paradise on earth?"

"That's grossly unfair," said Peter. "You malign good men."

Bannerman bent with great effort and a good deal of groaning to pick up Grace's leash. "If that's so, then you have my profound apology. You know how I am. Always devil's advocate." He laughed hugely. "That's a great joke, devil's advocate. But somebody is asking questions about you, Peter. And you are a passionate man. And passionate men fall in love. There are laundry maids and laundry maids. One can fall in love with heaven, if you get my drift, and have a roll on the celestial laundry room floor. Men find countless ways of making fools of themselves. Follies and indiscretions. But "—he sighed a great sigh—"in the end what does it really matter after all? What's left but a good glass of brandy, a piece of ripe cheese, and being allowed to break wind if you're flatulent. Take care, Peter. And if you want to talk, be free to come to me." He maneuvered old Grace back onto the path. "As you see, I'm a good confessor. I'm never far from Grace." Laughing at his own joke, he left Peter and his bench alone.

He sat for a long while after Bannerman left. Where was the truth of it? The truth was that New York was a sty that stank to high heaven. At Oneida a man had an enthusiasm for this little thing or that and he was encouraged to make a stab at it. Little industries, like weaving cane chairs and Newhouse and his traps. And the Community was making money. Out of the red. They worked as they loved; if times were hard they ate a poor table and still thanked God for it. They weren't afraid to laugh. And they danced, how they danced. They didn't bother to keep Sunday because every day was God's day! It was this generosity of spirit! And when they met and parted, they kissed each other. Not parsimonious little cheating social kisses, but with the full heart and openly. If that kind of love didn't come from God, then from where? There was nothing tainted about those feelings. Each time he shared them, he felt enlarged, enriched, his heart exploded for joy. And if that explosion could replace the explosion of his seed sexually, then where was the sin of it? These people, they knew how to love each other. Love to them wasn't a snide word, a mincing phrase. It was deeply felt in and out of bed.

He had come here to pray, he *tried* to pray and all he found in his heart was this litany of hate against his father. He'd been cheated out of love. A little child at night in a bleak world only wanting a little comfort in a way God Himself had designed, not with self-abuse but with God-sent dreams. And his father had contrived a little leather circlet, tied about the small member, so that when dreams stirred him and moved him, the circlet would tighten and wake him, strangling his sensual life forever, so that he was afraid to sleep, afraid to dream, his life was bereft of dreams, girded in realities and practicalities, ways to survive, swamped in a thousand guilts that prevented him from enjoying his pleasures even in a whore's bed, especially in a whore's bed. Unable to deal with women, leaping at love for fear it would be snatched away, or that the little circlet would tighten and tear at him. When he married, when he thought that the legality of marriage would release him at last, when he saw Katherine's body for the first time, he could have wept with happiness. And she had a parsimonious little heart, like her bitch of a sister, she kept her legs tight, denying him a thousandfold. And now Father Noyes said that there was a better way, another way. Note that he had been able for the first time in his life to spill out the things that were eating like vermin at his soul! Openly, and they understood! He payed for God to send him guidance. And for logic not to desert him. He lived in realities and tangibilities.

And now he had to leap into the void believing that the hand of God would sustain him. He was kept alive on teaspoonfuls of honey in a world of gall. He had a right, like the street urchins of his youth, to at least a bit of good meat in all the filth of the streets of his life. Or was he a liar, to the heart, following Noyes because he could sleep in beds of lust with impunity? He prayed for a sign. He confessed Christ: he hated his father, and sometimes he disliked his wife.

Amen.

Now he had to go home and open his heart to Katherine. To explain what he couldn't explain to Bannerman, that a better kind of life existed and he wanted it. That earth could be heaven again. That the present system had failed: note Lillienthal. Note the booming business of Josephine Woods and Madame Restell, business so good that they could afford the great Bannerman. Note his own marriage, where two people of common sympathies had fallen into cold disunion. No, there was only one decision. And he was considering Katherine as well as himself. So, therefore, they were leaving New York, without possessions. Everything he had he would give freely to the Oneida Community. Almost everything. He would lease out the house and give the rents instead. (He remembered the parable of the man who kept one field back in giving all to God and the terrible retribution.) But the man was not a lawyer. No lawyer could be expected not to cover all possibilities. But Katherine would have to give up the house, and her servants, and her luxuries, for luxuries of a more permanent kind. That in a month it was entirely possible that they would be members of the Oneida family.

He had to convince her of the benefits. Perhaps he would tonight. Or perhaps he would not. He was a lawyer after all. And until he had a positive sign from God, he would keep his doors open.

She brushed her hair, looking deep into the mirror for the face of her wounded soldier. He was healing now and they'd moved him to a little private room. A cubicle actually, there were so many other wounded to be cared for. But they would have some privacy at least so that they could plan their escape. He said he'd already written to his family in New Hampshire and that the house was being made ready for her and the children.

Peter opened the bedroom door. The image shattered. In the mirror, only her own face with Peter behind her. Her face . . . it reminded her of Momma's face, the way Momma looked before she died, like a frightened animal surrounded by hunters.

Peter stood there watching her. "Is your head better?"

Head . . . better? Berthe's words pounded in her temples. To protect her children she had to seduce her husband. She brushed out her hair and spread it around her shoulders. He used to want to see her hair that way. She laid down the brush. She opened the collar of her robe so that the whiteness of her shoulders was exposed. Nausea rose to her throat.

"We missed you at dinner."

Liar.

"Deirdre is still going on about *Hamlet.* I think she fancies herself in love with the bicycle rider."

"Yes."

"Did Else send up a tray?"

"Yes."

"After dinner I went for a walk in the park. The skaters were out. You should have been with me. You would have loved it."

Liar. He never wanted her with him. He hadn't for years. To the park? Lie upon lie. But she couldn't provoke him. She wanted Berthe there to advise her. She touched her bosom with cold fingers. Where was she to start? She was out of the practice of making love. Or she had never been in it, except in some fantasies.

"Rebecca tells me that Berthe was here today."

She answered faintly, "Yes." How should she begin with him? This was his court, he owned the jury, he was the judge. She was surrounded. She wondered how she could turn and look him in the eye without perishing, let alone go about seducing a man whose bed she had slept in for seventeen years. Seventeen years in bed with a stranger.

Peter pulled up a chair beside her dressing table. "We have accounts to settle between us, Katie."

Accounts. He'd said that before. She was a business transaction he had to complete. Where should she begin? Should she pull down her dressing gown and expose her breasts like the harlots of Greene Street? Should she lick her lips seductively or show her legs? It was ludicrous. She tried to clear her head. Berthe was wrong in one thing. Peter would never throw his children into the void. He meant to settle on them surely.

"Katie, why have there been so many unsaid things between you and me?"

"I don't know." Now the words took on a life of their own. "But I think it's too late to say them now. Just tell me what you mean to do with me and the children. I know that you love your children even if you have no love for me."

"Love!" The word exploded from his mouth, followed by a snort, a vicious sort of laugh. "You're the right one to talk about love." His face reddened, his fists closed. She was afraid he might hit her. She tightened against the blow. He didn't strike out. "What do you mean, settle? Settle for what?"

"I know you mean to leave us."

"I see . . . Berthe was here. So it was Berthe nosing around."

"She told me. Somebody had to."

To her astonishment, he fell to his knees and clasped his hands, like a child in prayer. "The only way there'll be peace between us is for me to confess Christ and to be criticized. I've studied it and I can see that's the only way. I want to unburden my heart."

She could hardly catch her breath with astonishment. "What on earth are you doing?"

"Don't stop me, for God's sake, while I have the courage."

"Get up!" she said. *"Please!"*

"It's like poison to the stomach, Katie, holding in feelings we've had against each other all these years. Bile collected under the heart. Confess. It's the only way back to health."

"Berthe was right! You've gone mad!"

[41]

"If madness is trying to come back to God, then I'm mad. Katie, there's a better life. We'll both be better for confession. So I confess that I've had little love for you for as many years as I can remember. You've been a cold woman, like your sister who's a bitch, how Hector can tolerate her I can't understand. You've kept a tight heart and tight legs."

"Stop this!" she begged.

"Early, when I didn't understand this . . . family trait of yours . . . I thought you had another man . . . a lover . . . and that when you were cold in bed with me you'd been sleeping with someone else."

"You thought *I* had . . ." she sputtered, incredulous.

"I used to leave the courts early in the day and drive the carriage into the square and look up toward your window, trying to see if there was another man in my house. I should have realized that you simply had nothing to offer any man. The jealousy was my fault and I confess it. And your coldness was your fault, probably fostered by your damn sister. And I freely forgive you for it. . . ."

"You"–she could have choked–"you forgive *me!*"

". . . freely. Whether or not you forgive yourself, that's between you and your conscience. But I'm holding no grievance against you. I give it up. . . ."

"You . . . *you* . . ."

". . . with all my heart. And I confess that because of your coldness I was driven to brothels. . . ."

"Stop!"

". . . to brothels and I've slept with strange women, but that I never in all my life loved one. In that I've been faithful. As for the rest, I consider myself a good husband in providing for you and my children. You've never wanted. And in point of fact, I'm faced with a great decision which affects us all, and it's your welfare especially I'm considering in making it."

"Liar!" she cried. "Filthy blackhearted liar! For my benefit you're running to the free lovers?"

He was getting uncomfortable on his knees. "They're not *free lovers.*

Of course Berthe would tell you that. I know I should have come to you sooner, but I've been debating my heart, and all the facts. And I assure you that you and the children are foremost in my decision. And I'm ready to explain it all to you now. But before I begin, if you can think of any other criticism of my conduct as husband and father, give it now. I can take it in good spirit." He rested his case. He lowered his head and waited for her comments on his testimony.

She was so outraged she couldn't bring words to her lips. She raised her fists to hit him, but she didn't have the strength. So she picked up the brush and threw it. It caught him sharp on the side of the head.

"Damn! What are you doing!" He pulled himself up. His knees were stiff. He shook them out. He touched his temple to see if she'd drawn blood.

"Blasphemer!" she screamed. "How can you use God's name and lie to me so freely! Berthe says you've joined the Socialists. You're no more a Socialist . . . than . . ."

"Not Socialist. Bible Communist. And control yourself. I can't stand hysterical women. Bible Communism is what they live. It's the Communism of the church of the apostles. They live by it. They're God-fearing. I've done a good deal of business with the Community and I've come to know them and to respect them."

"Business! Sleeping with a dozen women a night! Vile liar!"

"Keep your voice down. Do you want the children to hear you? I can see that Berthe's given you a pack of lies. Nobody sleeps with a dozen women. Leave that to Berthe's imagination. She'll have them doing it with the pigs."

"Oh . . ." Katherine moaned. "Oh . . ." Her nausea rose.

"Forgive me," said Peter. "I didn't mean to be so candid. I'm not used to talking about these things with women. I forgot myself. These are difficult concepts to grasp. I can hardly expect a woman to understand."

"No!" she shrieked. "And being a woman I wouldn't understand a man I've lived with for seventeen years who leaps from my bed to whores. . . ."

"I never leaped. You shoved me. I assure you that nobody in the Community is forced into loving beyond their conviction. There are members of the Community who've been celibate for more than twenty years. And if you'll calm yourself I'll explain what they mean by Complex Marriage."

"Don't tell me any more," she moaned. "I'm not your confessor."

He brushed off the knees of his trousers. "Neither are you my wife. You haven't been my wife for a long time. And as I've had the courage to confess my heart to you, although I can see you're not disposed to listen, let me tell you something about yourself, Katie. You're not only cold, you're becoming tedious. Your whole world is getting smaller and smaller."

She put her hands over her ears. "I don't want to hear this. Do what you want, go where you want, just tell me how my children and I shall eat while you're doing it."

"I happen to be more constant in my promises than you are. I never meant to abandon you. But I could see what was happening between us. And what would you do in the world without my protection? The only thing you know of the real world you've learned from your bitch of a sister or from those silly friends of yours. I know that you loved me once. And I loved you. I could have deserted you. Other husbands have left their wives with less provocation. I explained all this to my brothers and sisters in Oneida, and they showed me that the only way to bring us together again was for us to join the Community. It will be the salvation of us both, believe me."

"Told!" The horror showed on her face. "You told our most personal secrets to strangers?"

"They aren't strangers. And if things work out as I hope they will, they'll be your family as well as mine."

"My . . ."

"In a way you're more a child than Rebecca. What do you understand of life outside of your little paintings and your needlepoint? Outside the world is hell. And I won't have Paulie growing up in this garbage heap of a city, grubbing for gold like a blind pig. Not when there's a better life. I'm doing this for you and the children, I assure you, Katie."

"Oh, the outrageous gall . . ." She wept bitterly. "Using that righteous tone when you've confessed to living in sin!"

"Going to a whorehouse when your wife refuses you the bed isn't sin. It's a practical alternative. There isn't a court who would deny me. But that's over. We'll talk about it when you've come to yourself. We've had an offer for the house which I think is fair. As for my law offices . . ."

The house . . . she would faint . . . she caught gulps of air to keep from falling over.

"Or perhaps we'll simply lease the house. That would seem more prudent. In the event that I've been mistaken. I admit, I'm not infalli-ble. If at the end of a year, for instance, you feel that the life doesn't agree with you or the children . . ."

"You'd take me . . . and your *children,* into that . . . pestilence?"

"And where would you rather be? Your little morning room? That room as big as your heart. Your heart is shrinking, like a dried walnut. Soon you'll begin to look like Berthe. But I can see there's no use in talking logic when you're so overwrought. So I urge you, confess Christ and look into your own conscience. And calm yourself. Let me make the decision for my family."

"Never! I'll die first! I'll take poison!"

"Don't be silly."

"I'll take the children and live with Berthe!"

He shrugged. "If you want to live with Berthe I can't stop you. But my children go with me."

She would die on the spot! "You can't think of taking my children to that awful place!"

"Let me tell you something if you can listen with your little shriveled-up heart. There's been pox in the city. The influenza has been with us all winter. Do you know how many children have died of the pox right here in New York? The pestilence you talk of lives on the filthy streets. In the Community no children died. They breathe clean country air. They eat the food of their own fields. God protects children there. He loves children."

She moaned. She wrung her hands. "Who will protect my children here?"

"We've lived together for seventeen years. If we live like this any longer, with our hearts this hard against each other, we'll drown in our own bitterness. I've been dying day by day. I can't see any other way for us. I want to work with my hands, Katie. Don't you see that? I want to work with my son beside me. It won't be an easy life but I've been watching it for ten years, envious of what I've seen. If you haven't got the stomach for it, then go live with Berthe. Let her find you another Hector that you can suck dry. But the children go with me. If you want to be with us, then collect yourself. Amos and Sarah Smith, from the Community, are coming to New York to meet you. You'll be gracious and entertain them and you'll open your ears and you'll listen and if you have questions, you'll ask them."

"The horror . . ." she moaned. "The horror . . ."

"Do you hear a word I've said? You don't give a damn, do you, that I've been choked with questions since I was a boy, that I've suffered hell and now I've had a hint of heaven? You don't care. I never abandoned you and you've abandoned me. I don't mean to miss my last chance at happiness. Not because of a selfish woman who doesn't give a damn for anything except her little watercolors and her morning wine. Come with me and live. Or stay behind and go to hell." He walked out of the room.

She was too frightened to cry. She couldn't scream. She whispered: *Help me.* To whom? She begged her wounded soldier to come now, as he promised. She was ready. She ran down hospital corridors looking for him, into ward after ward. But the war was over and the beds were empty, the linen thrown aside. There was no one there. She called, "Help me!" But all she heard was the echo of her own fear. She ran to his little cubicle and flung open the door. The bed was empty. The linen made up. He was gone.

How long she sat at her table brushing her hair she didn't know. But after a long while Rebecca came in, Deirdre behind her. Rebecca leaned against her, stroking her hair. "Don't worry, Momma. You'll like the country. With pigs and horses, the way we had such fun when we visited Grampa Olsen once."

"What's Rebecca talking about?" asked Deirdre in alarm. "This is one of her dream stories, isn't it? I mean, Poppa has no intention of carting us all off to Virginia just when my voice is developing so well!"

"Will I be able to milk the cows this time?" asked Rebecca. "It's so funny the way milk comes. That God should have made milk come that way. Will I have a sled in winter? Will we still be there in winter? With wonderful hills to slide?"

"Why doesn't anybody tell me anything!" demanded Deirdre. "I'm not a child!" Then she saw her mother's face in the mirror and she fell silent. She watched her mother for a while and then she picked up the brush and began to brush Katherine's hair. "Momma, what's wrong? Tell me what's wrong? Please don't frighten me. . . ."

Peter moved through space without destination.

He walked the cold streets, up one, down the other. The night was no longer clear; fog rolled in from the bay and the gaslight made dim halos in the thickening white. The city. The city was not the center of the world. Outside the false boundaries of this false world Manhattan was the wilderness. Beyond the edges of this façade of life, the crystal

palaces, the white marble, the storefronts of A. T. Stewart's and
Tiffany's that disguised a terrible wilderness of the spirit was another
country. The law, as he conceived it and observed it and practiced it was
a construct, wrought by man, not engraved in stone like the Com-
mandments. Law could be twisted into any shape. But away from the
city, beyond the Appalachian, or even in the gentle rolling hills of
upstate New York, there was another world. The air was softer, the
grass more fragrant. He felt the liberation of the spirit. He was relieved
and suddenly hungry. Now he turned his steps toward a destination,
peering up at street markers through the thickening fog, toward a
sedate establishment. A knock at the door, an eye at the peephole and
the door would open to him. And if the existence of God were a fact,
he'd have much to answer for tomorrow. Tomorrow he'd pray in
earnest and confess and give it up once and for all. But tonight he
would lie in the arms of a woman who would make him feel welcome,
and at the moment that was the most consecrated act he could imagine.

"Barbarian!" Moira's little green
riding hat had been jolted to one side of her head by the bouncing
carriage. "Is this Fifth Avenue or Brooklyn Heights? You might as well
be riding in the country." She righted the hat, running a finger down
the length of the long green feather. "In Paris all the grand boulevards
are paved in asphalt. Smooth, without bumps. And the streets are so
wonderfully wide, they don't close you in. Ah, Paris . . ." She gave her
long theatrical sigh and closed her eyes in recollection.

Bitsie held her pudgy little hand to her bosom against the jouncing
of the cab. "Do you know Mrs. Schermerhorn's cousin? Her doctor said
that she could do damage to the vital organs riding on Broadway. He
forbade her to ride the streets because of her heart."

They stopped to look at the passing cab with the two liveried coachmen. "Is that *her?*" said a gawking Bitsie. Other carriages slowed, other women looked. "They call her Madame Killer," Bitsie said to Katherine.

"Impossibly provincial," Moira said. "If Madame Restell stopped providing her services, the best families of New York would be deluged with children they didn't want. In Paris such things are easily arranged."

Bitsie touched Moira's sleeve with dimpled fingers. "Have you . . . ever . . ."

Moira smiled her Moira-smile and answered nothing.

Katherine couldn't follow the gossip; she was too involved with her own heart. She'd been locked in the house too long. The tumult of the street confused her. Things moved too fast. Even Bitsie and Moira were strangers. Mouths opened, mouths closed. Bitsie had doused herself in a cloying perfume, too heavy for the close carriage. Bitsie, heavier than ever. Her taffeta skirts filled the carriage and her ruffled bodice bunched up under her chin; Bitsie's fingers on her breast dimpled with fat, like the wood-carved fingers of Rebecca's doll. Bitsie had such dainty hands, so bright and saucy as a girl, an easy smile and wild chestnut hair. Now the hair had been hot-curled so often that it was thinning and lifeless. And her eyes, in that puffed face, porcine. Katherine hated herself for thinking it but it was true.

"Ah . . . Paris." Moira, tanned frm the sea. Her tone implied that there were many deep things unsaid.

"I wish you didn't insist on going to Delmonico's unescorted. They're cutting me as it is," Bitsie complained. "Nobody's coming to the ball. And I bought gold livery for all the darkies. I still don't understand it. Just because President Grant put his gold on the market, whatever that means. Harry said Mrs. Grant swore she was in gold and her brother was even coming to my ball. Then gold crashed and Harry's in a state."

"Katherine isn't interested in Harry's schemes," said Moira.

Bitsie smiled her fat-cheeked cherubic smile. "Neither am I. Katie, something terrible happened to Moira on the ship. What a scandal! Make her tell it." Bitsie fanned herself with that scented handkerchief. Katherine wanted to stop the cab and jump out.

"Qu'est-ce qu'on peut dire?" asked Moira. "It was something that happens to women of the world, *n'est-ce pas?"*

"It was the ship's steward. Make her tell it, Katie."

The carriage careened its way through the crush of Fifth Avenue at lunch hour. "To the side!" Moira commanded the driver. Delmonico's vied for lunch trade with the Brunswick across the street and the avenue was jammed with carriages. They almost slid across the seats as the carriage made a veering turn. Julien, the maître d' himself, hair parted at center and oiled down, waited nervously at the side entrance. He rushed to where the cab had stopped, paid the driver, opened the door and offered Moira a hand down. *"Merci,* Julien," she said familiarly. He had to offer up two hands for Bitsie. Katherine wanted to escape but Moira had her by the arm and they were rushed into the corridor and up a small curved stairway to a private room. The table was set for lunch. "Our grand reunion," said Moira. "I tried to order absinthe but Julien said it was unthinkable."

"Please . . . madame . . ." Julien kissed her hand and bowed himself out. The waiter took their cloaks and wheeled in a cart with the iced bucket of champagne. He closed the door circumspectly behind him.

"And so here we are," Moira said.

"Did Edgar suspect?" Bitsie asked. "About the ship steward, I mean."

"Edgar is across the street at the Brunswick with all his horsey friends planning the greatest carriage parade the city has ever known. You know how he is about the horses. The opening of Harlem Lane was more important than the Second Coming. Sometimes when I ask him a question, I expect a whinny for an answer."

"It's a good thing I didn't dye all the sheep gold for the ball. Harry wanted a shepherd and shepherdess gold ball. I wanted Romeo and Juliet but Harry said some of the men were self-conscious about their thin legs. Tights can be cruel to men. And then President Grant was awful and everyone is angry with Harry because Harry was selling gold shares, don't you see?"

"Don't go on about it." Moira kissed Katherine's cheek. "See how pale she is. What on earth has been keeping you in seclusion, Katie? I'm so happy you wrote at last. If not, I would have come uninvited."

"You didn't even answer my invitation," said a hurt Bitsie. "I thought you'd given me up because I'd got so fat."

Poor Bitsie. Katherine embraced her in spite of the heavy scent, remembering what she was. "How could I do that? We've been friends forever."

"Longer than forever." Moira took the champagne bottle in experienced hands and popped the cork. "Forever and more." She filled the glasses. Katherine thought, *How confident she is, how modern.* Katherine took up her glass, waiting for the toast. All those old times, old places. Yes, she needed champagne. Champagne might stir her blood. She was a dead woman, a somnambulist. She had come for advice. How should she begin to tell them what she had to tell? She looked at Bitsie's jeweled fingers, Moira's self-sufficient smile. This was Moira's second trip abroad. And not a month went by that Bitsie didn't give a dinner or a dance. "How do you both manage so well?" She sipped at the champagne and then drank down the glass and offered her glass for more. "You want a trip to Paris and Edgar gives you one. Bitsie wants a dinner and the invitations are written. How? How are your lives so well ordered? What is it you do? Is there something, some gift . . ." Her voice betrayed her. She heard the edge of desperation and she couldn't stop herself. "Oh, Moira, what's wrong with me?"

Moira's mouth went slack in surprise at the sudden outburst. But the waiter knocked and wheeled in a tray of chilled oysters. "Not now!" Moira snapped. He quickly withdrew. "What on earth is wrong?" Moira asked. "I knew it was something when you didn't return my notes. I should have come sooner. Katie, what *is* it?"

Moira pulled her chair closer. Bitsie took Katherine's hand in her own warm soft hand. They had held hands as girls. Where was it all now? All the fun, all the good times. "Peter . . . he . . . wants to leave New York . . ."

Moira waited for more.

". . . to give up the house and move away from New York."

"Why?" asked Moira. "He dotes on that house. He drove everyone crazy, he had to have *that* house. And what of his law practice? I hope he hasn't got the migration fever and wants to go west to be a prairie judge or something."

They were waiting. Katherine felt that she would choke. "Upstate. He wants to move upstate."

"To Syracuse? Is it the courts? You'll hate it back in the country. And Peter will languish without company. There's no decent theater, no music . . ."

"Not to Syracuse."

"Where else is there?" asked Moira.

"Up to . . . Oneida."

The two waited with blank faces. "I have a cousin in Utica," said Bitsie finally. "I went up for the wedding. The house was so badly furnished. And there's nothing to do."

"You'd be neighbors to the *free lovers*," said Moira. "You might take a look into that, I suppose. What on earth can Peter be thinking to take you away from your friends?"

There was no way except to plunge into cold water. They had once, all three of them, when they were about Rebecca's age. In a little pond, just after the ice broke. They were so daring. Bitsie, the bright little swallow and long-legged Moira. It was just after the spring thaw. They screamed and joined hands and jumped in. "It's to the Community that Peter wants to take us. To the Oneida Community. As a family, you see."

The two were still blank. Slowly Bitsie's face turned red. *"Hic . . ."* Her flouncy bosom quivered with hiccups.

Moira slapped Bitsie's hand and leaned toward Katherine, her face a mask of astonishment. "You're joking! Surely you are!"

Katherine could only shake her head in denial.

Bitsie hiccuped and fanned herself. "I think I'm getting the vapors."

"Don't you *dare!*" said Moira.

"*Hic.* Please just loose a few buttons at the back," said Bitsie, "and untie my stays."

Katherine began to cry. "Oh, my dear . . ." said Moira, holding her as she wept. Now she wept it all out. The gates were open. All of it. "How have you managed your lives?" she asked finally. "What have I done wrong? What have I not done? What?"

"Do you mean to *say,*" said Moira, "that he actually intends to take you *and* the children *there?*"

"Is there something missing in me? Your trips, your parties. You seem to have so much control of your lives. I haven't, not anymore. Moira, help me."

Moira poured herself more champagne and downed it. "Oh, my dear Katie," she said wearily. She looked deeply at Katherine. Katherine could see the dark hollows under her eyes, as if she weren't sleeping well. "You think we've managed, Bitsie and I? You think we've managed so well?"

"Look how well you've managed the day," said Katherine. "You know Julien, you order the lunch, you understand Paris, you're at home on two continents."

"Am I?" said Moira with a tinge of humor. "My wonderful trips to Paris?" Moira bent her head over the empty glass. "Did you believe me when I told you about my wonderful trip? Oh, yes, why shouldn't you? I'm a grand storyteller, I always was."

There was a cushion of silence among them all. Now Katherine began to see them as they were, all of them, in the mirror across the room, shadows of their childhood still in their faces.

"My trip. Can you imagine a trip across the Atlantic on rough seas? Don't you remember how my stomach used to unsettle on rough water? I was over the side most of the time."

They used to go fishing with Bitsie's brother, on the diamond seas, Bitsie's fingers drifting in the bright foam. Katherine remembered, happy to be safe in the past again. "Oh, yes . . . yes . . ."

"I spent most of this last voyage in my cabin. I never wanted to go abroad. I'm dreadfully afraid of the sea. But Edgar had to go to Paris. Some of his racing friends, don't you see? I was sick in my cabin for days. He sat in the lounge drinking with his horse friends. He scarcely came to the cabin to see me. He didn't care if I was dead or alive. If it wasn't for a kind steward . . ."

"Oh, the steward," said Bitsie softly.

Katherine, through her tears, clasped Moira's hand. "A gentle steward, who fell in love with you. I understand that. A kind and gentle steward."

"*Do* you understand?" said Moira, her eyes dark with questions. Moira hesitated, words on her lips. Moira had been the bohemian of them all. Her long dramatic glances, her slender white throat and dark eyes and provocative smile. How she would shock them with the poems of Walt Whitman. Before they were married, Moira had taken to smoking cigars. At least one cigar, that Katherine remembered. *"Do you understand? I always thought that you were the one who got what she wanted, Katie. Peter was always so handsome and so attentive. You've been the envy of us all, did you know that?"

"If I was, it was false envy. You see that now. Peter and I scarcely speak, except in public. We haven't . . . slept together for a long time . . . and now this . . ."

Moira clasped her hands and bent her head. "Edgar loves his horses, and the men who ride them." She waited. Katherine tried to understand what she was saying. *"And* the men who ride them."

"Well, my Harry loves the stock market," said a perspiring Bitsie. "He's there day and night. He *loves* his stocks and his gold shares."

"Stop it, Bitsie. You know what I mean. He *loves* his horse friends. And he can't afford a scandal here in New York and things are so much more easily arranged in Paris."

Bitsie's face turned beet-red. *"Hic . . ."*

"I see," said Katherine softly.

". . . and as for me, if I were a horse he would have kept riding me. As it was . . . the young steward . . . there have been other . . . young stewards."

Katherine put a hand to her throat. "Oh, Moira . . ."

"Oh yes . . . Edgar pays them, don't you see. He paid the steward."

The silence sat like velvet on the elegantly appointed little room with its flocked walls and cut glass. The silence was weighted and palpable. "And you knew . . ." said Katherine finally.

"Oh, yes."

"And still you . . ."

"Yes," said Moira. "It's better than . . ."

There was no more to say. Katherine understood. Oh, she understood Moira so well. She understood Moira to the deep core of the heart.

Bitsie was fanning herself. "I do give grand balls and dinners. It's because Harry sells gold shares. He gives great dinners for his clients." She dabbed at her eyes with the handkerchief. "That's all I do. Dinners with twenty courses. Doves in plum sauce. You know. Once Harry put little gold bracelets in the napkins of all the women. Gold, you see. And when the dinners are over Harry comes and shoves bits of food under my nose and he says, *Oink-oink.* He says the only thing wrong with the dinners is the pig that sits *at* the table. He says that, Harry always does."

Katherine took Bitsie's damp little hand.

"I've tried to stop eating. I can't bear to be like this. Oink-oink, he says. And each morning I swear I'll stop. And each day is so . . . there's nothing to do. I go to church and pray God to help me. I even go to the Catholics. They have a saint for everyone. I thought perhaps they might have a fat Mary, a patron of fat women who would understand me. The Methodists are so terrible on gluttony. I thought, if there was a fat Mary she would understand how terrible it is to always want to eat and to have to hear oink-oink. I've even locked the food closet but I always find the key where I've hidden it. I've even tried to prick myself with a pin, when I couldn't stop eating. Look." Bitsie shoved up her tight sleeve and showed the rash of pinpricks on her arm.

The three of them sat numbly. Katherine could cry, she could laugh, she could do both. They were all exhausted with it. But for the first time she felt not *alone.*

Moira wiped at her brow with her linen napkin. "Well, enough of this. Let's not be fools, sitting around and crying into our wine. We have to manage, don't we? One way or the other. Exactly what does Peter propose for you and the children? How does he explain that?"

"He's explained nothing. I couldn't . . . we couldn't even speak of it . . . I was so shocked when he proposed it. What was I to say to him? He told me that his friends are coming down from Oneida in a few days and that I'm to ask my questions then."

"Monstrous," said Moira. "And that was all?"

"He said he wanted to work with his hands again. At the forge. To work at the forge."

"And where does he expect you to work, then? On your back?"

"Hic . . ." Bitsie poured more champagne.

"Bastards. Rotters. Anything for their own bloody satisfaction. They drag you through hell or worse. But surely he's thought of Deirdre. That sweet child. She's an innocent, Katie. How could he have the gall to even consider . . . I mean, does she even *know* of such things?"

"Oh, dear God . . ." said Katherine.

"Hic . . . they do serve wonderful strawberries though."

Moira put an arm around Katherine to support her. "Be serious, Bitsie. How can you make jokes now?"

"I am serious. They have marvelous strawberries and cream. I've been there."

"Do stop babbling," said Moira. "Been where?"

"You see?" Bitsie appealed to Katherine. "Just because I'm fat, people don't listen to me, or they don't believe me, or they say Bitsie stop babbling or Bitsie stop being a child. I have *been* there. I told you, my cousin got married up in Utica. I was trapped in Utica for a whole week and there isn't anything to *do* in Utica and so on Sundays everybody goes on a day's outing by the train. It stops in the Oneida station. They serve most marvelous strawberries. They're famous for it."

"Bitsie, are we talking about the same *place?* We mean the *free lovers!* Where they all fornicate in the same bed!"

"I don't care if they do it till they're blue in the face. They grow strawberries and pick them fresh and serve the grandest cream. People come by the hundred. They sit at long tables and bring away jars of fruit. They do fruit and quite good sewing silk. The women put the fruit up in their own cans. I think they make the cans."

"But you never *told* me!"

"You were in Europe and then Mrs. Grant got into gold and I was months planning the party. I never had time."

"Then you've seen the place? Actually *seen* it?"

"They do dress very queer, though. They wear bloomers, and they cut their hair like convicts. Oh, I *hope* he doesn't make Katherine cut her hair. Her wonderful hair!"

"Bitsie, don't ex*asp*erate me! Did you see the house? Where the women were kept?"

"They took us through the house. They were very kind I thought."

"You were *inside* the house!" asked a stupefied Moira.

"They have fine steam heat. Pipes all along the corridors."

"What did you *see* in the house? Did men . . . do things in plain sight?"

"What things?" asked Bitsie.

"Oh, don't be *tedious!* How did the women act?"

"Act about what?"

"Bitsie, don't exasperate me. Did you see the bed! Were there any women in the bed!"

"They didn't show us any beds. It's a marvelous great house, though. It has a grand ballroom and a proper stage. And they've just finished the children's wing. You can reach it underground, through a tunnel."

"Well, I should *think* they'd have a separate house for the children. There must be hundreds of children. Were they all pregnant? They msut be popping a child a minute."

"Nobody was pregnant. They took me through the kitchen. They all eat together, like a grand hotel. And one of the women, she was so kind to me, she took me aside and she said, 'You must confess Christ and pray for him to cure you of your *alimentiveness.'* She meant I was fat, of course. And she was so kind, she didn't say oink-oink. She called it *alimentiveness.* She'd heard Harry at the strawberry tables, you see. Harry talks so loud. He said to somebody that he'd got his money's worth of wife, and he wanted change. Two or three for the one he had. Everybody laughed. And the woman, she heard it. And she took me into the kitchen and she said if I confessed Christ he would take that sickness away from me."

"Peter said, confess Christ," said Katherine. "What did he mean? Do they do holy communion?"

"The heretics!" said Moira. "To use religion to cover up their lust. It's unthinkable."

"And they had a marching band," said Bitsie.

"A marching *what?* She'll drive me crazy with all this."

"I'm not! They can do it all they please, night and day in any bed. I don't know and I don't care. But they had a marching band and the children did an opera for us. Something about pirates. It was lovely. Oh, Katie, if I could lose this fat I'd confess anything."

"Is there something *to* this place?" Katherine asked. "I mean, Peter has always been so sensible about most things. Berthe said it was only a trap to get men's fortunes. That they lured them in to get their money. But why on earth would they need a marching band?"

"Berthe?" said Moira. "You told Berthe?"

"It was Berthe who found it out."

"Well, I'll wager she was pleased enough about that. To find out there was trouble between you and Peter, I mean. She was always jealous of you."

Katherine was astonished. "Did you think that too? I always thought . . . it was my fantasy."

"We all knew that," said Bitsie. "How could you miss it?"

What did she know? Living in an airless room with blind eyes, a somnambulist. So what could she know? "Then what I always sensed about Berthe was true."

Moira opened her bag and took out a gold cigarette holder and put a little brown cigarette in it. She held it between her teeth and took out a match and lit it.

Bitsie hiccuped and giggled. "She's so daring, she always was."

"Well, let's think this through." Moira puffed like a man and blew out smoke. She poured out the rest of the champagne and they all sat, exhausted, and let the liquor do its work. "Let's put it that there is such a place and it's not the hellhole it's been painted. I mean I don't quite see Satan serving strawberries and cream. But we know they all sleep together, that's a fact. Nobody denies that. So let's say that Peter's stumbled on this little mad scheme and being a man he's fallen in love with the idea and he wants to take you there. For how long? I mean you can't do that sort of thing forever."

"I don't know . . . I wasn't listening . . . he may have said a year."

Moira puffed out little pillows of white smoke. "A year isn't forever, is it?"

"Sleeping with strange men!" said Bitsie, a hand to her breast.

Moira reproached her with narrowed eyes. "That's not the worst thing in the world. In fact it has its advantages. What can you get out of it?"

"Out?"

"Yes. What do you want, Katie?"

"I want a divorce, without scandal! I want my house and something to live on!"

"Good. Then you have clear goals. And you're a sight better off than I am. And Bitsie's Harry will end up in prison sooner or later so where is she?"

"... *hic* ..."

"So ... if you decide to go with him for a year ... then get a contract.

"A what?"

"A contract ... that will hold up in a court. For the house and the settlement."

"You can't be serious!"

"I am dead serious. You must watch over your children, and you must have the house, mustn't you? So as long as you have no other choice"–she puffed on the little brown cigarette–"you might as well enjoy it."

Peter poured out two glasses of sherry. "Will you take a glass of wine with me?" Paulie was posing for his father's benefit in front of the parlor mantel in the dress uniform of St. George's. Blue serge pressed to a fine point, gold epaulets, hanging braid, a medal (at fifteen? For cleaning his room, Peter supposed). A gold eagle on his cap and that ridiculous sword. The sword caught awkwardly on the piano as Paulie came forward to take the glass. In spite of the toy-soldier costume, Peter thought with a kind of suffused pride, how good it was to be with his son again. And at this moment he knew irrevocably that God did not exist. No benevolent God could have commanded Abraham to raise a knife to his son; no father would have obeyed that command. Peter raised his glass to his son. This was a ritual, an ancient ceremony. "Have I called you away at a bad time?"

Paulie carried the wine carefully and sat at the edge of the wing chair. He hadn't taken off the sword. Peter had to hold his mouth tight to keep the smile from cracking. "We were right in the middle of maneuvers, in fact."

"Were you?" Peter trying to be as serious as possible. "And what maneuvers were those?"

Paulie watched his father stretching out his legs and Paulie did the same. "We're doing all the battles of the war. My project is Antietam. My friend Connory, you remember, Father, the fat one? He's got Chickamauga. I know Antietam yard by yard. I can tell you where the bodies fell."

"I'd rather you fight the battle of the algebra. Your grades are a trifle shaky, if I interpret the major's letter correctly."

Paulie sipped at the wine. "Algebra be damned." He watched his father's face to see if he would get away with the daring epithet. "Algebra can't save your neck under fire. A soldier has to keep ready. I mean, *semper paratus.* That's what the major says. I'm not having troops moving into my city to rape my women and children without being ready."

"Perhaps the major hasn't heard that the war is over," said Peter.

"It's not. Not at St. George's. The major says we're never to forget it. Two fellows' fathers have wooden legs and Connory's father has a glass eye and Lester has a father who went quite mad from lying in a wet field for three days under fire. When Lester goes home, he leads his father around the town the way you'd lead a child. I mean, his father actually babbles. But Lester is proud of it and they've given his father first place on the brass plaque."

"And what brass plaque is that?"

"Major Ambeson keeps it in the grand hall. It's inscribed with the names of all the wounded fathers."

It was such nonsense. "Paul, I've called you home on a matter of great importance to the family."

Paulie downed the whole glass and leaned forward, as his sword would permit.

"I've . . . never told you about my own life . . . about my childhood with your grandfather."

Paulie nodded that he understood. "It must have been hellish. Grandfather is so inflexible on God and women."

"Inflexible is the exact word."

"Good Lord, he's been lecturing me on self-abuse since I was ten.

But so does the major. He's keen on that sort of thing because it weakens the moral fiber."

"But that's exactly what I wanted to discuss with you! A very private discussion," Peter said. "On things of a . . . sexual nature."

Paulie sat bolt upright. The sword point jammed into the rug. "Is *that* it, Father? Is it about women? You thought I'd started on *that* sort of thing? I *am* relieved. When the telegram came I thought something awful had happened. That you'd gone bankrupt or something."

"Why on earth would you think that?"

"Well, Connory thought for sure. With all this gold fever. Even President Grant getting himself mixed up in it. Major Ambeson says that something terrible always happens when generals leave the battlefield for the countinghouse."

"You thought I was mixed up in gold?"

"Well, it happened to Ellis. You remember him? He had the scar on his cheek and all of us fellows thought it was a dueling scar and then we found out it only happened from a fall from a tree swing? Well, his father got caught in gold and they had to pull him out of the Academy. When he came back to visit, they cut him dead. He was simply finished."

"Poor Ellis," said Peter. "I know his father. I hope *you* didn't cut him dead."

"Certainly not!" said Paulie. "Well, not in private anyway. He was a good friend. But I couldn't even sit with him in the dining room."

"Why on earth not?"

"Because if the fellows had seen him, they would have cut me too."

"And you wouldn't have liked that," Peter said, his voice going slightly on edge. Poor Ellis, and to have his son snubbed by a bunch of young military fops.

Paulie put his empty wineglass down on the table. "Don't make it sound like *that,* Father. I have my career to worry about. I want to get into a good regiment. I can't take any chances socially. It's a matter of family honor."

Peter felt himself bridling. "Honor? Cutting a friend whose father was having a hard time? Where was the honor in that?"

A confusion was setting in between them . . . something . . . disturbing the sweet air that moved between father and son. He wasn't finding the boy so amusing now. And it was his own fault, for letting Paulie go. It was only that he knew he and Katherine had to settle this thing between them and he didn't want Paulie there to be disturbed by it. But the boy was at an impressionable age and he'd let him get into the hands of that idiot Ambeson. Now he got the full intent of what his son had said. "What on earth do you mean, *family* honor?"

"Please don't be upset, Father. I didn't mean it the way it sounded. I just mean that we fellows have to think with a war mentality, that's all. I mean that Major Ambeson says that life is a great battlefield and we always have to be ready. We can't be caught unawares. I have to train to be a winner. Because if you lose, you're dead."

"Major Ambeson is an ass. Did he teach you that? That winning was all?"

"You taught me that!" Paulie said, with rising alarm.

"I? When did I teach you a thing like that?"

"Well, you're a lawyer, aren't you? You always have to win, no matter if you have to lie . . ."

"Lie! When did you ever hear me lie in court!"

"Well . . . the major says . . . lawyers are trained to lie. They learn to lie and evade, that's their trade. That's what a lawyer is. Lies are his weapons. Father, why are you so angry with me! I didn't mean that you ever lied to us! I don't understand why you're angry!"

"And your major has a brass plaque and my name isn't on it. And you're ashamed because I don't have a glass eye or a wooden leg like your chums and you can't parade your vegetable father around New York?"

"I never said that!" Paulie's voice was rising. "I never said I wanted you wounded!"

"But I didn't fight in the war and I think you're ashamed of that."

"I *never* said . . . it was the major . . . you know how he feels about men who bought themselves out of the war."

"And you think I bought myself out because I'm a coward?"

Paulie was sweating. He gripped the arms of the chair. "I never thought that, never! I remember the war! It was terrible, all that fighting in the streets, all the riots and people hurting black people with sticks and rocks, just because they didn't have the three hundred dollars to buy out."

"But I did."

"You had us to take care of! I know that! I told Major Ambeson that you were only protecting your women and children! Mother is such a child herself, so scattered . . . She'd have perished without you! You needed to take us out of the city! That was why you didn't fight! It's just that the major said . . ."

"It didn't occur to you that I'd have to be fighting against men who were no more responsible for slavery . . . than I was. Men who were only cannon fodder, who couldn't buy *them*selves out . . ."

"I never blamed you! You weren't responsible, but I had to think of the family honor! It was you I was thinking of! Always! We're both Berger men and I wanted to help the Berger name by being brave and getting in a good regiment. I wanted to come back to you with wounds in my chest and never in my back so that you'd be proud and re- deemed . . ."

"Redeemed from what, damn you!"

"Good Lord, I didn't mean *redeemed* . . . not that *way* . . . why are you mixing me up like this? I only wanted to get into a good regiment and you need connections to get that and I thought you'd gone bank- rupt . . ."

"I refused to fight because I believed that life was sacred. Thou shalt not kill. Do you understand me?"

Paulie understood nothing. He was hurt, and he wilted under his father's abuse. Upset and defensive. "You had no right to accuse me. . . . I *never* meant what you said . . . you just twisted me up, that's all. And if you didn't want to fight because you needed to protect us, just say so. Don't lie to me about it. You don't believe anything is *sacred,* because you're an atheist. You said so a hundred times. So don't lie about it. Not to me."

He was swollen with his anger. "You dare . . . you *dare* to talk to me with that kind of disrespect?"

Paulie cringed in his chair, tears already forming in his eyes. . . .

"I called you home because there was a decision that affected the whole family. And you thought I'd gone bankrupt. When you thought I'd lost my money, did you think, poor Father, what will he do? No, you thought of your own skin, your reputation with the fellows and that pompous Ambeson. . . ."

Paulie drew in against the onslaught. "Father . . . please . . . *please* . . ."

"Well, now you just sit there and listen, do you hear me? I sent them an innocent boy and they've sent me back a fool. Antietam? You know Antietam? You mapped where the bodies fell? Do you know what it means to lie on a battlefield, disemboweled but still alive and screaming . . . and your major makes that a game of dominoes? No . . . I'm taking you away to a different kind of life . . . where you can learn a little common sense . . . *and* humility."

"But I don't want to leave the Academy!"

"I don't give a damn what you want. We're moving out of New York City. I'm sick of going off every morning to play the grab-game and leaving my son in the hands of strangers. So you betrayed a friend for the sake of position. Well, to hell with position and possession and war in the city. I believe in moral fiber. But there are other kinds of self-abuse."

"Just let me finish out the term then!"

"Not another day. You're a green boy. I support you and I educate you and by God if I choose to educate you out of the city, I will. Now have Else take those tin soldier uniforms and that foolish sword and throw them in the fire."

Paulie was crying. He couldn't control himself.

"No, take the sword. We'll beat it into plowshares, because we're going back to country life and that's the end of it."

"I hate you," said Paulie, weeping. "You sound just like Grandfather."

Peter slammed out of the parlor. Mirrors rattled as he shut the door behind him. He saw Rebecca and Deirdre scuttle for cover. Of course they'd heard; the whole house heard.

As he walked along the street the pain in his bowels rose upward into his chest. He thought he was having an attack. He heard the echo of his own voice . . . it *was* his father. He was sick. He'd lost control and twisted up his son with old courtroom tricks. An innocent boy like Paulie. Who only wanted an explanation. So the boy had taken himself a military hero. What boy didn't? Paulie, who vowed he would gladly take a rifle ball in the chest for his father's honor. Peter should have kissed him and blessed him. Instead, his father's voice had come up from hell to spoil his happiness. *Damn* you, he said to his father . . . *let me go!*

"Was it bold of me to come without an invitation?" Sarah was half into the hall before Katherine could think of an excuse to put her off. And Sarah had already taken off her coat. "But Amos has himself deep in chain link and bellows and I wasn't two miles from Gramercy Park and I felt cooped up and I had to stretch my legs. So here I am. Dear Katie." She held her arms to Katherine and came to her and kissed her cheek.

The final outrage in a day of outrages. The woman *must* have sensed that she wasn't welcome, but she wasn't put off. In fact she seemed totally at ease. *Where*, thought Katherine, *do women get this kind of self-assurance?* So she was being put on trial. This was a device for them to get a measure of her. Good. She would be found guilty and unacceptable and refused entrance to this heaven on earth and that would be the end of the whole thing and she would deal with what would be.

But her social obligation forced her to smile and nod and she invited Sarah into the parlor. No, not the parlor. There was something so embarrassingly personal in all this. She invited Sarah upstairs to her morning room. Was this the kind of woman Bitsie had described? Sarah was perhaps fifty, solid but without fat, tanned by the sun, wrinkles of laughter at her mouth and eyes. The smile seemed natural enough to her, not Berthe's forced smile. And the hair was as Bitsie had described: cut severely around below the ear and straight across the brow. Her dress was dreary. Katherine couldn't help looking at the hemline.

"Oh, dear, you expected the pantaloons. But we've done enough to scandalize the world. When we come to strangers, we do as the Romans. We keep a closet for travel, but we all share the same clothes. Am I too much out of fashion?" She said this without apology. "Last week two of our women took it into their heads to show off our style of dress in the Syracuse railway station, and to pass out tracts. Well, one of the ladies in the station took great offense, God knows why, and cried *Bloomerism!* and near started a riot. There were stones thrown. The police barely got them out. So I'm not about to come to New York City and cause trouble. We'll leave the strangers to their own ways."

"And do you also pass out tracts?" Katherine asked coldly.

Sarah smiled. "I'm too old for it. Mind you, you should have seen me when I first joined the Community. I was a firebrand. I'd already fallen in love with Fourier and then with Mother Ann of the Shakers. I was much given to passions. I drove my father mad. Then I met Amos and took the Perfectionists for my own true love and married Amos and we moved to Brooklyn where we worked the press and printed *The Circular* for years. Then when they built the Mansion House we had to be in on that. It was the best of times, I can tell you. The men did all the bricks and mortar and the women did all the lathing. Well, you couldn't haul plaster in skirts and petticoats. The bloomers are mighty comfortable."

Katherine stopped at the nursery landing. Had the children heard them? Paulie was locked in his room. The girls were somewhere about. "I want you to know that all of . . . this . . . is Peter's enthusiasm, not mine. I want you to understand that."

"Good," said Sarah. "Now that's clear. But aren't you in the least curious? I didn't think there was anyone in New York who wasn't."

She was relieved. Sarah was easy to deal with. She thought, it's all finished then. It's over. "Yes, I was curious. It's been . . . upsetting to the family. My son is home from school because of it."

"I quite understand. I'm here in New York to see my own son, in fact."

It was rare that Katherine took anyone from the outside into her room. She opened the door for Sarah. Sarah made herself at home, sensing that this was Katherine's private world. All that was communicated between them. Sarah sensed which was Katherine's own chair and took the other. She was a woman used to other people's needs. "I'm told you grow uncommon strawberries," Katherine said, to begin.

"That's all you want to ask? The only uncommon thing?"

Katherine sat for a while before getting up the courage. "You and Amos . . . you are . . . married . . . in the ordinary sense?"

"In the *extra*ordinary sense. We married early on, before we signed the articles. Almost at the time John Noyes married Harriet."

"Then people . . . do marry."

"We are all married in the eyes of God."

"And you share a room together? In the . . . ordinary sense? I thought . . . I was told. . ."

"Why on earth should we share a room? Do kings and queens sleep in a room together? No, royalty sleeps alone. And so do we, in the Mansion House of God. The rooms are small, but we need a small place to ourselves. I mean, it's such a bustle. We eat together, we pray and play together . . ."

". . . play. . ."

"Play. Croquet. We all have a passion for croquet. Do you fancy it?"

Katherine was flushed with embarrassment. "I was told . . ."

"When we retire, we do so alone. In the early days, when the Mansion House was still not finished and we had no place to sleep, someone had the grand idea of putting up a great round tent in the big hall. There was a central social area and we each had a small space separated by canvas. Well, you can understand the scandal that called on us from the outside. But Father Noyes said, if we're armed in a good morality, that would be better than walls."

"Then you don't . . . I mean . . ."

"Don't what?" Sarah asked candidly."

"They said . . ."

". . . we make love with one another. It's the fashion of the Community, not of the world. It's simply that."

"But you came into the Community with a child. You and your husband."

"Adam. He's quite wonderful. He has a splendid voice. He teaches our children's chorus. But Adam was restless and so the Community decided to send him to New York to study voice for the winter. Now he's had quite enough of strangers and he's longing to come home. I quite adore him. It's a great fault of mine. I've been criticized for it."

"How could loving a son be construed as a fault?"

"We don't hold with special love, you see. The children belong to us all. So that makes them quite free, as well as us. We are that, you know. Quite free."

"And Amos is satisfied to have his son . . . see how men and women live? I mean . . . the way they carry on . . ."

Sarah rocked up and back even though she wasn't sitting in a rocking chair. "But Amos is not Adam's father."

Katherine flushed. "I'm sorry . . . I didn't mean . . ."

"But you must ask. That's why I came to you. I knew that if Amos and I came to dinner, Amos and Peter would absorb the conversation. You'd be afraid to ask. I expected that. So I came alone, you see. About my son, I greatly wanted a child but in the early days we couldn't afford them and we don't believe in having children we can't raise properly.

But I was having internal problems and I felt . . . we felt that if I waited, it might be too late. And Amos and I . . . we are both so fiercely independent. They thought we'd make too bold a child, you see. And they were right, of course. So they chose a father for me. One with better characteristics for the kind of life we live."

Katherine's eyes opened in horror. "You were told who should father your child? But that's slavery!"

"How shocked you are," Sarah said. "Are you so satisfied, then, with the way things are in the world you live in? A man owns his wife and child. He only loves what he himself begets. These are all our children. We own them in joint ownership with God. You talk about slavery. To selfishly possess people, that's slavery. Amos loves me, I love him. Has that changed because someone else fathered my child? Let me tell you something, Katie. You may quarrel with Noyes's theology. God knows, most of the world has. But he's uncommon brilliant in his understanding of women."

"What sort of understanding? With his decision, he made your son a . . . a . . ."

". . . bastard? We hear it often enough from the outside. He's no bastard. He has a name. Bennington, for his father. Smith for Amos, who fathered him most, since his natural father is dead. Adam Bennington Smith. I should also add Noyes, since he adores Father Noyes."

"Why are you telling me these things? I haven't asked you to open your personal life to me! I told you, these are Peter's interests, not mine!"

Sarah leaned forward, her legs slightly apart, like a man. She clasped her hands. She had strong hands, with veins standing out on the back of them as if she'd been working the earth. "My dear Katie, you know Peter better than I. If Peter wants to come to us, I doubt anything will stop him."

"Then why are you bothering with me at all?"

Sarah's eyes took in the little room, Katherine's most personal things, her watercolors . . . particularly those. She felt as naked with

Sarah as she had with Berthe. "I'm not here because of Peter. My interest has always been with you."

"Me? How? We've never met."

Sarah got out of the chair and walked over to the wall where Katherine's little paintings hung. She took one off the wall and looked at it carefully. "I lied. I said I didn't pass out tracts. I may not be the idealistic girl I was when I first came to the Perfectionists. I'm older . . . I hope I'm wiser and a little more realistic. But I believe with my heart and soul that the world will come around to our ways sooner or later. The world can't survive the way it is, it's too crooked. Women won't survive. I've heard Peter talk about you for years. Bits and pieces. What you do, what you say. And your painting. Only he calls it 'finger-painting.' Something a child might do. Now that hurts me particularly. I love drawing. I never had the knack of it. Well, I suppose I made a picture of you in my mind, like this watercolor, somewhat indistinct, but I had the shape of it. And it came to me . . . I'm not clairvoyant but I'm marvelous good at instinct . . . some of us have the gift. I think God works in mysterious ways. I don't worry about Peter, he'll manage one way or the other. But you're too soft, Katie. I think that what God intends is not for Peter but for you.'"

Katherine didn't know how to respond. She wanted to be angry but she couldn't. Sarah was so candid and so fresh and so easy. And her painting was in Sarah's hands. Sarah's eyes had seen it and loved it.

"Knowing what the world is for women on the *outside,* I wondered what you'd do if Peter came to us."

"I've asked myself that question over and over."

"I suppose I said what I said to shock you, to get over the newness of it right off. So you'd get a quick measure of us. I've told you the hardest thing for outsiders to swallow. I haven't told you the best of it. It is heaven. I've lived this life for almost thirty years and I can swear to it." She got up and came over to Katherine and bent to kiss her cheek. "Don't throw stones at me, Katie. The world is full of surprises. If you should decide to come to us, we have a little nursery kitchen, not the great one where we all gather, but a little room with the fire always going next to the children's room. And I come down when I can't sleep at night for a cup of tea. I'll be waiting for you there." She held up the watercolor. "May I have this?" Katherine could hardly refuse. "You can have this in exchange." Sarah laid something down on her lap. "Don't get up. I'll let myself out."

Katherine was still sitting there when the door closed.

In her lap was a small pamphlet.

SLAVERY AND MARRIAGE: a dialogue

She opened the rough pages. She flipped through:

> . . . the truth is . . . Marriages give man the power of ownership over a woman, and such power is wrong in the case of marriage as it is in that of slavery.
>
> Marriage in pairs is only one form of sexual union and I believe that this method is arbitrary as the slaveholder's method of securing natural service; and it is a cruel and oppressive method of uniting the sexes. The catalogue of women's abuses under the tyranny of matrimony . . .

Then she started again, from the beginning.

In one of the upstairs bedrooms of Miss Josephine Woods's establishment on Clinton Place between University and Broadway, Bella Stravos stood nervously in front of a mirror trying to compensate with pins for the fact that the bodice of her dress was a size too large. She didn't work here usually. In fact, she knew that she wasn't "good enough for the place" as she told her mother before she left that evening. She was filling in for a friend who was "indisposed" by her monthly curse. In any case this was not her kind of work; she abhorred it. But she had "fallen" last year at sixteen by the butcher's helper, a black-eyed boy who lured her on sweetbreads and calves brains and finally with a whole side of lamb. She only "fell" once. Once was enough. She had a child and he went to work in Brooklyn. Her mother lived in a cottage near the East River and she could barely take care of herself, she was so sickly. But Bella knew that if she went to the city fathers for help, they'd take away the child. What she wanted was to make enough money for a passage west. They were urgent to have wives and they'd take a spoiled girl with a child. So that was the only reason she was here in this room. The other girls paid more than a hundred dollars a week for room and board. They could make two hundred a night, her friend said, which was more than Bella could imagine. And her eyes boggled at the room itself: silk sheets on the beds and real silk on the walls and a figured damask chair. And she was wearing taffeta against her skin. She wasn't sure exactly how to go about it, though. And Miss Josephine Woods was very nervous about taking her because she didn't have "class" like the other girls. Her friend said, *Just do it natural.* What *was* natural? They'd only done it once in the back of a wagon. He had blood under his fingernails from his day's work and the first time she saw "it," it looked like something out of the butcher shop, all white and unnatural. She couldn't believe *that* was the thing they made so much of. She never enjoyed it. It was over, and that was that. She was done for. A whole life ruined for what? So she thought, if she filled in for a friend on the odd nights, she'd have enough for train fare to Ohio or even California where every woman was a queen. She stood in front of the mirror teasing her hair and looking at her milk-white shoulders. Her friend told her to say dirty words when they were coming on. And to move her bottom around a lot. Miss Josephine Woods warned her to smile but not to speak because she was pretty enough but when she opened her mouth she spoiled the whole picture. She was very insulted by that, coming from the Madam of a whorehouse. But it *was* the best house in town. There was perfume on the dressing table, just for the taking. Bella put some on herself, enough so that she'd still have the scent when the night was over. And she sat at the edge of the bed waiting for the first gentleman. She wasn't allowed down with the regulars. She threw back her long hair and smiled to herself in the mirror and pretended she was a princess. Then the door opened. Miss Josephine Woods let a man in, and signaled to her to watch herself.

Deirdre brushed out her mother's hair. "Are you still angry with Father? Is everything all right now?"

Katherine took Deirdre's hand. "I know you've been upset by all this."

"I still don't know what *all this* is. Nobody's told me."

Both of them looked into the mirror. It amazed Katherine how much alike they were becoming. "Are you serious?" she asked Dierdre, "about being an independent woman and living a bohemian life?"

"Yes, I am. For a little while anyway. But I never said I wouldn't settle down and marry one day. I mean, I will when I get tired of the bohemian life. I suppose a woman can't go on that way forever, unless she wants to come back to the city alone with a child, like Miss Ada Clare, and send cards to her friends reading *Miss Ada Clare and son*. That's what she did. Honestly, Momma, I wouldn't shame you like that."

"Isn't there any other choice? Except to live the free life and be scorned, or be a wife, like me, with this kind of life?"

"*What* kind of life?"

Neither of them could answer. Deirdre took up the brush again and began to pull it through her mother's hair, long hard strokes.

Peter stood naked in front of the cheval mirror in a room of Miss Josephine Woods's establishment, inspecting his chest and belly. Being seen by prostitutes was one thing; being judged by the Community women, that was another. Would he pass muster? He sucked in his stomach. He still kept fit. Yes, he thought he might. "Have you taken care?" The girl wasn't one of the regulars. Jo said, *Only for you, Peter, because you know what you're about.* She was a pretty thing, very young.

She lay with the covers up under her chin. "Taken care of what, sir?" she whispered; he scarcely made it out.

"Of the necessaries."

She blushed, it was charming. "I . . . used what my mother gave me."

He sat on the edge of the bed and stroked her hair. "And what did your mother give you?"

"A sponge dipped in brandy, sir."

"Brandy! Doesn't it burn?"

"Oh, yes, sir, but I'm afraid of getting caught, sir."

He stroked her shoulders. "Well, you won't get caught with me. I assure you that there's no chance. So take it out."

She was bewildered. "My mother said . . ."

He bent to kiss her cheek. "Go into the other room where Jo has the French bowl and take it out! I don't want to get burned by brandy, do you understand?"

She didn't understand but she ran out of the bed so she wouldn't be seen in her naked state. He heard the water flowing.

What he was afraid of most of all . . . it was his vanity . . . was being given a teacher as Amos had promised, and appearing a novice, like a green boy, in this very thing at which he had considered himself a master all his life. He wanted to learn it first himself. And that meant keeping his mind on the act and not slipping away into fantasy. But for him the fantasy always preceded the act. He came on too fast as it was. That was the flaw in him. No staying power. That old horror of the little leather band was too much on him. Whores were titillating. He had to drift away to keep from coming on all at once. He had no control at all. Now he had to think of lying with honest women, women who understood the ritual meaning of this most glorious act. And to enjoy the lovemaking that came before, and to feel the pleasure of the entering, to savor it in fact, and then to be able to lie for an hour or an hour and a half in what Amos said could be cultivated into an exquisite art. What he had to exclude was the explosion of the seed, which for him had always been the goal of the whole game. To learn control so that he could stop and let the thing subside on its own. It was a new art for certain. He was up to it. And Jo had given him a green girl and not one of the regulars. He wasn't about to be laughed out of a whorehouse if he failed.

She came back to his bed looking uncertain and a little alarmed. He climbed into bed and lay beside her. It never took him long to begin. He always closed his eyes and fell into fantasy and he was there. But now he had to keep his mind alert for the various stages. He bent to kiss her breasts, which were to his taste inadequate, and ran his hand over her belly and then lower. But his mind was too occupied with realities and nothing happened. It annoyed him. "Start," he told her.

"Tell me what!" she said, confused.

He lay closer to the softness of her. He drew her hand down to him, but she was inexpert, and he was getting anxious. She pulled back her shoulders and began to roll her hips around like a machine. She said "damn" and "fuck," and looked down to his dormant part. "It's all right, sir. I'll get the hang of it." But nothing was happening. He went suddenly cold. What if this was the sign? That in invoking and then denying God, he's disturbed the fabric of his life, and he'd torn something and now he was impotent. He went numb . . . his arms . . . they were frozen . . . the way they felt when he was a child and they were tied to the sides of the bed. The panic rose. He *was* a child again, in the dark, before him visions of Eve, the naked Eve he remembered from childhood dreams, Eve with those parts exposed, only now he could visualize what those forbidden parts were, the brown curls between her legs. And on the ground, a green diamond-back snake, little forked tongue licking in and out, moving until it curled around her leg, and then up her leg, higher, higher, toward that *place,* and she smiled lasciviously and took the snake's head and guided it in . . .

"Oh, sir, *please!*" He tried to come to himself. "Please, I can't *breathe!*" He lay on top of her. In the last moment he must have had the presence of mind to remember the brandied sponge that wasn't there, and pulled out. He rolled off her. Dear God, she was covered with semen, the sheets befouled, he was sticky with it. He lay back with self-disgust. He was sick with himself. Foul . . . foul. He could have wept with frustration. He felt humbled to the heart's core. All his vanities dissolved in this terrible final act of copulation with a whore. He closed his eyes. He was the child again, but not the child tortured by a cruel father, a child who simply wanted to say his night's prayers. For the first time since that childhood he closed his eyes and prayed. In innocence. Without guile. A simple prayer that flickered like a single spark in the dark. *Our Father who are in heaven . . .*

The girl was horrified by the state of the silk sheets. She ran to the bathroom and came back with a wet towel. "Will they make me pay for it? Oh, sir, it wasn't my fault! I'm only paid by the *hour,* not by the *gentleman."*

She couldn't have been older than Deirdre. "What's your name?"

"Bella. Bella Stravos. It wasn't my fault!"

"No, the fault was mine. Don't worry about it. I'll tell Jo." In his wallet he carried a few hundred dollars in cash. He handed her the money. "Hide that away. This is for you. What are you doing in a place like this? An inexperienced girl like you? Can't you find another way to live?"

"I was spoiled, sir. By a butcher boy. I have a baby. I want to go west and make myself a new life."

"Get away from here before it's too late," he said.

He told Jo that his accounts would be settled by messenger and that he would probably never see her again. Jo, who was wearing pearls in her hair, smiled her elegant and knowing smile and said, "I've heard that song before." She offered him a glass of champagne for the road.

The sounds on the square became more and more intermittent, an occasional clip-clip on the cobbles; a shriek of laughter from a passing carriage; a clear high man's voice singing in the Irish brogue some lament of love which Deirdre listened to with a sense of magical expectation. Deirdre had opened her window because she was stifled and had to see stars. The moon was full. She was feeling upset and begged Rebecca to sleep with her. They lay curled together, the gaslight making shadow puppets on the wall and on the hand-sewn coverlet that Grandmother Olsen had given them while she was still alive and said would protect them always.

"Did you hear anything when you went to the bathroom?"

"Yes," said Rebecca.

"Was it Momma crying again?"

"No, I heard Paulie saying, *Now I lay me.*"

"Our brigadier. Our big major general."

"I'm glad he did. I don't want anything to get him in the night," said Rebecca.

"Do you think they're really going to take us away?"

"Tell me about Miss Ada Clare," said Rebecca.

"She was a free woman," said Deirdre. "She wrote poems and went to Paris alone and lived in cafes with all the artists and they stayed up all night drinking absinthe and talking about musical and artistic things and they slept together whenever they wanted."

"What's so different about that? We stay up all night talking and we sleep together when we want."

"You're so young. She took a new lover whenever she wanted and she died alone and unhappy. It was beautiful."

"What's so good about dying unhappy?"

"She had her memories," sighed Deirdre.

Rebecca cradled her doll and let the night pull at her eyes. "I'm glad

Poppa is making Paulie come with us. We're his women and children, so he had to go. Why am I the only one happy about going to the country?"

"She could smoke a cigar if she wanted to."

Rebecca was already floating on country lanes, watching the cow and her calves and listening to the lowing and the hoot of an owl in the barn rafters as she remembered owls when she was very young and in the presence of her grandparents who were now on the right hand of God in heaven. She rose out of her soft dreams to say, "Why would she want to smoke a cigar? My friend Emmeline at school says that if you smoke, you grow a mustache." She giggled at the thought of Deirdre with a mustache and sank happily into sleep.

Peter bathed and came into the bed he'd shared with Katherine, more or less, for seventeen years. He wondered whether she'd come, and finally she did, in her dressing gown, brushing out her hair. He wasn't angry with her now, or defensive. If anything he was empty of anger and concerned about her. "Doesn't it seem impossible . . ." (she sat at her dressing table and looked at him in the mirror) ". . . that two people could live together as long as we have and still be strangers."

"Yes." She brushed, looking at him lying there.

"I was damn foolish coming at you the way I did. But blame your sister. You caught me unawares. If we'd been more easy with each other, I could have come to you at the first and explained it better. I tried to make you believe I was a convert to God. I lied. I suppose you knew me better than to believe that."

"Yes."

He put two pillows behind his back and she came to sit in the little boudoir chair, her hands clasped in her lap, like a child waiting instruction.

"Amos said that Sarah was here today."

"She was. I liked her very much."

There was a new easiness to her voice that brought a small flame of hope. "Amos and Sarah have been with the Perfectionists almost from the beginning. There are three communes, one in Wallingford, Connecticut, one in Brooklyn, and the Mansion House in Oneida. In Oneida there are two hundred people living together in the kind of harmony you can't even imagine. Two hundred people who are all one family. Think of it, Katie. A family together. They call themselves Bible Communists. It's nothing like what Berthe described."

"Perhaps not," she said.

"They're called Saints, Katie. Noyes believes Christ has come back the second time; it's heaven on earth in these times to find people living with hope and expectation. It's like no other life you've ever seen. A man works at what he feels happiest. Noyes himself works in the bag shop or with the traps. And the women. Not idle like the foolish women of your set. They work beside the men. Deirdre can study her music, Rebecca will have the company of other children. They read the Bible every night, so it's not the kind of thing you thought it was. In fact, Amos's son studies voice. He and Deirdre will have a lot in common."

"Not Amos's son, Sarah's."

"She told you, then. Katie, I'm not going to argue how they interpret Scripture. It's not angels on the heads of pins that draws me to Oneida. It's the kind of life. They practice *Complex Marriage*. They *are* married, in the best sense. In the deepest sense. Not the kind of sham marriage we've lived under the world's system."

"But a woman is free to do as she wants. She can't be forced to do . . . anything . . . against her will."

"I swear it!"

"Nor my children. Not them either."

"Not your daughters," said Peter firmly. "Paulie is my son. I'll have him taught as I see fit."

She thought about that. "Then I agree. I'll go for a year. . . ."

He couldn't believe what he'd heard. His heart exploded with joy. "Oh, my dear Katie!"

". . . and at the end of that time, if you want to stay and I do not, you'll divorce me without scandal and give me the house and an allowance for me and the children."

Divorce! He felt himself flush with anger. But he swallowed his pride and tried to understand how she must feel. She wanted to give in, he could see that now, but she had to save face. "Yes. I promise."

"Write it down."

"How do you mean?"

"I mean in a contract."

"Don't be simple. There aren't any such contracts between husbands and wives. Isn't my word enough?"

"No," she said. "Not in this. Give me the contract and I'll get the children ready so that they understand what it is we're going to, and I'll prepare the house for tenants and we'll go to this place for a year."

She was being womanish. In a way it endeared her to him. It was a salve to her pride. Very well. He got out of bed and went to the writing desk and wrote her out a paper promising her the house and the settlement after a year spent in Oneida. In enough legal language so that she'd consider it binding. He blotted it and folded it and handed it over. She took it and put it in her pocket. It was a formal ceremony to end one life and begin another. "This will be an adventure for us both, Katie."

"Sarah said it was a good world for women."

"I can't tell you how happy I feel! We'll make a good life of it." He held a hand out to her now. "Come to bed."

She drew her robe around her and put a hand in the pocket that held the contract. "You said that women could choose to be celibate if they wanted. Well, that's what I choose. Good-night, Peter." She walked out and closed the door behind her.

He lay back feeling cheated. In everything he wanted. He got bits and pieces of life, never the whole. A contract? He was trapped, like Lillienthal. To ask for a contract, from him who had taken care of her body and soul for seventeen years . . . she was no better than her bitch of a sister. He turned down the gas and lay back in his solitary bed. He wished he could be back in St. John's Park. The park was the only place he'd ever been truly happy. Stealing out of his father's gate into the dark place he'd been warned against. The park was dangerous before the gaslights were put in, so they said. But he stole away to play in little dark caves of leaves, hidden between the thick maples on summer nights, feeling the feathers of the great cottonwoods like angels' wings on his nose and forehead, taking in the thick exotic odor of ailanthas leaves, and playing with his friends, the only friends he had, the faces and voices of his father's Book: he *was* Jonah, in the wet fishy belly of the whale, plotting his escape; he *was* the keeper of the ark, prodding the sluggish lions and the lumbering elephants and with his magical hand summoning all the great birds of the air; sometimes he *was* Cain, throwing a stone at his own father (he had no brother; his father had to suffice); he watched the green diamondback snake curl its bright body into the Garden and he *saw* Eve, her naked breasts and other parts which then he could only imagine, and he *saw* Adam eat the fruit and suddenly realize himself naked and reach down to cover that offending part that he and Peter had in common, the part that so offended his father.

Of course the park was gone. Three years ago. In '67. Vanderbilt bought it for a warehouse and destroyed more than two hundred trees, uprooted them and leveled the earth. When Peter saw the first ax cut wood, it might have been his own flesh. Vanderbilt offered $13,000 to every house that lost its view of the park. His father refused the money the way he refused all happiness. Peter fought to let this anger at his father go. He wanted to be out of this city. He ached to be out of it. He wanted a woman in his bed to protect him from the demons of the night, from the succubus who preyed on men in their dreams, who cohabited with the spilled seed from wet dreams and bred demons, misbegotten unholy children. . . .

No, all that was nonsense. He tried to picture the Mansion House at Oneida and a happy laughing table and the ringing of the forge and some wise warm woman who would take him in her arms, who would understand the depth of his need instinctively, who would hold him . . . hold him . . . he fell asleep in his father's lap, smelling the smoky odor of his father's dressing gown . . . when was it? It must have been long ago . . . when he was still favored . . . before he was cast out of heaven . . . he fell into a miasma of fragmented and confusing dreams. . . .

Katherine walked boldly to the hall closet and took out the quilt. She carried it up the stairs to her own little room and closed the door behind her. She didn't care who heard her now. She lit a fire in the grate. She had nothing to hide now; she owed no apologies to anyone. She poured herself a glass of wine and sat with the quilt across her lap, happier than she'd felt for as long as she could remember. Like a prisoner who'd been shut up and now was going to be let free . . . free to do what, she really didn't know and didn't care. Not at the moment. She rocked in the chair the way Sarah had. She was going to a place of her own. . . .

In her Fifth Avenue brownstone, the one with the great Grecian colonnades, Berthe creamed her face and rubbed cream into the backs of her hands. Brown spots, like rust, or mold, were beginning to appear. She was getting old. Aging from the inside out. All her bitterness beginning to show on the surface. Hector walked into the bedroom. She smelled his cigar before she turned. She heard him belch. She didn't turn her head. He farted. "Sorry," he said. She heard him groan as he sat on the green mohair bedroom chair to take off his slippers. The fire had made the room too warm, but he liked to sleep in the naked state. She detested that. He thought himself a stallion still. He thought the sight of him might make her excited. It was such a great joke. When she turned he stood there posing, his hairy chest like a gorilla, his belly, so tight with stuffed gut that he looked as if he might burst. He could scarcely breathe, he was so stuffed with meat pies. *Now as the time, she knew it.* Beneath the belly the round hanging fruit, almost hidden in fat and his little thing, getting bigger as he saw her staring. Hopeful, always hopeful. His florid face, his heart pumping to digest the greasy food and the cream pastries. What better time than now? Yes, now was the time. *The time was now!* Hector sucked in his belly and sat on the side of the bed. She took off her robe and hung it. She unbuttoned the pearl buttons of her nightdress, exposing her breasts. Poor flat breasts. Who else but Hector would find them seductive? That was something she could say for him. Now she drew her gown off while he watched her in astonishment. Now, while he was stuffed like a goose. When his heart could not stand the passion. Tonight she would be passionate. She would astonish him. She walked to the bed. He reached out to touch her. He was so laughable, she could scarcely contain herself. She bent and touched his thinning hair. She buried her mouth in his fat neck. She sat herself forward on his lap, like a wanton. She moved against him. He buried his lips in her breast, groaning in heat. She moved and ground against him, but she couldn't keep her mind on it. She thought of Katie. It was funny, now that the years had passed, that she still had love for Katie. She always wanted what Katie had, always. Hector's hands were moving down her hips. She closed her eyes and pictured Peter. She desired him, she always had. And seeing Peter in her mind's eye, Hector became Peter. Peter's hands on her, groping, wild. Then they fell sideways onto the bed. Once he was Peter, she stirred to ecstasy as she hadn't in a long while. Hector . . . no, Peter. . . was over her, breathing hard. She opened her eyes. She closed them. No, let him stay Peter until she had her satisfaction. Her cries only made him wilder. He was too heavy. She began to feel crushed under his weight. But she heard him moan and she felt his heart pumping . . . pumping. She would be crushed if he didn't stop! She was out of her reverie. "Not so heavy on me, ox!" She pushed him over on his back and straddled him, like one of the horses she and Katie had ridden on their father's farm in Virginia. She rode him . . . rode him. She bit her lip for fear she would cry *Peter!*

Later, when he wasn't dead from it, he snored and belched and farted in his sleep. She was betrayed. All that effort and he was alive still. Life was such a cheat. She drifted back to Momma's house . . . watching Katie . . . always Katie . . . Momma's eyes on Katie . . . Poppa's eyes on Katie. Betrayed . . . betrayed . . .

Bitsie lay on the clean linen sheets, her hair in a nightcap, watching Harry pace up and back across the bedroom rug. "He swore that Mrs. Grant had bought heavily in gold. The bastard, he swore it to me. His own sister was into gold and he swore that the president would never let us down. The bloody bastard. You can't trust anyone. From three hundred to a hundred-fifteen this morning alone."

Bitsie watched him pace. On the table next to the bed, hidden in a drawer, were her chocolates, small sweet dark chocolates with cherry centers. She prayed she would have the strength not to put one in her mouth.

"Well, done is done and we're well out of it, thank God. They can cut me dead today. Tomorrow I'll be solidly into real estate and they'll come begging at my door to buy. Then we'll give a great ball. I want a platform and a pool with swans. I saw one at Delmonico's. Such a grand ball they won't dare to cut us. I want swans swimming in the dining room. Do you hear me, Bitsie?"

"Yes, Harry." His back was turned and her hand was in the open drawer. Her hand had a life of its own. She popped the sweet into her mouth and closed the drawer. Then he turned and she couldn't chew. She didn't dare. She had to leave it melting there, moving her tongue a little, so as not to waste it entirely.

Harry stood evaluating himself in the mirror. He was trim for his age. He rode every morning with Edgar. He boxed a little. His mustache covered what Bitsie always thought was a weak profile. The mustache was very long and thick and it curled at the bottom just under his chin. He was terribly proud of having cultivated that mustache. He flexed his muscles and slapped his flat stomach. He turned to his wife with distaste and got into bed. He turned down the gas. Suddenly he turned it up again and sat up. "What have you eaten?" He sniffed, he caught a scent. She would have said, "Nothing," but the sin was in her mouth slowly dissolving. He pulled her roughly to where he could get at her mouth. He grabbed her chin with rough fingers and forced her to open her mouth. "You fat pig."

It was no use to say she was sorry. It was no use to promise she wouldn't do it again. So she turned away and wept into the pillow, letting the last of the chocolate melt away in her mouth. She swallowed it without pleasure. She thought of Katherine and that place with the wonderful strawberries. She thought of herself at Katherine's side, in the great kitchen, with women around her praying to rid of her of the sin of gluttony. To cure her of it. She saw herself sitting in that kitchen eating at the spare table with women around her to help her. She saw herself at Katherine's side melting, melting into her old self. Her real body. She was a girl again, able to bend and move and to dance. She could breathe again. She fell into a sleep, stirred only by the movement of Harry's body as he turned away from her and the derision in his voice as he said, "Oink-oink."

Bannerman soaked his heavy-ankled feet in a tub of hot water. He was troubled with the gout. His joints ached. His old wife, his Xanthippe, his wagging tongue for forty-odd years, bent over the pan of water, her iron-gray hair plaited down her back. As she bent to test the water, to see that it wasn't too hot, he put his hand on her shoulder and moved it downward toward her breast.

"Don't be an old fool," she said.

He thought of Peter with a troubled mind. In his hands he held a copy of *Bible Communism* and a handbook of the Oneida Community. Hard to find. Clerk had to look all over the city for them. Fantastical, this John Humphrey Noyes. How could a man twist Scripture to his own purpose? Noyes tried to prove by Scripture that he could sleep with as many wives as he wished. And he drew in converts as bright as Peter Berger. Well, he supposed that if a man fell into a midlife madness, he had as well fall into Oneida as into a Shaker Community where he had to remain celibate. But he supposed that Peter was not such a fool as to neglect to leave himself loopholes. Peter would find a way to keep something back for himself in the event that he wanted to return to the mundane world of one wife to one man. He'd probably sell his carriages and at least a part of his law practice . . . the cash, he could say good-bye to that. But the house, surely he wouldn't sell the house. "Poor fool," Bannerman said.

"And who might that be?" His wife climbed into the four-poster with a great deal of moaning, and settled the quilts around her.

"Peter Berger in fact."

"Peter Berger. I wonder if he is."

"Meaning exactly what, my sweet?"

"I read the book."

"What book did you read, dear heart?"

"The one in your hand. The Colony. The place where he's taking her. I read it all."

"Dreary reading, all that Scriptural nonsense."

"Not in the least. I found a lot of sense in it."

"You never cease to astound me! And you weren't shocked, sweet Adelaide?"

"Forty years in bed with you, Bannerman. What could shock me?"

He smiled. Past was gone but not forgotten.

"I think she'll get the best of it."

"Who will?"

"Katherine of course."

He was the one shocked. "She'll what?"

But his wife had turned her head and withdrawn into silence. She could do that, this iron woman. Best of what? Sleeping with a dozen men? Men had that sort of passion, not women, surely. At least not to his experience. Courtesans perhaps. Such women who had manly qualities, aggressive, demanding. But most women, he thought not. And what of brothers and sisters, since they were all angels in heaven? All could love all. *Male continence.* It was simply *coitus reservatus.* A man could bring on a nervous illness with that sort of foolishness. What would the celestial courts say about it? And what would old St. Paul say if he came back and saw what was being done in his name? Turn over on a cloud in horror. But it was a damned interesting theory, he had to admit.

He fell asleep in the chair, his feet in the water. Awoke cold and sneezing. What did his wife mean, Katherine would have the best of it? What was in the mind of the old woman? It gave one pause. . . .

Moira sat at her window watching Fifth Avenue at midnight. Still heavy traffic, men from their clubs or their saloons singing, a rill of some woman's laughter. Where Edgar was, she refused to consider. It was too depressing. And Katie was on her mind. She had in her lap Walt Whitman's poems, and a bottle of laudanum. She had several times considered taking an overdose and simply slipping into a permanent sleep. She would one day. But if Katie were in trouble, someone would have to keep a clear head and get her out. She took up her notepaper and wrote:

My dear Katie:
I have been floating in this sea of adversity so long that I suppose I have become a strong swimmer. Now I see you cast adrift, God knows where. I am with you in spirit. Write to me every night and I shall write to you. Talk to me in spirit, I will

hear you with my heart. Call for help, I will be there for you. Or better still, use the telegraph and I shall fly to you. We are so much alike, Katie, I am the darker side, you the lighter. But the same side when it comes to the marriage game. I am with you always,   Your Moira.

Pen in hand, she listened to horses on cobbles. Damned horses . . . damn . . . damn. She turned back to her poems, held the slim book to the gaslight and dreamed of Bohemia. . . .

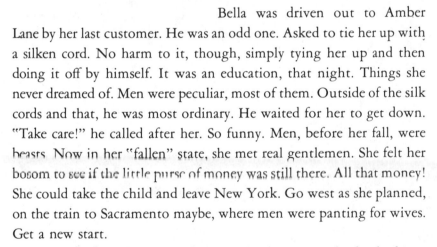

Bella was driven out to Amber Lane by her last customer. He was an odd one. Asked to tie her up with a silken cord. No harm to it, though, simply tying her up and then doing it off by himself. It was an education, that night. Things she never dreamed of. Men were peculiar, most of them. Outside of the silk cords and that, he was most ordinary. He waited for her to get down. "Take care!" he called after her. So funny. Men, before her fall, were beasts. Now in her "fallen" state, she met real gentlemen. She felt her bosom to see if the little purse of money was still there. All that money! She could take the child and leave New York. Go west as she planned, on the train to Sacramento maybe, where men were panting for wives. Get a new start.

She walked the lane in the full moonlight. She heard a dog barking. She was afraid to turn, lest it be something terrible, like a wolf. Full moon did awful things to dogs and men. The ground was soggy from an afternoon shower. Her boots were wet through. If she went west that was what she would find everywhere . . . wilderness . . . rustic towns . . . mud lanes . . . Indians maybe . . . living in log cabins with chinks between the logs that rats could get into. Bears and all that.

There was a light in the cottage. She could hear the child faintly crying. Her mother sat in a chair holding him, poor sickly thing. He had a cough that he couldn't shake off. It would be full summer before he would let go of it. He was so thin and pale. The western air would be so good for him. She put a bit of whiskey in the spoon and fed it to him. She took him out of her mother's arms. Her mother was three-quarters asleep and gave him up willingly, pulled her shawl around her and moved to the bed in the corner and fell asleep.

She lifted the child and kissed him. He had such wide and questioning eyes, like an old man. She wished she could put some fat on him. What if she took him west and he was ill and there was no doctor to be found? At least here they had a roof over them and good beds. The beds at Miss Josephine Woods's were purely wonderful. She wasn't likely to find better. After the child had fallen into an uneasy and rheumy sleep, she opened her trunk and buried the purse of money at the bottom. What if she went west and found that men were all the same and she had to take up the trade in some downtrodden saloon? Here, if she were prudent, she could buy herself a house and perhaps go into business for herself. With this as a small down payment. Nothing elegant like Miss Woods, but a small respectable place. And she would be the Madam. Nobody would tell her that she was common. So that in a way, one day she could be retired from actual business and just supervise. And when the child was older, she'd send him away to a good school, like Josephine Woods's daughter. In some private school in Europe. It was a business like any other. She counted the money in her head, making plans . . .

New York was settling in for the night. The gold fever had cooled down. Men were still berating themselves for being damn fools. But a gamble was a gamble. Done was done. People of substance were coming home from concerts and the theater, and from late suppers at Delmonico's and private suppers at clubs where they ate *coquilles St. Jacques* and wonderful *sorbets*. On

Broadway the Bowery Boys with their cocked derbies and their hair pomaded with Macassar oil came out of small theaters laughing and singing the tunes. And took their girls to Harry Hill's place on Houston Street, where gentlemen rubbed shoulders with low-lifes and desperate characters. *No loud talking; no profanity, no obscene or indecent expression; no man can sit and allow a woman to stand;* all the new tunes to dance to . . . late late into the night.

A great winged hawk came down out of the Appalachian and found its way to Central Park and came to rest on one of the tall cottonwoods, and then flew high above the city, circling higher and higher. The tip of Manhattan glowed palely with gaslight, all the way up to Forty-second Street, and then the lights became scarcer and dimmer. Beyond the park, wide plowed country fields; the forest seemed to be edging in. The green tip of God's peninsula had been gouged away and the forest wanted to reclaim it. The old range of mountains to the west, to the east a great expanse of sea. And this little oasis between, men scrambling for gold and finding it base metal; marble palaces surrounded by shantytowns as the city moved at its fast pace. The Indians had lived here. Now the forests of Manhattan were in the hands of the enemy.

In the Oneida Community, which was located east of Utica in Madison County, the moon shone white over the newly turned fields. Fresh vegetables were still scarce and there had been more than a few potato dinners. For the children, winter stomachs had to be cleaned out with a spring dose of sulfur and molasses. But the cows were doing marvelously well and there was plentiful fresh butter and cheese and good cream for the pies.

Sarah had come back from New York City with rheumatism in her fingers. It always happened. The devil was in New York City and when she let her guard down, he claimed her. The fingers ached terribly.

Mornings they were stiff and unbending. She stretched out those pain-ful fingers and ordered the devil to leave them. When he refused, she volunteered to do the milking. Mornings were still dreadfully cold. But she got up out of a warm bed and bundled up and went to the barn and sat before her lowing beasts and ordered her stiff fingers around the full teats. She *willed* them to bend. God smiled at her forbearance, gradually they relaxed and the cows were milked.

On the second floor of the west wing, Martha and Corinthe lay on their beds still talking about the new sister who would be sharing their room. Martha and Corinthe had both been Community-born. They were both sixteen almost to the same day. Martha was soft and easy with Community ways, Corinthe had been hard to live with for weeks. Now she was full of complaints. "I don't like outsiders. Couldn't she have shared a room with someone else? There's no more place in the closet as it is."

"Sarah says she's lovely and she adores the stage. If she sings like anything at all, she can join the chorus. We have pitiful few good voices this year."

"But things have been so nice with just the two of us, we've waited so long for a room of our own. And people from the outside can be so unsettling."

"I don't think it's the new girl at all, I don't think you're being honest about it."

Corinthe turned sulky. "What else would it be, then?"

"Do you need me to tell you? You know."

Corinthe knew. And if she didn't confess what she felt, she'd risk having a criticism from all the girls, and she didn't have the stomach for that, she felt so low. "I don't see why they won't let Adam and me lie together. I love him. I know he loves me."

"You know why you can't, Sarah told you. Adam was in New York too long, he has to come back to the Community ways. That's why he's still in with Mary. She's a good teacher for him."

"She's forty-five years old! She's too old to be lying with Adam."

"She's teaching him, that's all. The way you were taught and we all were taught. And you're wrong to complain. And I'll tell you something else, you have a fault of being too *exclusive,* not just with Adam, with others, I've seen it. It's a serious fault in you. Of course you love Adam, I love Adam too. And we're privileged to share the room and the closet. Think of how long we were in with the children."

Corinthe was close to tears.

"Amos is almost sixty and he's a wonderful and considerate lover, and he's taught us and we ought to be grateful. And if Mary is willing to teach Adam again, he'll be able to share his love with us. And if he loves you more than me, I'll be happy because I love you too."

Corinthe listened and her heart broke. Tears flowed. She knelt by the side of the bed and prayed. Martha came to kneel with her. Together they confessed Christ and begged to be made better and to be released from the sin of jealousy. And that Adam when he lay with Mary Darcy would be happy, and that Mary would be happy too.

Martha prayed with her heart and soul.

Corinthe prayed with her mind . . . the words were still gall to her heart. Her heart had a mind of its own and would not obey her . . . would not . . . would not . . .

ONEIDA – ARRIVALS, APRIL 15, 1870

'The new commandment is, that we love one another,' and that, not by pairs, as in the world, but *en masse*. We are required to love one another *fervently* (1 Peter 1:22) or, as the original might be rendered, *burningly*. The fashion of the world forbids a man and woman who are otherwise appropriated, to love one another burningly–to flow into each other's hearts. But if they obey Christ, they must do this. . . .

JOHN HUMPHREY NOYES, 1853
Bible Communism

The separation of the amative from the propagative places amative sexual intercourse on the same footing with other ordinary forms of social interchange. So long as the amative and propagative are confounded, sexual intercourse carries with it physical consequences which necessarily take it out of the category of mere social acts. If a man under the cover of a mere social call upon a woman, should leave in her apartments a child for her to breed and provide for, he would do a mean wrong. The call might be made without previous negotiation or agreement, but the sequel of that call–the leaving of a child–is a matter so serious that it is to be treated as a business affair. . . .

JOHN HUMPHREY NOYES, 1872
Male Continence

Neither do men put new wine into old bottles . . .
they put new wine into new bottles. . . .
Matthew 9:17

Moira, he did it cleverly. The trunks had been whisked away, we had nothing to take but our traveling bags. We left by night for an elegant dinner in the city, the children hardly understood what was happening. Peter ordered a party dinner at de Angelo's, five courses, and the children were allowed a glass of champagne. Deirdre was enchanted and Rebecca with those wide-open eyes, she couldn't get enough of it. And then he took us to the river and we boarded the night boat for Albany. Even Paulie in his bad temper couldn't ignore the St. John, it is a floating palace with galleried staterooms and that great mahogany staircase. They were all over the ship seeing the sights. And we floated up the Hudson, the great side-paddle turned, it was a marvelous adventure for them, and when they were bedded down Peter came to stand at the rail, smoking his cigar and looking cat-pleased. It was only me he had to conquer. Only I wasn't the gullible child. What did he expect? For me to throw arms around him and say, thank you for taking me on this voyage to a place where you can sleep with a hundred women and call it marriage? My silence put a lie to the river fantasy and finally he left me for the saloon to find more amusing companions. And I was left alone in my confusion. Where was I going? And then when I returned, what was I returning to? In my traveling bag was the contract of divorce, giving me the house. But I could no more go back to that house . . .

The moment I'd put the white furniture covers over the chairs, they became ghosts, as I closed the door to the house, it ceased to exist, as I stepped out into the carriage, I scraped the dust of Gramercy Park off my feet. I could have stayed on this boat forever, I walked to the rail and looked into the water. The white foam of the wheel in a wake behind us, the lights on the river as the moon moved in and out of clouds. Peter had dragged me away from the house for his own selfish desires, yet if he hadn't I would have melted into the wallpaper or sat forever frozen in front of a frozen fire. So what was my life now? It was unreal, like this voyage. Beside me at the rail my wounded soldier moved *against me telling me that soon I'd be safe and I'd understand what my life was all about, and that was as much shadows as any of Deirdre's childish romances. I bent so low over that rail looking into the black moon-diamonded water for a thing that did not exist, for the moment I thought . . . I could slip over . . . if I cried out my voice would be lost in the slap-slap of the side-paddle and that would be the end of it. And even then I heard Berthe's hard voice laughing and saying, What a waste of corsets. . . .*

The river fantasy was over in the dawn, their trunks put down on the docks at Albany and by carriage to the New York Central Railroad for the inland voyage.

The magic disappeared, the children looked bewildered by the loss of it. Paulie took a solitary seat at the end of the car, Rebecca held her Mathilda up to the window whispering things about the passing scene. It was Deirdre, poor bohemian, who was full of alarm, hanging onto Katherine with a moist hand. "I think Poppa must be mad to expect us to spend a whole year in the country." The tame farmlands moved by them, soft and without drama.

Rebecca crawled between them. "I don't mind, I like trains, so does Mathilda."

"You're such a child, you don't know what's *happening!*"

They lapsed into silence. Nor did Katherine know what was happening. Across the aisle Peter sat alone. He looked to her for some sort of confirmation. *No, not from her.* She turned back to the window. She saw small villages, bits of forest, shelves of rock, a deer standing ears-up listening to the lumbering of that great animal-train. She saw a lovely aquamarine pool, herons perched one-legged on the margin. She saw Indian women sitting near the tracks, babies slung before them, watching the trains as if they had nothing else to do in the world. *Moira, I have been a watcher of trains.*

She wanted to sit alone and reach out into shadows for *what it was she wanted.* But Dierdre wouldn't let her go. Deirdre lay hot and flushed against her arm, Rebecca held her Mathilda-child up to the window, whispering something. The tenderness of that scene filled her with shame. *Moira, it's more than Peter, it's myself. How much was I to blame for his unhappiness? Do you know what selfish thoughts have been with me this long voyage? I want to be alone in the room Sarah promised me, with no demands, to try to understand why my life has gone so empty. I wish Deirdre would let go of me. . . .*

She was so alarmed at her thoughts she hugged Deirdre and pulled Rebecca to her, she put her lips to Deirdre's forehead to see if she was feverish. Paulie, who had sat alone all those six hours, got up from his soliary seat and came, as if without design, to sit in front of them. Poor warrior, only fifteen and still wanted mothering.

Only Peter sat outside that magic circle, looking toward where they sat, now having locked himself permanently out.

They stopped at a place called Oneida Castle and waited on the platform for the Midland train that would take them the last short miles. Peter was busy with the trunks but kept looking toward her. Finally he came to stand beside her. "Do you believe when I say I'd never do a thing to hurt my children?"

"Yes, I believe that."

"I've been watching your face all these past hours. I'm not taking you to a prison, Katie. You'll see how wrong you are in that. Believe me, I'd make you happy if I knew how. So let's do this thing right, let's take a chance with it, with some sort of adventure, hand in hand. What do you say?"

She wanted to answer without anger, and to be fair. "The fact is that you're *bringing* me. I'm here because of what you want, not what I want. I'll hold up my end of the bargain, but I'm not deluded that you're here with anything in mind except your own lust."

The line of his mouth hardened. "Forgive me. I forgot. You're like the queen in Rebecca's little story. *Queen of Ice and Snow.* So what would you know of desire?" He walked away and stood alone.

She hadn't meant to say it that way. That was not what she meant at all. She was relieved when the Midland train stopped and the trunks were put up. Peter was more fortunate than she. At least he knew what he wanted. She did not. *Moira, I feel so alone. . . .*

The carriage of the Midland Rail-
way was due into the Oneida Community station in twenty minutes.
McMichaels, who himself had been the conductor on that run from its
inception until this past hard winter, pulled out his pocket watch,
snapped it open to check the time. The young man who now handled
that run, which went from Oswego to Norwich, was probably walking
the rolling aisles, checking to see that departing passengers were heft-
ing down bags, or helping to round up errant children. It was part of
the job, like the amusing patter a good conductor had to cultivate to
keep things light and lively. At this station a line that always got a good
laugh was *Oneida! Fifteen-minute stop to steal fruit!* Because sometimes in
summer when the trees were heavy, boys would jump off at the station
and run to the Community orchards and pick peaches and pears off the
ground. Not off the trees, mind you. Couldn't condone that, but if
God saw fit to let a fat-bodied red-cheeked peach fall, well, it was for the
picking, wasn't it? Of course it was a joke now, since the trees were
barely in bud. Not many passengers this time of the year, not like
summer when they had close to two thousand come for the strawberries and cream and vegetable suppers and to take in the entertainment.
They didn't serve much meat. Pity, he thought, himself who relished a
good joint of lamb or a beefsteak. But they put out fine bread and sweet
butter. And the amusements were best of all, to his mind. Grand
shows, not just hymn singing you'd expect from them that lived by the
Book, but a great chorus of swelling voices and quartets that sang the
newest show tunes. "Little Brown Jug," which everyone on the line
was humming, "Shoo Fly Don't Bother Me," or sad ones like "Now
the Day is Over" and "Birds in the Night." Of course, there was
classical music, dreary stuff, and some of the singers didn't always hit
the mark, but to liven it up there was a wizard comic who did recita-
tions, best thing this side of the New York stage. And the children,

even the toddlers, came out brash as you please and did their little pieces, sweet as honey those children and clever to boot. Women who came in from the city couldn't believe the children weren't brought up by their proper mothers. One woman claimed that the children were choked at night to stop their crying. Pure lies. Never saw better behaved or happier children. Or they said there was a big well out back where they buried their dead. Never believed a word of that, although they were uncommonly funny about funerals. Didn't take them serious. They said, Christ was returned to earth, heaven was at hand, so that a passing was simply a crossing over to Him so why make a long face of it? Or one of the women from out of town, she complained that there was an odd odor about the Mansion House and a Community woman who was sitting behind her said it was *the odor of crushed selfishness.* Well, he missed riding the trains in a way because he always felt that he had a serious obligation not only to make his passengers comfortable but to inform them. Stories he'd gathered all his life as a train man: where Washington slept or camped during the Revolution, or these and those birds coming overhead in their migration from Canada, or the stars. He was good on stars, always had been. Or when they passed Oneida Castle, he told about the Iroquois who had lived there. Called it Oneida Castle because there was once an old Indian Lodge on the spot and if you dug in the ground you could find Indian arrows and pieces of cooking pots. They were farming people, those Indians, and when the Oneida Community folk first came, it was the Indians who taught them a thing about farming. Now the Indians had been settled away, Wisconsin, he thought. He loved to amaze boys with his stories. And then this last cold winter his back acted up very bad and he wanted to retire but the company offered him a small salary for taking this little station, two trains and a freight each way daily, and of course he worked the telegraph. Midland stop in Oneida Community was only built because the railway needed a right-of-way through Community property and the "Saints" needed a station so they could haul in coal from Pennsylvania. Fifteen-minute ride from Oneida Castle, four miles, fifteen cents. Some who didn't want to squander that kind of money walked along the tracks. Station was pleasant enough and he'd made good friends among the Perfectionists. He was a bachelor, shy with women. Time and again he flirted with the notion of moving in with them, but he was born Methodist and it went against his grain to call himself Communist, even if it was Bible Communist.

But they lived in a wonderful stone house and they were good to their hired hands. In fact they started up a school for the children of them who worked in the trap shop and Noyes himself asked him to teach it since he knew numbers (he was A-1 in arithmetic; had to be on the trains) and he knew the passage of the stars and he knew history, at least that part of it he learned on the line. He loved teaching the trap shop school and time and again he cast about the idea of throwing in with them entirely. But what bothered him the most was that in spite of good living and music shows and such and the devout way they went about their religion, strange as it was, they were each one bone-poor. Used no money. They didn't store up treasures where the moth and the rust might corrupt. No, he firmly believed in putting away for his old age and trusting in no man for his burial, not even for God to provide. Bothered him not to have a few solid dollars in the bank. And as for his burial, perhaps Christ was back in flesh and spirit, perhaps not. He wanted mourners at his funeral, a bit of ground where his cousins from New York and Connecticut could come up on a Sunday and have a good cry. And the fact that they ate little red meat, just a bit of fish or chicken now and then, that was a problem. About the women: he couldn't condone it, not in good conscience. In his youth, he'd had women, well, a few anyway, and he'd gone to his share of whorehouses, but now in his declining years women weren't all that easy to come by, not for a shy man. At the Mansion House they had all they wanted. To have all you wanted of *that* sort of thing, well, he couldn't believe in his heart that it wasn't the work of the devil. Devil and pleasure went together, as he'd been taught.

He heard the distant whine of the Midland whistle. Soon the train itself would be hissing and screeching into view. Trains came, trains went, he had the sudden feeling that he was destined always to be waiting in stations. He wasn't prone to this kind of introspection and he knocked the ashes out of his pipe and buttoned his uniform, even the collar. Passengers or no, he had an obligation to the line. He went out onto the platform to wait for the train.

Peter expected Katherine's bitterness but Paulie's silence hurt him deeply. And the cold glances. And the averted eyes. It almost tore him apart. And to make matters worse, a man and a boy came on at Oneida Castle. A traveling man by the look of his sample cases, and a clear-eyed innocent country boy. The boy hefted the cases, found them a seat, sat head to head with the man talking and laughing, all affection, all courtesy. Peter watched them jealously. And then the man saw him staring, looked over to where Paulie sat, understood it all.

Peter was ashamed and went out onto the platform for a cigar.

The door to the platform pushed open and the traveling man joined him. Peter turned away, watching the landscape.

"Enjoy the cigar, you'll taste it in your sleep for months, I promise you." Peter turned, amazed. The man clapped him on the shoulder and offered him a hand. "Berger, I was sure it was you. We've been looking for you all month."

Peter tossed the cigar and took that hand like the most lost, the most lonely traveler in the world. "You're from the Community. I can't tell you how glad I am." The face was vaguely familiar, he ought to have known it. "I can't place your name. But we've met. Was it in the trap shop? When I came through with Amos?"

The man smiled, a long mobile expressive face, long-bearded, long-haired. "You tell me." The smile had a deal of amusement in it. "I was working the stamp machine when you came through, but we didn't meet there."

"Your voice is familiar."

"No doubt."

"Help me out."

"Think further back. See me another way. Hair short, small Machiavellian beard, mustache in the Italian style, dapper, I was mad for clothes in those days."

"In the city?"

"With Bannerman. I had offices with him for a while."

"With Banner . . ." It struck him like a shot. "Cunningham! Arthur Cunningham!"

The hand extended again. "The same."

"I'll be damned!"

"Not, I hope, on the road to salvation."

"But I've been in the trap shop dozens of times! Why didn't you say something?"

"As to that, I wasn't eager to be recognized."

"Did Bannerman know? He never said a thing!"

"Bannerman didn't know, he couldn't say. It's been six or seven years. Do you remember his mentioning me? What do you remember?"

"Let me think. Cunningham . . . you had a racehorse."

"Dancing Lady. Think you made some money on her. Bannerman said so."

"We met you once at the theater, you had a damned handsome wife."

"Mistress, not wife. Dominique. Gone but not forgotten. *Ahh.* What else?"

"You took ill? After some difficult case? Something of the sort, as I remember."

Cunningham stood back for inspection. "Do I look ill now?"

"Fit as a fiddle."

"More fit than I've been in my life."

"And it took the Community to do it."

"Good-bye New York, gave it my backside, out of the maw of self-destruction."

"I swear I needed to hear this. I'm a little shaky at the moment, I confess it."

"Understood. Great excitement, New York. And the courts. Darling of the juries, passion at the bar. And the shows and the music. *And* the cigars. That cigar of yours is five miles back and I can still smell it. I'm drunk with the city. They send me back from time to time to test my mettle. I've been a hard case."

"Cunningham! I still can't believe it! But how is it you left the trap shop for the selling game? It's not quite your line."

"They needed peddlers. I volunteered. One week out, one week home. But that's not what you're asking, is it? You're asking how I could give up the law for the peddler's life? Working a forge has romance in it, but brooms and silk thread and canned fruits? You find that demeaning?"

"Not exactly that way, but you know what I mean."

How shouldn't I know? Don't you think it's been the same wrench of life for me as it is for you? Do you know what job I started with when I first came? I cleaned out earth closets. Me, in the service of mammon, cleaning earth closets. I had a good laugh at that irony."

"Then the boy's not your son."

"He's my apprentice. Isaac. Fine lad."

"If only I could make my own son understand. You've seen . . ."

"Don't worry about it, he'll come around."

"And my wife still suspects my motives. If I could make them understand how a man needs something . . . clean in his life, one clean and unequivocal thing."

"Don't worry about her. She'll fit right in. As for the boy, he'll love the family life. He's about the same age as Isaac and Isaac is ready for the family bed. As soon as your son softens up, they'll find him a sympathetic older woman. She'll teach him. A good sexual life will bring him around. Does wonders for those young lads. No, it's you who'll have the hard time. Much harder for you than for them."

"I don't think so. I've made the decision, I've torn my life apart. I think the worst is past."

"You think so? Peter, let me tell you, you and I, we suffer from the sin of pride. The lawyer's affliction. I came in with a hard heart. The Community, they tried to soften me down. But I was a hard case, I told you. It was a long while before I was invited into the family's social life."

"Social life."

"The family bed. They made me wait until they were sure of me."

"But how long . . . I mean . . . before . . ."

"I know what you mean. Peter, I want to give you a piece of advice. And I wish someone had given it to me. It would have saved me a lot of grief at the beginning. Men come here for two reasons. One is sex, the other salvation. I don't know which has the greater allure. Our kind of sexuality liberates the spirit. You can't conceive yet of what it is to love freely and without reservation, without false morality and with the security of being *inside* the family. But salvation . . . ah . . . that has the greater attraction. And I don't mean personal salvation. We're here to be saviors to the world! Forerunners to a new age, because that's what we are, make no mistake. One day the whole world will live as we live, and there's an end to war and suffering.

"But here's the rub, Peter. We're proud by nature, men like us. I thought the earth closets would bring me humility and purify my spirit. Pride, Peter. I left the Community three times and three times I begged them to take me back. Learning to love women in the new way, that's easy. But learning to love your fellow man when you're bred for combat, that's a test to the spirit."

The train was rolling into the station. The whistle blew three times. "But the social life . . . how long . . . I mean . . ."

"I know what you mean. I waited five years."

Peter stood openmouthed, stunned. "Five . . ."

He followed Cunningham into the car. Bags needed to be gathered up. Cunningham's Isaac was busy with his, Paulie sat unmoving and sullen, leaving it all to Peter.

Peter moved to the bags, his heart pounding not from exertion. "Oneida Community!" called the conductor. "Five-minute stop to steal fruit!"

The train ground to a stop, screeching and hissing. Peter carried off the trunks with the help of a reluctant Paulie. But the girls clung to Katherine like aphids on a stem. *Moira, I am not the one to cling to. My world is a painting done on rice paper shredded in the wind.* Suddenly she was on the platform of a small byway station and Sarah came toward her holding out two hands, as a true sister would to a loving sister. "And so, you've come home at last."

Home? But this is not the same Sarah. A dress of plain homespun, a little lace at the throat, bound in at the waist with a simple belt, uncorseted, the skirt cut just below the knees and full-legged pantaloons . . . "As I am," Sarah said. Amos loaded the trunks and all into a wagon, they swung down the road through back buildings, past loads of boxes ready to be shipped away, the horses moving lively, manes flying, the clip-clop of soft country roads. Now the barns and the storage houses were behind them, the greenest kind of country, trees newly budded, in the distance the gardens and the orchards, and now before them the velvet lawns of the house itself, bordered by graceful trees and paint-color flower beds . . . and on the rise where a homely country place might have been . . . the Mansion House!

"We came from tents," said Sarah proudly. "We built this house brick by brick, if not with our hands then with our hearts. This is the Mansion House that we have raised for God and our family."

The house was a huge brick and stone square with a sheltered quadrangle inside the enveloping arms. Three stories in brick with twin stone towers rising at both ends of the main building, mansard roof, porticoes and porches, windows like eyes catching the afternoon sun. "The east side of our square is only just finished, we call it the Tontine, don't ask me why, we are inventive. That is where we are moving our dining room and our kitchens, wait until you see them, dumbwaiters and speaking tubes, like the finest restaurant." Sarah was so proud of it all. "Did you think us savages?"

The wagon stopped at the top of a long curved drive. A little group of the family had come out to greet them. For Rebecca a little covey of children bringing flowers. *Moira, what manner of women are these?* She had seen Sarah as something unique, but she was one of the tribe. *Their hair cut severely across the forehead or hanging just below the ear, the only decoration a pin or a clip. The short hair makes the eyes so direct! And of course, as Bitsie said, those pantaloons . . .*

Sarah had her securely by the arm. She was embraced by strangers, bewildered, caught in the crowd. Peter and Paulie had gone back to unload the trunks. Deirdre was taken over by two young women. The little children's troop guarded over by a mother hen with a wart on the end of her nose had snatched away Rebecca. She felt a sudden sense of alarm. Sarah read her clear. She tucked her hand into Katherine's arm. "What is it?"

"I'm afraid for the children."

"Your children have been seen to. Is that all?"

I was afraid for myself . . . and she read my eyes.

"And what have you to be afraid of? Have you been dragged down to the bowels of hell? Come." Sarah moved her through space, into the huge hotel of a house. "And what have we here so frightening? Our main building and public rooms. When Sunday visitors come, they come here. Visitor's room, parlor, dining room, conveniences for the gentlemen. To your left, the south wing where the children live with their nurses. To the right, the north wing where we have our private rooms."

"But this is so new to them. The girls have never been away from home. . . ."

"My dear Katie, this *is* home. But, you must be satisfied."

Moira, I walked through high-ceilinged halls, Sarah so proudly showed me heat registers; the whole of the house is laid out with steam, the whole of my life in fragments, and she showed me steam. . . . Up the steps to the great hall. Here in the house of who-knows-what is what seems a great theater, ceilings frescoed and twenty feet high, a stage with a harmonium and a piano, and standing center stage, facing an empty audience like a prima donna about to make her debut, our Deirdre. . . . "So, is that so scandalous? Anything to be frightened of here?"

"But Rebecca, she's such a child. . . ."

"Then we will have to see." Down again and across the endless corridors, stopping at this small parlor or that. "As Communists and always together, we do hunt out snug little corners."

Into the south wing, through an enormous long veranda where children played in bad weather, the sleeping rooms, the bathtubs all zinc-lined. "A bath every day. What savages we are." She opened a door for Katherine. Rebecca sat on a bed in a room of beds, her Mathilda by her side, and a new friend, and *her* doll, head to head. "So now what excuse have you?"

"I don't know . . . I . . ."

"Still more proof that we aren't here to snatch you up and do you harm?" Down the maze of corridors to the basement and the narrow tunnels that seemed to connect the buildings, into the *fourth side* of the square of a house, the Tontine, and up into the kitchens. *Moira, everywhere women greet me, embrace me. These mannish trousers. Women of our kind with our long skirts, we seem to float as we walk. Not they. They seem so solidly planted on the ground. They know where they are. If I did . . .* "Ovens for a hundred loaves and two hundred potatoes, scores of griddle cakes, how threatening." Sarah led her into the adjoining room where silk thread, long strands of shining colored thread, was being wound. "Look at the faces of our women. Do you see slavish looks here? Exhaustion? Fourteen hours a day on a pittance? No, you see women who work out of love for the family, whose own ingenuity has brought this business here. Don't you understand yet, dear Katie? You have been set free."

Free.

"No more," begged Katherine, "My head is spinning like the silk."

Sarah, her hand firmly on Katherine's arm, led her back to the north wing. *Moira, I was not only conscious of the women, the way they looked with amusement at my cumbersome clothes, but the men, they nodded at me with such a look, I must have blushed, I ducked my head, Sarah saw this and pulled me along, laughing. . . .*

Sarah paused before a door that was numbered 22. "Oh, dear, you find the numbers ominous? Like a house of ill-repute? How else should we find ourselves? There are hundreds of rooms in this house."

Sarah opened the door. *There in a corner of this amazing house was my room, it could belong to no other. A single bed, a small dresser, austere but clean, three chairs, a mirror, but on the bed was a pieced quilt.* "I saw it in your studio that day, I remembered how you seemed to prize it, and there was one like it in our linen room." *Above the bed, mounted and framed, was my own sketch, the one she'd taken from me in New York. And beside the bed a sketch pad and colored pencils. I could have wept.* She put Sarah's hand to her cheek. She was so without volition. She was so tired of so many things.

"I told you. Women flourish here. And now, questions. Things you couldn't ask me in New York. I mean for you to ask now, and freely. The room is yours. Not given you by your husband's leave. Even your children come to you only by invitation. And so . . . ask."

She framed her question out of the maze of questions, out of the clouds of questions, her head jammed with impressions and scenes. *Moira, you were behind my eyes when I said it.* "I can't help wondering . . ."

"Come, out with it. We're not hesitant here. Wait until you've sat in at our evening meetings or one of our criticisms. It will loosen your tongue. Your poor city sisters, sitting back so ladylike and mute. Not here, my dear."

"I've . . . seen women . . . like any women . . . hands up to the elbows in flour, at their sewing machines, in the fruiting room putting apples into cans and . . . ordinary women . . ."

". . . extraordinary women . . ."

". . . and how can I believe that at the end of the day these ordinary women of the house go to the privacy of their rooms . . . and . . ."

". . . and?"

". . . and . . ."—she sputtered it out—". . . and take off their clothes and wallow in lust."

Sarah had a laughing fit. "Oh, my dear . . . oh . . . but I shouldn't . . . I've heard this all before. Come, do you see the Sybarites' mirrored bedrooms? Beds steeped in lust? Do you see wanton women? You've come through a family house. You've seen so much. You should have a thousand questions. Do we have servants? Am I to wait tables and plunge my lady hands into the dishwater? Do I work at what I enjoy? Will we all eat together or in shifts? Will I rise early or late? Will I see my children? All of that, which is part of running a family in the Communist style, and what do you ask me? How women take off their clothes and open their doors to men who are not their husbands? Wallow in *lust?* Oh, my dear Katie, how am I to explain? Men and women in the Mansion House choose to work side by side because women are as capable as men. Hence the pantaloons. They deserve freedom of the body. But not only that. Side by side is a pleasant buzz of romance that makes the day so sweet. And where did that buzz of romance come from? From the devil's workshop? Never. God *is* love in all its forms. God decreed that we should love and flourish. Look at the way He created our bodies, what a masterpiece and marvel."

"I do understand man's natural desires . . ."

". . . and not woman's? This may amaze you. Women feel as men do. In New York women linger in romance, dreams and unrealities, while they languish without love—they corset their bodies and their natural desires. So you wonder, how does a woman fresh from the bread table go to this bed of *lust?* This isn't lust, Katie, this is *love.* A woman doesn't *give* herself in your sense. Sell herself. Dole out her feelings for gratuities, either on the street or in the house. She says, what a warm and loving feeling I have for this and such a man, if he invites me, I'm so happy to bring him happiness and he will bring happiness to me. Nothing selfish about it. Nor does the man want to leave her with a child. So she does her full day's work out of love of God, she eats at the table of food the family had grown out of love for her, she kisses all the children good-night and at night she opens her door to give and be given love and in the morning, the two of them wake in separate beds, so happy, so satisfied. While you and your city sisters . . ."

"I mean to remain celibate," Katherine said firmly.

"Many have and do."

"But you need to understand . . ."

"Nothing to understand. It's by your own choice."

"Nor my daughter . . ."

". . . as she chooses. You have choice in everything. I told you, women here are free. You can lie slugabed all day. I promise you, you won't when you get into the good spirit and let your heart go soft. Katie, you're still breathing the city air. You're filled with the same fears that imprison women outside. You are still *corseted* in so many ways. Wait unitl you breathe free. You'll plunge into the sheer joy of working. And . . ." *Moira, she was laughing at me* ". . . you shall be celibate as a nun in the most cloistered order, and if you're parched to dying, no one here shall force you to drink. Now unpack and rest yourself and we'll meet at dinner."

Moira, how can I say this? I felt oddly at home. I knew that somewhere in the house Rebecca was with strangers and needed me, Paulie and all that anger and nowhere to turn, Deirdre, who was to know where her fancies would take her without moment-to-moment guidance, and I had no more energy for it. I wanted to drop motherhood from my shoulders like a fallen shawl. I sat near the window of that soft little room. The door had closed out the rest of the world. And then, I heard the oddest sound. The click of balls against mallet. They seem to be fond of croquet in this house of lust. But lust had nothing to do with me. I was at peace. I realized what that sense of peace was. I had come among women. I was sheltered by women. And soon they would come to me in some sort of ceremony and cut off my hair and my cumbersome skirts and give me the veil, a veil in a house where a hundred women sleep with a hundred men. I didn't know whether to laugh or cry.

Deirdre moved in a veil of joy through the corridors of the south wing to find the children's veranda. Rebecca stood alone, looking out at the afternoon scene. Deirdre rushed to embrace her. "Are you all right? Are you frightened? They won't let me sleep near you."

"Curiouser and curiouser. Did you hear the croquet? It's *Alice in Wonderland!* The new book that Daddy brought me. The ladies wear funny dresses and there are so many doors, I half expected . . . no, Mathilda did . . . she expected a white rabbit to jump out."

"Oh, Becca, something wonderful has happened!"

"And do you know what they keep in the buttery, with the wheat-meal and the crackers? Pepper! I think it's to make you sneeze. And if that isn't *Alice,* I don't know what is!"

"Don't you hear what I'm saying! I was standing on the stage of the big hall with Martha and Corinthe and suddenly *he* walked in! I could have swooned, I was so shaken. He was tall and golden, his hair was all gold curls and he was smooth-faced and his eyes were blue and he wore an open artist's shirt, he was . . . oh, Becca, he was *David,* you remember the statue? Miss Moffat showed us the picture of it?"

"That was naked and he had parts covered up?"

"Don't be a goose. I meant *like* that, and he walked up and he kissed me, here on the cheek, I don't know what kept me on my feet, and at that moment, at the very moment, Corinthe squeezed my hand so hard, she almost broke it, and I saw her face. She loves him too, you see."

"Oh, love. Oh, that."

"And I knew that when love hit me it would strike like thunder and that it would bring me pain. And here we were, not just two new roommates, but two women battling for the heart of a man."

"Well, that's nothing new. Are you going to run off with him like Miss Ada Clare and come back *with child?*"

"You just don't understand love yet. I knew love would come to me someday, but to find it in this country place . . ."

"Will he take you to Bohemia?"

Deirdre took her sister's hand and stood by the long window, watching the wide lawns and the trees and the low-flying birds and a lamb that had strayed too close to the house and was bleating for its mother. "Don't you understand yet? This *is* Bohemia."

Peter Berger, whose life had been the city, whose pride had been locked into Gramercy Park, sat in a monk's cell of a room, shorn of glory, unhinged by the journey, facing an angry hostile son.

Paulie stood at mock attention, defying his father with a false bravado. "How do you expect me to treat you with respect after what you did to me. Making me sit in the back of the wagon with a . . . peddler's apprentice."

"It's the custom here. Children show obedience to their elders and that's more than I've seen from you for a long while."

"Obedience? To what? You're addled! To bring us to this kind of a place? I wouldn't be here except for Mother and the girls. Someone's got to look after them. Do you know what I've learned from your precious Isaac? What I wheedled out of him? They never fought in the war! Nobody from this place ever went! Not ever!"

"It was a point of honor, don't you understand? This is a religious community. They don't go out and murder . . ."

"Oh, is that what you think? Well, I happen to know the truth. That dunderhead Isaac. The Community fell between two counties and nobody realized it and they were never called! Well, *they* knew it, didn't they? And they didn't bother to rectify the error. Cowards, every one of them. Why can't you see that, Father? You're blinded by all this religious nonsense. And because of you I'm stuck in a room with that damned apprentice."

Peter was so weary. "Yes, an officer and a gentleman. I know."

"Well, I would have been a officer."

"Get out of here."

Paulie clicked his heels together in a mock salute. "I'll be happy to leave your presence." He pulled back his thin un-uniformed shoulders and strode out.

"Damnation." Nothing as he wanted it, nothing. Nobody understood. He closed his eyes to reach for God, the consoler. Not there. He felt pale and without energy. The dinner bell sounded. He put on his coat, he took his brushes out of his case and brushed his hair. His hands were sweating. The concrete foundation of his life had slipped from under him, he hung between worlds, he was nervous, like a boy. He wanted . . . he wanted . . .

As he walked the halls looking for Katherine's room, women passed him, gentle women, smiling women. Katherine could have come in good grace, she could have for *once* in her life tried to understand the turbulence in his heart. The glorious moment of his life and her bitter heart was tainting it.

He found her door and knocked. Lord, he was sweating, like a green boy. Katherine opened the door. Her elaborate hair, her voluminous skirts, so out of place. He had been wrong to bring her. She could have stayed at home and rotted, for all he cared. This was *his* moment. And to this woman, he could never in his life say what was in his heart. "Is your room satisfactory?"

"Yes."

"Sarah has taken you in hand?"

"She has."

Cold parsimonious little tone. "Wait a moment, I want to talk to you."

"The children are waiting."

"Just wait . . . I want . . . if you knew how I feel . . ."

"If you knew how *I* feel. Let's get on with it."

"No, dammit, that's not what I mean. Katie . . . you knew my father . . . you knew the life I came from . . . you could starve at my father's table, body and spirit . . . I . . . I've been waiting all my life . . . for this one moment. . . . You can see for yourself that the Community is nothing ominous as you expected . . . this is family in the most glorious sense. . . . Katie, please . . ."

"Please *what?*"

"Please don't shame me in front of my friends. Don't let them know that we . . ."

He'd said it exactly wrong. He saw the hurt snake across her face. "You know me so little," she said, "if you think I'd shame you in any way. We made a bargain. I intend to keep my part of it."

They walked side by side, strangers, as they had always been. Through a corridor of a hundred doors, and behind those doors people loved. Outside on the great quadrangle, sheltered by the stones of this blessed place, men and women easy with each other, touching, speaking head to head, so easy . . .

The girls were waiting outside the Tontine. Paulie, seeing him, nodded with cold politesse and gave the girls his arms and they went in. Peter offered an arm to Katherine. She nodded and took it.

They walked into the dining room as a handsome family.

The oblong tables at the center of the room were filled already. The round tables at the sides were filling up. Eyes raised, voices called greeting, hands waved. The whole room was redolent of warm yeasty bread, good stream-caught fried fish, the potatoes steamed, the huge cheese, good home foods, home . . . he breathed in *home* . . . more than the food. This was his communion, his First Supper.

The children were already seated at Amos's table. Sarah waved. He pulled out a chair for Katherine. She smiled graciously and took her place. He was still standing there when the room stilled. Across the room John Humphrey Noyes had risen, his napkin still in his hand, and signaled to Peter. Noyes, the man whose single vision had created this kingdom, whose words thrilled more than food, his innocent child's eyes, the generous mouth beneath the spatulate beard. He raised his hands, amusement in his eyes. Peter held onto the back of the chair. He was trembling.

"Brothers and sisters, dear children. Peter Berger, who has been so good a friend to us, has come to join us now with his good wife Katherine and his fine children, to be with us in body as well as spirit. Welcome to our table which is now your table."

From all corners of the room cries of welcome and applause and laughter.

Noyes raised his hand for silence. "Not done yet. When have you known me to give up the podium without a Home Talk?" He waited for the laughter to subside. "Now Peter as you know is a lawyer. And you all know the special feeling we have for *legality*. Legality, my dear brother Peter, to us means doing things not from the heart but by the rule. *Legality* is bending to law. If we make sacrifices here, we don't sacrifice out of *legality,* but because we love God and each other. So in joining us, Katherine and Peter, try to understand the Community spirit. Rules and *legality* go together with a hard heart. Our critics say that because our women dress alike we're regimented. Don't let that fool you. We love the spontaneous, new ideas flourish here. Get a fancy to take your dinner out on the lawns, or out to Joppa for a picnic, you'll have a dozen ready to join you. What I'm saying is this: let your hearts go soft. We love soft hearts here. Cast off the shadow of that old cold world. Let our ways seep into you the way water seeps into roots after a dry season. Let us embrace you. Outside women kiss in railway stations, one cheek, the other cheek, the conductor checks his watch with impatience, waiting for all that vanity to be over. Is that love? Here our embraces are more warmly felt."

Father Noyes left his table. He walked between the tables toward Peter. Peter's knees trembled, he was a trembling boy. He was afraid there might be tears in his eyes. Noyes opened arms to him and took him in, embraced him and held him.

Peter Berger was filled with glory. This was as close as he would ever come to God.

The family had gone into the big hall for the reading of Mr. Dickens's book, *Martin Chuzzlewit.* And then to a spelling bee which Martha said was the week's activity. But she and her new friends had better things in mind. Like closets and drawers.

Deirdre unpacked her cases, most of the clothes would have to go down to the clothing room to be shared. She didn't mind. Well, she didn't mind *much.* Her heart was too filled with other things. She was in love with Sarah's son, Adam. The first and only man. And he was to teach her music. They would be together every day. She tried to recall the details of his face, the timbre of his voice, the expression of his mouth, the way he held his hands. . . . She bounced on the bed. It crackled. "What's in this?"

"Cornhusks," said Corinthe with a sour face.

This was part of the test. Cornhusks. So be it. Fate meant to try her spirit. And it spoiled the moment that Corinthe hung back hurt and silent. Deirdre wanted to hug her and say that they could still be sisters, even though they loved the same man. But Corinthe was full of storms and angers. "They won't let him lie with you," she said.

It was a moment before Deirdre realized she didn't understand the meaning of those words. "How . . . lie with, how? How do you mean?"

"How can you be so unkind? Martha reproved her. "Deirdre hasn't even been told yet. Sarah said so."

"Then what right has she to be here? What right?"

Deirdre's cheeks flamed, her hands went cold. "Told me about what? What was I not told?"

Martha was furious with Corinthe. "No, she doesn't understand and it's for her mother and father to tell her, not you. I know fully what's in your heart. You're jealous. It's wrong and hurtful and you'd best confess Christ and beg him to soften your heart."

Corinthe ran to her bed and fell on it, her face into the pillow, crying.

"How?" Deirdre demanded. "How does she mean *lie* with?"

Martha said, "Don't think of it yet. It's a long way off. Only you must know that here jealousy is a sin. If Adam is happy, I'm happy. If I'm happy, Adam is happy. If Corinthe sees Adam happy she should rejoice in her heart. It's jealousy that goes against God. And that's the thing you must know about us. All the rest will come in good time. In Father Noyes's good time."

"*Lie* with . . ." Her heart was beating wildly. "Do my parents know . . . about *lying* together? Do you mean making *love?*"

Martha said nothing more. She embraced Corinthe, who accepted the embrace contritely and the two of them fell to their knees and silently prayed Christ. Once, Martha opened her eyes and looked to where Deirdre still sat on the edge of the bed and she said, "God *is* love. Don't you understand that?"

Katherine sat with Sarah in the little nursery "pocket" kitchen, talking about the next day's work. It was Sarah's thought for her to try out every job, a *sampler,* Sarah said. "For a woman of your class, it may well be a novel experience."

"My class? You know what my class has done for me. I think you saw that in me."

Sarah said, "Yes."

"I can't wait to get my hands into something."

Deirdre burst in on them there, full of her usual drama. "I've been looking for you everywhere." All hot with emotion, such an actress.

Sarah smiled and nodded to Katherine that she understood the nature of pubescent daughters, at least daughters on the *outside.* And left them alone. Deirdre dropped into a chair, twisting her fingers in distress. "You said this was to be a year in the country with fresh air and good food. Why didn't you tell me the rest?"

"Have they been talking to you already?"

"What do you *mean,* have they been talking? Why didn't you tell me what kind of a place this *was?*"

"What kind of place *is* it?" Katherine said. "I think you understand it as much as I. It will be a good country year."

"I mean about the *lying* together!"

"As to that, it doesn't concern us."

"I think everyone in our family must be mad! Men and women *lie* together without being married and it doesn't *concern* us? You think I'm Rebecca or some child and it's not necessary to tell me?"

"Deirdre, I would never in my life have chosen to bring you here. This was a decision forced on me also. And I didn't tell you about . . . other aspects of this Community because I didn't understand them myself. I'll tell you as much as I know, but you and I need not be troubled by it. Your father promised me that. It's all by choice."

"What is by choice? *What?*"

"All the husbands here   are married to all the wives."

Deirdre's face was flushed in bewilderment. She shook her head in disbelief.

"Married . . . in that they look out for each other. Sarah explained it to me. For instance, if a man is here without his wife and needs care, then one of the women becomes the wife for his clothing and another becomes a wife for his room, and so forth."

"But what has that got to do with *lying* together?"

"I've never spoken to you of . . . personal things . . . between men and women. I had thought . . . that before you married I would. It was something my mother never even dreamed of discussing with me, but these are modern times I suppose."

"Oh, *bother!* I *know* what kind of things happen between men and women. All my friends talk about it. I mean . . . nobody has . . . actually . . . but we've figured it out."

"Well . . . you have to know that things between men and women aren't easy . . . the way they are in your fantasies. . . . All the lovely things you've been telling me about your bohemian idols and their lovers. Lovers become husbands and they are often . . . unkind to each other."

"Unkind . . . you mean in the bedroom? How?"

How. "In that it seems so . . . romantic and then . . . I'm sure you understand."

"You're telling me that all the men and women here . . . they all go to bed *together?*"

Katherine took a deep breath. "Yes. A man may request . . . but always through a third party, and a woman may refuse or she may accept."

"But then they can all have babies? Why isn't everyone about to have a baby?"

She couldn't explain. "I . . . I'm not sure myself. The men are responsible for that. I can't . . . please, Deirdre, it has nothing to do with you and me. What we do is by or own choice. And we choose to be celibate. Just accept that and put the rest aside."

"But I'm not a child! And you brought me here and thought I simply wouldn't *know?*"

"No, I didn't bring you here, your father did. And it's to him you ought to complain."

"And what of Father? Does my father mean not to be . . . involved in this marriage thing?"

Katherine averted her face. She had no answer, "No, he means . . . to be involved."

Deirdre put a hand to her throat, she gasped and fell back against the chair. "Not my father! I don't believe it . . . I never will!"

Katherine had no desire to malign Peter. Whatever their private angers, he was a good father all in all. And she knew he had his own private anguish, she granted him that. But Deirdre had to know the truth. They had been such a pallid kind of mother and daughter, dancing their dance with grace and beauty. There was nothing of truth in it. *Moira, help me to be fair and yet to say for once what I have to say, this child is the same age I was when I met Peter and thought I was in love. . . .* "Deirdre, listen to me. It wasn't my choice to bring you here, now I think it may have been a great mistake, for you especially, but you might as well understand the world as it is. You've talked endlessly about Miss Ada Clare and her Bohemia. Did you never stop to think what that meant? Your father is a man, for better or worse. His needs are very strong and I can't fulfill them."

She heard Deirdre's little intake of breath, her face paled, she was shocked to the core.

"I would never in my life have spoken to you like this, but what choice have I now? So you'd better understand the truth of it and accept it. Your father may sleep with other women. He has before. I don't care anymore. I haven't cared for a long time."

Deirdre burst into tears.

Katherine embraced her and drew her in. "I suppose that mothers, seeing their daughters so steeped in romance . . . Deirdre, how can I speak the truth about marriage? Romance doesn't last. Shall I be cruel and tell you that? How you live in such a fairy-tale world, like Rebecca, with all your talk of love. Men and women . . . men play at romance until they've caught their game. And then, it's all compromise. I'm not able to do that anymore, and neither is your father. At the end of this year, your father may stay on here and it's possible that you and I and Rebecca, we may . . . I don't know what yet . . . but believe me, what's between your father and me has nothing to do with your father and you. He adores you. He adores all his children. He's simply a man, for better or worse. And it's time you understood men."

Deirdre pulled away from her and ran out of the room.

Sarah had not been far away. Sarah came and sat beside her again. "Leave her to her sorrows. She'll have to face her own life and learn how to deal with it. I've sent Adam after her."

"This is all madness," Katherine said.

"No, the madness is the world you brought her out of. It was exactly as you described it. Don't you understand that behind these walls there exists a life between men and women that does succeed? If she had been brought up here, as my son was, she would have every reason to continue her fairy-tale dreams. Here dreams are possible. Here dreams are fulfilled. Katie, open up your eyes."

Deirdre ran, down corridors, faces watched her, they were a blur, she was a stranger in a strange costume with a stranger's hair, someone from another part of the world, and a terrible blow had been dealt her. She found the outside door at last. She couldn't cry until she was alone.

She ran across the lawn, she fell behind a small oak where she could lie on the grass unobserved, she lay face on arm and wept out her heart. Her father! Giant of her life! No better than a lecher! And her mother betrayed? How could it be possible? She let herself fall into a deep hole of despair.

"Deirdre . . ."

She knew who it was. She was too distraught to raise her head.

A hand touched her shoulder. "Deirdre, please . . ."

"Leave me alone." She was mortified.

"My mother said you were upset . . . I saw you run out of the house . . . I had to come after you . . . please let me help you."

She raised her eyes just enough to see Adam squatting beside her. "Just leave me alone. . . ."

"I won't do that. We don't believe in solitary bouts of self-pity."

She pulled herself up. How unfair! "*Self*-pity? Is that what you think? Well, it isn't that."

"Much better. What is it, then? Homesick?"

Her chest was still heaving from the deepest tears of her life. "You can't understand . . . it's too horrible."

"Try to tell me." Now he sat beside her and looked into her face, although the light was dimming as it was coming on dusk.

She tried to turn away. "It's something I could never explain to another soul."

"I hear that so often on the outside. Now tell me what sacred subjects can't be told to another soul. Something between you and God?"

She shook her head.

"Something totally private."

"Yes."

"Something to do with your body, you mean? You've found out about our sexual theory, something you didn't know?"

The word took her breath away. She gasped, she heaved, she thought she might faint.

"You *are* a tender little thing. Sarah said you fancied yourself a bohemian. Are you bohemian? Father Noyes writes about sexual matters all the time. We all discuss it. It's central to our life here. You'll get over the novelty. What is it, then?"

She choked it out. "They didn't explain. They were beastly not to explain. It's . . . my father . . ."

"Oh, I understand." He settled himself beside her. He lay back and looked up at the darkening sky. "I think I understand. You learned that your father wants to take part in our 'social' relations, which means he'll go to bed with other women, women who aren't your mother."

"You're horrid to say a thing like that! How *dare* you!"

"Is the truth so horrid, then?"

She couldn't answer.

"No, I think it's more than your father. It's you, isn't it. His little angel, his dear, his sweetling. And he's pure, isn't he? He loves Mother and you and you expect him to stand forever like a statue on a pedestal never changing so that you can always look up and see him exactly there for your comfort and convenience. How selfish and unloving of you."

"I! I selfish? How unkind and cruel!"

"Unkind to tell the truth of the matter? Cruel to tell you something for your own good? Well, my girl, if you intend to live with us, you have to realize that you're open to criticism. We all are. We criticize very readily here, and if you're not careful you'll have a public criticism and you'd better have a strong heart for that. No, hear it from me, in the dusk where you can hide your shamed feelings."

"I have nothing to be ashamed for!"

"Haven't you? Dutiful daughter. And you let your father pamper and pet you and give you presents on your birthday and you give him presents and you think that's love? Well, love is something more. Love means that you want him happy, even in a way that cuts you out."

"I do love my father! I always have!"

"Self-deceit is the worst kind of deception. I don't think that you understand that your father is a man as well as a father. And if you love him as a *man,* you'd be happy to think of his finding pleasure in someone else's arms."

"That's crazy! I thought you were all so religious!"

"Stop thinking with the old lies they've stuffed in your head. Think with your eyes and your heart and your body. Marriages are petty and mean and selfish. Men stray all the time. Women hold in their desires. You know that's true. Man isn't monogamous, and that's the pure truth of it. Neither are women."

"Liar!" But when he didn't respond right away, she took that little silence to think about Miss Ada Clare who had desires and was destroyed by them. "Women do have desires . . . and they have to suffer and sacrifice if they want to have them."

He laughed, a laugh so musical and appealing that she almost lost the thread of her anger. "You goose! Why on earth should people sacrifice and be punished for loving? People on the outside call us *free lovers.* We're not. We believe in love but inside the laws of the family. Nobody does anything wanton here. Nobody is hurt by love. If a man wants a woman, he asks for her company.

"If she doesn't want him she says no and nobody's offended. But the whole Community knows about it, it's out in the open. If she takes him, on the other hand, he gives her pleasure and she gives him pleasure. And if either of them behaves badly, they have a bang-up criticism. And so they're pleased and the family is pleased and God is pleased. Amen."

"I never heard of a thing so *outlandish!*"

"What's outlandish is what happens in New York! Do you know there are more than six hundred whorehouses? And nobody knows how many women are out on the streets because of your way of living. Listen to me, Deirdre. If you love your father, really love him, you'll say, well, this and such a woman made him happy in her arms and so I'll thank this woman for giving my father that joy. And what's the harm? He doesn't love your mother less, does he? No, he's satisfied and he loves her more. And he loves you more and he loves his work. And what if your mother should lie in someone else's arms? Would she love your father less?"

"You don't know my mother. She never would."

"And what about you? If I asked for your company, you *never would* either?"

She may have gasped audibly. She couldn't find the words to answer him.

He pulled himself up and offered her a hand. "Don't think I haven't anguished over questions, as you are doing. That's why I went to New York. But I've seen the world *outside,* and this is the only answer. Be kind to your father. Think how you can show him love, not the other way. It will soften your heart."

It was late when Cunningham knocked. "I thought you might want to talk."

"Yes . . . been lying here . . . I . . ."

"But you survived the first day. Hardest."

"Barely."

"And you feel . . ."

"Tired, frightened, exhausted, insecure . . . what else?"

Cunningham pulled up a chair beside Peter's narrow bed. "I may have erred in making . . . certain remarks on the train this afternoon. Want to talk about it?"

"I don't want you to misjudge me. The family bed wasn't my only reason for coming."

"Good Lord, man, do you think you need to minimize your need for sexual comfort to us? No, it's something else I want to talk about. I told you this was a hard philosophy. I want to tell you something . . . very personal. I think it may make you understand the kind of challenge you're up against. Peter, do you remember anything of my last case? Did Bannerman mention it? Just before I . . . fell ill back in New York? I had taken on a client, a boy from a wealthy Connecticut family. The boy was accused of killing a prostitute, ghastly crime of passion, done with a knife. The parents were prostrate with grief, it was unthinkable that their clear blue-eyed boy should have done such a horrendous deed. And I quite agreed. It was the boy's misfortune to have slept with the whore just before she was slashed to death. I prepared a brilliant case. Gentleman of the jury, this boy could be any one of you. Alone in the big city, lured to a whore's filthy room, dragged into sin and then fleeing in guilt and shame. Only to learn that the whore's next client had slit her belly open with a knife.

"The boy got off, of course, but in the process I made an enemy of the police captain who was trying to get the boy hanged. But so goes the law, the family paid me a handsome fee, I celebrated with my Dominique, dinner and show on the town. Finish.

"A few nights later, knock on the door at midnight. That same police captain. He invited me to dress and come with him. Case that might interest me. I was intrigued, of course. He drove me out to Five Points. Building ringed with police. Led me up a filthy stairwell, all piss and garbage, to a room, and what I saw in that room changed my whole life.

"On the floor lay a woman who had been butchered, her belly, her breasts slashed, her eyes open to death, the horror in those eyes went beyond death. And in the corner, my client, that blue-eyed boy.

" 'This is the lawyer's art,' the captain said. 'You and your slick tongue. He was guilty as sin and you knew it, and you got him off free. Now I want you think about this pretty picture when you go back to your fine apartment for a good night's sleep.' I was so filled with horror that I almost retched on the spot. I walked over to the boy. He sat without expression. Then he smiled up at me. 'I had to do it, she was a bad woman. Somebody had to do it, didn't they?'

"I walked out of that hellish room and threw up my dinner. I threw up until my throat was raw. I went home, I bathed; I couldn't get myself clean. I began to have nightmares. Every night, that dead woman's open eyes burning into me, accusing *me.* I developed a tic in my cheek. I feel into a terrible depression. And why? Society didn't condemn me, I had no responsibility for the deed. And what was the death of a whore in Five Points to the modern world of 1864? When so many were being murdered with impunity. But I couldn't get it out of my head that I was responsible. I went to a physician. All he could recommend for my terrible nights was morphia. I couldn't practice, I wandered the streets in confusion. And then I went with a friend to hear John Humphrey Noyes. He shook me to the core.

"I began to read philosophy. I read all the startling works of Darwin. Were men merely animals, then? Was that it? Was that why they carved each other up and ate each other up and developed a system of law that would get them off with impunity? I read Malthus, I wondered about women who had to live on the streets as that poor whore had done. And men like my client were free to visit them while despising them. And all the children these poor creatures had been forced to bear because of the lusts of men in the city. I thought of nations filling up with unwanted children and the attendant horrors.

"Noyes moved me more than I can tell you. He explained human nature and man's relation to God in such a sensible way. As if man had been conditioned for years to think in a particular way and here was a new truth so eminently clear and so eminently sane. *Man was responsible for his brother.*

"But here is the crux of my story. I came, as you did, fired with salvation. Ready to clean out earth closets. But that enthusiasm didn't last. I was a proud man. I was independent and competitive, as you are. Three times I left, three times I came back, sick of the same nightmares, caught between worlds. They forbade me the family bed, they weren't sure of me. Finally my heart softened down. The nightmares subsided. I had fallen in love. At last a modicum of peace. I was accepted into the family, heart and body. And the source of all this love was the most gentle creature. Her name is Annie Lee. The kind of tenderness I felt I'd never known on the outside. Of course she was obliged to sleep with other husbands and I slept with other wives. The family way is not to be exclusive.

"And then the Community prospered enough to begin to bear and rear children. They had not for many years. Annie asked to mother a child and she asked me to father it.

"But I wasn't approved, you see, I was too outward in my nature, too independent. It was suggested that someone more . . . spiritual should father the child since the child would have to be content in this life. They chose the man who was my roommate, Esrick.

"My disappointment tore me apart. My hatred of him was debilitating. I began to dream of the murdered prostitute again. And then I began to realize that those two events were somehow linked together for my salvation. I'd never been truly forgiven for my crime, or I would have known it in my heart. It came to me that man can never abdicate his responsibility to his fellow creatures. I was responsible. If I had descended from the apes and evolved into a higher spiritual being, then another deeper change was necessary. I had to learn the nature of true love in its deepest sense. That was the next natural step in the evolution of man. That was the only way society could ever truly change.

"So here I stand now. The baby is a year old, the child that should have been mine. Esrick and I are reconciled in word, but not in my heart. I'm still eaten by my resentment, I'm a hard case. But I tried to tell you on the train, love is a hard nut to crack. Love for women is easier, women were made for it, there's an easy path to loving a woman. But with man, ah, Peter, to love your fellow man *without* reservation *and* competition . . . it's lack of that kind of love that's destroying the world. Do you see what you've come into?"

Long after Cunningham left, Peter lay searching out his own heart. He wanted to purify his soul the way Cunningham was scouring his own soul of sin. The elements of his nature were shifting. He wished that someone could see the upheaval of his spirit, the rending of old cloth, the beginning of this new tapestry of his life. He felt anxious and excited and nervous and frightened. He wanted a woman's body beside him. He needed solace. He detested a solitary bed. If he could make love to a woman, it would drain away his anxiety. He wanted to sleep but images crowded in on him. That sad little whore at Jo's place. He tried to shake Jo's place out of his head. That was not the road to salvation, nor to easy dreams. But he couldn't let it go. Amos had promised him he wouldn't have to wait too long for "social" acceptance. So Cunningham's dire warnings were for nothing. Soon he'd be taught, like Isaac, how to make love. He let his fantasy drift to the golden angel who would teach him. She wouldn't be too young, a mature Madonna, an experienced lover. She would know how to arouse a man, she would teach him to lie inside a woman with patience and skill. He let himself move close to that gentle sensuous creature . . . he was aroused . . . it would be hell until he could lie in a woman's bed again.

Deirdre lay filled with astonishment. How could she be so blind to the world she had lived in? Her father, who had been so ordinary, just a father, now a newly mysterious creature who had loved strange women, and her own mother with this scar on her heart, just suffering in pain and silence. So those were the footsteps Deirdre had heard, her mother climbing those stairs in the night, to lock herself into the upstairs room, with her woman's secrets?

Adam had as much as said he wanted her. Soon she would feel his sweet lips on her lips. Soon he would come and say he desired her, in body as well as in spirit. And since this was the rule of this blessed place, how could her mother refuse her? If her mother in her pain and suffering chose to remain cloistered, Deirdre could understand it. But as to herself, she chose love, and always would. She was the happiest of women.

Rebecca Berger *'fessed Christ* and tucked Mathilda neatly in beside her. The moon came in through the high windows, she could see the tops of trees and the sloping lawns. Did spirits knock in this big room? Well, what if they did, with all the sisters sleeping nearby.

This place was called *Oneidacommunity.* God lived here.

It was nice to live in the same place God lived.

Amen.

This was war and Paulie had been sold into the hands of the enemy. His father was addled, shellshocked with religion like his friend's father, who had been shellshocked in the war. Paulie had fiercer gods . . . thunderbolts from the mountain. In the bed next to him Isaac the apprentice slept deeply. Paulie would bide his time. He had lost the battle, not the war. In the end they would see Paul Berger's mettle.

Moira, this has been the oddest day. I want to show you the nature of this place which is not what you and Bitsie thought at all. All sexual matters aside, I was standing at the window listening to the night sounds. The footsteps of a watchman who makes the rounds, tending to the safety of the house. From some far place the pale sounds of a flute, someone in the house is practicing, you seem never to be far from music in this place. Outside country sounds, you know, cows lowing, wind on the grasses. And as I looked out at the moon-washed lawns, I see a man coming down the path, an odd figure wearing a flopping jacket and a wide-brimmed hat. He walks with a cane, dragging a foot somewhat. Well, you remember my grandmother, who was full Irish and filled me with stories of the little men? It was that magical kind of moment. He stops beside a little pear tree that grows near the entry, he puts his hand up to the tree to get his balance. So I thought. But no. He strokes the tree as you might stroke a pet. I thought, what an irony of this kind of life. Where the gentleness and kindliness of the folk shines in them and is reflected in every action, where a man stops in the dark to stroke a tree. All we see in this place is their bizarre sexual life. Well, that has nothing to do with me. Let them take their men in numbers. It's this other I find so appealing, the love of nature and their extraordinary kindness. I understand a little what Peter finds so appealing here. They act, not out of legality or obligation, but out of love, spontaneous, from the heart, in all things. As to Peter and me, it was always legality. I know that now. And therefore, without the benefit of this divorce contract, I consider my marriage over. As for men, I'm done with them. One of them was more than I could bear. And they take a hundred to bed? They must be saints.

THREE

*O*UTSIDERS

Their promiscuous intercourse of sexes is so shocking to all sensibilities we cannot defile these columns with their recital . . . a perversion of scripture so blasphemous as to chill the blood . . . The beasts of the field are better than these people who preach it.   *New York Observer,* 1852

For more than thirty years the attention of the American people has been directed toward the strange and abominable practices of the Mormon sect, and all lovers of morality have, with one accord, been outspoken in its denunciation. But while attention has been generally directed toward this particular form of vice, another and more dangerous evil has sprung up and has been silently growing in our midst, unnoticed by those whose duty it was to crush it in the bud. . . . Encouraged in this way the evil principle of Free Love has spread with marvellous rapidity . . . whether they be Oneida Communists, Individual Sovereigns, Berlin Heights Free Lovers, Spiritualists, Advocates of Woman's Suffrage, or Friends of Free Divorce, we find them all united in the accomplishment of one object . . . the total destruction of the marriage relation.   *Free Love and Its Votaries*
                              JOHN B. ELLIS, 1870

. . . an unmanly sight to see a great prosperous newspaper . . . gather together the two wings of its hebdomadal flatulence . . . for a doughty descent upon this starveling and harmless fieldmouse!
                              HENRY JAMES (the elder), 1852

My dear, *dear* Katie:

What have I done? I've sent you off to God-knows-where on the flimsiest of information from Bitsie, who never got a thought clear in her life. I was sure that this "adventure" was simply one of those trials that all women must go through in the marriage game. I thought, well, I've always seen you as a sort of sad heroine who would rise from adversity and find courage to persevere. It was your *goldenness,* I suppose, and the fact that you've always kept yourself aloof and inviolate from the haggles of this awful life. At least I had thought so. Now Edgar has just come back from dining with one of his "horse" companions (I shall call them that for fear of offending the sensibilities with any other name), one of his occasional companions who is a writer of sorts just back from London and he brings with him a manuscript about to be published which shall soon be in the hands of the world, a manuscript that so shocks me and berates me for having cast you into the hands of devils that I am quite beside myself. The book is called *Free Love and Its Votaries* and Mr. Ellis who wrote it visited your little "community" and the truths he tells have so disturbed me that I shall never in my *life* forgive Bitsie and her simplistic "strawberry feasts," and you yourself for your little domestic letters, the silk room this and the trapshop that. What I have read of the "vile and unnatural practices" has excited my nervous system into a visit to my physician. I was so certain, Katie, that no matter what happened, you were strong enough to keep yourself inviolate and make free choices and that you had no alternative, considering your delicate marital "situation." I never for a moment thought you'd enter into the "free love" in spite of my what-shall-I-say "worldly" wisdom. You know me, Katie, how I do put on.

But now I have read the book, and I have learned what they do to the children. If I have given you any bad advice, if any vile old hand touches our Deirdre, I'll kill myself on the spot. Send me word quickly. Are you safe? If I don't hear from you in a week's time, I'll be there with a carriage and several strong men (not Edgar's friends, I assure you) to take you away by force and you can stay with me until you sort out your life. I am always yours, now in abject fear for your safety and the safety of your children.

Your Moira

Dear Katie:

My head is so bad today I can scarcely think. Have I done the terrible thing Moira says I have? I can't think so, but if she says it's true, I am beside myself. I am enclosing with this letter a box of chocolates to comfort you until Moira comes. I would come myself except that Harry has just bought up part of Brooklyn Heights and to sell the land we are giving a grand ball in the Venetian style. I think he is digging a pond out behind the house and is sending for a gondola and some men to sing in it. I had an awful time getting at the chocolates, the larder is locked most of the time, but I have found the key. Please write me and tell me you are not ravished or murdered in your bed.   Your Bitsie

My dear Peter, you poor addled fool:

I have collected the rents as you directed but I have sent only part of them to the Community. I have held back a portion and deposited them to your account because I recognize that you are not of sound mind and body. I don't know how to name your disorder but I have no doubt that I could convince any jury that you are temporarily insane. You write of Arthur Cunningham in your support of this venture. Arthur Cunningham has a serious illness and fell from sight. I myself had seen him pleading in the courts, he was brilliant in his time, but he suffered a stroke that left him with a palsy and when I saw him after I was totally shocked. So it's not wonder he's hidden himself away in that place. Also I have had my clerks do a bit of research into the life of this *saint,* John Humphrey Noyes. Your eyes are so veiled with romance that I beg you to sit and read this letter without passion and with what is left of your clear mind. Peter, the man is convinced he's St. Paul! He was thrown out of the church for good reason. When he was still young and hotheaded he published a letter in the newspaper which has become, as my clerical friends tell me, infamous in the religious community. They call it the "Battle-Axe Letter." I quote. Exhibit:

I call a certain woman my wife . . . she is yours, she is Christ's and in Him she is bride of all saints. She is dear in the hand of a stranger, and according to my promise to her, I rejoice. My claim in her cuts directly across the marriage vows of this world. . . . When the will of God is done on earth as it is in heaven, there will be no more marriage. The marriage supper of the Lamb is a feast at which every dinner is free to every guest. . . . In a holy community there is no more reason why sexual intercourse should be restrained by law than why eating and drinking should be. . . .

My God, Peter, can you be in your right mind to have brought Katherine and the children into this perpetual Dionysian feast? Do you need more proof that the man is either a charlatan or a lunatic? He married a homely woman for her money and proceeded to use it to set up this heaven on earth so that he could play God. He's announced himself to be *perfect!* Are you paying attention to me, Peter? More than that, his wife had four stillborn children and so he dreamed up his outlandish system of *male continence* which is no more than *coitus reservatus* so that he could with impunity have his fill at the *feast of the Lamb* without impregnating her. Do you honestly believe that men are able to perform this thing? It's known to cause nervous ailments. And a man can profess to do it, that is one thing, but what he does in the privacy of his closet, that is quite something else. My dear Peter, you have had your little romance, you've likely worked yourself to complete exhaustion at the forge by this time. If you'd been intended for a blacksmith, you would have been one, and not wasted your years at Harvard. Peter, my dear boy, look at the reality. The intellectual man understands full well where he stands in the universe, side by side with the animals, his time finite, from dust he comes and to dust he shall return, he cannot bear the thought, being egoist as he is, of ending so ingloriously and so he creates a God in *his* own image, a God powerful enough to snatch him up off this vale of tears into the clouds of heaven, a heaven replete with winged angels of the most lovely aspect who will do nothing but stroke the harp and sing hymns. (What a detestable picture of a hereafter, and who would want to spend eternity with it but my maiden aunt.) I have to say this Noyes's fictional paradise is a cut above. I have just read a marvelous new poem by the English poet Browning, called "Caliban upon Setebos" in which he shows Caliban living on an island creating a god in his own miserable image: a bitter vengeful angry god, a more accurate picture of what you may call God's kindness to man, God's mercy. What has God sent us, my God, but plague, war, disease and misery? The truth of it, Peter, is that we are all Calibans, half-man, half-animal, living in a pit and trying for a lifetime to clamber out of it. God is the creation of frightened men who cannot deal with the reality of an abandoned universe. Do you think that one poor perverted megalomaniac who thinks he is Christ or St. Paul can change men in all their *in*glory, as they have shown themselves for two thousand years? Read your Scripture and you will see the same apocalypse as we see today, the same gross nature, the same proscriptions to save men from violences of their fellow men. You argue that man is altered to a more spiritual nature, you argue music, art, etc. Beethoven for all the music which thrills us was a man of the grossest kind of nature. Ben Franklin, that great statesman and marvel of good sense, why, the man left bastards all over the place! He was a lecher, running after women until the day he died. The concept of man floating up to the heavens is a phantom. Search for heaven, Peter, you will end in despair. And Noyes isn't the only apostle who is promising the world a hole in the sky to climb up and crawl out of this inharmonious world. Note the Shakers, the Mormons, New Harmony etc., etc. This one has no sex, this one had nothing *but* sex, this one has a hundred wives, this one none. Dreams and fantasies.

And when you come out of this dream, I intend for you to have something with which to feed your wife and children. To that end I am taking it into my own responsibility to manage your affairs here. Peter, my poor dreamer, awake!

And my wife asks that you send her some of that good blueberry jam. What the blazes does she mean by that?

Bannerman

FOUR

THE *Softening of Hearts*

Let us say that all appetite of every kind is equivalent to magnetic attraction. The charm of food, of music, of friendship, of love, of thought, imagination and religion . . . the union we seek with these things . . . is like the coming together of positive and negative poles in magnetism. We are thus a magnetic relation to every thing.

. . . Shame is factitious and irrational. If attraction is the result of a magnetic force, then in a pure medium, love between the sexes would stand free of much of the prudish sentimentality that now besets it. . . .

. . . There is a strong scientific probability falling in with the plain intimations of the Gospel that death will sometime come to an end. Let the magnetism that rules between man and nature become harmonized and freed from disturbing elements so that his passions can exercise themselves in the pure medium of the love of God, and everything must contribute to his improvement and beautifying, instead of his decay.

The Circular
October 8, 1863

Katherine was awakened from a dream of death by the sweet sounds of a clarinet. She sat for a moment bewildered and saddened. And then the clarinet brought her to life again. She threw open the curtains. A clarinet was calling a bee. What marvelous grown-up children they were. This morning they were called out in the early light to weed the vegetable garden. Not just the clarinet, the oom-pahs and the boom-booms of the marching band. *Bitsie, no one would believe you who hadn't seen it.* The marching band would pace them to the gardens. The band was warming up on the lawn, she ran for her robe and joined the women in the hall on their way to the bathroom. Mary Darcy waved. Mary worked beside her and Sarah in the sewing room. Heavy-armed and heavy-bosomed, that warm double-chinned smile, Mary always looked so fresh from her night's sleep. Sarah joined them, rubbing her stiff fingers.

"How are they this morning?"

"The devil and I, we wrestled through the night, I thought he had me once or twice, but then I heard the clarinet. It was a sign. By the time we finish weeding the garden, I'll have him on his back."

Lines were already forming as she reached her place. She heard calls of "Where's the captain of this squad?" and "Where's my division? And, "Remember right foot forward!" She found her *platoon* (*Moira you will never believe this.*) Six women, aged from eleven to seventy-five, the leader being the best baker of bread in upstate New York, who reminded her "squad" of the meaning of "double quick" and "right and left wheel" so as not to foul up the precision of the forward marching. Then the tuba gave up its practice sounds and fell into something that was almost a tune.

The "titmouses" and the "little prattlers" came flying out of the children's wing, their "mothers" trailing behind them, trying to fasten a scarf on the run, or button a shoe. Katherine saw Rebecca, hand in hand with her new little friend. Rebecca waved.

The drums took up the boom-boom-boom, the tuba picked up the rhythm and then all the instruments joined in, some in tune, some not. The poor cornet. It struggled on.

The band played "The Balle of Gavelotte," more or less. They had been playing *at* it for weeks. The Mansion House seemed to be filled with two hundred musicians, there wasn't a corridor which, in the evening, didn't echo with the strains of notes practiced or choked out of instruments, there were in the house two orchestras and countless singing clubs and the soloists . . . of which Deirdre breathlessly prayed to be one. One had only to lie back in bed before the house closed up to hear the scratchy strains of a violin or the tinkle of a beginner's piano. But what was brassy or tinny or insecure inside the house was thunderous and marvelous in the brightening light and the sweet dampness of the wet clover, marvelous and martial under the bright banners of hanging branches and the waving of tattered clouds, and the staring cows, and the huddled wide-eyed sheep.

The whistle sounded. The leader called, "Step out!" The children shrieked with delight, Katherine forgot the foot, she had to double-step to get even, they all high-stepped in the Prussian style across the lawn, past the little pear tree, down toward the hedge that was the limits of the younger children's free playground, down the slope. "Wheel right!" They wheeled right to the bleating of the big-eyed lambs; by the time they had wheeled left again they were at the gardens, there was pushing at the call of stop because some did not, the children fell to the ground laughing, the band stopped, but not all together. The cornet ended alone.

Katherine breathed in the sweet morning and went to find a piece of garden to work. The strawberries were already well attended, the onions, the potatoes, the fat squash. The night before in the great hall there was a great debate about the pumpkins. Someone said they were really *pompion*. And since they were all in the throes of spelling bees for self-improvement, it was suggested that the pumpkin thereafter be called *pompion*. But they all decided finally that the homely *pumpkin* suited them more.

Katherine chose . . . the carrots. She had most of the carrots to herself. She took a hoe and began to scrape around the feathery tops. But bending over carrots didn't suit her spirit. She found a little three-pronged tool and fell to her knees. How comfortable, the pantaloons. She thought of the old Katherine and how women of her class were trapped by "fashion." She put her hands into the soil. She worked it loose with the fork, pulling at the weeds, working and reworking the soil down the row until it was sweet dark loam. The earth was so rich she lost all sense of others and fell into the reverie of her task. She turned up fat worms, she picked one up and held it on her palm, how good of nature to have put them there to wriggle their way into the soil and make paths for the fingering roots; she let her mind travel with the cycle of the seed: the sleeping seed buried in the hard earth, then feeling some bit of warmth or water, stirring and then beginning to swell and finally bursting with the blind urge to reach toward a sun it somehow knew existed, that reaching the sun it would be free at last from the underworld.

A fragment of her dream returned to her. *Fingering . . . fingers . . . something about fingers . . .*

The weeding was done and others were regrouping for the march back to the breakfast table. Katherine bent to her work. The music moved away, and the voices, and the laughter, her mind was still occupied, like new shoots searching for something, some little space not impeded by rock, to push down and down . . .

The dream came back to her like a thud in the breast. *She had dreamed of her dead babies.* Her two dead babies were being lowered into the ground without coffins, she and Peter in the empty graveyard carrying their poor dead babies, little arms hanging, those fat little hands with dead fingers . . .

She had killed those babies before they were born. Because she did not love Peter and her heart denied his seed. Even though she prayed for the courage to accept those pregnancies, her body would not and refused to nourish them. Her poor innocent babes. They were born dead. Twice. Twice she'd murdered by withholding love, by neglect of feeling. Oh, murderer! Twice she had seen her babies lowered into the cold dead ground.

But she could feel now the earth was neither cold nor dead. She could feel with her hands plunged into the worked soil that the earth was alive! Full of roots and movement, worms and mealy bugs, making way for those roots to stretch . . . with a cry she plunged her fingers into the soil, deep down, trying to find the fingers of her dead babies who reached up to be reconciled with their mother. She pushed her fingers down, working the soil. The earth was warming now. If she could touch those fingers once, those poor dead fingers, and let the babies know that they were loved and now they could push up their shoots toward her and grow . . .

She came out of her reverie dazed. *Someone was watching her.* A man, resting on his hoe, watching her. She should have been embarrassed, or angry, that someone had intruded on so intensely personal a moment. But she recognized him. The man at the pear tree. The one who limped. He touched the brim of his hat to her, turned and walked away, using the hoe for support. He'd seen her there when everyone had left, he thought something was wrong, he was concerned. There was no guile in this place. It was innocent. She saw him limping back to the Mansion House.

By the time she'd washed and changed, something sad in her had come to an end. The dream was finished. She wondered at the nature of her anger with Peter, so strong an anger that it could kill something in her. But that was finished too. She was done with him. She felt happy and buoyant. She went down to the best breakfast she could remember.

And you hath he quickened, who were dead in trespasses and sins! Peter's hand lifted the hammer high, sweat from his chest and face hissed in the orange licks of fire, his city muscles agonized by the weight of the hammer, the blow rang like music, chain jumped in his hand, the link closed . . . *wherein . . . ye walked according to the course of this world . . . lusts of our flesh fulfilling desires to the flesh . . .* He wasn't fulfilled, oh, Father, you saw to that, the hammer lifted, the iron rang, *walked according to the prince of the power of the air.* Prince of the power of the air, his father had given that prince dominion over him. Ephesians 2. His father had that engraved on his soul. He was more familiar with that airly prince, god of whores and lawyers. Bannerman would have liked that. He tried to hammer out his stubborn spirit but in his ears the argument rang on.

He'd been too many nights without a woman. The strain was on him.

Newhouse tapped his shoulder after the bell rang for the noon meal. "Time to stop, man." Newhouse didn't like him. He didn't know why. He admired the rugged backwoods man whose traps were the mainstay of the Community. Peter fastened chain to spring. The spring was machine-made. Newhouse appraised him with narrowed eyes, and spat. No one chewed tobacco. But they chomped on rope, straw, anything that kept the jaws moving and spat as if the chaw were in the cheek. "Old days," Newhouse said, "took two strong men two hundred blows to make a spring. But God gave man a brain, had to use it."

"Must have been glorious out there in the woods, those old trapping days."

Newhouse chomped on a piece of hemp. "Glorious? City man could die of it. Little gnats that got into your skin and eyes. Little punkies so small, you could go mad. Had to make a paste of pennyroyal and lard, only way to survive. Use to say John Brown Tract Whiskey, that would kill the pain. Took the lining out of your mouth. If you could stand the whiskey, you could stand the pain, vice versa." He spat. "Trapping is a poor man's game. Man can make a few dollars living free, better than going off to war and killing his brother."

Peter raised his hammer and hit metal hard. Poor man's game, not entertainment for the rich. That's what Newhouse thought of him. No way to get through these hard heads that he was sincere.

Newhouse smiled, playing with him. "Trapper all my life. Red fox, silver fox, raccoon, fisher, wildcat, mink, possum, housecat, wolf, marten. Know who buys up all those pelts?" He spat. "John Jacob Astor. Made his million off poor men's sweat." He spat again and walked away.

Amos came by and put an arm around Peter's shoulder. "Have something to eat and I'll have you a game of chess."

Peter wasn't hungry. He worked on for a while and then put his hammer aside and turned the barrel for a chess table and began to set out the pieces. "Why doesn't Sewall like me?"

Amos settled his squat bulky body into a chair. "Doesn't know you yet."

Peter was nervous. His muscles ached from the hammer. He led out with a Wilhelm Steinitz move, the champion's opening, his nights had been spent in the Community library, he wasn't used to letting his brain go fallow for so long, he had been playing solitary chess to keep his languishing mind occupied. Amos countered him, rook for rook, bishop by bishop, but Peter was too good at the game. Amos didn't have a prayer. The old sweet familiar taste of victory was on his tongue. He played cool, straight-faced. Everyone in the shop watched the match, family men and German hired hands alike. Three moves he'd have the game. He reached for a knight. The bell sounded. Meal was over. Amos swept the pieces back into the wood box.

"What are you doing? It's my game!"

"Game's called when the bell rings."

"But I'd have had you in three moves!"

Amos smiled, Newhouse winked, the spectators nodded, amused, and ambled back to their work.

"But that's not fair! It was clearly my game."

"Rules is rules," Amos said. "We play for the game, not for winners."

"Come *on,* Amos, winning is the point of it!"

"The point for you," said Amos, "is to learn patience. We don't play to win."

Patience, his arse. He'd seen Amos on the croquet court slamming away at his neighbor's ball, cracking like thunder on the mountain. And if that wasn't the desire to win, nothing was.

He went back to the forge with these unclean thoughts. His battle was not with Amos but with himself. He struck iron for humility. He would hammer himself out clean if it killed him. Sweat hissed into the fire. It was *his* life he was bending like wrought iron, *his*. Newhouse clapped a hand to his shoulder. "Take it easy, man. This isn't a contest."

Peter struck iron. "The contest is between me and the devil. Leave me alone." *Prince of the power of the air.*

Newhouse peered at him from under those bushy brows, as if Peter were a specimen in a trap. Then he put a more gentle hand to Peter's shoulder. "Nice and easy. You'll have the devil on his back."

When the day was finished and the hired men walked off, the insiders sat back, stretched out legs, took a cider, chewed on straw, made small talk of this and that. "Peter," Amos said, "did you try the applesauce at this morning's table?"

Applesauce. He was exhausted, body and spirit, he wasn't in the mood for applesauce talk.

"Early Joe's," Newhouse said. "Sweet old apples. Weren't those trees on the place when you bought if from Jonathan Burt?"

"Best of the apples to my taste," said Amos. "Sweet, but not too sweet, sometimes the tart edge on them, but a deep good flavor." He nudged Newhouse.

Newhouse twisted his mouth into a smile. "Apples like women. Don't know why the old church was so hard on them both. Both fine to my taste."

"For the lesson, man. Apples and women to teach us all." Amos smiled at Peter. "Her name is Mary Darcy, she'll be waiting for you tonight."

Peter felt his legs tingle, the way they did when he was in court and he knew the tide in a bad and stormy case had turned to his advantage. He kept himself quietly contained but the others were amused at his expense.

"Best bed this side of Eden," said Newhouse. The others agreed and nodded their well-wishes.

Mary Darcy. Best bed this side of Eden. She would be a mature beauty. La Gioconda, a woman who pleased men, not young but tight-bodied, firm mature breasts, not the poor pitiful things of that whore he'd slept with last. The sweetness and tart of Early Joes. He prayed he wouldn't embarrass himself, that he'd prove his manhood. Mary Darcy. He would ask discreetly which one she was.

It happened as Deirdre knew it would. She was alone with Adam in a little rehearsal room, he was trying to modulate her voice. He would jump up from the piano, show her how tight she kept the muscles of her throat, then down again to play. And then he stopped. He took her by the hand. "Let's get out of here."

They ran hand in hand, laughing. Anyone seeing them would have thought them children. They walked for a long while into Cragin's Meadow. And when the world was too far away for them to care about it, they fell to the grass. The first kiss was long and hard and she felt it in all the hidden places of her body. It was the end of her child's life and the beginning of her life as a woman. Finally Adam released her and lay back in the meadow grasses. She couldn't bear the parting, she bent over him and kissed his mouth and his ear.

"Have mercy . . . Deirdre . . ."

"I love you with my whole heart."

He put her away but touched her face with the tips of his fingers, they were such wonderful long musician's fingers, his slim long wrists, and the long column of his throat and the smooth sun-gold skin and in the depth of his eyes were little gold fires and his cleanly defined mouth, his full lips still moist with her kiss, the way his hair curled and fell, it was so precious, so wonderful, she couldn't leave it all alone. "You're going to be a trial for me," he said. "Loving you comes at such an inconvenient time."

"Then you do love me, oh, you do!"

"Who could help loving you, but God knows how long before we can be together."

"Now, we can be together now. I want to. And if everyone lies together here, then us. Please."

He raised up on one elbow, the shape of his reclining like that, he was a portrait, he was Hamlet full of moods and shadows and she was in his eyes, she saw herself, she was there forever, no, nothing was forever, she was not that much of a child, she was there now, and now was all she had. "You know what my life is, Deirdre. You know how much this life means to me, and until the mood here changes . . . I mean about us being together . . . we'll have to wait, and the wheels grind exceeding slow."

"Then let me join and be a proper part of the life here, they can't stop us then."

He turned his face up and lay back chewing on a piece of long grass. "You don't know what you're saying, you have no idea of what a commitment like that means."

"Then teach me, I want to be taught."

"To be with me, you'd have to be taught by one of the older men, don't you understand that?"

"My mother said a woman can remain celibate, so let me lie with you and be celibate with others."

He turned to her, eating her up with his eyes. "You're such a delight, you absolutely charm me."

"Then let's . . . be together . . . you and me."

"It's not possible, not now."

"Then come away with me! We'll go to Paris!"

"And what will we do in Paris?"

"We'll be lovers."

"And how will we eat in Paris?"

"I'll go on the stage, I'll sing and you'll play."

"Be serious. Singing for an audience of trap shop workers and Sunday visitors isn't a career."

"I'm serious, I adore you with a deep and abiding love."

"Deep and abiding . . . you sound like a *Harper's Weekly* romance. If you were part of us, Deirdre, part of the family, *deep and abiding* would mean something else. Listen, adorable child, this isn't the Berlin Heights free lovers that the Presbyterians are always screaming about. This is a deep and abiding ideal and I'm born into it, it's part of my soul, my whole soul is given to it, do you understand me? When the world is less stupid and ready, we must be here to teach them. So you see, no matter how much I desire you . . ."

"Then you do desire me!"

"You idiot." He kissed her again, with his mouth open, until she couldn't breathe, until she could feel his whole body against hers, she knew passion the way bohemian women knew passion, she abandoned herself to it. But he stopped himself, and her. "I can't, not until you've been taught."

"Then teach me!"

He took a curl of her hair around his finger. "You see why you're dangerous for me? Not just the need for your body, it's the need to be the only *one* with your body and the temptation to that would destroy me. But the thought of anyone else in your bed, I couldn't bear that either. So, we'll see." He stood up. "We'll wait and see."

He walked away and left her there without looking back.

Since his return from New York Adam had avoided his mother's room. It was the same little dormer room she'd had all the years in the Mansion House. When he came to her from the children's room, it was here, the little window seat, warm and filled with her presence. Bittersweet memories.

This is where she received him now, a leg in those brown sensible pantaloons tucked under her, leaning her cheek against the window, looking out over fields and meadows. So girlish in the way she bent and seemed to be dreaming. But she'd aged, her hair had gone quite gray, her face was deeply lined. It hurt him to admit it. And he hated being harsh the way he was now. "He's keeping me away from women. Ever since I returned, and you know why."

"It's not Amos keeping you, it's the committee. They thought you ought to wait awhile longer. Be patient, Adam."

"Ah, the famous committees of the Oneida Community. Committee on trouser buttons, committee on the rising and setting of the sun, and a grand committee to keep Adam out of the family bed. Amos *is* that committee, and you know it."

"Try to understand, you were in New York too long, he feels you've been contaminated, he only wants you to wait and regain your soft heart. And I don't hear a soft heart now."

He let slip a little laugh of disbelief. "Contaminated how? Body or spirit?"

"Since when did you learn to carp and find fault in that tone? It's better to be silent than to find fault like that."

Now he could see in the way she leaned and turned that her body wasn't girlish, the slump was genuine fatigue. He drew in a breath of self-control. "I'm sorry. You're right. Tone, yes, the difference between a good honest criticism and carping is *tone*. I'll soften my tone. The matter remains the same."

"The difference, my dear son, isn't tone, it's *intent*."

"My intent is to be home in every way. I've been carefully inspected by Theodore Noyes, M.D. Theo certifies that I am uncontaminated in body. And in spirit? I've come back to God. You'll have to take my word on that and Amos has no right to deny me my word."

"Give him a little time . . . he'll come around. He never meant to deny your sincerity."

"Why do you always excuse him? You never excuse yourself and God knows you never excused me."

The implied criticism was of her too, and the tone was wrong. He tried to soften his heart. "I've spent months thinking this out, I'm sure of what I believe yet the moment I come back here with the archangels, you make me feel a child again, forbidding me this or that, and I have to speak harshly to make you understand."

She started to answer back, but she was too well schooled in the art of criticism, and she knew it was her duty to listen.

"I learned something important in New York. I learned that the Community is the next best thing to heaven, but not heaven itself. And the fathers aren't gods, but men and therefore fallible."

"Which men in particular? Let's have it all."

"Father Noyes, and Amos."

"Amos. You're suddenly smitten with a girl and Amos wants you to wait and suddenly you find fault with a man whose whole life has been the Community?"

"Whose tone is angry now, Mother?"

She started to answer, and then corrected herself. She softened her tone. "Where and in what has he become inflexible?"

"In the matter of the 'social' theory."

"Are you sure he isn't right in keeping you from the family bed? You've come back with some strange ideas. It takes time to let go of the city."

"You come to the same thing over and over again. I've been to the city. The devil in New York, haven't I heard that often enough? Mother, listen with an open mind, just once. I'm not denying the community ways, not the essentials. You're dealing with a new generation now. You and yours came through fire to make this holy place. You were forged in fire, scourged from town to town, you had the courage to break with tradition. But when it came to raising us, you gave us the easy life. Easy and gracious. It was natural that we'd question our traditions, wasn't it? And our traditions have Corinthe sleeping in Sewall Newhouse's bed, despising his old body . . ."

"Corinthe is free to refuse, you know that."

"Is that true? You know how you work on Corinthe. A little suggestion that she must consider Sewall's goodness to the Community, or is she being selfish by withholding her love from a good man.

You have your ways." She couldn't turn from his accusing eyes, it wasn't her fashion to turn away from accusation. She was direct. And if she'd spared him, he would have spared her now. But between them was all those days when he'd come running from the children's house to leap into her arms and she'd cover him with kisses and hold him and rock him in the blessed window seat, the same seat she sat in now, his head to her breast, and suddenly she'd move him away from her, her passion cooling to affection, and she'd remember the sin of loving too possessively and she'd say, *You mustn't be too sticky, or they won't let you come the next time.* So truth stood between them in its sharpest form. "A little pinch of conscience from you, a reminder to duty, and Corinthe accepts and sleeps with Sewall."

"It's not an easy philosophy. We all love one another, why should she not love Sewall?"

"Because he's sixty and she's sixteen. If I didn't believe in this hard philosophy, heart and soul, I wouldn't be here. But we have a right to fight our own battles—no, not battles, skirmishes. Little procedural things. Like this business of older men teaching the girls. That comes from John Humphrey Noyes, not from God. So let's have a committee of girls who will propose a few changes. It's nature for a young man to want a young woman in his bed. And Amos and his cronies are bent on prior rights to that bed. That's not Perfectionism, that's downright medieval and you know it."

"It's always been our way to let mature men teach the girls."

"Mature? Esrick is mature. Cunningham is mature. Amos is sixty, mother, and he likes to lie with young women."

Her face shifted, she lost control of it, he'd never before seen such black anger. "Don't you accuse him of a thing like that! I forbid it!" It startled him, he was unsettled, she was a goddess, beyond that kind of loss of control.

"Why is it you'd plunge your hand into fire for what you believe, or mine, but you're bent on protecting Amos? Where's you faith in him, then!"

Shame overtook her, she put her hands on her breast, horrified at the hardness of her voice, her whole affect shifted, she was suddenly the soft mother he'd remembered waiting for his visit. She held arms out to him. He came to her tentatively, afraid to let himself love her too much. "I am afraid."

"How long since Amos slept in your bed?"

"Very long."

"And in the beds of other women of your age?"

"Very long."

"And you don't think that calls for a criticism?"

She couldn't answer.

"And something more disturbing yet. And you know what I mean. Father Noyes's *special love* for Theodore."

She lowered her head, saying nothing.

"Theo and I went away at the same time. We both questioned God and the Community ways. He to study medicine and find God in the marvelous bodies of men, and me to find God in heavenly harmonies. Well, I found my God, Theo didn't. I understand his doubts and they're deep as canyons. He's not a believer, he wants nothing more than to be allowed to practice medicine, but he respects his father too much. He's being groomed for leader, he hates the idea, everybody knows that Father Noyes disbelieves in *special love* and they see it happening and no one dares call it a fault. How could they? He is our rock and foundation, if he flounders we sink. Don't you see what's happening? Father Noyes must be criticized. Amos must be criticized."

"Are you so sure," she said, "that you see with the clearest eyes? You're still so young, Adam. Father Noyes has his inspiration from God and St. Paul. If he wants Theodore to replace him, God must have a reason. And as for the young women and their young men, isn't this in some way tied to your love of Deirdre, which is evident on your face? You speak of skirmishes and war. This isn't a war we're fighting, not against each other, God forbid it."

She pierced him with that. But the wound bound them together more than all the cementations of filial and maternal obligation. They both wanted the Community to survive. She was the old physician, she knew the gangrenous spots and how to excise them. She was unwilling to hurt Amos, whom she loved so much. She loved him too, Adam knew that. But no matter how much she loved them both, when the moment came, she would cut.

He also knew that his love for Deirdre was compelling and he wanted her in his bed.

Sarah, that good guiding hand tucked into Katherine's arm, led her across the fields.

"And where are you taking me now?"

Sarah had been so much into herself, Katherine knew her moods by now. "Do you find me too directive?" Sarah asked. "Do I push you too much this way and that? I do believe God works through me."

"When I came here I was a woman walking a rope bridge across a chasm, swaying in the wind. You've built me a nice stone bridge. You may push me, in *almost* any direction."

Sarah laughed, that good-earth-woman laugh of hers. "As to that, did you know that Peter had asked to sleep with one of our sisters?"

"With my blessing."

"Spoken like a good Oneida woman!"

"Don't deceive yourself. It's not my love for Peter that makes me generous. I just don't care anymore. His bed habits are his own, they always were, I suppose. And where are you taking me now?"

They headed toward the grove of sweet-blooming peaches and plums and pears. "Martin our nurseryman has agreed to take you to work in the orchards. He's short a hand. Mind you, these are *his* orchards. He is our only exception to the rule of *personal love.* The trees are his, he tolerates us merely."

"Yes, you know me so well, you knew I'd like that. I used to stand at my window in the city looking at that locked park."

"Ah . . . there is our St. Martin of the Fields."

The man with the flopping coat and the wide-brimmed hat. The man on the cane. "My monastery monk!"

"Monastery monk? I wouldn't call him that, but I could see how someone would. He's a solitary soul. He hides in the groves. I'm afraid that one of these days he'll take root. And he's so careless about his clothes. We've offered him a wife for his trousers and handkerchiefs but he's declined. But he's a gentle man and marvelous with trees and we all do love him."

"And you have ulterior designs, I know you so well."

"As to that, you are so aloof from your brothers in the Community . . ."

". . . and you thought to find me a safe and gentle creature to be my friend."

". . . if a friend is what you want. I've had so many invitations for you, Katie."

"All of which I gratefully decline. Don't speak of serious matters, what a day this is!"

Martin gave a shy nod of greeting, pulled his hat still lower on his brow. He was not bearded but unshaven, untidily hirsute. He motioned them to follow him into the groves. He spoke to Katherine without looking at her. "Are you fast with names?"

Not even a word of greeting. She looked to Sarah. Sarah indicated that she was on her own. "Yes . . . I suppose . . ."

"This is the family Babcock. I want you to see each grove as a family." He bent a branch so that Katherine could see an insect-scored leaf. He searched between the leaves until he found the insect that had scored the leaf, and then made them listen for the bird that ate the insect. "You must introduce yourself to the grove softly, let the trees know that you're here. They'll understand you by the way you act toward them. Do you believe in *animal magnetism?*"

"Here he goes," said Sarah, chidingly.

"Animal magnetism? You mean *mesmerism?* The parlor game?"

"It's no parlor game. Good old Ben Franklin gave it a bad name. But it's a hard science now, like phrenology."

"Watch him," said Sarah, "he'll have you reading the bumps on the trees."

Martin pulled Sarah to him and kissed her cheek. "No, phrenology is for your hard head."

"Well then, I'll leave you with him," Sarah said, "and if you talk to any trees and they answer, you shall tell me at dinner."

Martin led Katherine through the orchard, showing her this twisted branch and that excoriated bark, how this leaf showed signs of illness and that one robust health.

"Do you mesmerize them?" she said. "Do you conjure them to give more fruit?"

He gave her a sidelong glance, under the brim of the hat, to see if she was serious. She tried not to smile; he was so earnest with it all. "Feelings"—he put his fist to his breast—"all feelings are carried from here . . . in a kind of subtle fluid. Nervous feelings, loving feelings, the deepest sensations of the heart, on this subtle nervous fluid. It's more developed in some people than in others. So that one person, if the other allows, can have influence on the other during sleep, the way waters in two adjoining chambers equalize with each other. Trees are deep-rooted, they reach down to the earth's most subtle fluids. And when we touch them and try to make connections with them . . ."

"Like knocking on wood?"

She saw him smile. "Yes. Do you?"

"Knock on wood? I did when I was a girl. I had an Irish grandmother."

"How wise she was to teach you."

"You think you can knock and the druids of the tree will give you back magical gifts?"

"But they do," he said. "You knock, you take the magnetism from the tree, you give it back something of yourself, and it gives you out its treasures. Like the little pear tree at the entry. I took it from the grove, away from its brothers and sisters; it needs loving and stroking, wait and see what a yield of fruit it gives up."

"What a gentle way to think," she said. "I saw you touching the little pear tree at night."

He nodded and said no more. They started off again; he showed her how to recognize trees by their configuration, this branch stretching out an arm, this turning back on itself. She followed him in the happiest way. It was the best of afternoons. A good day all in all. They worked together learning genus and species. She couldn't wait to get her sketchpad in her hands.

But she was feeling tired, her arms ached from the stretching. "I'll go back now, if it's all right."

"Yes, I'll come along with you."

When he reached to take her arm, he shocked her. Instinctively she pulled away. No one touched her without invitation. She was more shocked when he fell. She saw him falling, she realized at once that it wasn't for her sake he reached out but for his own. She was moving too fast, his leg wasn't steady. He lay for a moment and then pulled himself up and sat. She was so ashamed. She fell to her knees beside him. "Are you all right?"

He pulled up the trouser leg to assess the damage. "Nothing hurt. Just my pride."

"It was my fault, I am so sorry."

His hat had fallen off. She had thought him older, perhaps fifty. It was the hat and the unshaven face. He was less than forty, pale watery eyes, blond hair washed out by the sun. "Why should you be sorry? It's important for me to fall sometimes."

She sat beside him on the grass.

"It reminds me of things that need to be remembered. It brings back the stench and the gore of war. I'm apt to forget in all this peace." He offered her a hand, to be pulled up. She stood and helped him to his feet, picked up his cane. She walked more slowly now, pacing him. He held onto her arm.

But once outside the grove, she became self-conscious and he let go of her. The sense of intimacy was all in the grove. The grove was a magical place. They both paused at the pear tree and touched it.

She went inside alone.

At dinner she smiled at him, he nodded but didn't speak.

Sarah saw this. "It's all right, there's no need to puzzle it, life has a pattern, it all works out in the end."

It was ignoble and stupid, sitting at a bench doing women's work. Isaac sat next to him, stuffing tomatoes into jars, as if there were nothing better to do in the world. Paulie's gorge rose, he was overwhelmed with the idiocy of it. He pushed away from the bench. "I want to go to the river for a swim."

"And don't I," Isaac said. "When we're done, let's have a swim before dinner."

"I mean now. What do they do to you if you leave?"

Isaac dropped a tomato into a jar. "What do you mean, *do* to you?"

"I mean, what's the punishment?"

"Who do you mean, *they?*" He fancied he saw a smile play around Isaac's mouth.

"They. The jailors. The gods. Keepers of the workhouse."

"Nobody does anything."

"You mean you can leave and nobody *does* anything?"

"Why would you want to leave when there's still work to do?"

So they worked on honor. Well, who was he to honor here? So if nobody was about to take away his rations, which were poor at best, he'd have himself a swim. He started out of the canning shed, he heard Isaac call after him. To hell with them all. If they didn't like it they could send him home.

His bravado oozed away as he walked the dusty road in the warm sun. Where was home? He walked along backroads, across tracks, across meadows, he followed the creek for a while, kicking after frogs,

watching water swirl over rocks, he climbed down to the good swimming hole under the vine-wound tree.

He sat near the jack-in-the-pulpits and the wild lilies. He wanted a
cause, something he could believe in, he wanted a banner, he wanted a
reason to be proud in this bastard world.

Well, he wasn't going to sit there being sorry for himelf like a weak
girl. He stripped down; the afternoon light thinning, shadows growing
deeper, the water invited, he stood like a Greek warrior on an overhang-
ing rock, he let out a warrior's cry, he jumped.

He cut through water, his head must have grazed the rock, he felt
impact not pain. He didn't lose consciousness immediately, he was
aware that his world was slipping away. He was *below* the world, the
water was *above* him, the thin skin of the water, the underside of
floating seeds in the thinning light, each of the seeds he thought as he
slipped away, had thin-veined wings, angels, he thought, as he gave up
his grasp of things and sank down . . . down . . .

. . . coughing . . . he came up coughing. Someone had him doubled
over, pounding his back. He retched pond water, he tried to catch a
breath. When finally all the water was out of him, he retched bile, he
choked, the back-slapping kept on. "Let up . . ."

It was Isaac who let him slump back on the ground. He drew in air
painfully. His throat was raw, his chest and back ached, now he
touched his head and felt the lump. And Isaac sat there smiling,
drenched from the pond, the slime of wet leaves and seeds in his hair.
"How," he asked Isaac, ". . . how . . ."

"Well, I guess I know *you* by now. When we saw the swimming
hole the other day you said you'd jump from the deepest spot and I
warned you about rocks but you wouldn't listen. You never listen. So I
came after you. I guess that the state you were in, the devil would have
had you for sure. Well, he gave you a proper lesson."

He lay back in awful humiliation, saved by the enemy. Isaac, the
country fool, with that stupid grin on his face. "Why did you?"

"Why did I *what?*"

"Jump in and save me? I'm nothing to you."

"You're my brother," Isaac said.

"I'm not your brother, I've never given you a civil word, I've never given you the time of day. I've been wretched to you."

"I know you have, but that's because you've lived on the outside so long and it's still on you. But God sent you a good lesson, didn't he?"

Well, he was damn well not going to be beholden to Isaac. "What do you want?"

"How do you mean?"

He pulled himself up, he was damn sore, his head was splitting from the smash, he was wounded in battle. "What do you want? I owe you for saving me and I want to buy myself off."

Isaac got up and brushed off what mud he could and pulled some slime out of his hair. "You can buy yourself off from God. Confess Christ and see what He wants."

"*Isaac* . . ."

Isaac began to slosh back down the road. He turned and called out, "And we did have one man in the war. Mr. Hasselman. So if you want war stories, go down to the orchards and talk to Martin Hasselman. He'll tell you war stories. . . ."

"How did you dare?" Newhouse accused him. Peter was riveted to his chair, around him Amos and Cunningham, their eyes on fire. But his own anger matched theirs. What a monstrous joke, to give him into the hands of a fat old woman.

"Did you think, man, that you were hurting her when you turned your back on her that way?"

"I didn't even speak to her . . . nothing . . . I just . . ."

"You said everything with your eyes." Amos stood over him like thunder. "With your eyes and with your body. You know that well enough, we do not treat another in that careless way, we do not wound, we do not scar, this isn't a battle, man, this is heaven on earth. We're tender with each other."

"I only wanted to know who Mary Darcy was!"

"And you looked at her with disdain, you hurt her to the core and then you walked away coldly. How did you dare?"

What was he to say, he was too hurt and too angry and too confused.

"Well, here is the crux of it," said Amos. "And you sit there and listen."

He opened his mouth to respond but Newhouse's black fire-toughened fingers pointed to him to desist. He sat back, a prisoner, unable to testify in his own defense.

"From the moment you came," said Amos, "you've shifted and changed. When you came only to visit, you were taken with us and our ways. But once inside you were superior to everything you saw . . ."

"That's not . . ."

"Quiet, man!" boomed Newhouse. "This is a criticism. This is not our anger but this is for the good of your own soul! Don't you know that!"

Newhouse's voice shocked him, was this for his soul? What he had done to Mary Darcy was wrong, he knew it the moment it had passed, that thing he felt as he looked into the flabby aging face, at her body and her arms, the repulsion he felt, she saw it, he regretted . . . but it was too late . . .

". . . you came in superior. Your wife has fallen into our ways in the best spirit. And your daughters, but there is, in the Berger men, a stiff-backed pride that defies God and shows a hard spirit."

"I've tried to tell you," said Cunningham. "We're hard cases, we have to give up a lifetime of critical judgments. Outside I would have been chagrined to be seen with Mary Darcy. Here I know she's an angel, I see her with different eyes. I told you it would be hard. You owed it to yourself to wait for a while before making harsh judgments. You want too much too fast."

"You work in too much competition," said Newhouse. "You

work for excellence, yes, but not for the joy of doing it, only to impress your fellows. It's in your eyes, man."

He wanted to shout out, he wanted to stand and run, but he was pinned.

"Listen," said Cunningham. "Don't turn your thoughts inward. Listen!"

He was on the surgery table, they cut him with knives. He was competitive, he wanted to impress, yes. He shrank against their accusations.

"You crave approval in the eyes of men. You use women for your own vanity. How would it seem if you were associated with a woman less than beautiful, as you see beauty? It was to *use* Mary that you sought her out. And because she might not seem lovely to the general, you ran from her."

"You've never listened to a woman. You've never really made love to a woman. Only look at your own wife, it's in her eyes. The woman is starved to be loved."

"Liar!"

"Even your own son won't talk to you. Your wife avoids you, she came out of fear, not out of love for you. But her heart has been softened. And yours? Full of vanity."

"Vanity, self-aggrandizement, disdain, pompous egotism . . ."

They stopped. He was shaken. No, these weren't lies. They held a mirror up to his heart. He used women. He always had. He saw the accusing faces of the whores he'd bought, years of whores, that last poor girl, not much older than his daughter, sold into slavery by adversity. But he didn't consider that. She said something about a child. And he'd bought her off with money. For her? No, to salve his own conscience, at having taken her . . .

Cunningham looked him straight in the eyes. "Peter, you deceived yourself. It wasn't for the new kind of physical love you came to us nor for the Communism, nor for God . . . you came for *this*. You couldn't say it to yourself, you needed us."

Trembling, like a child. Vanity, vanity, every motive of his life.

How he used women. But hadn't women used him? His mother, she came to him while he was tied to the sides of his bed, he begged her to let him out, but she only bent to him and said, *Understand your father. He means for the best, he wants to help you, understand.* . . . She was no more his mother, she was the devil's handmaiden.

And so his heart had hardened. He became a voice in the world of law where men were tried or punished. He waited for more, he wanted to hear it all, while his skin was open.

"You've never loved a woman," said Cunningham. "How could you? Nobody taught you to love. Mary would have done that. Go to her. Excuse yourself. It's easy to walk blind looking for heaven, and with your eyes closed miss the gate."

He waited. But it was over. Amos embraced him. Newhouse clapped an affectionate hand to his shoulder. Cunningham shook his hand. And they left him there.

He was an empty vessel, everything drained out. It was a long while before he understood that this was the first step to his salvation, that they had helped him to drain out the bile of his vile sins.

Finally, when he came to himself, he went to look for Mary Darcy.

It was already dark when Paulie found the gardener burning a pile of leaves. The fragrant pungent odor of smoke, the fire in the gardener's eyes as he leaned on the rake, the fires of holy wars and the smoke of honor curling up to heaven. "Sir . . . if you don't mind . . ."

The gardener pushed the hat back from his brow. "Are you the Bergers' boy?"

"Yes, sir . . . and I thought . . . Isaac said . . ."

"Has your mother sent you?"

"I came on my own . . . I understood . . . I thought . . ." His eyes went down to the shattered leg, the gardener limped over to a fallen log and sat. Paulie came to sit beside him. "I thought you'd understand my feelings about the war," he blurted out. "Nobody else does, nobody around here had the honor to risk anything, and since you did . . . and I do admire . . ."

"What's your name, son?"

"Paul. Paul Berger. Corporal of St. George's Academy. I was before my father pulled me out."

"Corporal of the Academy. And you're filled with a sense of honor and in love with war."

"Not in love with . . . I just understand the meaning of courage, that's all."

"Up on the hill," the gardener said, "is an old man who's very ill. Too ill to tolerate the noise of the house. His leg pains him terribly. He's scarcely able to stand. And he knows he's dying. Not that he minds. He says he's lived out a good life. But he's bound to keep his body alive until God takes him, and every day, on that terrible pained leg, he gets up and walks across the room. But that's not the courage you want to hear about."

"I only thought . . ."

"The war. I volunteered for the great war. Back in '63. But not from the Community. I had a farm in New Hampshire. A wife, two sons, not unlike yourself."

"Your sons must be proud of you, sir."

"Perhaps, perhaps not. When I felt bound to duty, my wife wasn't sympathetic. It wasn't my cause, after all. She took the children and went back to England."

"How awful," said Paulie. "I would have been proud."

"Would you? Would you like to know the circumstances of my wound?"

"If it wouldn't be too painful."

"I was fighting up near Stoneman's Switch."

"That's near Aldie, between Bull Run and Kittoctan Mountain."

Martin Hasselman tossed a twig into the burning fire. "You know your war."

"Learned it all by heart."

"Well, I had been fighting for about a year. Never once met a black man, let alone saved one. We marched, we saw men fall, never took a bullet, we were a lucky bunch, we moved through battle after battle and weren't even touched.

"By that time I was more interested in the local trees than in the war. We supposed we were immune to death which was all around us. Well, we were on a morning offensive, the sharpshooters up front, we, the farmers and shepherds, we followed behind. Suddenly something happened. Noise and shouting and shots and smoke. The rest of the bunch seemed to fade away. We were alone, shells flying, hitting the ground. The man to the right of me, storekeeper from New York, he grabbed his belly and fell. It was a terrible gaping wound. He lay there screaming, his insides coming out. The man to the left grabbed his eye, he had been hit in the eye, but alive. He fell to his knees, unbelieving."

". . . and you in the leg . . ."

The fire caught Martin Hasselman's eyes. "I? No, I stood between them, so shocked I was frozen to the spot. I couldn't move. Suddenly a man stepped out of the smoke. Not a man, a boy. Your age. Maybe even younger. The age of one of my own sons. This boy had a gun in his hand. He looked at the three of us, the man on the ground who looked at his gut spilling out, screaming to be put out of his misery. The boy raised his gun, I saw his face go white and he shot. Like shooting a wounded horse. The boy turned and retched. The man with the wounded eye, who was an accountant form Pennsylvania, he fell unconscious. The boy raised his gun and looked me in the face, puzzled as to how he should do this thing. I was too amazed to cry out. I stood there, he stood there. And then he said, 'Howdy, sir.' It was ludicrous. I said, 'Hello, son.' And he said, 'I'm from Georgia, my father made me go, I was apprenticed on the farm . . .' as if to explain why he had to kill me. I said I was a nurseryman from New Hampshire, and he said he was fond of trees and wouldn't mind going into the nursery business himself. All this while mind you the battle was moving away while he was trying to come to terms with his life and his God and murder and war, just as I was. Then a voice called that if he didn't hurry, he'd lose his company. He looked at me in agony, and then, he raised his gun to my head, and at the last second he moved his barrel down and shot me in the foot. I held out my hand to shake his but he'd turned, and as he did the man on the ground, the man with one eye, came to and raised his gun and shot off the back of the boy's head."

The fire was almost burned down, only a few last leaves crackling and smoking. "And I thought, what has this to do with slavery? How did it help the black man if the white man became an animal? I got up and limped away. I had my leg bound up and I started for home. They must have thought I was killed with the others. Nobody asked about me. When I got home, my wife and family were gone. Back to England. I sold off the farm. Then I met one of the Perfectionists and he brought me here." He touched his crooked foot. He pulled up his trouser leg and showed Paulie where the ankle had been shattered and badly set. "The boy, he's here in my leg. He reminds me of one single moment when the urge to keep life was stronger than the urge to destroy it. I don't know if this is the kind of war story you want to hear, but this is the only one I have to tell."

Paulie sat looking into the dying fire. "Yes, sir."

"Paul, if you want to see real courage, go and visit the sick old man on the hill. There's more courage there than you're likely to find in any war."

Peter stood humble and contrite before Mary Darcy's door, a soul plumbed for sin, all vanity turned inside out, ready to exorcise his black heart in contrition, at least part of him did. The other side of him, through the looking glass, heard Bannerman saying, *I've heard of men falling from Grace, but to fall toward Grace . . .* That other half saying, *Why are you here? Fool, you should be back in New York dressed in your own good clothes, a good shine to your boots,*

eating oysters and stuffed quail in Delmonico's, or taking a wine with a colleague to celebrate a good win in the courts. As to the rest of it, dammit, he should have done as the others, to hell with his wife if she was cold to him, he should have taken a mistress, one of the pretty shopgirls, and set her up in a cottage in the country. Either this was just desserts for his folly or the cosmic joke of the century.

The door opened. Mary Darcy, pudgy and double-chinned, her downy face, her hair all blowsy from lying down. He didn't know whether to laugh or cry. Was she angry? What was he to say? "I'm here to apologize . . . if I said or did anything . . ."

"Come in." It was more an order than an invitation. Her room was no different from his own, plain, spare . . . was this what Amos meant by Eden? Where was the truth of it, it was driving him mad!

"Sit down!"

He sat, he couldn't think of another thing to do. "Thank you," she said. "I have a lot to thank you for."

Her voice was so sharp and direct, he didn't expect it from a creature like her.

"Oh yes, to thank you for." She pulled her robe around her and pinned him with her glance. He sat like a truant scholar on a hard chair next to the bed. "Because I've been so happy here I've forgotten what men are like outside. I'd forgotten what it was to be looked at like *that*. To be nothing, to be canceled out by a man's eyes because I didn't suit his idea of beauty."

She called back his sense of shame. "Believe me, if I said anything inadvertently to embarrass you or cause you distress, it wasn't my intention . . ."

"Oh, I don't think you intended. You simply were what you are. You are what men are outside this place. Selfish, cruel, when a woman doesn't suit your fancy. What is a woman to you, more or less, than an instrument to masturbate yourself."

He was shocked by her frankness. If his face flushed she was quick to note it.

"Oh, we don't mince words on that subject here, Mr. Berger. The world outside is a wretched place for want of love. Man doesn't love his fellow man, he uses him, sometimes badly; he doesn't love his work, he tolerates it and sometimes it eats him up. And women, Mr. Berger, most men have never really loved a woman. I know you and your kind, I know you from the outside, I suffered by your kind, oh, believe me I have. And I've learned something about men, thank God and Father Noyes and the family. I've learned that a man, if he cannot love one woman, can love no women. And you've loved none."

"I assure you I've loved women all my life." He heard his own hard voice.

"Love? Do you love your wife? Do you love your children? How could you, not knowing what love is in the slightest way? You sub-stitute and your substitutions, like all the substitutions of all the men starved for love in the world, those substitutions make wars and make bloody business in the banks and make whores who sell their bodies for you by the hour. Is that what you call love? And what did you expect from this room? Velvet hangings? Mirrors on the ceiling? When Amos said that Mary Darcy would teach you how to love, did you think we had a new trick that the women in New York hadn't found yet? He meant love, *love,* poor man, which is the same love and the one love and the only love, which starts with love of God and moves through love of your brothers and sisters to your love of work, not a vain satisfaction of beating out your fellows, but a true and deep and soul-satisfying feeling which is what you should have lying beside your wife or any wife and looking at her body and having her look at yours. You know nothing of that. Love of work that is an art, love of God that is a gift, love of a woman that is like music or painting or good conversation, it is like good old wine, it is a deep and satisfying thing and you do not know it."

He sat dumbfounded. He didn't know what to respond.

She looked at him pityingly. "Perhaps . . . it was my good fortune that you looked at me that way. It made me thank God for the good life He's given me. And perhaps, it was also fortunate for you." Her eyes softened, she looked at him with much compassion. "Perhaps this was the only way you could have come to me."

To her. She sat heavily on the bed, large warm breasts, dimpled fingers, a doll-like quality to her. She held out a hand for him to come to her. She reminded him . . . not of a whore . . . but of a mother! Who calls a child to bed in the evening, to snuggle in beside her and to hear a story or to be petted before sleep. She looked at him in so unconditional a way, so loving a way, so accepting a way . . . not a look he had ever got from his mother . . . the devil's handmaiden. His mother stuck in him like a canker . . . he was tied to the bed and he begged her to release him. *But we must obey your father . . . your father knows what's best.* . . . She was no mother to him, she should have been soft and warm and she should have taught him how to love, and for that he had no teacher. Mary Darcy was right, had he loved anything or anyone? Satisfaction, vain satisfaction. Something had been left out of the making of him. He understood now that this room was not a *place* but a state of *mind.* It was the state of mind a man retreated to when all his defenses were gone, when he had no other place to retreat, when the shallow privacies of a public love were shorn away. Mary Darcy wasn't a woman who had been offered him as a lesson in *male continence,* he had misunderstood. Mary Darcy was *women,* the symbol, the essence of women, yes, she was Eve in a way, Amos said, Eve and the apple, they were symbols, and Mary Darcy was a symbol of the body of woman, of something he was supposed to respond to that he had never been shown, he was a child again and she saw it and she understood. That was who Mary Darcy was.

She knew that in the loving, in the total inmost privacy of the loving, they were all lost children and that he was most lost of all, she read it in his eyes, she let her arms—where she had crossed them in her angry speech—she let her full arms fall and her robe fall open. She read in his eyes what the vacancy was and what her role was and her heart softened to him and then she offered her arms to him and she said, "Poor, poor Peter . . . poor lost boy . . ." What had begun with Amos

and the others in the trap shop, the excoriating criticism, was com-
pleted here. He gave up the *egocentric* core of his nature, which was the
only part of him that the prince of the power of the air could cling to,
and that hard core like a hard cold diamond came loose and the fingers
of the devil came loose and all his confusion and pain came loose and
was swept away and all that was left was a lonely child who had cried in
the middle of the night for a mother who was her husband's handmaiden and that lonely child laid his head on a warm sweet breast and
was taken in . . . home . . . finally . . . and for the first time. . . .

The amazing thing about her day,
as Katherine considered it now, sitting at her window listening to the
sweet sounds of evening, cicadas and lowing cows and the rustling of
branches, the *amazing* thing was that she had learned to dry out a pie
tin! Imagine, if you dried it bottom side up over a warm fire, you would
think it should come dry. But no, the vapors were trapped in the tin
and they might rust. The amazement was not in the pie tins but in the
vapors rising. All those indolent years at her useless window or in front
of her fire with her claret and her vain dreams, her head was filled with
nothing. Now considering the rising of vapors, she had space and time
to understand the beauty of things. And now she could consider all the
kinds of vapors and how they should rise and her fingers moved like
imagined sketching pencils as she saw vapors rising from the cold
ground in the early morning, or vapors rising from a wet marsh in hot
summer, or from the graceful bent arm of a teapot spout, or from the
nostrils of horses on an icy morning. In her head came a whole family
of pictures called *Vapors Rising*. Colors and shapes formed themselves in
her head, she was so excited she was loath to sleep.

Her sketches were spread out on her bed and it was late, she needed
to sort them and put them away.

"Mother!" Deirdre tapped at the door. "Mother, may I talk with you?" She didn't want to talk to Deirdre, she wanted to think about nothing but her sketches until she fell asleep. But Deirdre's insistent knock brought back her old *self* in a rush and she felt the tension rising, the dual tug, desire and duty. She put on a robe and opened the door.

Deirdre pushed in, distracted, pacing and wringing her hands, she was always dramatic, a born actress. She spun around, she was so charming in the short hair, she was such a beautiful child, Katherine wanted to take up her pad and make a new sketch, to see Deirdre not as *daughter,* which made such immediate and painful demands on her, but as subject. But Deirdre moved and paced and sighed. "Mother," she said like a stage Desdemona facing a whole audience, "Mother, I love Adam."

Deirdre was most noted for love. The boy at Madame Sasone's Dance Academy and then the boy who cared for the horses in Central Park when they took their morning canters and then the bicycle fiend and then and then. She kissed the top of Deirdre's head. "Oh, I'm sure you are."

"Oh, you never take me seriously." Deirdre plumped her bottom down on the bed, on the sketches which crumpled under her. Katherine's work destroyed and Deirdre went on about love. "Mother, did you hear me? What should I do?"

"Do about what?"

"About Adam! I adore him and I want to be part of the Community! I told you!"

"You can't be *part of* in the sense you mean, that's not possible, especially where Adam is concerned and you know that."

"But you don't understand!" She pulled a scrap of paper from under her and crumpled it and threw it on the floor. Katherine's sketch of a crooked oak, crumpled and thrown down like trash. "I love him terribly and I don't want to be outside of things. Why did you bring me here if you wanted me to stay outside of love?"

"Deirdre, you're being impossibly childish."

"You can stay apart from the social life if you want. I want to be with Adam."

"Adam is Sarah's son, he's married to the Community."

"I love him and he wants me. All the other girls do it, so why am I here only to be kept from the joy of things?"

"I didn't doubt you'd fall in love with someone, you always do, but to act out your little romances, it never occurred to me you'd do anything so foolish. You'll have to leave. Your father ought never to have brought you."

"No, that's not what I mean! I love being here! I only want Adam. And I don't know what to do."

"Adam is out of your reach. One day you'll want to marry. Adam could never come and court you, he's married already, don't you understand?"

"Why should I want to marry? What's in marriage? You're married, and whatever good has it done you?"

The question was a slap in the face. "You ought not to talk to me that way."

"Why ever not? That's the whole point of this place. Everyone gets criticized. And I want to know the truth. If marriage between men and women is so awful, why would you want me to go out in the world and get into it?"

"It's a matter of luck, I suppose. There aren't alternatives. Sarah says this life is the only answer. But think what that means. Husbands to the right and left. This is an oddity. Outside a woman marries. I can only hope that you find a happier marriage than I have. That you can find someone you truly love."

"But I truly love someone now!"

"Only think of the consequences of what you're suggesting."

Deirdre jumped up, the bed sprang with her, the papers were destroyed, the colors smudged, the sheets smudged with color. "I can't talk to you. Why did you bring me here if you didn't want me to be happy? Father is happy, isn't he? He's sleeping with someone, everyone knows it. If he can, why not me?" She stamped out of the room.

Katherine should have run after her, but her eyes were on the ruined sketches. "Damnation." *Moira, did I say that?* She gathered them up and stuffed them into a wastebasket. But Deirdre was only a child. How was Deirdre supposed to understand?

She stormed out of her sanctuary with the same anger Deirdre felt. She asked for Peter and found him finally in the library, sitting with the *Times* in front of his face, dreaming. She pulled up a chair beside his table. He flushed, he was flustered, he floundered, guilt all over him. Like jam on the face of a truant child. That was his business. Deirdre was hers. "Deirdre is in love with Adam."

"Katie . . . I . . ."

"Don't *Katie I* me. I haven't the patience for it. She's in love and she wants to sleep with Adam."

He looked around to make sure they weren't overheard. "That's preposterous."

"Tell her. She wants to know why her father is living the Community life and not her."

"Then explain it to her!"

"First you explain it to me and then I'll explain it to her."

"No, first get that hard look off your face. I've been sitting here . . . trying to think how to explain . . . how can I tell you this new view of love . . . the narrow petty view we've always had of love . . ."

"I've had no view of love at all. I haven't a grand opinion of love in the world as I've known it. Nor do I want one now. What am I to say to our daughter? I came for a year. I expect her to leave with me. Now I realize that there may be serious consequences."

"Do you know, Katie, that I've only just begun to realize that the reason I came to this blessed place was you? Your unhappiness? I was faced with it day after day. I had no way to understand."

"For me! That is more than I can swallow. The gall to say you have a soft heart and what you're doing is for me. What of Deirdre? The child whom you would never harm in the world!"

"Deirdre is perfectly safe. She can't sleep with Adam. She'd have to be trained first by an older man. Older women for boys, older men for girls. It might be someone . . . anyone . . . even Newhouse, if you can picture it. Deirdre is the world's leading romantic, she's fallen in love with her music teacher. Can you imagine our Deirdre with Sewall Newhouse? That would shock her out of romance. And Adam would never agree. He's honor to the core, he wouldn't act against the Community."

"And you don't find all this . . . bizarre in the least?"

"I find it all spectacularly sensible, if you intend to make a life of it. But Deirdre is a child, she's giddy and silly. She was the same in New York. It will pass. It's you and me I want to talk about, Katie. Why is it you never listen to me? I can knock on your attention and you're always floating in clouds."

"I listen. I don't hear. Explain to me why a man is entitled to the Community life and not his daughter when he protests he believes and takes the benefit."

She could see his eyes evading. "That's something different. You and Deirdre, you came here as sojourners. I came searching for my honor and to find the reason for my unhappiness and yours."

"Honor? Is it honorable to live with one foot in and one foot out? She is your daughter, you talk with her and explain it. I want to be left in peace for once."

"Damnation, you've got yourself a sharp tongue."

"And you've a forked one. Which isn't exactly the right tongue to have for heaven."

Moira, you would have been proud of me. I even astounded myself. She fled to her sanctuary room and closed the door and took out her sketchpad and began again.

Deirdre and Rebecca sat near the Pirate's Stump out in Cragin's Meadow. "Did you see Momma today?"

"I saw her two days ago. I want to, but I'm afraid I'll get too *sticky.*"

"What nonsense. Where are all your little friends?"

"Two boys are getting a *criticism* in the children's room."

"Why aren't you there?"

"Mathilda didn't want to watch. Anyhow they'd done something terrible and I didn't even understand it. They got into the canning shed and found the little tin can tops and made money out of it."

"And so?"

"God doesn't love money. Not in *Oneidacommunity*. I don't *know* why. They bought things from other boys and made boys do things for money. *Outside* Grandpa Berger gave me money on my birthday and he's never talking anything *but* God. It must be a different God."

The grasses smelled so sweet, and the bees buzzed around them in the clover. "I know. Things are so backward and upside down."

"It's through the looking glass," said Rebecca. "Did you know that people are *horizontal* and *vertical?* If you stay with someone older to be instructed, that's vertical. If you play too much with your friends, that's *horizontal.*"

"Only love is the same both sides of the glass. She doesn't understand that, Momma I mean."

"Well, you're older, so that makes you *vertical* but you're my sister, so that makes us *sticky.* I'm going to find it all out, though."

"How, by asking the white rabbit?"

"The white rabbit lives in a book. I mean really find out. I'm going to ask God."

"I wish I had someone to ask. I wish Aunt Moira was here."

"Oh, they wouldn't let her in," said Rebecca. "She smokes cigars."

"Are you happy here, Becca? Would you stay forever?"

"I have to stay forever! I can't leave, ever!"

"Why ever not?"

"You're so silly! Because the devil lives in New York! I'd be afraid to go home again!"

It was only Cunningham he could talk with, it was only Cunningham who understood. He knocked at Cunningham's door.

"Come in, don't turn up the light."

"I need to talk to someone. . . . My heart is . . ."

". . . no more than mine," said Cunningham. "Something's happened and I owe it to you."

"How so?" Peter asked.

The two sat alone in the dark, only the moonlight through the window, in an intimacy Peter could not believe could exist between two men. "When we spoke," Cunningham said, "you stirred up fires in me. The thing I told you . . . Annie and the baby . . . it began to press my mind. And suddenly this evening I was filled with a great turmoil, troubled and anxious. I thought . . . I ought to talk to Father Noyes, but this seemed to be between God and me. I walked the corridors, I wasn't sure where I was going. And then the tug led me to Annie Lee's room. As if some preternatural message was being sent to me, it was a signal. I stood outside her door. I heard voices. The child was still with her, she was nursing, he wouldn't go into the nursery until he was weaned. And when Annie entertained a lover, the child was fitful and awake. It was Esrick, I knew it was. Suddenly, Peter, it came to me in an epiphany, it flashed like lightning, the meaning of the perfect love. It was a gift from God. I knocked, Annie was surprised to see me, but she greeted me with such a warm smile. Through the door I saw Esrick, alarmed and dismayed.

"I walked into the room, I *clamped* a hand to Esrick's shoulder as a signal that all was well. I went to the child's cradle, I lifted out the child, and kissed him. This was Esrick's son, but I knew absolutely at that moment it was my son as well. I loved it as well. The child responded, I wrapped him in a blanket, and I took him out to my room.

"For an hour I rocked him until the child was asleep. Peter, a sense of . . . peace . . . I can't tell you . . . it was a shower of rain to a burning skin, it was a drink of water to parched lips. I had been forgiven, to the bottom of my soul. I was a tree planted in God's good earth, my taproots were sunk deep into the source of life. I've been reborn, I know it. I'll never have that nightmare again. Finally Esrick tapped at the door and came in. The way our eyes met, it was a perfect understanding. I carried the child back to Annie's room. She was waiting for me with a smile so sweet. She and Esrick and I, we loved the child and each other. Do you understand? No matter who lies in her bed or whom I lie with, the strands of that love are interwoven in a fabric of the most perfect harmony."

"I feel so cheated," Peter said. "I see it in you, I want it and I can't feel it, as if something's been left out of me. Why do I doubt so?"

"Let go, just let go. You hold on too tight, Peter."

"If I let go, I'll fall. I understand the world as I know it, I'm not much on faith. I know that I'm beginning to learn love, I've begun the journey into love, but I can only go so far."

"Don't fight it. You're still afraid of getting hurt. Why should God want to hurt you? See how he's sheltered me."

"Can I ask you something . . . most intimate?"

"What could be more intimate than what we've just shared?"

"Is it possible . . . to find real satisfaction in the bed without the explosion of the seed? I can't believe men love that way. When they finish, do they . . . in the privacy of their rooms, do they . . ."

"I can only tell you this. Until you've learned to love a woman in the Community way, you've never loved a woman. I practice it, other men do. If some fall, then that's between them and God."

"I can't forgive my wife for a life of cold years. I feel as if I've come on loving as a novice."

"Until you forgive your wife you'll never love a woman. Until you've loved a woman, you'll never love a man. What a perfect chain it is."

"She doesn't understand, she never understands that I watch over my family, and her, in spite of everything. What has she to do but walk through gardens and make her little pictures? Do women ever understand man's struggle in this hard hard world?"

Paulie was trying to sleep, Isaac was all over him, thumping and tickling. "Leave off! All I did was to bring the old man some water, damn you. It was part of the bargain, to buy myself off from you."

"*I* didn't ask you to be water boy for a poor sick old man, God did. You carried the water up the hill out of a good spirit. Why are you denying it?"

"Someone asked me to carry the water. I don't remember who. And . . . since I get my rations here . . . and they're pretty bad I can tell you that . . ."

"Why are you so ashamed of having a soft heart?"

"Why don't you jump in the lake," said Paulie.

"If I did you'd pull me out."

"In a pig's eye."

"You've got yourself a soft heart for sure, so as long as you do, why not just confess Christ as well?"

Paulie turned toward the wall and pulled up his blanket. "You do it for me."

Isaac went back to his own bed. "I already have," he said. "Anyhow, you're cutting off your nose to spite your face. The sooner you come around, the sooner you'll be able to make love with the women."

After a while Paulie sat up, the blanket around him. *"What women?"*

Moira, how I wish I could bring this to you. You of all people would understand. I have to send Deirdre away for the rest of the year. But there is so much . . . confusion . . . in your way of life. You understand . . . for a girl I mean . . . a girl who does not understand compromise. . . .

Dear Berthe:

I hope you and Hector are well. I am writing to you on a matter that requires extreme delicacy and I hope that you will treat it as such. You've so often offered me and my children your hospitality. I am well and reasonably happy, but in Deirdre's case . . .

So there was no one Deirdre could turn to. Her mother lived in clouds and her father was willing to take his own pleasures and she was sure he'd have Paulie in the family bed. It made her so bitter. She thought love was different here. But it was all the same. Women suffered for it. Adam had said love was easy here. It wasn't. It was the same everywhere. So she'd have to decide for herself. They'd send her away, she knew it. Where? Where else but Aunt Berthe and she'd die first. She loved Adam as she'd love no other man. She would never love another . . . never. She wanted to give him the gift of her body and to do that, she'd first have to sleep with an older man.

What older man? she wondered.

FIVE

A Virtuous Woman

Who can find a virtuous woman? for her price is far above
*   rubies.*
The heart of her husband doth safely trust in her . . .
She will do him good and not evil . . .
Strength and honor are her clothing . . .
Give her of the fruit of her hands; and let her own works
*   praise her in the gates.*

Proverbs 31: 10–31

They are not wives, they are simply mistresses. Yet the Saints impudently tell us that these women are better, purer, nobler, happier, freer than the pure women around us whom we call wives. . . .

"Why do they not go back to their friends, or out into the world to seek a livelihood?"

Few women once sunk in vice, especially in a vice that has so many allurements, have the moral courage to change their lives.

Free Love and Its Votaries
DR. JOHN B. ELLIS, 1870

The fact that victims of marriage are attached to it, and could not be induced to abandon their situation, only proves their degradation. The Hindoo woman chooses to be burned with the body of her husband, because she knows no other way, and prefers death to the odium of unfashionable behavior.   From "Slavery and Marriage:
a dialogue," 1850

The house itself was a graveyard, the rooms were darkened with death. Shadows slanted in between the half-drawn drapes made gravestones of everything. She walked between the stones of furniture seeing in her eyes' mirrors the inscription that had turned her to ice: *Be ye also ready.* Berthe would not have thought Hector's death would have stunned her like this. Cold to the soul. Chilled with guilt and remorse. No, not remorse, well, she had to be honest, even in this extreme. She'd wished him dead. She'd said as much to Katherine. She should have bit off her tongue before she'd let those words slip, to give into Katherine's hands and eyes to hold against her. But death wasn't what she expected. He lay there on the bedroom floor with bulging eyes, his fingers into claws grasping out to hold onto life. She'd buried him quickly with as few people about as possible, just the social necessities not to call contumely down on her own head. She stood with dread while they closed his coffin. Even then she was sure she'd heard a faint knocking, it would be just like Hector to come back to bedevil her. Oh, they'd closed the eye lids all right but behind the dry lids the eyes bulged, accusing her. His voice was in whispers everywhere in the house, in the shuffling of her soft shoes on the carpets, in the moving of curtains. So she'd gone back to the true church, she gave *confession* but those words choked in her throat. It was bad enough that Katherine knew. God, she was sure, having seen so much of life, understood what it meant to be a virtuous woman in today's society. Hector had forced her into obscenities. And God now wanted her to take up a better life. So she'd locked her jewels away so she couldn't take pleasure in touching them. For the time being. She'd dress the season in black, fashionable black, after all, you couldn't provoke, and she would simply wait until this spasm of horror passed. She supposed all widows faced this sort of thing.

But gnawing at the back of her conscience was the need to make restitution. Katherine's letter burned in her pocket. If Katherine wanted to throw herself into the maw of sin and degradation, that was her hard luck. But poor Deirdre. Katherine had no sense altogether. Now Katherine had come to her for help. Invite Deirdre to spend the year with her? The house was empty, she would adore having Deirdre there.

And then it occurred to Berthe that this was indeed God's design in taking Hector, who hadn't much to offer in the way of charity. No, she would not *invite* Deirdre, she would adopt her. What court could refuse her appeal, knowing the danger to Deirdre's soul?

And then, with Deirdre hers, wouldn't Peter be a constant visitor? It was only chance that had separated them. If she had Katherine's face and Katherine hers . . . it was a small act of fate that wanted remedy. With Peter she could have been soft, she was clever enough for him where he was wasted on Katherine, she wouldn't have gone shrewish. She never wanted more than to be a good wife, but to a man not a pig. Peter was a gift to women, and Katherine had so carelessly thrown him away.

And so, she would open her heart and her fortune (close your eyes, Hector, and be still) all to her niece and *that* she could confess with open heart to the nice young priest, and God, who had engineered the crucifixion of His only begotten son to teach the world how crosses were to be borne, He would smile on her since He was the one who struck Hector down and left her still alive, and if that wasn't a clear message, she didn't know one.

"Don't . . . oh, dear child . . . you delicious child, have mercy!"

"You're a jolly old bear, I love to tickle, oh, sir, you are a tiger, you set me all to tingling."

Bella went about her work with true professional dedication. Since she'd learned to talk to gentlemen, Miss Josie Woods had taken her on, she had a good room, it cost her seventy dollars a week with board but on a good night she took in two hundred which was more money than she'd had in her life, and she had nice gowns, and she wasn't going to let this gold slip by her. And she felt she was doing so much good in the world. For instance, this sad tub of lard who lay spread-eagled, helpless on his back on her satin sheets, his stomach bulging like a pregnant woman, he couldn't even turn over proper without help, his legs they were huge hams, but still he was a funny old bear and she had to mount him carefully and work with great skill or he'd have a fit and they'd have to roll him out on the sheets, no, he was too big, they'd have to bring in blankets and drag him along the floor, two or three of them would do it, and so she had to concentrate all her skill to cool him down because if she lingered too long at this stage or that, he'd kill himself on it. She tickled him, but not too close to the source. "Oh, sir, you make me hot with desire." She loved the taste of "hot with desire"—one of the girls taught her that. She sat lightly on his upper hams and leaned over the mountain of gut trying not to laugh, but smiling childish and coy as she'd practiced so long in front of her mirror, it was just like being an actress and he was moaning and rolling up his eyes and she had to calm him down. "Oh, sir, my friend told me that you know a kind gentleman who came here, he was my first, a gentleman lawyer . . ."

"Slower, child, have mercy . . ."

If she went much slower she'd fall asleep on him.

"If you see this gentleman, sir, please tell him that I asked for him. . . ."

He was moaning and groaning, yes, they'd have to roll him off onto the floor and onto a heavy blanket but how they would get him down the steps, she couldn't think. He moaned in ecstasy and she speeded up to get things over, it was disgusting when you thought of it, but who these days had a line of work they really enjoyed? And it was an act of kindness, a poor old fat thing like him.

When he came he let out a huge cry and a voluminous fart. She fell back in disgust, if he soiled her sheets with it she'd make him pay. The whole room stank, she'd have to air it out and lose her time, she hoped he'd consider that when he came to paying up. He moaned and opened his eyes, thank God he was still alive. She ran to the French bowl to wash, although she knew how to use her sponges now and how to jump at the critical moment, back and to one side so as to divert the seed.

When she got back she was softened by his look of appreciation. She knew what a service she did, these poor old men with their shrews of wives. God had given her gifts to please men. And one of these days her son would get into one of the fancy schools, and be a gentleman himself. She'd have her own house up in Brooklyn Heights, and her mother could sit in the sun on the front porch warming her bones.

He smiled at her, wiped at the huge hairy nose with his fingers. "Did I give you pleasure, child?"

"Oh, sir, young men don't know the way of it. I shouldn't charge you, the pleasure you gave me."

She had to help him to his feet and put on his drawers for him. As she was pushing one huge leg into his trousers, he asked, "Do I remember right? Did you inquire after a gentleman lawyer?"

"My first He brought me into the business. A tall dark handsome man."

"And his name? This doer of favors?"

"Oh, we never ask the family names. But Miss Josie said his first name was Peter."

He laughed so hard she had to thump him on the back. She hoped she didn't ask wrong, she was still new and she couldn't risk her position. "Was I bad to ask, sir?"

"You asked right, child, perfectly right. This is the very gentleman I've been trying to save from salvation. He's rushing blindly toward heaven on the primrose path and when the Keeper of the Heavenly Books notes that he's brought you into the profession, that will take some sorting out."

She didn't understand a word of it, but he took a huge wad of bills from his pocket and was going to peel some off but he looked at her and she gave him her most coy kittenish look and he left the whole of it.

"Who knows where the truth will emerge? And I need God on my side for this battle . . ."

The thought of him in battle uniform made her giggle.

". . . the ultimate battle of a long illustrious career. Bannerman the knight errant who will take on John Humphrey Noyes. And if anything is better than an act of love, it's a passionate case of law against a man who has not only taken possession of another man's child but another man's soul. And as for the lawyer chap, you can thank him yourself when you see him."

"But, sir, he swore he'd never be back!"

"Those, my child," he said, patting her on the backside, "are famous last words."

"You cow, I said if anyone asks, you never saw the papers, you never heard me mention land on Forty-ninth Street and you never met Mr. Tweed! Let alone seen him, do you understand me, Bitsie?"

Bitsie wiped her eyes with the tips of her fingers. "But everyone's heard of Mr. Tweed and I did see the papers, Harry, they were land papers, I read them."

"You never *saw* them, you stupid woman, and you can say you and your silly friend gossiped *about* Mr. Tweed, you read about him in the papers but you never laid eyes on him."

"I did. I brought coffee to Mr. Tweed, I remember because his name was like a cloth, you remember I said that, I said, isn't it funny your name is like a cloth. Moira says Mr. Tweed is into graft, please don't get into graft and go to jail!"

Harry was fuming, his hair was all funny where he'd forgotten to comb the little remaining strands over his shiny head. "If I go to jail you'll be stuck without a roof over you and nothing to stuff in your mouth, so you remember to disremember Mr. Tweed, if you know what's good for you."

She was so unhappy, and her corsets were pinching. "I hate it when you talk rude to me."

He bent over her with his ugly mouth. "Do you hate it? Well, think of me, Bitsie, sitting across the table from you every day, how would you like that?" He yanked her harshly to her feet. She begged him to stop. He dragged her over to the mirror, he made her face it, he took her cheeks in both his hands and pinched them. He pinched the fat on her arms.

"Don't, you're hurting me!"

He dropped her back into her chair. "Now if you don't want to be out on the streets, you'll be a good little wife and go to Utica as I told you."

"I still don't understand."

"Stupid woman, you tell everyone you're visiting your cousin, you go to that place where Katherine is staying, you say to Peter, I need a lawyer in confidence, I need a lawyer who knows me, I don't dare put a thing on paper but if he comes here and takes my case there's a pretty penny in it for him. Do you get it, Bitsie? Can you say that?" He reached for her box of candies and took a chocolate and stuffed it between her lips. "Can you do that trick like a little doggie? Here's your reward."

She didn't want to eat candy, she was feeling bilious. "Oh, Harry, you are taking graft!"

"Moira is a bitch. This has nothing to do with dishonest graft, Bitsie, this is honest graft."

"Oh . . ." The candy was melting in her cheek and she couldn't bother with it, she was so upset. "Oh, I didn't know there was any honest graft."

"Of course you didn't, piggy, because you're too busy eating to know anything, aren't you? Honest graft is taking your opportunities. It happens that my party is in power, and they just casually do me a favor of mentioning this street or that where a park or a car line is going in and I just happen to buy it and I pay my commission and that's not graft, it's business. Are you satisfied?"

"Everyone says Mr. Tweed is a crook."

"The hell with Mr. Tweed. You're my wife, you owe me love and honor and obedience. Isn't that what you swore?"

She could feel the melting candy on her lips. "Yes, Harry."

"Then write to Katherine and tell her you'd like to come."

Bitsie ran the bathwater and cried for so long. She took off all her clothes and forced herself to look in the mirror. Her fat arms stood away from her body and her breasts were sagging down and she had a terrible shelf of fat under her belly. She was obscene. How could this be Bitsie?

She stepped into the tub. She still had dainty feet. She lowered herself into the tub and washed the chocolate off her mouth. How did it happen? She had been so happy in her father's house, she used to ride the chestnut mare across the meadow and go to dances, she was so light on her feet, and then Harry came to the house and her father liked him and she married him and promised to obey and now she was fat.

She sank lower into the water and the queerest thought came to her. Harry might go to jail. If a man goes to jail, she wondered, was the wife divorced? Yes, she'd promised to honor and obey, but if he broke God's commandment to *shalt not,* did he break the bargain first? Was graft a sin against God? She clasped her hands and prayed to be relieved of the prison of fat. Then she got a vision. She saw Harry in jail and she got the giggles and hiccuped. She lay back in the warm water, remembering herself on the mare in the cold spring morning taking one of the fence jumps, her hair all flying out behind her. She dropped lower in the water and she said, "I don't like you, Harry." She didn't care if he heard it or not.

Moira was tired of shopping. She wanted to go home and read Katherine's letter again and to write to her.

She was fishing in her bag for the fare when she saw the black victoria, the driver slumped in his seat, the reins looped around his wrist. *That* black victoria, with the green painted horses around the sides. She'd come home too soon. It would be prudent to tell the driver to take her to the park for an hour and give the black victoria time for escape.

But she felt perverse. She paid off the cabby, she let the doorman open the door for her and her packages, and she went up. She had known exactly what she was doing in marrying Edgar, so she had no one to blame but herself. She had spat in the face of convention. She detested the good homely hypocrisies of her family, she wanted the bohemian life. She had written what she thought was splendid soul-rending and shocking poetry and she pined for a garret in Paris. She'd had plenty of beaux but one after another turned away from her cigars and her absinthe. She offered herself to sin, she frightened them off. And so she waited for the right lover to come and then she was twenty-six and her parents died in an accident on the road, under a carriage, poor things, and the money was gone and she was a spinster. She panicked. Then Edgar came into town, a beautiful figure on his horse, and amusing, she adored him, he enjoyed her, and what else could she do? She spun not, neither could she weave. She'd found out . . . about Edgar . . . before they married. But, she thought, how marvelous and bohemian. She would take her own lover and have the best of both worlds. But the lover never came. And she'd sunk lower into his degradation.

She let herself into the apartment. The bargain between them was over. The crisis of the spirit was not only Katherine's. It was all coming to the boil. She knew it in her bad dreams and in the way she looked when she rose in the morning . . . gray and shrouded with a sense of finality.

The rooms were dim, all the lights had been turned down. The double doors to his bedroom were closed. The two beasts had copulated and now they slept in their sweated sty.

The inspiration came to her purely. She was sick of it all. She hadn't the courage to take pills, it took too much conjecture and writing of letters and in the end, her sense of irony always turned her around. Now she went to her room and with the silver key on the chain around her throat she opened the little trunk that held all that was left of romance: the pressed roses, the thin bound volumes of her sad poetry, and among the old shawls she found the leather sheath, the stiletto given to her by the gentleman who went back to his wife and children in Venice, the same knife, he assured her, by which he'd vanquished several of his wife's lovers in duels. Likely story. But it was sharp and final; she pricked the tip of a finger with it, the bubble of blood oozed, it was that easy.

She would plunge the knife into their two beastly hearts and then into her own. No, better, she would cut her throat and bleed to death over their sleeping bodies, they'd wake and find her thus, and in the slight remote chance that there was a God, she wouldn't damn herself with murder and find worse in the next world.

She opened the doors softly.

They lay in sleep together, facing each other, naked, the soft gas-light flickering on them. She was mesmerized by the sight of them, the way the light fell on the sculptured planes of their two bodies . . . they were a study in a French painting. The boy was lovely, slender in the hips, his gold hair over his brow as he curled into the pillow and the hair of his chest like gold shavings, one slender arm resting on Edgar's breast, and his legs . . . their legs touching lightly. Edgar, his dark brooding face in repose, so . . . content, yes, content at having loved and now being still joined with his lover. There was between them a palpable love that flowed, like ribbons, binding them as they drifted in another place.

She closed the doors.

She was cut to the heart with something sharper than the knife. The sudden and absolute knowledge that her own conventionality was no different from her parents'. She thought Edgar incapable of love in the ordinary sense. Edgar did love, there was nothing sordid about it, he loved with a deep and genuine passion, but not her. And she would never know that passion, she understood that too.

She raised the knife to her wrist . . . one quick slash.

No, she hadn't the courage even for that.

She had lost something . . . something she had at first with Edgar . . . what? Yes, her virtue . . . not in the conventional sense but the virtue that she had *self,* the part of her she'd held inviolate through all humiliations . . . that thing . . . now she even disremembered what it was.

She was still standing there when the messenger came with a note from Bitsie.

Adelaide Bannerman put down her silver-backed brush.

"What, is Berthe mad? Custody of Deirdre? But Peter would never allow it!"

"Given the nature of the case and the moral implications, the nature of the common man, jury of our peers, she has a damned good chance of pulling it off," Bannerman rambled.

"And Peter, he knows nothing of this?"

"Just learned it myself, so I'm off to see the place, to warm the pot before I put it on the fire, so to speak."

"Has she had the nerve to ask *you* to file the suit?"

"She's asked a colleague, she knew damned well I'd find out, what the woman has in her mind, one can only conjecture, she's that devious."

"And you mean to defend your good friend."

"I'm after bigger game than that, I'm out for Noyes. I want to do what the Presbyterians have been trying to do for years, what Professor Mears in Syracuse and all his good fellows have been after. I want to expose Noyes's feet of clay, to turn out that bunch of impostors and get Peter out entirely."

"But why, Bannerman? What will you get out of it? There's no money in it, surely. And Peter's a grown man, he's well able to make up his own mind."

"Nonsense, he's blinded by the light, his father's biblical harangues at an early age have taken him out of his right mind."

"But it's his life."

"It's not just his life, by God, it's the destruction of the institution of marriage!"

Adelaide Bannerman laid aside the brush with which she was giving a hundred good strokes to her long gray hair, she turned to her husband in astonishment. "The institution of *what?*"

Bannerman, sitting on the edge of the bed which sagged with the weight of him bellowed out, "Marriage, by God! The institution of marriage!"

She moved the brush aside, she placed her hands on her dressing table and laid down her head and laughed until her chest hurt.

"And what the hell do you find so amusing, old girl?"

"Oh, Bannerman, you've always given me a good laugh, I'll say that for forty-odd years of marriage, and some of them were odd, you'll admit."

He unbuttoned his trousers and took a deep good breath. "I fail to see the humor in this."

"You and marriage, dear heart. You've made my sides ache."

"And where, pray, have I failed in my husband's office? I've seen to your bed and board for forty years, no small feat, your bills in the shops are beyond credulity."

"Is that the institution of marriage you're defending, the bed and board? And my bills at A. T. Stewart's?"

"You know better than that. I fancy we've had the best marriage abroad."

She began to brush out her hair again. "And what makes it that, do you suppose?"

"Well, you've never complained!"

"Why on earth should I complain? What have I got to complain of?"

"So you see? You say so yourself."

"I have nothing to complain of because I created it. Marriage isn't an institution, Bannerman, it's a fiction. And by the by, when you pack your bags, put in your stomach pills. You remember that train bill of fare is less than expectations."

"And what do you mean by fiction!" he fumed. "What kind of fiction? Define yourself!"

"Bannerman, let it go."

"No, by Jove, *define* yourself!"

"Leave me in peace."

"No, dammit, I will not. I've given you the best of life, good companionship, a fine table, and I fancy I've satisfied you in bed, when you wanted it, before age overtook you."

She held the back of the brush to her lips and smiled against it.

"Well, you never had to take a lover, had you?"

She pulled the brush through the long gray strands of her hair, she took it all and twisted it and turned it and fastened it with a comb, the way she used to when it was black. "You're the master of definition, my dear, define *lover*."

"Blast you, don't joke with me. Why would you take a lover when I always satisfied you!"

She opened her drawer and drew out her box of paint. She took a brush, looked at it, dusted it off, it was long unused, and opened a pot of color and began to paint her eyes. "Define *satisfied*."

"Don't mock me. Sense of humor doesn't become a virtuous woman. I've always had the gift of satisfying a woman, I have it still."

"If she says so she's a liar and you're a big fool. Now take your powders and get some sleep, you'll be miserable on the train tomorrow."

"No, by God, I want an apology from you or an explanation. Have you let me think I had a constant wife and then betrayed me? When?

Behind my back? With whom? I want names!"

"Ah, a virtuous woman. A proper marriage. Shall I define marriage for you, Bannerman?" She painted herself a small beauty mark. "A marriage is a domestic arrangement between two people who are moderately atuned to each other, moderately, to expect more is folly, who can in some way respect each other's code . . . two imperfect people."

"Then at least you respected me."

"Your *code.*"

"My code? Which was?"

"The code of the jungle. Two people who band together against the dark and the cold nights. Yes, a woman finds a man she can tolerate and then she creates the marriage. She sets the tone, she sets the stage, she creates for herself a hero and then she makes him believe it, she overlooks what can't be helped and she finds a little gentleness where she can find it, and if her friends ask her if she has the perfect marriage, she assures them she has, so that they can envy her, when in fact she has what they have, no more and no less. It's in the nature of the *institution.* So you see, it's a fiction at best."

"You wound me, Adelaide, to the heart."

She put down her brush and looked to see the shape of her eyes. "Don't be so vain, Bannerman, you've had your good years, why ask for heaven." She came to him and kissed the top of his head.

He caught her hand. "But you never took a lover, assure me that at least."

"Ah, Bannerman . . ." She stroked his thinning hair. "Assure me that in all those good early years *you* never took a lover, I don't mean one of your whores, I mean a proper lover."

His nose reddened, he belched. "Never," he swore.

"Well then," she said smiling, arching her painted eyebrow, "nor did I."

"What a treacherous woman." He bent to take off his socks, she saw his plight, sighed, and knelt with effort and pulled them off. He touched her hair. "You were splendid in your salad days."

"I was, wasn't I?"

"Sweets, would you like me tonight? I mean in bed?"

She pulled herself up. "Heaven forbid, save yourself for the journey tomorrow. But thank you for the mad impetuous suggestion." She climbed into bed and told him to hurry.

He dropped his trousers, pulled on his nightshirt, and got in. "And you don't mind being alone for a few days, good old Adelaide?"

She lay back against the pillow and pulled out the comb that bound her hair, she smiled at him with her painted eyes and her old Spanish smile. "Define *alone.*" She winked, turned and pulled up the covers.

SIX

THE STRAWBERRY FIELDS OF HEAVEN

NOTICE TO VISITORS

The Community do not furnish spirituous liquors or tobacco in any form. Smoking in the Mansion House is especially offensive and ought to be wholly avoided.

Card-playing is offensive to the Community and to many visitors.

Purloining of fruit and flowers in the gardens is contrary to good morals.

Careless driving of carriages on the borders of the lawn and swift driving in crowds are serious annoyances.

Scribbling on window casements or walls is not in accordance with the tastes of the Community.

Visitors should remember that all of the small rooms are occupied by the family as private apartments.

The Circular
July 2, 1863

The Community beg to announce that as more of their members are residing at home than at any time for many years past they have promised themselves the pleasure of making an unusual effort to entertain the crowds of friends and visitors who make summer excursions to their place. They will furnish refreshments, a variety of vocal and instrumental music, some theatrical performances, opportunities for dancing with suitable dance music, etc.

SCALE OF PRICES

Community Dinner, Full . . . . 60¢

Community Dinner, Plain . . . . 35¢

Grand Entertainment . . . . 25¢

Full Dinner and Entertainment . . . . 75¢

Lunches, Ice Cream, Soda Water

at popular prices

Oneida Community Broadside

Thank God, Katherine sighed, no corsets. She moved with sureness and a sense of belonging among the visitors who filled the halls with the odor of heavy scent and the swish of voluminous taffeta skirts. *Was I like that? Artificial curls, bound bodice, heavy breathing after too many strawberry shortcakes and cream?* She felt light and alive. The halls had been jammed with Sunday visitors most of the summer. The *outsiders* stared at her, queer woman with her short hair and her outlandish pantaloons. And her red strawberry-stained fingers. She'd been hulling McAvoy's Superiors all morning.

The visitors' dining room was noisy with people from the early train. She made her way through bulging skirts and cigar smoke to Sarah, who was taking money at the front table. She helped Sarah to gather coins into sacks and the two of them moved out of the dining room. She held her breath until she got outside. "Why don't you insist that cigars be left outside?"

"Haven't I often? No luck there. Outsiders are tied to the filthy weed. Our women said, 'take tobacco, no beds.' That was the end of it. It spoiled the lovemaking."

"I don't know why you put up with the gaping crowd. I thought the Community was well off these days."

Sarah checked her sums. "Oh, it's not the money. This is our way to bring them in."

"And you don't mind the intrusion?"

"What a selfish way to think. Outside this place there is a world of women who are hurting in a thousand ways. And they call us the mad ones. We lure them in with strawberries, we let them poke around and nose around to see we aren't the monsters we're painted out to be. And sometimes they come away with an idea. Look at your friend Bitsie who was so much taken with our ways. And look at you. Are you the woman you were when you came?"

"I suppose not."

"And the wonders you've worked on Martin, you ought to recognize the power of change."

She sorted out the nickels from the dimes. "What have I done for Martin? It's quite the other way. Do you know that he's teaching me to draw and he doesn't know how to draw himself?"

"How? By animal magnetism? Does he put you in a trance?"

"I'm not the type for it."

"How then?"

"He puts my eyes on detail. Little veins in a leaf. How the sides are different, the one toward the sun and the one away. How the little veins are waterways in a sense. Liquid flows. And it puts me in mind of all things flowing, streams, rivers. And then arcs. A rainbow. The little arc of my fingernails. And curves. How my left thumb curves a little. And the curves of a branch."

"And in exchange you've civilized him. And taught him to dress proper."

"I? I wouldn't dare to suggest so personal a thing. No, I think he was simply in shock over the war and he's begun to come out of it."

"Would it surprise you how many women have begun to show interest in Martin's bed? What do you say to that?"

"I say well and good. If Martin is happy, then I am. I owe him so much. He's like another pair of eyes to me."

"And if he's happy in someone's bed, you're happy for him?"

"Of course."

Sarah kissed her. "Spoken like a true Oneida woman."

"If he were my own brother, I couldn't be more happy. Why do you always draw Oneida into it?"

Peter in his shirtsleeves, a green accountant's shade over his eyes, rose to meet her. He took the heavy ledgers out of her hands and made a place for her at the table.

She sat as far as she could without offending. "Have you spoken with Deirdre yet? I'm still uneasy about her. She's so much the coquette with Adam, and so seductive that she quite frightens me."

"You've nothing to worry about. Why don't you trust me a little? I had a talk with her last night. She has quite a spirit. Do you know how many will be in the big hall tonight for her debut? Nine hundred. And she's able to handle that. She has raw courage, she's my daughter, no doubt of it."

His daughter. When it came to raw courage, Deidre was *his* daughter. While she, the timid one, had her *little drawings*. She supposed he'd said things like that before, but she'd managed not to hear them. She was only now coming out of the haze of herself. Things that had been a mass of undifferentiated anxiety got themselves into genus and species, like the strawberries.

"I've tried to reason with her for a month. About Adam, I mean. How did you manage to get through?"

"I forbade her."

Through the closed door she still heard the noise of the Sunday people. "You did *what?*"

"I forbade her. I'm her father. She's too young for that sort of thing. And that's the end of it."

"And you didn't think she'd find that contradictory? That you've brought us here to a new kind of life and you've taken all the advantages for yourself and when your daughter asks for an explanation, you simply *forbade* her?"

He moved his chair closer, she moved back and away. She didn't want to be overwhelmed by him. Her head was clear until she got too close to him. He was an energy force she could not contend with. "Why are we always on the wrong foot? I had to forbid her. I won't send her away. I won't have the family broken up, I told you that. Try to hear me out. Try to keep your mind on what I'm saying. Intimate things in my life . . . are shifting. We came here under different circumstances, you and I. My life was corroded by acids. You came because I asked you to, and I'll always thank you for that. But look at you, you haven't suffered for it. You haven't had to go under the knife as I have. You haven't had to twist yourself into knots as I have. So it's me who's had to bear the brunt, don't you see? Look at you. Fit from working in the fields. You never looked better. And Rebecca takes to the life like duck to water. Do you see what I'm saying?"

"Yes, I see. I'm not a child that I don't understand what's explained to me. You had intense personal problems. You came to solve them. We dragged after, this gave you a chance to explore your life freely and with impunity, since you hadn't deserted your wife and children."

"That's unfair and too harsh. You've gained from being here. So have I. Although I have to admit, I've had a bellyful of the forge. And I'm appalled at the way they do business, now that I'm looking after the accounting. They owe a big bill. Not a prayer in the world of meeting it. They say God will provide, walk about happy as larks, shoving the problem on His shoulders. Somehow providence always steps in but it keeps me deuced nervous."

"I want you to go to Amos. Tell him that we're here on trial and that Deirdre is not to be considered part of the family circle in that sort of sense. Let him take the responsibility. He can warn Adam off."

Peter fiddled and fidgeted. "That would be difficult. I mean, Amos is such a purist. For the time being she can hold her romance to the stage. Once she's made her great debut, she'll fall in love with someone else. You know her." He was looking at her in such an odd way. "While I was talking to her last night, I was thinking . . . Katie, do you remember when we first met? You were so like her, all innocence, so beautiful."

"No, I don't remember, it was too long ago."

He reached out and took her hand. She should have seen that coming, now she couldn't draw away without offending, and he was being earnest. She was trying to keep a soft heart. She would even have considered offering him friendship, for the children's sake. But the other, that was over forever.

"You were so innocent then, more innocent than Deirdre, and you trusted me to teach you about life. I was stupid. I didn't know how to love and you suffered by my ignorance. And you've languished all these years. It's no wonder you almost went daft."

"Daft!" she exploded. "I was daft? *I?*"

"In a manner of speaking. Locked in that little room. If I hadn't rescued you when I did, you'd have taken to drink. So you see how fate has arranged it all?" He pressed her hand with a passion that alarmed her. "Katie . . . only let me learn a little better how to love in the Community way and I'll come to you. I won't let you die a virgin of the spirit. Sometimes when I look at you I remember that old Katie, and wonder what our life might have been if I'd only *known.*"

She ran all the way to the orchard. She didn't breathe until she got there. She raked leaves until the anger drained away. Until she got the sounds of city people out of her head. Until she could hear a mourning dove and the funny cry of the spruce grouse.

How shall I my true love know, from another one?

Two simultaneous quartets were practicing, she couldn't get her tone. And the *words* were wrong, she would die if she forgot her lines:

> *How shall I your true love know, from another one?*
> *By his cockle hat and staff, and his sandal shoon.*

She *must* remember that Ophelia being mad because of her father's death is asking her mother: *How should I my father know?* Or something like that. (Did Ophelia have a mother?) And where was Corinthe, Corinthe with her wreath of flowers? They had sewed her a lovely dress with a high bodice, she was the poor gone-mad Ophelia, Hamlet had given her tokens of love and now denied her *utterly.* So she *was* Ophelia, and she *was* going mad from it. Talk to her mother? She might as well talk to a wall. And her father, a perfect Polonius, pompous and arrogant, *forbidding* her to love her dear Hamlet and lie with him. *Forbidding!* So she understood Ophelia as nobody understood her.

And around her quartets were trying to tighten their harmony and the little ones in their costumes were all over everywhere, and if she couldn't find her note, she would faint on the stage, she would let her knees go slack, keeping her back straight she would crumple . . . a huge cry of alarm would go up from the audience and Adam would rush to her, bend to her face and say, *Now the Community be damned, I'll come to you tonight, my dear heart. . . .*

"All I could find were hollyhocks and verbena and the hollyhocks were too coarse so I picked some of the peppery roses at the back of the house and I've been picking off thorns, I'm all cut." Corinthe handed her the wreath without much grace.

"The thorns are still in them! Look! I'll cut my head and bleed! Oh, Corinthe, what a dunce you are!"

"I'm not a dunce!" Corinthe was upset.

"I didn't mean it like that, it was just a manner of speaking."

"Well, we don't speak that way here, and everyone says your head is big with *prima-donna fever.*"

"Bother everyone," said Deirdre. "Then let everyone sing a solo in front of the whole audience who's paid to hear it."

Corinthe was pouting. "Well, you do sing sweet, but you don't have everything."

"Well, you might as well tell me what *that* means because I haven't got time to guess and you'll never let loose of it. I know you, Corinthe."

Corinthe set a smug face. "I've had Adam, that's what I mean."

She felt the blood drain out of her, as if someone had opened a vein. "What do you mean?"

"I mean Adam has been with me, two times. I mean he can lie with me and he can't lie with you. So have your solos, I don't care."

She would faint. She had to hold onto Corinthe to steady herself. Corinthe was alarmed to see her face.

"Deirdre, I didn't mean . . . I . . . it's only . . ."

It was true, Adam couldn't come near her, and so he went to Corinthe. She could die on the spot, she wished her heart would stop beating, quick, what were the words of her song? It was all out of her head:

> *He is dead and gone, lady,*
> *He is dead and gone.*
> *At his head the grass green turf,*
> *At his feet, a stone.*

She felt the tears down her cheeks. Corinthe threw her arms around her. "I didn't mean to be cruel, I want him as much as you, and you're not part of us, you have no right to everything." She took back the wreath and searched out the thorns and pulled them until her fingers were pricked and bleeding and put it back on Deirdre's head and ran through the practicing children and the comedian with his red nose, the toddlers playing leapfrog. And Deirdre stood as mad as poor Ophelia, wishing for a stream to drown in.

Adam came through the quartets and found her. "Now remember, keep your voice small and if it wants to swell at the end, then let it." He saw the tears. "That nervous?"

"You slept with Corinthe."

He put it aside. "Sarah's been on me, it was a kindness, it has nothing to do with you."

"And what of me, then?"

"Amos is softening. Just wait, be patient. I love you, you know that."

She only knew that he was lying in Corinthe's bed when he should have been in hers.

"I have to see to the little ones, sing sweetly, I'll be watching you and listening." He kissed her cheek, and then her hands and left her.

Tragedy was in her breast. She had never in her life felt pain like this. She wished with all her heart she could talk to Aunt Moira, who would be the only one in the world who could understand it.

"Let me catch my breath," Bannerman begged. "I haven't had to walk this fast since the war."

Peter had an arm around him, old Bannerman *here*, he was so delighted. "What war? You were an army lawyer, in Washington."

"Yes . . . yes, but my office was miles away from the barracks, it was a punishing walk to the breakfast table. Have mercy, let me sit."

"The shops are just here."

He led Bannerman in, he overturned two kegs to sit on, but of course Bannerman's posterior would overspill and so he turned three kegs and put a board on them. He held onto Bannerman until the weight was tested. "I can't believe you braved the journey and left Delmonico's for two solid days just to see a friend."

"By God, you look fit, Peter. I suppose you're fucking the women every night and eating well, that has to be good for the figure. And is this the famous forge you gave up a glittering career to work in? When you've had your fill of pastoral life, can I bring my horses to you for shoeing?"

Fit? He was loose and happy, the sight of poor Bannerman panting up the path made him feel it more, but damn, he was happy to see the man. "In fact I'm out of the trap shop."

"Graduated from forg-ery?" said Bannerman, clapping his fat thigh.

"I've moved to the business end, to use my skills more profitably."

"Healthy sign. And what great and momentous business decisions are you faced with?"

Peter smiled with the irony, as Bannerman would see it. "In fact, we're facing a major crisis. The German workmen are threatening to leave the trap shop."

"Life and death," Bannerman said. "Lazy louts at best, always asleep over their lager beer. Is that a loss?"

"They're good workers, backbone of the shop and the shop is backbone of the Community. No one suspected they were unhappy. We pay high wages here, we've started a school for their children."

"Ruin the entire labor market with practices like that. What's the complaint?"

"The food. They don't like it."

"Couldn't agree more. Good for cows, all that greenery."

"They want veal and fried potatoes and they want the other men to stop calling them krauts."

"Earth-shattering." Bannerman had taken two cigars from his vest pocket and held one under Peter's nose. Peter declined but Bannerman insisted, it was more than flesh could bear, he took the cigar, guiltily. Bannerman fished for matches. Peter bit off the end. The taste brought back another world. He would have to make amends for this fall from grace. Tomorrow. Bannerman lit it for him, Bannerman's face in the glow of the match, that also brought back something. Peter drew in smoke, into his lungs, into his belly, into his veins and arteries. Oh glory, it was fine.

The moment was too precious to ruin it with conversation. They smoked for a long while. "And so," Bannerman said finally, "here I am winged Mercury bringing messages from the outside world."

"Have no interest in the outside world," Peter said.

"Not even from a gorgeous little baggage at Josie Woods?"

He licked at the end of the cigar. "And what gorgeous little baggage is that?"

"A green one who says you brought her into the business. It seems you gave her a great sum of money and she's eternally grateful."

He watched the smoke curl. "The one who said she had a child and wanted to go west? She promised me she'd go to California. Ingrate."

"So much for humanitarian gestures." Bannerman brushed some

ashes from his trousers. "And there was another message . . . can't for the life of me think of it." He sucked at the end of his cigar, watching Peter. How Bannerman loved to draw out the moment. "Ah yes . . ." Finally. "Ah yes, it's come to me. Your sister-in-law . . ."

"Berthe? What's that bitch up to?"

"She's taking you to court."

Peter pulled a shred of tobacco from his lip. "Taking me to court for what?"

"I mean, St. Sebastian, that you're about to be flayed. She's suing for custody of your daughter."

Katherine shriveled like a leaf in the fire against the onslaught of accusations. "Did it occur to you that your sister is bitter and vindictive and wouldn't pass a chance to do us harm? Did you stop to think before you decided to meddle?"

"I, meddle? This is my own daughter!"

"I told you I'd see to it! And you took it on yourself to ask Berthe, of all people, to take Deirdre off our hands?"

"How *can* you twist it so? What did you think when you brought her here? That she'd be blind and deaf and dumb to what was happening? So you forbade her to fall in love. A girl like Deirdre. You might as well forbid the tides!" She could see Bannerman sitting at a farther bench on the quadrangle, with his mocking smile. "And I don't believe Bannerman understood Berthe. She only means for Deirdre's best interest."

"She's put the claim into the hands of an attorney. And did she bother to write you that Hector died?"

"Oh *no* . . ."

"The funeral was days ago. Loving sister."

"Poor Berthe."

"There's nothing poor about our Berthe. She's inherited his money, that's what she wanted."

"And now she's struck by conscience and wants to share it with Deirdre, that's all it is, I'm sure."

He waited until some of the Sunday strollers passed, he lowered his voice. "Please don't try to work out the intricacies of Berthe's devious mind. Just leave these matters to me. I'll have to go to New York, and it's a bad time for me. Don't you understand that things are happening . . ." He made a fist of his hand and pressed it to his breast. "I'm sorting out my life, can't you see that?"

"But I'm sorting out mine too."

"It's not the same. A man has responsibility for his family. He's out in the world battling all the connivery. You were gentle bred, you don't understand connivery."

"Then explain it to me. All the years of our marriage we never had a discussion of any true importance. Tell me what the world is. We have matters to sort out between us. You said that to me once. We've made a serious mistake. I'm not saying it was wrong for you to bring me here, but it was wrong for Deirdre. And these are matters I'll have to deal with once I have my divorce."

He gestured for her to keep her voice low. "What's this nonsense?"

"The divorce . . . at the end of the year. I'm not certain . . . I may even remain, but Deirdre surely can't. You can put the matter off until your own heart is clear, but she'll have to go. And when I'm on my own, I'll have to know how to handle these things."

"There is no divorce between us. It was only a way to get you here. You say yourself it was the right thing to have done. You don't regret it."

She felt a flutter in her breast, the wings of a little trapped bird. "But I have a contract."

"There is no such contract between a man and his wife. Listen, you've prospered here as you could in no other place. You're my wife. We're joined together forever. Did you think I'd ever set you adrift? Let's go the year, as we planned, and we'll decide then what's the best life for us."

She could scarcely breathe, her heart was beating so hard. "How can you tell me that I'm yoked to you forever whether I want it or not,

[209]

when the whole meaning of the Community is that one human being cannot possess another."

"Poor Katie . . . it's too much to explain, only take my word for it. One day it will come clear, it will make sense in the end. And Deirdre is in a romantic explosion, it will pass. I knew that this life was impossible for her in the long run. But a year isn't too long for her to wait. As for you, you love your little paintings and your gardening. And as for the family bed . . ." He bent to kiss her. It was no brotherly Community kiss. She knew enough of his lips, she knew enough of his hands. ". . . as for that, be patient. I told you I'd come to you when the time was right."

She took in deep long breaths until the spasm of anger passed. He'd gone into the house to pack his clothes, but Bannerman waited for her and offered her an arm to walk her up the path. "Katherine, may I speak frankly, as an old friend? Be careful that you don't destroy his career." She stopped, she withdrew her arm. "I'm not sure it wasn't on your account he came here and risked what he'd spent half a lifetime to build. How it must have maddened Peter to know you'd kept the best of yourself away from him."

"What do you mean by that?"

"I mean . . ." He took her arm possessively and put it in his again. "I mean that you can keep the truth from your minister and your physician, but never from your lawyer. He's a good man, Katie, believe me he adores you, and you can catch more flies with strawberries than vinegar, if you get my drift."

"Bannerman, you're an idiot." She left him standing there.

Deirdre was tense with anticipation. The lights of the great hall dimmed. The talking stopped, a few coughs, and then silence. The single light moved toward her until she was caught in its bright circle. Now she was alone. More alone than anyone knew. Adam had been in Corinthe's bed. In her mind she saw them there, his ardent kisses on Corinthe's lips, the sweetness of his body on Corinthe's body. The thought of them together tore at her like tigers' claws. What was she without Adam's love? An empty thing. She *was* mad, like Ophelia. The wreath of flowers still had a thorn or two, she felt them at her forehead. But they were nothing to the thorn Corinthe had plunged into her heart. She prayed that the thorns would make her bleed and that Adam would see it. She clasped her hands. Behind her, the little flute began its air, she sang from the deepest, the emptiest place in her heart:

"How shall I my true love know . . ."

The wrong words. It didn't matter. They were truth, she couldn't deny them. . . .

> *From another one,*
> *By his cockle hat and staff,*
> *And his sandal shoon . . .*
> *He is dead and gone, lady . . ."*

He was dead to her, gone from her, hope of love had fled, the lament came up out of her, swelled up, she sang without art, without guile, the song was a natural stage of her lamentation.

When the last notes of the sad-voiced flute died away, she stood in silence. And then the roar of voices and applause, the rush of chairs as they stood and thundered, "More!"

It was as natural as breath; she turned and gestured to the flute to begin his "Greensleeves." She knew now why she took Miss Ada Clare for her heroine. She was born to the tragic herself, denied by her own cruel father, by her careless mother, held off by her lover for a girl he didn't even desire. She took the wreath from her head as Ophelia did before she drowned herself, and with the sweet instrument behind her she began her monologue: *"There's rosemary, that's for remembrance, pray you, love, remember."* She turned and saw Adam watching her from the side of the stage. It was to him she turned. *"And there is pansies, that's for thoughts. . . . There's fennel for you, and columbines."* Beside him awkward Corinthe all dumbstruck in her guiltiness. She offered Corinthe a sprig. *"There's rue for you; . . . they call it herb-grace o' Sundays . . ."*

She finished with the rendition of "Greensleeves" and ended on a soft and quiet note. As the applause rose again she dipped her head in curtsey; it wasn't graceful in the pantaloons but they didn't care, they loved her. So this was her sorrow, to be loved by strangers and never by her own. She walked into the arms of the others in the evening's program. She walked between them not acknowledging their strokes of affection, she couldn't, she was too drained of all feeling. Adam came through the crowd and put arms around her. "I've never heard you sing so sweet." She drew away from him also and left them all there and walked out of the room, alone with her sorrow.

"Gentlemen of the jury . . ." Bannerman began his summation in his elegant fantasy, as he sat on the black horsehair sofa in the visitors' lounge waiting for Peter, who would join him for the journey back. *"Gentlemen of the jury, it would be unfair of me to deny Mr. Noyes his genuine accomplishments in this bizarre and unnatural experiment which has been allowed to root and proliferate these thirty years, a canker in the mouth of all righteousness.* (Canker in the mouth was a vile phrase, he struck it out.) *A thorn in the side of all righteousness.* (Much better, Christlike implications, strike at the man with his own weapons.) *"Gentlemen of the jury, I found the physical surroundings to be pastoral and beautifully tended, the kitchen a delight of cleanliness, as spotless and ordered as any man could wish of his wife or servants, the business most admirably run, although gentlemen* (he would lean toward them as if in confidence), *gentlemen, doesn't it strike you as ironic that the mainstay of the business of this holy community should be traps, instruments of destruction to God's gentle creatures, and manufactured by a man who is even at this moment applying for patent for a new breech-loading gun? What can I say? Mr. Noyes*

runs a tight ship (bad analogy), *Mr. Noyes reigns supreme over an orderly state. Orderly in the physical, oh, gentlemen, it is the eyes of his converts I ask you to consider. The women, heavy-eyed with lust, and worn out by their nightly passions, each night in the bed of another, and in the unholiest, most pernicious way, I ask you to bear with me in the plain speech I must use to present this blot on the escutcheon of holy matrimony.* (Blot on escutcheon was heavy and trite, but it depended on the jury of course, he held it in abeyance.) *In their unholy intercourse the seed is withheld, do you know what damage this does to women? I read from an article by that learned man Dr. L.F.E. Bergeret of the Arbois Hospital of France who attests that a woman, denied the completion of the natural act of sexual intercourse, is prey to the following disorders: acute metritis, chronic metritis, leukorrhea, menorrhagia, fibrous tumors, polyps, uterine hyperesthesia, neuroses, mammary congestion, and diseases of the ovaries. Mr. Noyes attests that women who suffer constant pregnancies under the old law of holy and Christian matrimony are oppressed by the privations of child-raising. Gentleman, think on your own mothers! What woman doesn't glory, yes, glory in the very pains of bringing forth life? God constructed her for that purpose! And to nourish and guard her children through the years of her life, what more satisfaction in life could a woman desire? No, gentleman, what Mr. Noyes desires, and I use the word desire in its most potent form, what Mr. Noyes and his fellows desire is the sexual slavery of women. Only look at the faces of the men of the Community. Wet lips, eyes cast about them knowing that every woman, no matter how young and innocent, is prey for their lust. Each one working his mouth as if he had a sweet under his tongue. . . .*

That last he had lifted from Ellis in *Votaries,* but no matter; he was carrying the same banner. He'd have a bit of a problem with the children, who were the most delightful and the healthiest he'd ever seen. But then they were forever out in the open air which was notably good for infants . . . where the deuce was Peter? The room was empty of visitors. They'd miss the Midland train. They'd have to take a carriage all the way to Utica and he'd never survive it. His gout was acting up, he yearned for his own bed and a decent meal.

Glory of glories, John Humphrey Noyes walked into the visitors' room. The head satyr himself! Unmistakable, that regal bearing, born leader, that short spatulate beard, the visionary eyes. Poor misguided fool. A man who could have done any other thing with his life. Captain of industry if he wished. How could Bannerman describe him? *Gentleman of the jury, I saw this man, I knew him by his figure and his eyes, not much taller than average but he seemed tall, regal, I'd say. And the eyes, those eyes were preternatural and bore into me.* . . . "I say, Dr. Noyes, do you have a moment!"

Noyes bent over a table talking to the pantalooned woman who was in charge of Sunday visitors. Bannerman waited. Noyes looked up, acknowledged his presence and came over to shake his hand. "Mr. Bannerman, I see you're still here. Won't you miss your train?"

"Mr. Berger is coming with me."

Noyes was disturbed at that. "I don't feel it's necessary at this point but I yield to his concern."

"Sir, this meeting is most fortunate. I've asked for an interview."

"Unfortunately I have a paper to prepare. You'll excuse me, I know."

No, Noyes played too clever a hand, but it needed a proper beginning, this duel between them, an opening gambit, as Shakespeare's kings always said before the slaughter, *Words before battle!* "Sir, I'm an admirer of yours, I've read *The Berean* and most of your other pamphlets, impressive, I must say."

Noyes nodded his acknowledgment.

"And you write these wonderful Home Talks, which I suppose fall into the category of sermons."

Noyes gave him a careful, wry smile. "As you wish, I write and speak as God wills."

"God and St. Paul." Bannerman noted his response.

"Both welcome to my heart. And if you will excuse me now I have pressing affairs."

Bannerman saluted him a farewell, waited until he had gone a few paces and then called, "Oh, Dr. Noyes?"

Noyes turned and waited.

"Dr. Noyes [how he relished this!], Dr. Noyes, how is it that they have taken away your license to preach and you keep on preaching?"

Noyes let the blow settle, he searched out Bannerman with his intense gaze and then his face relaxed to this beatific smile he projected. "Mr. Bannerman, God took away your license to sin, how is it you keep on sinning?"

Bannerman let the reply sink in and then he burst into laughter. By God, an opponent at last, a worthy opponent. It would be almost a pity to vanquish him.

Absalom, Absalom. Peter stood at Paulie's door, finally he knocked. Isaac answered and called to Paulie that his father had come to see him.

Paulie stood in the open doorway, his usual feigned carelessness. "What do you want?"

"There's been some trouble in the family. I have to return to New York for a few days."

"Good Lord, not Grandfather! He hasn't died or anything?"

"No, something of a more . . . personal nature."

"It's all right. I'll watch over Mother and the girls."

"No, it's not that. I want you to come with me."

He'd caught Paulie unprepared. Now Paulie closed the door and stepped out, so that he wouldn't embarrass himself in front of Isaac. "Why do I have to go? You always do what you want without consulting me, so what's the point of it?"

"The *point* is that you are my son and we have trouble in the family and your place is with me."

Paulie's mouth went soft.

"Because one of these days you'll be the head of this family and you'd better start learning what kind of family it is. Your Aunt Berthe isn't the easiest one to deal with, neither is your grandfather. So we might as well start now."

Paulie's face shimmered, as if he were underwater, the child coming to the surface, the little boy face that Peter held in his heart.

"And because I love you and I've missed you and I want your company."

Paulie broke. He threw his arms around his father, they held each other in the sweetest reconciliation, and as they did Peter realized how much he loved his son, and that no new life that he could carve for himself could exclude Paulie.

Deirdre walked and walked, where she walked she didn't know. And then she came to a decision. Love had its price. She understood that. She had always understood that. And now she was prepared to pay it. She argued with a manlike logic. Adam was the only love for her, that was the truth of it. And she could only come to his bed by paying the price of membership in its cruelest form. She knew the hunger of desire that only Juliet in her own young years could have felt. What did older people know of desire, they were so dry and empty of it.

She slipped into the side door and made her way up to Amos's room. She would appeal to him directly, and he would guide her. She stood outside his door, cold as death, and then she tapped. He opened it. He was such a kindly grandfatherly gentleman, she could speak to him in candor. "Sir, I've come to you for advice."

"Come in, child."

She was sorry to bother him so late but, if she hesitated, she'd never get the courage again.

"I love Adam," she said, taking a chair as he sat on his bed. Yes, she could trust him, he was Adam's other father, he loved Adam too and wanted them happy, she knew. Only the laws of this odd Community kept them apart like the laws of Venice kept Romeo and Juliet apart. "I want to come into the family and be with Adam."

"But you understand our ways, child. You know that if you love

Adam, you love all his brothers and sisters as well. We don't hold with selfish love."

"Then I'll share his love, but I have to be a part of it. Don't you see it in my eyes?"

"Poor child," he said in great sympathy.

"So then who shall teach me?"

"You've prayed for guidance? You know that this is what God wants of you?"

Her whole body was cold and clammy. "Yes."

He nodded that he understood. She knew he would. Adam was wrong to think he wouldn't understand and he would find her someone gentle and kind. He was so bearlike and woolly, he was a good uncle, and she trusted him. "Tonight you sang like an angel, child, how could we refuse to take you in?"

What had Peter called her? *A virgin of the spirit?* What had he said? *I'll come to you when the time is right?* To her bed, did he mean? Did he think he could just step back into the husband's role as he pleased? And the divorce was only a joke to him? To humor her the way you humor a child?

Well, she'd let Peter make her a child, hadn't she? Lolling around the house in Gramercy Park, full of migraine, so why should Peter have respect for her feelings? And Deirdre, how could you come to a child and say *Let me guide you in this* when she's seen you as nothing but a decoration. And now she couldn't think of sending Deirdre to Berthe. *Then where?* There were always the Virginia cousins, and who knew how scandalized they were by the Community. They were staunch Presbyterians.

When she heard the knock on the door she was afraid that Peter might have returned. But it was Martin. She was so relieved to see him. She drew him inside and closed the door.

"Sarah said something had happened and you were upset. What's wrong?"

"Everything is wrong."

"I can see that. Too many Sunday visitors? I heard that you had an old friend in from New York."

"Peter's friend, not mine. I've been frantic looking for you. I need someone to talk to."

He settled into a chair and reached down to his bad foot. "Mind if I take off my shoe? Too much walking."

"Take it off. Martin, can I ask you something? I mean something of a delicate and personal nature?"

"Who can you talk to better than me?"

That was true. He had become her best friend, like a close brother or a good cousin. "My sketches . . . my little pictures . . ."

". . . as Peter calls them . . ."

"You've noticed that?"

"Of course I've noticed that."

He was so sensitive to slights, it was his foot, she supposed. No, he was sensitive to her feelings. He was the kindest of friends. "Are they any good? I mean truly?"

"Haven't I always said they were?"

"But was that meant to flatter, to smooth down my feathers?"

"You know me better than that. I speak straight out. What on earth makes you ask a question like that? Haven't you a sense of what's changing in your work?"

"I thought I did. Peter always confuses me."

"You're always in a dark mood when he's around."

She pulled her chair up close to his. "The question is more personal than my work. And I can talk to you. You remind me of someone . . . a dream I had . . . I used to dream of someone like you. I mean a man I could speak with frankly."

He set the shoe on the floor. "When? When did you have this dream?"

Why had she mentioned it? She couldn't think why she had. "Nothing . . . it was a long while ago."

"It's more than nothing. Dreams come from the roots of the soul. What did you dream?"

Was that so? Did she dream a premonition? He was a wounded soldier, although certainly not in the same sense. "I dreamed about a soldier . . ."

". . . who was sympathetic to you, someone you could talk with."

"Yes."

"Was he wounded in the leg? Which leg?"

She felt her face flush. "No."

"Where then?"

"Oh, it was nothing, only a dream. Let it pass."

"Are you being shy with me? Why on earth? Haven't we shared the greatest intimacies between us?"

"What intimacies? Trees and flowers? How are those things intimate?" Oddly, in a way, it was true. She couldn't explain how. "He was wounded in another place."

"What other place?"

"In a personal place, please don't embarrass me."

"You're such an anachronism, Kate. You no longer live among the gentiles. Shame belongs outside. Don't we speak frankly of sexual things at the evening meeting? So what on earth are you embarrassed about with me?"

"I'm not embarrassed, it was a personal wound."

"Well, let me guess. I'm a good Daniel. I'll read your dream. With all your fears of being touched . . ."

"When have I . . ."

"Come, don't avoid it, from the first day. And I've honored that feeling, haven't I? In your dream your wounded soldier was safe and emasculated. And you see that in me. Safe eunuch Martin."

"Don't put it that way."

"What way shall I put it?" He smiled, he had such a gentle way of making fun at his own expense. And in truth she had thought of him that way. And he'd seen it.

"Since you've opened the subject . . ."

"Yes?"

"When you were married . . ."

"Ah . . ."

"Did you rule your wife? I mean . . . *rule* her?"

"I was a normal man, a man of my time, I tried to rule her. And failed. She was stronger than I. She ruled me with her *legality*. They say that here. My sister used to call us Martin and his martinet."

"I don't think marriage works, do you?"

"It works here admirably well."

"I mean between one man and one woman. I mean between a man and a woman who want to be friends. You can't mix friends and lovers."

"But that's not true. *We* do, you and I."

"We're friends, but not lovers, so you see . . ."

"And if I took you to bed, would that change anything?"

"But that's not a problem between us, thank God."

He bent to rub the foot on his crooked leg. "Yes, it is. I've asked Sarah to speak for me. It's time we went to bed."

It took a moment for the impact of his words to reach her. Betrayed! Twice betrayed! She wanted to bring back the rage she felt with Peter, but somehow she couldn't. No, he wasn't serious, he said it so lightly, he was teasing with her. "I can't believe that all this time you've just been softening me up for the attack."

"Is that how Peter treated woman? Of course it was. He didn't understand the art of loving, nor did I before I came."

"Then, Martin, I want you to know, if you are serious, and I doubt that you are, that I vowed never to let a man touch me again."

He leaned back in his chair; he was a slender wiry man, sinewy like his trees, his eyes were pale, the color was all under the surface, but he was so comfortably sure of himself, no posturing, no vanity. "Then I won't touch you, but I want to make love to you just the same."

"To love without touching? How queer."

"Isn't that your dream? You were loved without being touched?"

Curiously it was. "I don't need a lover, my life is overfull as it is. Deirdre needs me, I'm not resolved with Peter."

"The family will resolve Peter. He needs a good criticism. And Deirdre has a hundred mothers. Let her go. I'm talking about you. You're a half-finished woman. Part of you is still asleep. Ask me, I'm an expert on somnambulism. Like this talent with your hands, which has just come awake. Sleeping Kate. Let me wake you up."

"What are you saying? That you'd make love to me and never touch me?"

"I have been making love to you, for a long while. Don't you know that?"

In a way she did know that. Or else how could she be sitting so calm and talking this way so intimately with a man not her husband? They'd never touched, and yet they were intimate. And she and Peter had joined bodies, and there was never an intimacy between them, not an easy sort of intimacy like this.

She had come to the line dividing two opposing halves of the world. What *outside* was thou-shalt-not, here became the command-ment *thou-shalt*. Where was the truth? The truth was in her own senses. *Outside* the world was a bloody battleground, a chaos of body and spirit. *Inside* the strawberry fields flourished. Love was *inside,* in everything that grew, in the children, in gestures, in soft hearts, everywhere. Even in Deirdre's dream of romance. It was only the world's standards that prevented Deirdre from that consummation with Adam, poor child. Love was everywhere here, the kind of love she could only conceive with a wounded fantasy of a soldier.

And she was so tired. Tired of worrying about Deirdre, tired of being badgered by Peter, too tired to hold her body tight against a man who had been bringing her back to life. She understood that now, all those hours in the orchards, their walks together, the easy way she spoke with him, the way he saw her art, yes, her *art,* which was exactly part of herself, and the most intimate part, she could thank him for that.

He began to take off his shirt. "Would you rather we went through Sarah? Would you like the chance to refuse?"

"You said you could love me without that. Don't spoil it by

making this physical. It's good sitting here together in a closed room. That's enough for me."

"I'm not going to pounce on you. You've come such a long way in looking deeply into things. Look into me now, trust me a little, I want you to see me exactly as I am. Look at me the way you've looked at trees and flowers and birds, with that same kind of observation and understanding. I want you to know me, Kate."

She was filled with such a lassitude. "Why do you always call me Kate? Do you know you're the only one who does?"

"Of course I know. Peter calls you Katie. Katie was the frightened bird who came that first afternoon. Are you the same now?"

"No."

"Then Kate is who you are."

He unbuttoned his trousers and dropped them and drew them off. And then his drawers, until he was naked. The first shock of seeing him naked sent odd waves through her. Had she never *looked* at Peter naked? She'd averted her eyes, always. And then as the shock passed, she began to see Martin through an artist's eyes. Mesmerized by his body, as an artist who sees a thrilling subject for the first time. And she thought the oddest thing. With those private parts in fullest view. She wondered, *Could I paint a figure?* Peter always demanded some passionate response, Martin did not. He allowed her that kind of room. And so she lowered her eyes and looked at his most intimate place with the same eye she used on McAvoy's Superiors. He was aroused, but he never moved, never changed aspect, and he sat relaxed in the chair as if they were talking about some casual topic. He gave her time to see him bit by bit.

He was a slight man, his skin wasn't brown like Peter's, he was pale, not graceful like Peter but tough like the limbs of trees. Peter was always ready to spring, Martin was rooted to a place. His chest wasn't muscled like Peter's, it was solid though and taut in its own muscled security. His hands were hands of the earth, knotted and spatulate, his eyes, all the color was under the surface. The crooked leg was a curiosity. It grew straight and there where the bullet had shattered the bone, you could see how the bone grew crooked, like a tree grafted, and the skin grew thick over it. Yes, something else had been grafted into him when he sat at the borderline of life, she could see that now, and that thing had changed his nature as the tree is altered.

And then her eyes were drawn again to the . . . taproot. She was amazed it didn't fill her with alarm, quite the opposite. It was a lovely thing. At first she thought, like a great finger to plunge into the turned bed so that the seed could be planted, but they didn't plant that seed here. What with Peter was a weapon here was used only to bring pleasure to a woman. She wondered, why did they so rarely paint this thing in portraits or carve it in stone? Always covered, with a leaf or a vine across. When here was so clearly the source of what God meant when he said *love* and *creation*. She would have liked to touch it, it was so ripe and lovely.

She was Kate who dreamed of a wounded soldier and now his wounds had healed and she was still unfinished.

She was hot through her clothes, his eyes were magnetic; he had mesmerized her, she thought so. But she didn't care. She wanted to be stroked now. He had loved her without touching her. She wanted the rest of it. She wanted it. She opened the buttons of her bodice and skirt and let them fall. She undid the buttons of her pantaloons and then the rest. She was naked. She saw herself in the mirror. It wasn't the same Katherine she remembered from those early days when she stood and saw herself in the mirror and touched her own breasts in girlish passion, all romance. This was not romance. Nor was it lust. It was something different from what she expected, just simply an air that had shifted in the room, all electric, all warm, a new aroma, an aura, as if she were meant to be naked like this, all hot in the loins, wanting not so much to be touched as to touch. When they met he waited until her hands could learn what her eyes saw. She closed her eyes and learned his body, bit by bit. Through the skin to the muscle, the configuration of the joint, the brow, the lips, he ran his tongue against her fingertips, and the sensation ran all along the nerves of her body electric and alive, when he moved against her finally it was quietly, belly to belly, breast to breast, when he put his arms around her finally, it was breath to breath, when he took her to the bed, it was in soft movements, he lay beside her for the longest while, they breathed each other, he didn't enter her until she asked him to, the rhythms of their bodies were universal rhythms, when she came to her passion for the first time, he laughed with pleasure for her. And they began again. He told her what gave him most pleasure and she set about learning it.

Later he sighed and kissed her and left her body. "But you . . ." He smiled and shook his head. "This is the way."

"You're not dissatisfied?"

He kissed her again. "Do I look dissatisfied?" He kissed her breast and her throat and lay back. "So good . . . so good . . ."

"And you're not cheated out of the final act."

"You don't know what you're saying. I feel as if the war is finally over for me. I've fought a very long battle, now I've come home."

She lay awake a long while thinking. When the tap came at the door she thought he'd returned, with one last sweet thing to say that she could sleep on. She opened the door to Deirdre. Deirdre in the dim hallway light, her face white as chalk. "What is it? What's wrong?"

Deirdre tried to speak, she tried to form words, she put her hands up to her face as if to hide it, and then turned and ran. . . .

Adam was almost too hoarse with his emotion to speak clearly. "You knew . . ." he choked, "you knew that Amos and Deirdre were together and you never tried to stop him?"

Sarah paced the little pocket nursery kitchen. She was brewing some strawberry tea, but the water took so long "And how did you find out so soon?"

"Because . . ." Adam's face was twisted with rage, she'd never seen him filled with fury, "because he told me so himself. He thought I'd be pleased."

"And you think he was lying?"

"He did lie! He let her in his bed but the sin was on you. Do you know what you've done, Mother? You've sacrificed an innocent to your gods, you've gone counter to everything you've said or believed. Doesn't that turn your stomach? Doesn't that make you want to retch?"

The water was on the boil. She put in the leaves to steep. "Quite the contrary. Where is she now?"

"Locked in her room, she wouldn't let me near her. I think I could kill him."

She took a cup and saucer. "Could you? Kill Amos? And for what? For acting according to what we believe and what we've always believed? You came back here so smug in your new convictions. You said, 'Mother, you and yours came through fire, we were brought up softer, give us leave to fight our own battles now.' So here you have a battle. Deirdre has done no more, no less than every girl in the Community. Now, you've come back to us. So you say. You complained bitterly that Amos was keeping you from the family bed. You were *returned* in every way. Then you fall in love. And when the woman you love asks to come into the Community of her own volition, when she asks to be one of us for *your* sake, you'd *kill* the man who brought her in? Go to New York, Adam. Take Deirdre with you. Marry her. Live with her there. Because you don't believe in us. If Amos had thought he'd done something against the Community or against Deirdre's best interest, would he have come to you? He's not vindictive, there's not a cruel strain in him. He's foolish, yes. He's become a bit . . . inflexible. But when he came and told you about Deirdre, he was saying the woman you love has joined us now and soon you can bring her happiness and she will bring happiness to her other brothers. That is what you say you believe. That is what we are! We are Communists! We share and live by sharing. We don't believe in selfish love."

"She came to ask Amos to find her a teacher. It could have been anyone pleasing to her. You could have talked about it with me first. Would that have compromised Amos's grand ideals? And it would have made a friend of me for life. As it is, I'll never look him in the face again."

She had to put down her cup, it rattled in her saucer.

"I've made the Community my life and well you know it. Amos should have been your proper father, but for the good of the Community I turned away from him. The Community must survive! If you believe as you say you do, sacrifice your own *special* love and live our life! We won't survive unless we convert our own children. Amos came to me and I asked myself hard questions. Yes, Deirdre is an innocent, she didn't know what she was asking. But she's no more no less than any Oneida woman. She couldn't do better than to be among us. If she could let Amos love her and learn to love him as she will love you and others, then she's true to us."

"You sacrificed her for a principle."

"As I sacrificed myself to it."

He knew she was right. He couldn't look her in the eyes. "You know the ledger Father Noyes keeps in his study? The big ledger?"

She knew which book.

"He writes his failures in it. Nobody reads it, it's a secret ledger. But it's all there and we know it. What man failed in his duties. What man sits secretly in his room and squanders his seed. Which men and women are selfishly in love. What man cheated in the business and was silently sent away."

"And what of it? It's not a perfect system. But we work *toward* truth in order for men and women to live together in peace on this planet. Sometimes we lose a little to gain much."

"I wanted to love Deirdre. She wanted to love me. What would have been the hurt? To have helped to teach her, that's all I asked. Amos is the jealous one, jealous that he'll have to give over power to my generation. And that was why he made love to Deirdre, knowing how I felt."

"I won't call you a liar, your conscience will tell you that."

Now she poured him a cup of tea and cut him a piece of currant cake the way she did when he came to visit her as a child and she wanted to please him. "It's you who are being tried in all this. When you were small, you came running to me, you were all the joy I asked in the world. But there were other children I needed to love as much as you. If the house had caught fire, I would have picked up the first child I found and left you to someone else's arms. You were all our children, we were all your mothers. Either you give up this selfish love or go back outside and make a life there. There's no between."

She left him to work it out.

She'd survived her hard years, now these were his. And there was nothing she could do to help him.

Katherine walked Moira and Bitsie out to Cragin's Meadow. The afternoon buzzed around them. In the vineyard they were heeling in the raspberry vines for winter. And the potatoes were being taken up and stored. She should have been working. "How can I thank you for coming all this long way. My dear good friends. I was desperate. Deirdre said she'd talk to no one but her Aunt Moira."

"I rode a horse in Central Park," said Bitsie, who was dressed in a riding habit with a great leather bodice and a tight wide-hipped skirt, her eyes all dazzled by the afternoon. "It took two men to hoist me, but once I was on him, the riding came back. I've lost six pounds. I have, Katie, and I mean to get my figure back."

"That will vie for attention with the Second Coming. Her dieting pills are full of laudanum, she's been floating in space like this all week."

"After it happened," Katherine said, "I found her in her room absolutely devastated. She refused to talk to me, she said I wouldn't understand. And Corinthe was hysterical. I had to find out through Sarah. I telegraphed you directly. Has she come out of the shock yet?"

"We had a long long talk. And it took me awhile to piece it all out. From what I gather, she went to him of her own free will, expecting this gross old man to pair her up with someone presentable, not too old but not Adam, her own love, in order to be part of the family and enjoy his bed. She thought she was asking him to find someone *else* for the office. It wasn't a seduction, Katie, it was a comedy of errors. He was as upset as she, and now she's embarrassed to death. She wants it silenced. Nothing has happened to her, she says, that didn't happen to all the other girls. At first I thought, what a mad way to carry on. And then, Katie, I thought of how brashly I advised you when you first came here. I'll tell you something, I never realized how much I lived under the same cloud of convention as my poor mother. And I thought, she's lost her virginity. And that's a tragedy because a girl must keep her virginity to sell at the marriage auction intact. The folly of that. When you and I know what marriage is. And I thought of New York, not its myths, its realities. There is no ideal marriage, we married as virgins and what has it done for us?"

"I don't like Harry anymore," Bitsie said.

"So her virginity is gone. No use crying over that. It can't be mended. If it could, all the good ladies of the city would pay to have it done and then only go out and lose it again. And make more business for Madame Restell. Well, here you can have your strawberries and eat them too. No pregnancy. It's ingenious, I wonder why nobody thought of it before. Done is done for Deirdre. Now what?"

"She'll go to Adam, I suppose."

"Not quite so. This was an eye-opening event for her, all the romance is washed out of her. Now she says she doesn't know what she wants. But until she does, in the oddest way, she's protected here, isn't she? She has concerned people around her, she has you, the other girls, and the winter's coming in, it's in the air, the house is close and warm. This is an idyllic place and she could do worse than be here."

Katherine looked across the meadow toward the orchard, down along the Oneida Valley toward the creek with its soft border of trees, back toward the Mansion House, the flowering quadrangle and the two towers. "Yes, it's a place apart. They come on the train to see the circus and the marching band. They never see what's here."

"Nobody believed me," Bitsie said, "because I was fat."

"The thing that worries me most," Moira said, "isn't Deirdre, it's Peter. What will he do when he finds out?"

"I can't think, it frightens me."

"Can you keep it from him?"

"Nothing is secret here. If a man sleeps with a woman, the family knows. So that if something's amiss, they can call a criticism on him."

"On a husband too?"

"Especially that. And the wife is called to testify. And he has to sit and listen."

"It's a wonder the women of the world aren't breaking down your doors." She touched Katherine's hair. "Katie, I believe you're happy here, only look at your face. You've come back to life and left me and Bitsie behind."

"If it weren't for Deirdre."

"Deirdre's done something wonderful in a way. She made a decision, no matter how foolish, and she plunged right in. Look at the three of us, we've wasted a lifetime looking for love. So you've got your painting and Bitsie is recreating herself so she can go riding in Central Park and what about me? What's left for me?"

Katherine looked at Moira in the clear and critical way she saw so many things these days. Moira was pale and so hollow about the eyes. "Your lovely poems, what of them?"

"They were child's poems. There's no more romance left in me."

"Romance is a dangerous thing. Write a novel, then. Like George Sand in Paris. Write of things as they are."

"You'd have a reason to smoke your cigars." Bitsie giggled.

"How can I write anything? What do I know? I don't even know my own husband. So, what will you do now?" Moira asked her. "Stay on here, do you think?"

"If only they would all leave me in peace I could be happy here. Poor Deirdre. Now she understands Miss Ada Clare. All those lost dreams. Thank God Rebecca is still a baby and no cause for concern. She still lives in an *Alice in Wonderland* dream. I suppose she's the only one who hasn't been affected by this odd little world."

So they were finished talking. The afternoon closed in on them, little freshets coming in from the west carrying away not only dry autumn leaves but all their cares and necessities. She would have liked to paint them all like this: Moira looking off into the fields, the long line of her throat, her mouth a question; Bitsie bending over a buttercup.

But she'd forgotten Bitsie. "Dear Bitsie, you had a message from Harry for Peter? To leave with me? I'll tell Peter directly he comes back. What message?"

Bitsie had found a daisy and she was pulling off the petals. "He did give me a message, Harry did, but you know me, I'm a fat cow, I'm an oink-oink." She smiled her sweetly dimpled smile. "And can't remember what it is."

Sarah held the weeping Rebecca. "Come, child, now, what is all this?"

"We didn't *think* it was bad, it wasn't Rachael's fault, I only thought . . ."

"What were you doing in the warehouse chamber? That dirty dark place."

"Rachael and I . . . we only went . . . we were calling spirits."

Sarah took Rebecca on her lap and kissed the top of her head. "Were you? And didn't you know that calling spirits is a dangerous thing? That you might get the wrong ones?"

"Oh, no, if He came, we were going to ask Him Scripture. For a test. We were going to ask Timothy III, about being disobedient, and the devil wouldn't know Timothy. When it comes to Bible games, nobody knows Timothy."

"Calling who?"

"We only wanted to talk to God."

"You wanted to talk to . . ."

"Was that wrong? We thought, since He's always so good to children . . ."

"God forbid that I should stop you from calling His blessed name into your presence. Why were the dolls there with you?"

Rebecca hugged her Mathilda. "She wanted to."

Sarah rocked Rebecca on her lap. "You don't mean *want*. Surely a doll can't want. A doll isn't flesh and bood."

"Well, she's not flesh, exactly, but she is real."

"Dear child, a doll is a lifeless thing. If you love to play with babies, go to one of the new mothers. Ask to play with a real child."

"But she *is* real!"

"Child, I know you mean well, you've fallen quite into the family life. Confess yourself and ask Christ to guide you. And put your doll aside for a while. Find some older person and help in the kitchen. Find some good instruction that will help you to a good spirit. I have great hopes for you, little Rebecca. You have a fire in you that God loves, and I love you too." Sarah kissed her. "And if God does come one day and speak with you I shall not be surprised."

"Does He live in New York too?" Rebecca asked.

"Does who, child?"

"God. Does He live in New York, or does only the devil live in New York?"

She was so precious, so dear a child. "If God lives in New York City, then there are a lot of women who have sorely missed finding him. Let the devil have New York. You belong with us. You are an Onedia Community child if ever there was one. Remember that."

SEVEN

Visit to Three Houses

She that is a widow indeed, and desolate, trusteth in God, and continueth in supplications and prayers night and day. But she that liveth in pleasure is dead while she liveth.
Timothy 5:5–6

A bishop then must be blameless . . . ruleth well his own house, having his children in subjection with all gravity (for if a man know not how to rule his own house, how shall he take care of the church of God?).
Timothy 3:2, 4, 5

. . . women adorn themselves in modest apparel, with shamefacedness and sobriety; not with broided hair, or gold, or pearls, or costly array; . . . I suffer not a woman . . . to usurp authority over the man, but to be in silence. For Adam was first formed, then Eve. And Adam was not deceived but the woman being deceived was in the transgression.
Timothy 2:9, 12–15

Two weeks and he was still whispering around the house, berating her for this little thing or that. (Hector, please be *still!*) It made her doubt that there was still a reward in heaven or else he'd have gone there and stopped bedeviling her. "Did you put Mr. Berger into the sun room? Did you bring him the best Madeira?" She had tried three dresses, black made her sallow, she begged God to forgive her the single strand of pale gray pearls. Dolores stood behind her doing the clasp. Her punishment was in seeing Dolores's face, those dark Spanish eyes, the skin like cream, that pouting provocative mouth, men followed her like puppies, tongues out. It was so unfair, that for a thing as shallow as skin was given all the prizes; this one marked for love, that one passed by. She let down her hair, she shook it out. Her hair was still good. But her face . . . she pinched it to make it let go of its stern lines.

She opened the double doors and entered slowly, her widow's face, a small linen handkerchief to stem any possible flow of tears. Paulie jumped to his feet, he overturned his wine, so clumsy, she waved away his apologies. "Don't worry, Dolores will get at it later." He came to her and kissed her, sweet child. She dabbed at her eyes, not too hard, the skin beneath was getting so thin. She turned up a cheek to receive Peter's kiss; no kiss was forthcoming She raised her eyes modestly. "I would have written, but I knew from Katherine's letter that you had troubles of your own, I didn't want to put my sorrow on your shoulders." She settled herself on the sofa, patted the cushion for him to sit beside her but he took a chair opposite, and sipped his Madeira trying to make her out. "Berthe, what are you up to?"

How could she signal him that the days of bitterness were over? "It was only a matter of expediency, and love, I love Deirdre, you know that."

His eyes mocked her over the wine. "Love of what? Of my daughter? I often wondered why you didn't have children of your own."

She would not let the old bitterness come through her tongue. "Yes, love, I love my sister. Katherine was never strong, I've seen her weakness growing year by year, the demands of family life were too much, she wanted to retire, with her hobbies and her . . . glass of wine." She tried not to look at the urine stain which was spreading on her carpet. "Deirdre is in danger, you know that, and the house without Hector is so empty. . . ." She dabbed at her eyes, she hoped they were moist at least. "Deirdre wants a home to protect her reputation until she marries, and one day she'll inherit from me."

He put down his wine. "And that was your only motive?" She fancied, she thought (or was it only desire?), was his manner softer? She rose to that hint of softness like a hungry fish to bait, she adored him, with all her heart, he should have been hers, oh, what a life she would have had, and what she could have made of him. "My only motive, Katherine is so helpless, you know that, Peter."

Paulie who was sitting on the arm of a chair, rose and bristled with indignation. "My mother isn't helpless . . . well, not very helpless, just a little . . . artistic."

"Exactly what I meant."

"And Paulie and I are here to say that Katherine overemphasized the matter. Deirdre is well with us and quite safe. So that your gesture of love . . . is appreciated, but not needed."

"But she needs a home!"

"She has a home, with us in Oneida."

"Home? You call that place a home?"

He looked at her, no, not ironically but with a sense of pity. "Is this?" She knew what was in his head, Hector had put it there, Hector who never took much comfort here and always ran to Peter with his tales. It was cruel, too cruel.

"Honestly, Berthe, there's no danger to Deirdre's reputation. Oneida is a loving family, she'll be protected until we decide . . . until my son and I decide finally what's to be done. And as for Katherine, you wouldn't know her, she looks wonderfully well."

So he was still defending her, who had done *nothing* to make him happy, who had driven him to that existence, that pastoral half-life, only by dint of her face . . . they were two sisters equal in their father's house, their father came into the room and his eyes would fall on Katherine's gold hair and her soft child's mouth. Katherine needed protection, Berthe was so self-sufficient. His eyes were on Katherine and they ate her up. Because of a nose or a mouth, those women were eaten up with eyes; and the ones not eaten, they had to make their lives by their wits and tongues; that's what a shrew was, a woman standing forever in abject hunger for *those* eyes which another captured only because of this brow or that shoulder or a sweep of a lash.

". . . so I can count on you to write to your lawyer and tell him it was a mistake. Deirdre will stay with us through the winter at least."

Peter finished his wine, he looked around the room and said, "Poor Hector," in such a way that she knew what he meant. Whatever passed between her and Hector in this house was put on her head, that was the way of marriage. And now Berthe knew for certain that Peter's manner might have changed but not the way he felt about her. She saw her dreams fall away. Dreams. Was Katherine the only one entitled to dreams?

He and Paulie took up their coats. Now Peter came to her with a kiss of condolence, and the doors closed behind them.

She sat for a long and empty while in that room, a room full of autumn shadows. Katherine had always managed to land on her feet, like a cat. It was not fair. Never in her life had a man looked at her the way Peter had looked at Katherine, the way Katherine was still reflected in his eyes.

No, that wasn't so. Hector when he was young, not with Peter's stature, his hair already thinning, unprincely eyes, when he came to her for the first time, he looked at her that way.

And for the first time since Hector died, she wept for him. Grief overtook her, she pulled the pearls from her throat and threw them down and she wept.

When she came to herself, she wondered whatever had come over her. It took half an hour to find all the pearls. And she thought, Well, the matter wasn't over yet. Who knew what might happen to Katherine in that awful place. And Peter had kissed her, a duty kiss on the cheek but he'd never done that before.

She put the pearls in a box and decided that it was time to take off the black; she was out of mourning.

The house was an anachronism caught between the Vanderbilt warehouse and his memory. The yard was overgrown with weeds, why? In spite of time and the city his father had been so careful with this garden. Now the chrysanthemums were blooming wild and untended, caught between reedy weeds and rangy vines that had captured the garden. The front windows were painted permanently shut and shuttered, as if . . . if the warehouse couldn't be seen it didn't exist.

The weather had turned so quickly, the wind scudded the sidewalks pasting bits of paper and leaves around their legs. Paulie turned up his collar. But Peter was cold not with wind but with memory. "This wasn't a happy house for me."

"Well, I should think not, Grandfather Berger is so stern."

The curtains parted. Did she know they were coming? She was preternatural with anything concerning her husband. He thought of Mary Darcy's soft and enveloping arms. The woman who opened the door was a thin sparrow in a dun-colored dress, that ubiquitous apron. He neither loved nor respected her. But he prayed for a soft heart, to allow him for once and all to give up the resentment that crowded everything else out of his heart.

She berated Paulie for not coming more often, she inspected him for faults and imperfections, how could Peter have permitted him out with so thin a coat, didn't he remember there was consumption in the family? Peter thought how wise they were in the Community to forbid "sticky" grandmothers. Finally she turned to Peter, not so much in love, but frowning. "I was afraid you might come when you heard from the bishop."

Lovely welcome. "What's Father been doing now to meddle?"

She raised the apron to her face. "How can you say a thing so cruel. He's been so ill."

"Ill? With what? Why didn't you write?"

"He wouldn't let me, not to that place. Oh, Peter, if you knew how you were hurting him, give this life up for his sake."

For his sake. The bile flowed. No *Dear Peter, we missed you,* or *let me kiss you,* only *Peter, you hurt your father* . . . guilt . . . and more guilt. "I want to see him, let's settle this up for once and all."

"Oh, no!" It horrified her to think of confrontation; she doted on her husband, everything else in the world could go hang. And then he heard his father's voice boom: "Who is it! Don't stand out there dawdling."

Sweet, as usual. *Christ, grant me a soft heart and arm me with truth and love.* The great double oak doors of his father's study opened, and his father stood in the doorway holding onto the doorjambs with both great hands, tall as an oak, grown into wood, the ramrod back, like an aging Samson holding up the pillars of the Temple.

"Oh, Grandfather!" Paulie blurted it out before Peter realized. He was stunned by his father's face. His father must have suffered some sort of stroke, and it had settled on his face. One side was drawn up in a terrible smirk, the two sides had become different. His father's handsome face; it was horrible. That patriarchal face with its white patrician beard, now it was a caricature of itself, one half up toward God, the other in a permanent indecent mocking wink. So this was God's justice. And this was why his mother hadn't wanted him to come.

"Father, why didn't you write to me?"

His father faltered, he led him back to the study. Peter couldn't believe that the man had fallen, he had always seemed unshakable and infallible. Now his mother hovered nervously, fluttering about the ruined old man with that look of anguish and helplessness. "Take the woman out," his father said in disgust. "I can't bear her around me."

She put the apron to her eyes and began to cry. "He doesn't mean it, he's gone out of his head, he never spoke like this."

Paulie took his grandmother out to comfort her. "It's all right, Grandmother, it only wants a little courage, he'll come out of it."

The hand he raised to Peter was also twisted and drawn. Peter closed the doors and came to sit beside him.

It was a terrible divine justice, the dichotomy of those two faces. "The devil mocks me," his father said. "He marked my face the day you went over to the antichrist."

So his father would scar him with this also. But how could he debate an old man who had this horrible affliction on him? "Let's not wrangle this time, I only came to see you."

"All my life devoted to the church but God was saving me for this last trial. My dear boy, my dear Peter . . ." Peter realized that his father's voice reflected something like affection, he was shocked by it. "My dear son, at last you've come to me for salvation!"

Salvation! He drew back, had his father gone mad?

Perhaps it was easier in madness. Mad men were like children, open and candid, unable to control their memories or distort them with lies. Did his father truly think he was bringing Peter to salvation, with those terrible . . . "Father," he blurted out. "Father, did you ever love me?"

His father's good eye opened wide in surprise, the other eye smirked and mocked and laughed. "Love *you?* What else did I love? God and my son. That was all I loved in my whole life."

That wasn't the answer he expected. Never in his life a soft word that denoted love, and yet his father said *love?* "Then when I was a child, when you . . . did those terrible things . . . when you tied me . . ."

His father's face turned inward, it pulled in on itself. "Terrible . . .

most terrible . . . how I suffered with you . . . I used to go out into the garden and cry. Once I made a lash of ropes and whipped myself until the blood ran . . ."

"You whipped *yourself?*"

". . . . to have heard your cries and not to have been able to comfort you."

"But *why* not! It was you who tied me!"

His father seemed not to be able to understand him. "But how else could I save you, don't you see? I saw the devil holding you over the pit, you were held by such a slender thread and once let go, your soul would have suffered eternal damnation." He plucked at Peter's sleeve with the clawed hand. "I would have had to see my only son suffer eternal damnation . . . *eternal* . . . the torments of the damned . . . and so I had to listen to your cries night after night . . ."

Peter was amazed . . . his heart was *filled* with amazement. His father had acted out of *love?* What was love and what was God? He had struggled with the question night after night with Amos and with Cunningham, trying to let go of his logical heart and throw himself into the hands of a God and he saw that God had a thousand faces in this fragmented broken mirror of a world. God depended on the angle, the moment, God was compassion, God was torment and punishment. His father had spoiled his childhood out of some distorted vision of *love?* If this was God, who needed the devil?

"You've come to me for salvation, praise God, let me pray for you."

He knelt happily, he was grateful for the respite, to be able to turn from his father's awful face. He hoped it would be a long prayer.

The miracle, as he saw it now, was that the anger against his father had drained out of his heart. At least in the present world. He also knew that the child in his breast would weep in the night forever, he had no control over dreams.

So he rose, having received a benediction from a madman. He understood that he would never be entirely resolved, he would always live in two parts, like his father's face.

Amen.

He embraced his poor ruined father. His father's claw of a hand fluttered toward him. "Will you leave that Antichrist now, my son?"

"Father, you misjudge Mr. Noyes."

His father's eyes blazed with the light of a true believer. "Then I will come and meet him face to face. And let him tell me why he is keeping my son from God."

For a long while Peter and his son sat in the carriage outside of Miss Josephine Woods, smoking and talking. "It was Grandfather and my own stupidity that drove me here. Do you understand?"

Paulie, in his new wisdom, nodded that he did.

"I wanted you in the Community so that you'd be taught the ways of the bed in better places than this fancy whorehouse. I didn't see that you had choices. You'd go to a place like this and buy love for money, or you'd wait until you were married and suffer privation, or you'd cultivate other *habits* which are bound to bring on nervous ailments, blindness, God knows what. What disappoints me is that I thought you'd agree to the family bed long before now."

"Well . . . Isaac and I . . . we've talked a lot about it. And the way I see it, I don't intend to make Oneida my life so it would be dishonorable to sleep with the family girls. And the old women, they don't interest me."

"You're sure you couldn't make a life of it?"

"Can you? Those dreary jobs when your mind's fit for better things? I mean, don't you just champ at the bit for a good play or music that isn't amateur entertainment? Their music breaks my ears."

"And in the spring, what do you mean to do? Go back to St. George's? I leave the choice to you."

"That place? Not likely. That ass of an Ambeson glorying in war when it's so immoral. I thought I'd like to go into history or teaching . . . I'd go into the law if it weren't such a bitch."

Peter puffed at his cigar. "Would you like a look inside? So that you can understand the world of men? So that you understand the kind of thing I did before I saw the light?"

"Lord yes, I've been dying for a look inside."

They climbed the steps, arm around shoulder, father and son, Peter and Paul, not Paulie, never again Paul*ie,* two generations cemented forever.

The peephole opened, the door opened, Josie herself swept them into the anteroom, the velvet and the crystal, the music and the bosoms. "Didn't I know you'd be back with us sooner or later. And what have you brought? Son and heir? I have just the one to break the ice, don't you know."

Paulie was all eyes, a look-in, eye-winks back at him, soft laughter, braided pearls in black hair. "No. My son only wanted to see the place. And I wanted to ask after a girl. Do you remember? She was a novice, a green girl. What was her name? She had a child."

Josie swept her long train from underfoot as she took him aside. "Am I likely to forget? I was mad to take Bella off the streets."

"Then she's not here now?"

"That greedy girl? She made a good living here, but she had to take business off street corners as well. By the time my physician had a look at her, the disease had already taken hold."

"Oh, poor child, she's not more than seventeen!"

"Poor child! Devil take her. Think of my dozen customers who were with her before we found out! She got her desserts."

"That's an odd position for you to take, Josie, considering your profession. I shouldn't think *desserts* would be the word for you."

Josie bristled, she snapped her fingers for her doorman to bring her a glass of champagne from the sideboard. "You want to talk morality, Mr. Lawyer? Talk morality to the bastard who came in and gave it to poor Bella. And how the hell am I ever going to tell Mr. Bannerman?"

He and Paulie sat up a long while in the smoking car, the click of the wheels, the sweet tobacco, loath to give up the last of this new intimacy. "I wouldn't blame Mother too much . . . about this thing with Aunt Berthe, I mean. She's probably right about Deirdre. Deirdre can be damned silly."

The moonlit landscape moved by, shadows on shadows. "I may have underestimated your mother. I don't know many women who could have come into Community life and made the most of it."

"Do you think Mother *does?*"

"Does what?"

"You know . . . sleep in the family bed."

Peter smiled a knowing kind of smile. "It's not her way."

"I shouldn't think so either. She's awfully good friends with Martin, though."

"The crippled gardener? She's a gentle sort, your mother. She would pick a friend who needs her gentleness."

He had only now begun to understand Katherine. She was a damned strong woman in her way. And admirable. There was no one in the Community to touch her for looks.

When he got back he would ask Sarah to intercede for him. She'd love that kind of courtship, she feigned not to, but he understood women. It was time for him to teach her how to love. And he'd teach her as no man had taught woman, since Adam.

He was disappointed, the next morning, that Katherine wasn't waiting for him at the station.

ℱIRE

Can a man take fire in his bosom and his clothes not be burned? Can one go upon hot coals and his feet not be burned? So he that goeth in to his neighbor's wife; . . . a wound and dishonor shall he get; and his reproach shall not be wiped away. For jealousy is the rage of a man . . .
Proverbs 6: 17–35

. . . my doll seduces me to a heedless spirit. [We] were criticized for neglecting to come down to breakfast in time, and the reason why we did not was that we stopped to dress our dolls before dressing ourselves and that made us too late . . . I have asked Christ to help me do the thing that will please him about it, and should rather put my doll in the fire and see her burn up than play with her any more. . . .   Letter from a child

Oneida, 1851

Peter . . . come on . . . get up . . . you
can't hide from us forever."

Cunningham and Newhouse tried to prod him awake. To hell with
them, damn them in eternal hell. He curled under the covers, encased
in stone, his face to the wall, because if he opened he would explode,
the fury of his anger would spill molten gall, he would spew fire. For
three weeks he'd hardly slept. If he closed his eyes he saw his wife's
naked body with that crippled gardener bent over her. If sleep overtook
him, he was lost in old nightmares, drawn and quartered and nailed to a
post while the snake curled between her legs and then the snake became
the gardener, and the gardener turned leering at him, little forked
tongue whipping in and out, and the gardener-snake ravished her while
he laughed. Only morning released him, he spent his days splitting
logs, bringing the ax over his head, every piece of oak was that damned
cripple's head, he cracked bone, he smashed gristle, he wanted blood, he
had the lust to kill, he raged, he was a volcano, or he despised himself
for a cuckold and spent his days in the horse barn, his nose filled with
stench of manure.

Cunningham shook him. "Can't you face the truth, Peter? Are you
so afraid of the truth?"

He spoke without turning. "You bastards, you knew what was
happening, you only waited until I was out of the way. Is that how you
planned it? Is that how you planned to humble me? I hope you rot in
hell."

"Very pretty," said Cunningham, "very nicely spoken. Is that what
you really think? To humble you we've seduced your wife and daughter. Well, who is the seducer here? Who is the deceiver? Who's been
cuckolded here? Why did you come? To embrace us or was it to seduce
our wives and daughters, because you've had your share of those . . ."

He threw off the covers and sat up, his fists clenched. "Damn you!"

"You seduced my wife and Sewall's wife and Martin's wife. They're our wives, only you didn't do it when we were gone, you did it under our eyes, with a handshake and a backslap. You took our wives and daughters in lust not love, and you intended always to keep your wife and daughter from us."

"My wife was innocent! She never intended to sleep with any other man! You *knew* that! Who worked on her? How did you do it? With Scripture? Or did Sarah use her little *persuasions?*"

"Then you never loved Katherine, nor Deirdre. They were only your possessions, no different from your horse. Your horse could stand hungry or dying of thirst, no other man could tend it, only you and in your own good time."

"I did love Katherine, I can't bear to look at her now."

"I shouldn't wonder," Cunningham said, "because she's happy now. And how could you bear to see that, since someone else made her happy and not you."

He covered his eyes with his hands, he pressed his hands into his eyes. "It was for me . . . for me . . ."

"And your daughter, your sweet Deirdre, can you not bear to look at her also? She came to Amos of her own volition. . . ."

"*What* volition? She was only a child, she came to Amos for guidance and advice in my absence, didn't he realize that?"

"And if Deirdre had been in the city and gone to another man, which might well have happened, and if she'd been truly ravished and perhaps left with a child, what then? Would you have turned your back on her as you've done now and left her on the streets for another man in his lust to use her? You don't understand that we love Katherine, Amos and I and Martin and all the others. We *love* her, we want to see a look of pleasure in her eyes, we cherish Deirdre, she's protected by us. Do you understand a word of what we're saying?"

His heart was pierced. It spilled blood.

"And what of God?" Newhouse asked. "Did you ask God to give you understanding?"

"God! My wife is used, my daughter ravished and you're asking me to speak to God about it? If I ever believed in God, I give it up now. So you see, I can't quite view this from your eyes."

"No, you can't," said Cunningham. "I told you when you first came, on that first day, this is a hard philosophy. You didn't listen. You've been betrayed by a man whose only crime was to make your wife happy, and in your rage you're ready to kill. Blood. Lust. That's the world I came from. You said you wanted a haven here. And you took all our wives and daughters and withheld your own. Get out, Peter. This isn't the place for you. Take your family back to New York. But if you do, you'd best learn to deal with them because we've set them free, and if you want to cage them again, I suppose you'll have to catch them."

"I'm gone away for to stay a little while
But I'm coming back if I go ten thousand miles,
Oh, who will tie my shoes, and who will glove my hand,
And who will kiss my ruby lips . . ."

Deirdre stood alone center stage, her eyes closed, her arms about herself, letting the sound of her loneliness fill the corners and the arches, the faces on the ceiling frescoes looked down, understanding her sorrow. She sang on, even when the music stopped.

5"The rocks may melt and the sea may burn,
If I never more return,
Don't you see the lonesome little dove
Mourning for his own true love,
So why not me for mine . . ."

Then she saw Adam look up from the piano, watching her with those awful soulful eyes. "What are you staring at? Why don't you play?"

He rose from his seat and came to her side and tried to put arms around her but she averted her face from his lips. He sought them out, but she kept her mouth tight and unyielding. "Why?" he begged her. "I don't want you to be unhappy. Let me come to you now. Let me love you, properly, with my whole heart."

"No."

"Please don't act this way."

She tossed it off. "What way? Oh, don't think about it, I'm not." She pulled out of his arms. "I don't feel like singing anymore."

"Deirdre, I love you. Don't harden yourself against my feelings. What was it all for, if not for us?"

She made a sour face, she tried to find a sharp and biting answer, but her heart was bitter, little wounding phrases came to her lips but wouldn't pass through, so in the end she simply walked out of the room.

"Deirdre!" But Deirdre barely looked up and then, seeing Katherine, moved deftly around her and down the steps without acknowledging her at all. She turned and followed but Deirdre was down the hall and out the door. From the doorway she called, "Wait for me!"

Deirdre kept walking, but she turned a little, giving that stagy shake of the head. "I can't! I have something to do!"

"I want to talk with you!"

"Well, I'm very busy now."

Katherine caught her by the shoulder and spun her around. "I said *talk* to me."

"What about?" Deirdre had come back to that old familiar dramatically bored voice of hers. "What have we got to say to each other?"

"I want to help you, don't cut me out of this."

"What can you possibly say to me?" Her voice was soggy with irony. "You live in clouds, oh, do just leave me alone."

But Katherine had her sharply by the arm, without caring if anyone recognized that there were no soft hearts here. "No, I won't leave you alone, and I don't live in clouds, not anymore, or perhaps you hadn't noticed that."

Deirdre tried to explain. "You don't know anything, you think I'm a child."

"Well, aren't you acting like a child?"

"I mean about Adam, you thought, *Oh, Deirdre, how silly she is, she falls in love with everyone.*"

"And was I wrong? Didn't you?"

Deirdre shook her head, trying to sort it out. "I did . . . that was another time . . . that was a million years ago. I loved Adam and you wouldn't understand that."

"You're quite right, I didn't. But I do now. I spent my whole life lying beside a man and I never conceived of what love could be. But I understand now. I'm lying with another man now and if it's sexual passion you mean, then ask me. Because for the first time in my life my head knows and my body knows very well what that is. And if I belittled your passion for Adam, I beg you to forgive me. And you have been a silly girl, you always were, how could I have known you'd changed."

Deirdre's shoulders sank.

"Any more than you could understand about me, I suppose."

"I did come to you, but you were busy with your little pictures.'

"Don't *say* that to me again! My painting is as important to my life as your music is to yours. What's the law that says a daughter's life is more important, that a mother has to drown herself in fulfilling her daughter's desires and throw away her own!"

Deirdre's eyes were full of bewilderment.

"I haven't slept a night since this happened, I lie awake trying to think how it was my fault. Something has happened to us both, so talk to me now. Don't think *Mother* if you don't want to, just think that I'm a woman who cares about you very much. I have a right to know what's in your heart."

"You and Poppa, you tried so hard to keep things as they were, even here."

"It's too late for that, the veil's been shredded and put aside for both of us. Now talk to me frankly, tell me."

Deirdre's mouth fell open, quivered, tears filled her eyes, Katherine put an arm around her. Others passed and saw them, but faces turned away. Nothing was secret to the women of this Community family, not her sexual passion for Martin, nor his for her, not what Deirdre was feeling now. It was like living in a fishbowl.

She and Deirdre sat together on a bench. Little bits of dry seeds were falling from somewhere, catching in eddies of wind, swirling in the dust, like little voices out of the air coming to scold or counsel her.

"It was terrible," Deirdre said finally. "His body was so dry and withered. I could have died. I saw it all happening, I was afraid to say *no*. He thought he was being so kind, it was awful, he was so carried away. And afterward he asked me if I were happy. I couldn't tell him, that sad old man . . ."

Katherine smoothed her hair, it had gone all curls. "Adams loves you, he knows the sacrifice you've made for him. I suppose you can have Adam now, there's no more harm in it."

Deirdre pulled away. "I've been a child and a fool, I can see that now. But I'm not a fool anymore. It's you and father who are the children. He's skulking around like a wounded bear. He doesn't care a bit what happened to me, he's just ashamed. And if you loved Martin truly, you'd run from this place. It's a mad place; it has no logic in it, not for young people, not for Corinthe and Martha and me. I deserve what happened to me because I've been such a fool. I don't care about Adam anymore, Adam was a dream and now I'm awake. So what more have you to say to me?"

There was no other answer. Martin had mesmerized Katherine. That crippled bastard had some mystical hold over her; there was no other explanation. He wanted to take Martin's neck in his hands and crush the life out of him.

Mesmerized. Taken her when she was in a trance.

No, there was another possibility. And now he caught on to that and held onto it to ride out the maelstrom. *Revenge.* Katherine had taken the perfect revenge against him.

He understood revenge; he hadn't understood Katherine. She had fire, she had a tongue, she had her own passionate nature. And for all those cold years she'd languished in his bed while he went to whores. And how was she to take the perfect revenge? By taking to her bed this poor excuse for a man, knowing how it would gall him.

She was all in all a woman. More beautiful than he'd ever known her. She had flair, she had courage. It had to take courage, didn't it, to lie with this half-man with the crooked foot.

And now he saw the pristine logic of it all. And who was to know if she actually had sexual union with this man?

Who was to say that they didn't simply lie side by side like children, she and that cripple. But that, in Katherine's eyes, that was sin. And now she and Peter were even, sin for sin.

In that way it could be said that their marriage was born again. As to the family bed, he would thank Mary Darcy every night of his life. But it was becoming a bore. There wasn't another woman in the community who could hold a candle to Katherine. And he had to sleep with women he didn't fancy in order to sleep with the ones he did.

So in summation:

If Katherine's only fall was this cripple Martin, it was still to him to bring his wife to passion. And he was ready to do that now.

He rested his case.

As to his daughter, he couldn't bear to think of it. He would wear that scar the rest of his life.

Katherine ran toward the icehouse, Sarah close behind her. "Wait . . . don't be alarmed . . . she's not hurt."

Sarah caught her arm and slowed her. "It was a child's prank. She was playing a game, Snow Princess."

"It's a story her father used to read her. How could it have happened?"

"Who knows with children? The door to the icehouse was propped open, the men were cleaning it, she went inside, with the doll, and the door slammed shut. The men are there by now. She'll have a good chill and a good scare, nothing more."

By the time they reached the icehouse, two men had Rebecca wrapped in a blanket. Her little friend Rachael stood by crying. Katherine reached for the sobbing Rebecca. "Let me have her."

"Come," said Sarah, "don't pet her for something she did that was clearly wrong. She's not hurt. She's not sugar candy. She's a strong little one."

Katherine pushed Sarah away and carried Rebecca off, hugging her and petting her and soothing her. She found an overturned packing box and sat the crying child on her lap and wrapped the blanket tight around her and rocked her until she was warm again.

"It closed," Rebecca sobbed, "the door . . . it closed . . . and the handle was slippery . . . and I couldn't open it . . ."

"Shhh."

". . . and the devils were in there . . . all the humping lumping things . . ."

"Why did you go into the icehouse? What on earth made you do it?"

"She made me, that bad Mathilda."

"But why? It's a terrible cold place. Were you playing a game?"

"The Ice Princess had to be punished."

Katherine kissed the cold forehead. "Punished for what? What had she done?"

"She didn't know," said Rebecca. "But it must have been awful. Her father was so angry."

Katherine rocked and held and soothed. "Her father."

"Yes, her father was angry, everyone was angry and she didn't know why. God must be angry to make everybody act that way."

Sarah stood by, arms crossed, watching. "It was the doll," she said. "Those dolls, they urge the children into heedless spirit. Rebecca knows that. She ought not have been playing with her doll. She was told to put the doll away for a while and to let her heart get closer to Christ."

"I *did* put her away . . . but . . ."

". . . but . . ." said Sarah.

"Please let her be," said Katherine. "What harm is there in a doll? She loves the doll."

"Does she?" Sarah asked. "Let the child speak. Do you love your doll so much that you'd sacrifice your good spirit?"

"I wouldn't!" said Rebecca. "She made me go into the icehouse and the door shut! I . . . I . . ."

Sarah bent beside Rebecca. "You would what, child? Let God speak through you. You're an inspiration for us all. You love that doll and the doll enticed you into a cold place where your heart was almost frozen. You don't want a cold heart."

"I hate my doll!" Rebecca said. "I want a soft heart! I don't want my father to be angry anymore! I'd rather throw my doll into the fire! I'll never play with her anymore!" She pushed the blanket off. "I'm all right. Let me be." Mathilda was in her hands. She held the doll to her and ran back toward the house.

"You were too hard," said Katherine. "There's no harm in a doll. She adores that doll, she's had it forever."

"She's iron, that child. I marvel at her. What she said came out of her own desire. She'd destroy the doll if it meant keeping a good spirit. We need a revival spirit in the children."

"Are you so bent on your mission," said Katherine, "that you'd sacrifice a child's doll to it?"

"You underestimate your daughter. Let me tell you, that one will be a firebrand for God. It's in her. As to my mission, I've sacrificed myself to it, what is a doll more or less, when the salvation of the world is at stake?"

Clothes were carelessly thrown about the room, shifts and dresses, Corinthe must have chosen from theirs, she didn't have the nerve to go to the clothing room and explain that she was running away. "Did she write where she was running *to?*"

Martha held the note close to her. "It's private."

"If you're a Communist nothing is private. Tell me."

"It was Adam. She loved Adam and Adam loves you. And she can't bear it, the sin is too much. Oh, what will she do, Deirdre? She's never been out of the Community. She hasn't any money."

"What a dunce, why didn't she ask me? She can have Adam for all I care. What city was she running to?"

Martha sat down on the bed, holding the note to her. "What do you *mean,* she could have him? I thought you were mad for love, that's why you went to Amos!"

Did she mean it? She didn't know what she meant, not any longer. She had a blank spot where passion used to be. She would never love a man again, never. "I want a career, that's all I want to think about. Why would Corinthe do anything so stupid? Well, she wasn't much of a Communist, was she?"

"Oh, don't say that. She was troubled in her heart. And she always had a rebellious spirit, like Lucinda Umphreyville. She loved that story."

"Lucinda who?"

"It was long ago, during the high tide of the spirit, before Father Noyes found the social system, when the Perfectionists first came into their beliefs. They didn't sleep together then, women were spiritual wives. They thought they could love men in spirit not in body and Lucinda and a friend ran off in the dead of winter, in the snow, to their minister's bed and lay with him all night to prove that nothing could happen if they didn't wish it to."

"Did anything happen?"

"Oh *no!*"

"Did anybody believe them?"

"I don't think so, I think Lucinda went mad from it."

"Well, as long as people thought it, she might as well have been killed for a sheep as a lamb."

"How hard you sound," Martha said.

She felt hard, she'd been hurt so bad, she couldn't bear to let Adam touch her now. "Did you get pleasure . . . I mean . . . do you . . . when you sleep with men?"

"Sometimes I do . . . if it's someone I feel that way about . . . sometimes I do three or four times."

"But with older men?"

Martha didn't answer.

"You must tell, I have no one to ask."

"Not with the older men. But if my heart is right, I have to give them happiness too, don't I? But in my dreams . . ."

Deirdre took her hand. "What in your dreams?"

". . . in my dreams it's only one man and we live in a house all of our own, and that's a sin, I have to root it out. It all goes so well when Father Noyes explains it, but I don't understand why we can't live a good life just two by two. If I were ever to leave here, would men treat me as a slave? Did your father do that to your mother? She certainly seems happier here. I just don't know what to think."

Neither did she. She might go to Paris and be a singer, but her rational mind told her that was a child's dream. What if she wanted a proper marriage? Could she hide that she wasn't a virgin? She didn't want marriage anyway.

Troubled in their thoughts, they tidied up the room and went to tell Sarah that Corinthe had run away.

The noise of the band rolling up and trilling up and fluting up for the great loud flourish filled the big hall. "Don't fret yourself," said Sarah, "she's fine. She had a criticism by the children and now they're having cakes and milk and throwing pillows as if nothing had happened."

On the center stage of the big hall, Mr. Newhouse had set up the table for the weighing of the babies. He hefted up the big kitchen scales. The drum began its martial roll. Annie Lee carried her baby up to the scales, placed the child carefully in. Mr. Newhouse steadied the child with one hand, and adjusted the weights with the other. He bent to read the numbers. He raised his ham of a hand. The drumroll finished. "Arthur Cunningham Esrick has gained six and one-quarter ounces!" The band struck up a tune, the audience applauded, the baby reached up to play with the weights.

"Have you made your peace with Peter yet?"

Katherine was half listening. "It's not likely that he'll ever speak with me again."

"And that doesn't displease you?"

Martin sat near the wall, sometimes watching the stage where it was his job to help with the ceremony when needed, sometimes watching her. "To be frank? No."

"The anger he feels is not uncommon. Men have gone through it before. It's part of the softening process. He'll come around. But it would help him so much if you spoke with him. You have no cause to be angry."

She didn't answer. The second baby was being handed over.

"I have an invitation for you. Mr. Newhouse requests the pleasure of your company in bed."

She was so grateful for the band's roll and flourish, it saved her from embarrassment, and unkindness. Mr. Newhouse cradled the baby in his

great arms, that rugged backwoods face, the way he combed his thinning hair across his head, his trap shop manners. When the audience
settled, she said, "How kind of Mr. Newhouse, please thank him and
tell him I'm forced to decline."

"Are you sure? Mr. Newhouse is a good lover, all the women prize
his visits."

"No, thank you," Katherine said.

"He's a fine man, Katie. You and Martin don't want to provoke
criticism by being too exclusive."

"Oh, Sarah, don't be so officious, it's my privilege to refuse any
man. I didn't go half a lifetime being moved around like a chess piece
only to be moved around again."

"Then you mean to be exclusive and tempt Martin into personal
love."

"I mean that when I receive an invitation that appeals to me, I'll say
so."

"Then I have another, and this time I urge you with all my heart to
accept. The invitation is from Peter. It's not easy to come from his kind
of life to this. He feels he's on the rack, he needs you and we all think it
most loving that you accept, for your sake as well as his."

She saw Peter sitting across the hall watching her. She wanted to
make a soft answer. But the hard-edged word slipped out of her.
"Never." She left Sarah and walked away. She looked for Martin, where
he had been sitting, but he was gone.

The Indians were bringing in the
dried cornhusks which the Community used to remake the beds. Martin helped them to store the sacks in the shed near the orchards.
Katherine raked leaves until they'd finished, she set a fire and stood
back, watching the smoke rise and watching the Indians, their wide-

cheeked faces and their leather skins. She thought she might do some Indian studies.

She waited for Martin, and when he came toward her finally, she gathered him in. He kissed her not on the mouth but on the back of the neck. She felt the magnetism of that kiss moving like electricity down her legs, she felt like falling to the leaves, she wanted to make love in the daylight, she wanted him to make love with her there, shameless . . . no, that was not the word, shameless meant something else. Without shame. The wonder was that her feeling for him was without shame.

He threw a few rakesful of leaves into the fire. "You shouldn't have refused Mr. Newhouse. You'll start a buzz among the old women."

He was teasing her. "And if I accepted?"

"He's a notable lover."

"Sarah said that. I have as notable a lover as I desire."

"There are women who claim he's prodigious."

Or perhaps he wasn't teasing. She tried to look into his face, but he made himself busy with leaves. "Surely you don't seriously expect . . . you're not asking me to play Deirdre's game." His face was smoky, his eyes all the paler. "You know I could never do that."

He walked with her across the fields, leaning on her arm. He turned his face up to the sky as if he were trying to take in the magnetism of the elements, he pointed out cranes in flight, he found a place for them to sit underneath an old chestnut, he lowered himself to the ground with effort, "Do you want to be part of the family, Kate?"

"Not in the sense you mean. I've only loved one man in my life, that man is you. One man is enough."

He plucked some strands of grass. "Peter detests me. His hate makes me cold to the bone. I'd quite forgotten what it's like with men on the outside."

"That's his worry, not yours. If you're cold to the bone, you've got me to warm you."

"It's just that I'm not used to hate anymore. I suppose that this place is like a great hothouse and I'm a hothouse plant. We don't suffer the winds of war or man's contumely. Do you mean to become part of the family, to stay on after Peter leaves? He'll leave sooner or later, or be booted out. You know that."

She felt a flutter of alarm. "How much do you believe in all this?"

He plucked at the grass. "What do you mean by *all this?*"

"I've never asked you, are you religious?"

"In Noyes's sense? Giving my *self* to God? Probably not."

"But in the Communist way; you're a Communist by conviction?"

"I like sharing the work, there's nothing to touch it. I like taking my share, I'm not much at competition, you only had to ask my wife. She said I was a fool in business."

"Then why is it you have to stay? Do you need a hundred wives to make you happy?"

He ran the backs of his fingers across her cheek and then softly over her bosom. "You make me happier than I've been in a lifetime."

"Well then."

"Outside I'd be a man who stole another man's wife."

"Peter and I are nothing anymore, we were finished before we came."

"Not to his eyes."

"I have a contract in my trunk to prove it."

He took her hand, he looked at the lines in her palm, he pressed his hard palm against it. "I'm at home here, do you understand what I mean? I don't know how to deal with the world of men anymore."

She listened carefully to hear what he was saying.

He hit at his crooked ankle. "You know what I'd be in the world outside. I see it in Peter's eyes now. It shrivels me up."

"I never asked you to be something you were not. I love you just as you are are, we're perfect together, you know that as well as I do."

"Yes."

"Then what's the question?"

"The question is . . . what would I be in the world outside?"

It was a more profound question than she realized. She left him pondering it and went back to the house.

Peter had spent the whole after-
noon in the woods with Rebecca hunting mushrooms. She'd taught
him to find the great white "button" close to the ground, she said it
was the *Agraricus campestris,* all the children learned it because you
must find the ring around the stem and the flat umbrella must be pink
and not brown because that was poison. The mushrooms would be
fried in butter with sweet onions and fixed with cream.

When their sacks were filled he said, "Can we talk about Mathilda
now?"

Her eyes were dull to it.

"You don't have to throw your doll into the fire. Nobody says you
must. You made a promise, but I'm taking that promise back from you.
The sin is on my head. Give Mathilda to me and send her back to New
York and have her put away until later."

"The moon's watching us," said Rebecca.

"What do you mean, sweet?"

"The moon, he sees your heart, so you can't take back a promise."
She struggled off his lap. "If anyone sees us, they'll think we're getting
too sticky."

The clearing in the woods was a
buzz of activity, Katherine searched the clusters of children for Rebecca. The whole family was alive with *revival fever,* the wagons had
carted them and the picnic out into the woods, the big ovens had been
set up for the roasting of the potatoes, and the tables covered with linen
and the bread set on and the cider and the pies and the fiddlers tuning
up . . . a celebration for the death of dolls. She wanted Martin . . . she

wanted someone to explain this monstrous thing to her. She saw Peter making his way through the revelers toward her. She had no time for personal anger, this was a problem with the children, and they were tied with bonds of steel where the children were concerned. "Did you find her?"

"She's fine, we've been talking all afternoon. She's made of iron. She won't let me send Mathilda home."

"It's terribly cruel, it's so unlike the family to do this. It's the first time I've felt anything of cruelty in this place."

"Not cruel to their eyes. She's simply giving up Satan's idols for God's grace. They see the choice as good."

"Do you?"

"How could I agree with a voodoo ceremony like this? Katie, I never meant to hurt the children."

"Then why haven't you spoken to Deirdre?"

"What should I say to her? Tell me what. The fault is mine."

She listened to his voice, she heard only sincerity. "I do believe you."

"And I never meant to hurt you either."

"You haven't hurt me. But you do hurt Martin. Please leave him alone."

"Martin can go to hell. I should have come to the Community alone. Cunningham warned me that this was a hard philosophy. I didn't understand. Rebecca's going to take some raveling out when we leave." He tried to take her hand but she kept it to herself. "It's all right between us now, isn't it, Katie? I mean, we've come full circle, you and me. So something good must come of this. We're even, in a way."

"There's no contest between us. Let it go."

"I never imagined you'd flower like this. You're the woman I first met. There was such fire in you then. It's taken the Community to bring it out. So we've profited, if you see it that way."

"Oh, don't go on. I believe you meant well and still do. If you mean well for me, then let me go."

Her words only seemed to ignite him more. "Then I'll have to court you again, won't I? I'll have to woo you again. You need a real man, and you'll have that in me. Katie . . ."

A flash and a roar. The fire had been set.

Rebecca with Mathilda in her arms stood with the other children, poor little victims of a philosophy that had no middle ground. Rebecca caught, Martin caught, herself caught. The only one free was Peter. He moved through all the worlds at his own speed. She wished she had that kind of freedom.

The moon had come out white and clear, the fiddlers struck up a tune, the children danced before the fire, all but Rebecca and Rachael, who clutched their dolls, waiting for doom. She needed Martin so desperately. Where was he? Peter's presence, his physical magnetism, was trying to draw her back into the Katie-of-the-locked-gate body. She felt his presence and his desire palpably. She was grateful that Sarah found her there and put an arm around her so that Peter had to stand aside. "Your Rebecca is a wonder. You ought to be so proud. She's an example to us all of what love can do. The novel writers say so much of passion in their romances. Let them look to us for passion. Passion for truth and passion in God's truest sense."

Passion. Peter's excitement rose with the flames. This was a ritual act. If it was recognition of the sacrifice demanded of Abraham that turned Peter against God, then it was this pagan sacrifice of a doll that turned him against John Humphrey Noyes. Noyes was no more father to him. This single act more than Bannerman's deprecations brought him to his senses.

In a surge of clarity, in the bright flash of the flame, he understood his nature and his relation to the universe. There was no God, there was no devil: *he was free of all guilt at last.* There was only man to fear. Man made war, man put out his greedy fingers for more: man, center of the universe. He was as much his own god as any. And so it was for man himself to construct: a home for his wife and children, a world of ethical kindness; that was heaven enough. He was free to go home now. A surge of energy filled him. *Free to go home! Salvage* was the word. If Deirdre had lost the precious bud needed to make her a good marriage, then her father had to provide dowry enough to make up for the loss. His head was full of ideas already. He would mend his fences, build his own Mansion House of the spirit. With honor, to make his son proud of him. It would be pure joy to court his wife again. The only thorn in his side was the gardener. If Martin had petted her with soft romance, with sweet and gentle lovemaking, if Martin stoked the fire, he would stir the flame. He would give her passion as had never been written in books.

The fiddlers struck up a tune. Newhouse was calling the figures. He had to put his hands on Katherine again, he felt a surge of sexual desire. Where was she? She stood with Martin near a tree, she between Martin and the tree, his arm resting on the tree close to her body. No more. He shoved through the crowd, he stood where Martin could see his face. The man flinched; bastard, coward. Peter moved between them and put his arm about Katherine's waist.

"What are you *doing?*"

"Inviting you to a dance." He didn't wait for a reply, he led her out into the crowd, made their way to the clearing and set her in place and took his place across from her. He saw her turn and search out Martin, he saw the cripple leaning, ineffectual and stiff, against a tree, the music struck up, the first figure was called, the first couple moved into the center, swung around and then danced down the line. The whole family clapped and laughed, the fiddler was wild with revival fever, the music echoed through the trees, the white eye of the moon watched them all, the orange of the fire was on all faces, on Katherine's face, he clapped the time until they were at the front of the line, she moved forward toward him, he moved forward toward her, he took her by the elbow and swung her around, then he took her by the waist and lifted her into the air. The crowd shouted and stamped. She tried to take his hands and push them off. "Let me down." But her words were lost in the music, he spun her around, doing a step in time with the rhythm, he was dizzy with desire, he couldn't let her out of his hands. She hit his hands with her fists. He lowered her to the ground, there was a roar of laughter, he danced her down the line. His blood was up. So was the part of him that desired her.

He looked toward Martin. The gardener had not moved. *Lean there, bastard, watch a man take hold of a woman. . . .*

The dance was over. He was in a sweat. He tried to stay by Katherine's side but the children had lined up before the fire. And Father Noyes called his flock together invoking God into the clearing to see how children could show their love for Him, blessing the children in the name of Christ and St. Paul. There was a silence. His heart was still beating.

If this was the Garden of Eden, then he was Adam, he was the first man, he had not been stirred like this since he was Paulie's age. It was the perfect circle. He had come back to the beginning and fate had given him another chance at life. He raised both hands in the air not in hallelujah, but like a boy suddenly coming to his full manhood.

Deirdre held Rebecca's hand as she walked to the fire. "Please . . ." Deirdre begged, "don't . . . oh, Becca . . ."

"She won't be dead," Rebecca said. "It's just a passing over. The way Miss Molly passed over, you remember, and Miss Sarah said, Oh, what a nice day for Molly to be passing over. She'll go into the fire and God will take her and make her into a real girl and then one day I'll be walking along in the woods . . . you'll see . . ."

"Please, Becca . . . please . . ."

But Rebecca pulled away and took her place in the line of children. Deirdre went to stand with her mother. "I can't bear it," Deirdre said. She covered her face. But she had to look. Poor Becca! Rebecca moved up the steps of the ladder, closer and closer to the fire. Rachael's doll was burning. Rachael stepped back and away and ran to the cluster of children. Boys stood near the bonfire crying, *"Yea!"*

"Oh, Momma, how could they make her do it!"

Rebecca looked down into the fire. You could smell the wax, and the hair, some of it was real. Mathilda twisted in her arms to be set free. One last look at the little rosy smile and the plump carved fingers, and then she lifted Mathilda and threw her in.

She hadn't thrown her far enough! Mathilda landed on the edge of the fire. She wanted to climb down and get her and throw her into the hot heart center but Mathilda's clothes had already caught and burned slowly. Rebecca heard her own mouth scream. The stuffing had caught. Where Mathilda's heart had been there was a bright red flame. She prayed for it to be over now. The features melted slowly, the smile was gone and then the hair caught, the paint curled and bubbled, the porcelain head burst. Her marvelous Mathilda turned into a humping lumping thing.

No, Mathilda was pure and good. Now she was melted down. Now she could go to heaven. Someone tried to pry Rebecca off the stand but she froze there, she had to wait until nothing was left but ashes, and then she turned and ran down and pushed through the crowd and ran toward the trees and the forest. She ran down the road, but not too far to see the lights and hear the music, she ran until she found a little glen and a tree stump to sit on. The horror was so much on her that she felt she couldn't breathe, if she breathed, Mathilda's cries would come out of her mouth, the screaming as the fire burned her . . .

Rebecca saw the edge of calico in the moonlight, somebody . . . some*body* was sitting at a base of a tree, just off the road. It was a girl, she sat there with a shawl around her. Then she heard her name.

"Rebecca . . ."

Mathilda had come back! God had triumphed! She'd thrown her doll into the fire with full faith in God and the doll came back to earth as a real girl. "Mathilda, is that you!"

She ran to where the girl was sitting, huddled and cold, her hair wild, her face black with dirt, her shoes . . . it wasn't Mathilda at all!

"Rebecca, I want to go home. Take me home."

"Corinthe, where have you been? Everyone's been looking for you for the longest time!"

Corinthe was so cold Rebecca hugged her around. "I . . . was afraid to come back . . . I've been in the woods so long . . . I heard the music, I'm so hungry and I've been so alone . . ." Corinthe began to cry, Rebecca was so touched by her crying, poor Corinthe was away and lost, she kissed Corinthe and hugged her and said, "You're home now, let's go to the fire and get warm."

But Corinthe didn't get up. "I'm sick, Rebecca."

"That's only because you went to the city and the devil got you. If you feel sick, just say, *Devil get behind me.* And you'll be well. Are you hungry, do you want me to get you a potato or something?"

Corinthe slumped over and fell out of her arms and lay on the ground. "Corinthe, please get up."

But Corinthe wouldn't move.

Rebecca ran back to the clearing. "Help!" The music was so loud, nobody heard her. She ran right into Paulie's arms. *"Here she is!"* Paulie called.

"Put me down!"

"You're the bravest girl in the world, Becca."

"Oh, something awful has happened!"

"I know but Momma and Poppa are going to set it right."

"You don't understand, it's *Corinthe!*"

Paulie set her down *finally.* "What about Corinthe?"

"She's back there! In the woods!"

"Where? Where did you see her? Tell her to come here!"

"I can't tell her, I can't! She's *dead!*"

The Mansion House should have been asleep for the night, the good watchman making his rounds, but the house was still awake, long past midnight, little whispers and buzzings here and there, footsteps, a small light in the pocket kitchen, the teakettle on, in the library a few hearty souls still into a book, or half dozing in a chair. Something . . . somewhere . . . a ghost was in the house.

Dierdre sat in the visitors' parlor in a shawl although the house was steam-warm in spite of the strong wind which had come up outside. She waited for Adam. Aimlessly she put little double-pictured cards into the stereopticon slide, pictures of Niagara Falls and Wild West Indians, and one terrible picture of devils, someone's idea of little fork-tailed imps. Rebecca adored these slides. Rebecca was forever talking of God and the devil, could Rebecca's devil have come off this slide?

Adam stamped in, fell into a chair. She rushed over to him. "What did Theodore say? What's wrong with Corinthe? Why is she still in the clinic and not back in her room?"

Adam pushed his fingers through his uncombed hair. "She's ill, very ill, he wants to keep her there for a few more days."

"But ill with what? Is it the ague? Did you see her?"

"It's not the ague. She's got diphtheria. That's why he's hiding her in there."

Diphtheria. Diphtheria was death. "Is he . . . a proper doctor? Can he take care of her? Ought there to be a doctor from the city?"

Adam looked ashen. "Theo's a fine doctor. That's the problem. Father Noyes has built him a fine clinic but he won't let him use his medicines. Father Noyes is bent on a faith cure."

"What sort of mumbo jumbo is that? Faith cure? You mean with little prayers and things?"

"We do cure by faith and have for thirty years. People have come to us with crushed arms, from machinery in the city, and all sorts of ailments. I've seen them give up the pain through faith and move dead fingers again. The devil brings illness and there's a devil in the house now."

"You *don't* believe that. You don't believe the devil had anything to do with the dolls and that God wanted the dolls thrown into the fire. You can't believe such a thing."

Adam passed a hand over his eyes as if he were pulling aside a veil. "I do believe. I came back professing my faith and I turned my face away from Corinthe who needed me. I turned against everything I swore to honor. It was my fault that sickness came into the house."

"But that's not so! Corinthe ran off to the city! She didn't take the proper clothes, she didn't eat for days. . . ."

"The devil's in the house. I invited him in. Something has been wrong since I returned. I've asked too many questions. I encouraged Corinthe to rebel. And I can see so clearly now, the old ways were the right ways, the only ways. And because of me, so many will be taken . . ."

"Oh, don't be crazy now. I can't bear it. It was my unkindness that drove her away."

Adam said nothing. He took the palm of her hand, he looked at the lifeline as if he were trying to read it. "I think you were sent to test me. And I failed. And now others have to suffer. You will suffer too, because of me."

"You frighten me when you talk this way."

"You're right to be frightened. You don't have the faith. It's only the faith that will sustain us in the dark night. Your sister's taken ill."

The cornhusk mattress rustled under them as they moved together, as the slow dream-tide swelled in them, as the wave swelled and almost broke, not yet, not yet, Katherine moved, Martin moved, she breathed, he breathed, they touched, lips, tongues, thighs . . . she didn't want the wave to break for her if it could not for him.

He sensed her holding back. He left her and lay breathing deeply, coming back to earth. . . .

"Please speak to me tonight," she said. "I'm afraid of silences."

"I am speaking to you, I have been speaking to you, don't you know that?"

Yes. But she was so full of questions and fears. "There's something in this strange world I don't understand and never will. It's wrong for me to be here, half in and half out. I love you so dearly, what shall I do?"

She waited for an answer. He turned on his side toward her, touched her face. His eyes, which were always windows, now were mirrors. Something was closed. His eyes were full of that bonfire, he was watching Peter holding her in the air, taking possession of her body. She didn't know how to erase that picture except by loving him. "If you believed in the family ways, you'd have forgiven Peter and not resented him. Peter is in your eyes. You're a good man, Martin, but you're not a saint. Come make a life with me, I do love you so."

He didn't answer. Something in him closed up. Something was troubling him deeply.

The knock on the door disturbed the moment. She wished it had not come. They had to sort things out. She started to put on her robe but Martin held her back.

"It may be Peter."

"It may well be. He'll have you back one way or the other."

"Never," she said. "Not in this life."

He pulled on his trousers and opened the door. If it was Peter, she was glad for it. They had to confront each other sooner or later. She waited, she listened. She heard him speak in whispers and then close the door. She knew she was the stronger one now. She called him back to the bed, she drew him down in a fierce embrace but he put her apart. "Don't be frightened," he said. "Trust in God."

Don't be . . .

"Rebecca's been taken ill."

The hand of the devil took hold of her heart and turned it to ice. "That's not possible. I saw her an hour ago."

"It comes on that way."

"Is it the ague, then?"

"It's diphtheria. There's no cure for it but faith. Let yourself go soft, Kate, put yourself in God's hands. And God help me . . ." He kissed both her hands and her mouth. "Remember me."

NINE

City Streets

It is not you alone who know what it is to be evil;
I am he who knew what it was to be evil,
I too knitted the old knot of contrariety,
Blabb'd, blush'd, resented, lied, stole, grudg'd,
Had guile, anger, lust, hot wishes I dared not speak,
Was wayward, vain, greedy, shallow, sly, cowardly, malignant,
The wolf, the snake, the hog, not wanting in me,
The cheating look, the frivolous word, the adulterous wish, not wanting,
Refusals, hates, postponements, meanness, laziness, none of these wanting.

"Crossing Brooklyn Ferry"
(first called "Sun-Down Poem")
Leaves of Grass
Walt Whitman, 1856

My dear Friend:

How I would like to give you courage in these your tormented moments, that delightful child ill to the death with diphtheria. I *cannot* counsel you to come to New York for treatment. This new, this fresh, this promised land which sends from its shores visitors to the Old World has received visitors in turn, lurking in the holds of creaking ships, let loose like rats at the dockside. Typhoid has come to New York. Putrescent typhoid. I tormented myself all these weeks about how to tell Adelaide, my dear heart, about the vile thing that had come on me. But God relieved me of that onerous chore. Adelaide is dead. The typhoid took her. And I am left bereft of a wife, a friend, a congenial spirit, a lover (in the old days). I can't tell you, my friend, how broken I am. Did you see me write *God?* I begin to doubt my own skepticism. I was in the midst of preparing the greatest attack of my life on that Noyes of yours. *Was it God's intervention?* I thought much later: What had Noyes done in reality? He tried to prove that man was not monogamous and was thus created by God, and made a system that rectified that mistake of society. Well, who can argue that, knowing us and our follies? I was blinded by my ego when I lifted a pen against him. And Adelaide was struck down. They put the cups to her to try to take away the fever. She said, *Don't let the leeches bleed me, Bannerman.* I said, *Dear heart, there are no leeches.* And she said, *Don't be a fool, I mean the doctors.* And in the end she said, *Bannerman, I've had good times with you, we've run our course, if I don't go to heaven I'll make the best of it in the other place, and I'll wait for you there, dear, they're bound to set a good table.* Can you believe that of a woman? And I deserted her for whores and got my reward for it. *Mea culpa,* I sit here in Delmonico's, I can't bear the house these days, and know that Noyes is not the worst scoundrel in the world. *Do not bring your sick child to New York.* It's a pestilence. And I, poor fool that I am, alone with an old dog who can scarcely walk. I am broken, Peter, broken. I was thinking of taking my life, dear boy. But how? I wondered if a man can eat himself to death on oysters?

Keep the child there. Let them do their magic over her. All that physicians can do is prognosticate, they cannot cure. If Noyes says he can, he's as true as any. They used the hot cups on her until her skin was burned in terrible circles. She died in my arms.

Death cannot fade nor custom stale her infinite variety. Oh, the loss, Peter, the insufferable loss.   Bannerman

                     The little house was proper enough, not her dream of a white-pillared mansion with porticoes and dormer windows but she had to make the best of it in altered circumstances. Her mother took the back room, poor thing, where she could sit at the lace-curtained window and watch the three red chickens scratch and squawk, and see that the child didn't fall into the mud or get at the good fresh eggs before she could gather them.

The child still looked wan and listless and he was eating a fresh egg a day and cream from the nursery down the road. You could smell the cows but what of that, you couldn't have everything, and this wasn't Five Points with its rats and vermin, was it? The child was still rather slow to her eye and he needed meat and potatoes and she spent hours a day getting him to eat, he was that peckish.

She'd fixed up the front room for herself, she'd papered it in red velvet (which cost her a pretty penny but business was business) and she'd bought a good gown, well, she didn't need two, they rarely come back a second time because she was so careful only to choose sailors who were shipping out with the tide, because they'd take it to foreign places where all the women had it. Her mother sleeping in the back was deaf as a post but she made the room so nice with silk shaded lamps and that sort of thing. Once the child wakened and came into her room and stood by the bed, the poor sailor without his trousers covered his thing with a *doily*, it was a sight, and the child said, "Is this my daddy?" It was so sweet.

And she wasn't sure that the cure *hadn't* taken because she didn't get caught with babies anymore, the doctor had said that the scarring did it, so something may have closed up on her.

Well, it wasn't Miss Josie Woods, it was adjusted expectations, it was life in the city.

She wondered if she hadn't made a big mistake by not going west but then she thought, men are bastards, they aren't going to be different west of the Mississippi. And she'd always have the satisfaction of knowing she gave as good as she got.

"La . . . la . . . la . . ." Bitsie skipped around the little study, she was putting up horse pictures, she was practicing skipping to see if she could without getting out of breath, she could take an entire deep breath without hiccuping, she stopped at the table to take a little sip of her tea and a little bite of her cucumber sandwich and she skipped to the mirror and looked at her self which was melting day by day and she pulled at her bodice and she could find slack so that meant this dress would be burned . . . she burned them all as they got too loose and put on a tight one, she patted her face so that the skin wouldn't sag, "La . . . la . . . la . . ." When she heard the tap on the door, she pulled back at her shoulders, her breasts weren't so prominent now, she had a greater field of vision, she looked down at her dainty feet and skipped to the door.

"Madame . . . I'm bringing in the coffee . . . are you sure . . ."

She took the tray and with a little kick of her heel she walked toward the dining room and let Ida open the double doors, Harry looked up, quite red in the face, la . . . la . . . la . . . and Mr. Tweed like a bull elephant looked up angrily and said, "What the hell is she doing in here!" And she brought in the coffee tray and laid out the cakes on the sideboard. Mr. Tweed was gross, she passed the table where their papers were spread out and she said, "Mr. Tweed, I hear that you're going to run for governor," and Harry said, *"Will you get out of here?"* He didn't say it, he hissed it, and she said, "Mr. Tweed, I read that awful editorial in the *Times*. I know it's a lie." And she turned and walked out and closed the door and out of her pocket she took the little notebook and in her round large hand she wrote *"November 18, 1870,"* and a period. And then she changed the period to exclamation mark. And she put the notebook back in her pocket and then she went to her room and dressed for church, she would go to the Catholic church and light a candle for Rebecca, she didn't think her own church would have anything as definitive as smoke rising in prayer and if she got back to the same weight she had when she married, she was converting anyway. Amen.

TEN

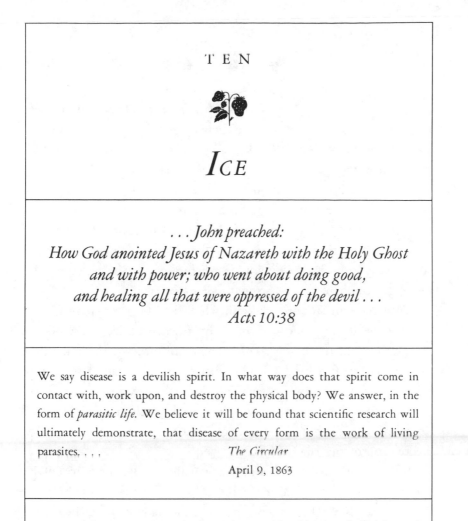

*I*CE

. . . John preached:
How God anointed Jesus of Nazareth with the Holy Ghost
and with power; who went about doing good,
and healing all that were oppressed of the devil . . .
Acts 10:38

We say disease is a devilish spirit. In what way does that spirit come in contact with, work upon, and destroy the physical body? We answer, in the form of *parasitic life.* We believe it will be found that scientific research will ultimately demonstrate, that disease of every form is the work of living parasites. . . .

The Circular
April 9, 1863

. . . we ought not to tolerate in our society a spirit which breeds division and disunion . . . a meddling, interfering busybody . . . a disturber of harmony. *Disease is precisely of this character.* It is the intervention of a foreign substance, breaking up the unity of life. The great difference between God and the devil, between pure, interior life and unclean vampire life, is *that God gives life to everything he touches and the devil sucks and destroys all life he touches.*

The Circular
January 1, 1863

*W*heel of fortune. It rang in his head all night, it was the song of the old rags-and-old-clothes woman who used to sing in St. John's Park. *Round and round the wheel of fortune, where it stops it worries me . . .* He had never been so close to Katherine, the irony that his dying child should have brought them together. *Dying child . . .* the words stung his eyes with tears, he was so helpless, trapped on the *wheel of fortune,* on the rack of fortune. He sat by the hour holding Katherine's hand, she looked like death herself, when he put his arm around her she didn't push him away. She welcomed his strength. But there was no strength against death.

Then the rain stopped, the rain which had been slapping against the windows through most of the night, frost shrouded the windows, the weather had turned very cold. Theodore came in to look at the children. He tried to read Theodore's face, the man hadn't slept in so many days he was himself ashen. Theodore whispered that the ice was very low, could he see what was left in the icehouse? He'd kissed Katherine, put on his coat and boots and he went out to see if the shallow end of the lake had frozen over.

Ice cracked under his boots where little puddles had frozen. He opened the barn door and let in the cold, the horses snorted, one of them nuzzled him. He lit the lamp. The wind had taken off the clouds, the moon was clear, he hardly needed the light. He hitched the wagon and loaded the saw, and let the animal into the predawn.

In the eerie light the horse, tossing his mane, looked like a phantom. He turned into the lake road, the horse knew its way. Phantom horse taking him into the depths of a phantom forest.

He had no one God to talk with, he spoke with older gods, gods of mythology, capricious gods who sent their thunderbolts without reason, at their whim, *wheel of fortune,* that was the game. He was a rationalist. And his reason told him that the wheel would turn and where it stopped, there hung Rebecca's life. Some were taken, some were not. He had as much chance as the next man, he could have led a sordid life or a blameless life, what did it matter to the wheel? It stopped on a number, that was it.

The horse stopped at lakeside, snorted, pawed the ground. The air cleared out his head, he was awake. A man could not put his fate into the hands of a deity that did not exist, he was caught on the *wheel of fortune,* he had his wits, his hands, his heart, he made his own heaven or his own hell. What a man could do was jump down in the just-dawn and test the end of the lake with his boot to see if it had frozen.

The light was just beginning to make the world clear. It was a fairy world, all ice, ice had covered every living thing while he'd sat beside his dying child, every branch, every reed cased in ice, the musical ice clinked in tinkling notes over his head, he raised his hand, ice shattered and fell in showers. He wanted to say, *Look, Rebecca, how wonderful.* He wanted to lead her to little frozen puddles where she could break the ice with the heel of her shoe. He wanted . . .

. . . his child was dying.

He hefted down the saw and hatchet, chopped a hole and began to saw ice. . . .

Katherine sat beside the bed, she dozed, she awakened. Rebecca's breath came so heavy, she wanted to breathe for her child, she found herself breathing in and out, as if to help the poor congested lungs. She put a sliver of ice into Rebecca's mouth, Rebecca mumbled something about the *queen of ice* . . . if ice would only help . . . if anything would help.

She must have dozed. When she woke, Martin was beside her. She was so grateful, she needed him dreadfully. "I would have come sooner," he said, "I didn't want to intrude."

"As if you could. It's terrible to sit here alone and not be able to help her."

"You can help her. You have the power. You're the healer, only ask me. Haven't you healed me?"

He never spoke idly, did he mean it truly? She grasped at any straw. "Do you believe that people can heal? That men and women have such a power?"

"Without a doubt."

"Then show me, tell me how to heal my child."

"Not your child alone, all the children."

He was right, he sensed what was right always, it was in his nature. He shamed her.

"You and I . . . we work with elemental forces . . . we plant, we watch the seasons, who knows better than we do the power of natural things." He went on in this vein, he spoke softly to her, she took him in with more than ears, she soaked him up like a rain after a dry hard season. "When you make pictures, you pull images out of the air and you shape them in your head. That takes energy, it's a kind of power, you know that."

"Yes."

"Then concentrate those forces, draw in the magnetism of the air and the power of the earth, draw it into yourself and then focus it on the children. *Want* it with all your heart, *want* her well."

Yes. He was right in everything. His instincts were right. She closed out everything, even him. She drew in the magnetic forces of the earth and sky. She focused on the earth, on the ground, on the roots pushing through the black earth, on the wind, on the storms, she pulled the electricity out of the sky and into herself. She breathed in. She smelled foul pestilence and turpentine, she cast them away, she sent her thoughts up through the roof to purer air, she filled herself with healing forces, she felt the image of that force in her head, the force that started Rebecca growing inside her, she remembered that growing child, she wished it well, she thought of all the children wheezing in their sickbeds, she drew the sickness out and filled them with good deep breaths and cool heads. She did that until her force waned and she felt faint. She opened her eyes, his were still closed. She touched his arm. He came up out of his own vision.

Rebecca stirred, she opened her sticky eyes. "Hello."

Martin bent over the sickbed, he dipped a cloth in a bowl of water and wrung it out and washed Rebecca's hot face. He put a sliver of ice between her lips. "Hello."

She smiled up at him. "Are you the white rabbit?"

Dierdre took up her courage and knocked at Theo's clinic door. It was a few moments before she heard the *Come in.* She walked in softly, so as not to disturb him. He'd been awake so many nights. He looked awful. Poor Theo, he was nothing like his father. Father Noyes with his patriarchal beard and his constant smile and good spirits and those absolutely childlike eyes. Theo was shorter and bulky, full of alimentiveness, his eyes were red and tired, he had the migraine, he would sometimes squeeze his eyes shut and put his fingertips to his head. She hated to disturb him. "Theo, I want . . . I came to ask . . ."

"Sit down," he said. "How is Adam? How is the madman?"

"He frightens me. Everything frightens me. I don't understand."

"How could you understand coming from the *outside?*"

"I want to know . . . can you cure her? My sister? I mean can you cure *them,* the little ones with that terrible sickness."

"Cure? How? By medicine or by faith?"

"Is there a medicine for diphtheria?"

Theo leaned back in his chair, his vest was unbuttoned, his tie hung open, he looked absolutely gray. "No. For smallpox, now they have a prevention. But for diphtheria? Nothing. Alum and brimstone, there's a canker in the throat, they choke up, they need to vomit, sometimes the physician is forced to cut the throat to let out the poisons."

She swallowed hard, she dared not cry.

"Father says, 'No alum! No brimstone! No throats cut!' He says we're only suffering from the hypo and the devil."

"What nonsense is that?"

"Hypo. Fixing your mind on illness instead of wellness. He wants the smell of turpentine steam out. He wants the windows open. He wants an *indignation meeting* to rout out the devil. He says we've got the devil cornered in the house, and if he wasn't cornered and quailing, the children would be dead by now."

"Do you think that?"

"I found an article in a French journal . . . you keep ice in the throat to keep the canker down. I've been feeding the children ice. That's what's kept the diphtheria at a low level. It's ice, not God. I can't make him understand that. I show him the microscope, so that he can see for himself that it's not the devil but parasites that cause illness. He looks into the thing with wonder, the way he looks into every miracle and he says, *'Ah, animalcula. God's miracle, the microscope. But who sent the parasites! Tell me that! If that isn't the devil's work, I never saw it.'* Do something with a man like that."

"And you don't believe it?"

"Adam and I, we were sent to find answers for ourselves. Adam came back entire, I didn't. But I love my father and he counts on me. I can't make my father see the logic in fox and hens. Fox eats hens, God made the fox *and* the hens, Sewall with his traps kills the fox, no one imputes the hand of the devil to the fox! Well, the little *animalcula* feast on us, they're also part of the natural creation."

"But Adam says you've had a faith cure, you and he both, when you were children."

"Did he tell you that? Yes, we had the whooping cough. Well, that whooping cough was a delight to both of us, let me tell you. Little Communists, sharing everything, toys, room, books, trying not to be sticky on our mothers. Then he and I caught the whooping cough, we were put to bed and pampered and petted and given custards and our own toys, unshared by the uninfected ones. We adored it. We stayed sick long after the cause. And then one day, Father came into the nursery and he held an indignation meeting. You have to see one to believe one. His hands raised in the air. *I have had enough of this whooping cough! Haven't you! Let's get rid of it now!* It was splendid. We were both so shamed by it we jumped up and went out to play in the snow. So much for miracles."

"But my sister . . . will she . . ."

"She holds her own. There's nothing more I can actually do for her. Just the ice. But I know what my father wants of me. He wants to show me that an indignation meeting will rout the devil and make a miracle cure. And with that I'll come back to God. If the children are cured, it may be the ice. Poor Father, he will never let me go."

"But Adam. Does he actually believe all this?"

"Deirdre, my dear girl, take Adam, marry him, get him out of the Community and back to the city. He's possessed by God, he's possessed by my father. Can guilt and desire bring parasites or send them away? My father listens to St. Paul. And Adam, even though he *knows* my father's fallibility, chooses to believe by faith. If anyone brought the devil illness into this house, it is my father. He needed a crusade, if not a children's crusade, then a good *indignation* healing. Too many young people question him. We used to be strong, we struggled in the fields, we slept on hard cots, we ate crusts, it was good for the body. Now we're prospering and we're going soft. That's why he's got all the marching bands. But he won't admit to natural law. No, there's nothing like the grim hand of death to stir up fear of God and that's the truth."

Little rain fingers tapped at the window. "I'm afraid," Deirdre said.

Theodore Noyes slumped back in his chair. "So am I. Not for the same reasons. This is a noble experiment. My father believes, heart and soul. He loves mankind. He believes he inherits the spirit direct from St. Paul. He's made himself a little heaven, and he's afraid he'll lose it for all of us. Heaven is also a trap. And it happens that I love my father. And I'm trapped in it."

Sarah poured Katherine a little elderberry wine. "The trial is yours as well as Rebecca's. You know that."

Katherine let the wine warm her. She had been cold so many nights. Cold with fear. Cold with dread. "I've thought it all over and over and over. I think that part of me always denied my children."

"Ah, that," said Sarah. "But it's human nature to think of yourself first as woman and then as mother. Haven't you learned that from us?"

"I should never have married. I wasn't cut for it. I was all romance, like Deirdre. Reality is too harsh in marriage."

"Then stay with us, Katie. You're natural for us, and your children will be well."

"How? Like Deirdre is well, like Rebecca is well?"

"Rebecca is ill but not dead, Deirdre is herself, no more no less. Better, if you ask me."

"It's not in me to sleep with a score of husbands. I'm not built for it. I love Martin, and that's the end of it."

"And Martin loves you, but he can't love you alone, it would destroy him."

"He loves me now, it doesn't destroy him. How clever you are with words, you love this place so much, not that I blame you, it's a marvel in its own way, but not for me and in the long run not for Martin."

"He's protected here, he's in our orchard. He nurtures the trees, they nurture him."

"Overprotected," Katherine said. "The world is still there outside, one has to deal with it sooner or later."

"You wouldn't say that if you'd seen him when he first came. Have you thought of that?"

"A thousand times."

"Then be practical. Take what you can. Love us all, let Martin love you and then all his wives, and you'll fall into the pattern. Open yourself to the faith, for you as well as for Martin. Take another man to bed. You'll see how easy it comes."

"I wonder about you, Sarah, if you're such a rock as you seem. Are you so sure of everything?"

"I'm sure of this. Your child's life is in God's hands and yours. Come to us. Confess yourself of doubt. Take Martin. Take us. It's more than you had when you came. Rebecca has the faith, let her give it to you. What have you to lose?"

Deirdre sat outside Corinthe's room as her penance. To do errands, or to bring soup, or to write little poems to send in, or to paste up cut flowers, any little thing.

She saw Adam turn the corner and, seeing her, stop. They looked at each other like the most lost Romeo and Juliet of the world. How ruined they both were. And she didn't know why. He'd told her that this new life was the answer to love and it was just as much a conundrum as the other. He should have taken her from the first, what was the harm? They could have been lovers together in the best sense, even if they had to part. They had brought illness to the house. No, it was herself, their family who ought never to have come. This was a different world, they brought in the wrong air, the wrong wind. They had brought the pestilence. She wanted to comfort Adam but she had no way to do it. It was wrong for their eyes to meet this way. It was wrong for her to provoke him in any way. He was meant for Corinthe, who lay at death's door languishing for him. She was shallow or had been. Now she could be better. She lowered her eyes away from his, folded her little portfolio of paper and paste and walked away without saying a word to him.

She walked outside into the gray cold morning. They were the greatest fools in the world. What a most terrible waste of love. They'd got nothing from it and poor Corinthe had to suffer. It wasn't fair.

Adam confessed Christ his sins and knocked on Corinthe's door. Miss Baker was tending her. Sweet Miss Baker who had been mother of the children's house when he was a child. He wished he were back there now, he wished he'd never floundered in his faith but he supposed that *that* was also part of God's design. He wanted to stop the exhaustion of questioning, he wanted to root Deirdre out of his heart, he wanted to lie back in firm belief and be carried in God's hand.

Miss Baker answered his knock. "You again? Get some sleep, child, she hasn't changed."

"Father Noyes, he wants the turpentine out, he wants the room aired, there's to be an indignation meeting."

"About time. This smell is the death of me. There's nothing but the *hypo* in these foul smells. Clean out the room, let me bathe her and bring in fresh air. That will rout the devil."

"Get yourself a cup of tea first, I'll stay with her."

She came out and closed the door. "I don't want you near her, Adam, you're not above taking it yourself."

"I had the diphtheria."

"You have *not!* I've known you since you were in diapers."

"I was six months, mother cured me by faith."

"*Did* she? It was before I came. Isn't that like Sarah, never mentioned it."

"You know Mother."

Indeed she did. "Marvel and an inspiration. I could use a cup of tea, I'll take down the turpentine and bring up fresh ice, it's almost gone."

The kettle was still on the little gas stove, he poured water into a bowl, put some ice water in it to cool it, he dipped in a cloth and washed her face. He put a sliver of ice in her mouth. "Corinthe?"

She was breathing hard, her eyes were almost shut with mucus. She tried to open her eyes, she tried to speak, he saw how she rallied to his voice. The truth was so plain, all debates were vanity. Thank God all the debates were over. He confessed love for Corinthe and Sarah and Amos and for all his other brothers and sisters and fathers and mothers. He blessed the family. He turned back the covers and got in beside her. He turned her toward him and kissed her on the lips.

"It's middle of the night, Sewall. Tooth that bad?"

"Look at it now."

"Been plaguing you for weeks, why didn't you let me take a look at it when I asked?"

"Got the call. Take it when it comes." He opened his mouth wide and turned his face into the gaslight.

Bob Hamilton peered in. "Rotten clear through, could have told you that. You've been wincing with it for a long time."

"Pull it," Sewall said.

"Pull it in the morning."

"Pull it now."

"Got a bottle of the new stuff coming in on tomorrow's Midland train. Pull that tooth you won't even feel it."

"Don't want anything. Just pull the tooth."

"Pure foolishness to stand pain when you don't have to, this isn't the north woods, man."

Newhouse set his jaw, tested it, winced. "Why is it foolish? A little pain is good for the spirit. Builds the spirit the way chopping wood builds the muscles. If you duck the pain here, God will get you with it somewhere else. Might as well face it head on."

Bob Hamilton picked up his pliers. "Well, it's your jaw."

"That's right." Sewall Newhouse confessed Christ a stalwart heart, dedicated this tooth to the sick children, spat out his imaginary plug and opened his mouth.

The ice made her throat feel better, but Rebecca still drifted in a fuzzy place. Once in a while she opened her eyes and she saw Deirdre, or Momma, or Poppa, but she drifted in a place called *sick*. The white rabbit had stopped coming now but she was hot and fitful. Now she opened her eyes and saw that the room was filling up with people, and they were smiling and laughing. *That* was odd. They should be very worried because she was so sick. She reached for a piece of ice. Had Poppa brought ice for her? Did she dream that?

Miss Bertha came to the side of her bed and said, "Sit up, child."

That was *very* odd. You could smell sick in the room. She thought perhaps God was ready to take her to heaven now. Somebody opened the window. Cold air came in. She looked to her mother's face. You couldn't have cold air if you were very sick! But her mother only smiled. Then Father Noyes came through the crowd. He stood over her bed. He raised his hands over his head and called out, "I am tired of this diphtheria!" And everyone shouted, *Yes they were!*

Were they? Well, good heavens, so was she!

"I have had this diphtheria around long enough! Now somebody has invited this diphtheria into the house and it's time we told this guest that his welcome is worn out!"

She was amazed. People didn't joke about a terrible sickness. The cold air was on her. She wanted to cough but she didn't dare.

Father Noyes stood at the foot of her bed and raised his hands for silence. He looked down at her so sternly. "Rebecca, the devil is some-where in this room. It's time you sent the devil away. Now the devil is a parasite. Do you know what he feeds on? Guilty secrets. If there is anything in your heart, any guilty secret, let it out into the daylight. Let it shrivel and die in the light and the devil will starve to death."

She knew what the secret was. The devil knew it too and was eating up her chest, the secret hurt so bad. The whole room became quiet. "I . . ." she choked but she said it out, ". . . I . . . didn't want to burn Mathilda . . . I loved her . . . I talked to her every night . . . I 'fessed Christ I wanted to throw her in the fire, and that was a lie."

The faces in the room became very soft and Father Noyes came and put a hand on her head. "Child, the devil is routed and you are well now."

Was she well? Well, he must know what he was talking about. Everyone smiled as if she were well. Momma was shaking her head *yes*. She was wide awake now. Somebody brought her a shawl and told her she could stand up. She stood up wobbly but a cool breeze had come over her and somebody asked if she was hungry and she was. "I'd like some pudding, please."

And she was told that now she could get a little sleep because she needed to be up soon to do her chores, that all her chores were waiting and she was well and had to get at them.

She ate a spoonful of pudding and then got back into bed. God must have blown His cool breath on her. She was so happy. Mathilda was in heaven now and had forgiven her. She wanted a little sleep, she curled in her blankets, her arm around an angel Mathilda and slept the sweetest sleep.

Katherine was so grateful for Peter's arm supporting her to her room. She had gone numb. When Theodore said that the fever had broken, all feeling left her, she was a rag, she would have fainted, but somewhere in her head was a little ringing sound to warn her that she'd best be in her bed and let her body work it out there.

"Was it the faith that saved her? Was it Father Noyes?"

Peter half-carried her down the corridor. "Theodore says that they took a light case, that the ice had already brought the canker down, but the children were in a torpor of illness and the indignation meeting simply cracked that. In a way it brought them back faster, but it was the ice."

"You brought ice for her in the middle of the night."

"She's my daughter. I would have gone through hell for her."

He opened her door and helped her in. She'd never known her body so unresponsive, her head seemed drained of thought, she thought she might be paralyzed. Peter sat her at the edge of the bed and began to rub her hands. It was an odd old familiarity, she didn't fight him now because she knew how he had suffered, she knew how he must have blamed himself for bringing them there, beyond that, she couldn't think. She was grateful for his strength, he turned back the covers for her and bent to take off her shoes. "Wasn't she funny, Peter, her head was full of *Alice in Wonderland* in her fever dreams and I remembered how you used to read it to her before she went to bed at night." It also came into her head how many times Rebecca had come to her and she'd had a sick headache, her cheeks must have flared with that guilt. Peter reached up to touch her head, to see if she was taking a fever. He sat with her and unbuttoned her sleeves, she felt like a child in her father's house, she remembered as a child getting so tired at a party and her father driving her home in the buggy, she slept with her head in his lap on the seat and when they got home she was so warmly snuggly comfortable she didn't want to raise herself to go into the house and so he carried her and undressed her and put her to bed. So it was now.

Peter unbuttoned her bodice and the buttons of her sleeves. "I can manage now. But I couldn't have got through the night without you." To her amazement he began to cry, face in his hands, he lay back on her bed and let out his feelings. All through the hard nights he'd sat ice-faced, grim, never a tear when Rebecca choked and gagged, and then he went to cut the ice. Now his child was safe and the numbness and reserve had broken. This was a tenderness she'd never seen.

"Let me stay awhile."

The thing that had tied them together was broken, she knew that no protest on his part could ever drag her back to Gramercy Park. She knew that she possessed her own body now, he had no claim to it. But she couldn't erase what existed, it was like a painting on the wall you passed from time to time. Could she remain friends with him? The children would be a continuing link between them. He had comforted her sick child and now he wanted comfort. She was beholden to him in that.

As for her body, what was it now? It was hers, she *gave,* no one took, and he was part of the family, he made love in the family way and she was filled with gratitude for the life of her daughter and she would give him a gift in celebration.

The tears were wet on his cheeks. He lay there passive, watching her. All those awful times he'd watched her before, all that sexual madness. She knew that she was part of his distress, it was an equal blame.

She would give him pleasure in the family way. This one time. It would be a relief to know that the silent sexual anger between them was finished.

She unbuttoned the rest of her bodice and let her tunic fall. She unbuttoned her pantaloons and let them fall also.

She wanted this act to be a firm and conscious decision, not to lie back and be taken, but an aggressive act, and there was no harm to it, Peter had mastered the man's part, Sarah had said he did it wonderfully.

So with his eyes on her she took off her underclothing.

"How could you so have changed," he said, marveling.

"I have. You can thank the Community for that. And Martin." She hadn't meant to say his name, but truth was truth. And it severed them forever. *Katie* was gone. She was Kate, who freely gave herself this one time.

He undressed. She saw his body as she could never have seen it through a quailing wife's eyes. Tall and lean and muscular, the long flatness of the belly, the tight muscles of the legs, he moved with a kind of magnetism, a different sort of tension. Where Martin was air and sunlight, Peter was storms and hurricanes.

He made a place for her on the bed beside him. She was curious now, how he would make love different from Martin, now that he was trained in the *family* way.

He seemed so grateful; his hands touched her body, slowly, slowly. Good. Mary Darcy had taught him. She tried to let thoughts out of her head and fall into the rhythm of the sea, which was always good for her.

Peter's hands weren't Martin's hands. They were too stiff, and too fast. They woke her from her water dreams. She couldn't relax. There was a persistence in him that returned, a remembered urgency. She was alert to danger as she always had been with him. She ordered her body to let that feeling go, to give pleasure as Martin had taught her. But his rhythm wasn't her rhythm. He entered her. She tried to slip away from reality. "We'll go home in the spring," Peter said, moving her into the inferior position so that he was above her. She wanted to say no, that she would rather do it differently, but he was on her, in her, carried on his own passion, she tried to move him off, she tried to tell him to stop and do it differently, he moaned in his passion, he moved, the seed exploded in her. . . .

His eyes opened, he was dazed, her own horror reflected in his eyes. "What have you done!" She struck him with her fists, she hit his head and his shoulders and his face. *"What have you done to me!"*

He waited until her blows were spent. "I'm sorry . . . I don't know what happened . . . I was exhausted . . . up all those long nights . . . Katie, I was so happy to be back in your bed."

"Are you mad? I could have a child!"

"We're man and wife. What's the harm in it?"

"Harm! You brought me to a place where this wasn't possible . . . you swore to me . . . you swore . . ." She opened her hand and slapped his face.

He caught her hand and kissed it. "I love you. And I forgive you freely for what you've done. We'll go home in the spring. I swear to you that I'll love you better than I did. And . . . if you should have a child . . . from this . . . reunion, then it will be a sign, won't it, Katie? God's blessing on us. What would be so wrong in that?"

"You goddamn fool," said Theodore. "How could you do a damn fool thing like that?"

Adam smiled up at Theodore from the sickbed. "I've never heard you use that language before. The devil is scared to death because I've challenged him."

"Put the ice in your mouth. Adam, do you hear me?"

"Pray with me," Adam said.

"I'm in a madhouse. When this gets around you'll feel worse than a fool. Wait until Sarah hears."

"Sarah will rejoice for me. You know my mother. I've taken on the devil. It's you who have to carry the family on your back, poor Theo, and you can't do it without faith. I'll survive without the ice and you'll come back to God."

Theodore was wild. "And this is the legacy my father wants to leave me?"

"He'll have you in the end, Theo. You'll be His messenger in spite of yourself. Now get out and let me sleep."

Katherine held Sarah's hands firmly in her own. "You must make Adam take the ice. Do you hear me, Sarah? He's your son, your only son."

"It's Adam's decision. I cannot take his glory from him. And they are all my sons, don't you understand that yet?"

"*Listen* to me! Theodore says that Adam has a heart murmur. Did you know that? His heart won't stand the struggle. He cannot survive unless he takes the ice."

"He only wants to prove his faith. He will live without the ice and bring Theodore to God."

"Oh, no, he's doing this thing to glorify you. I don't want to give you criticism when you're struggling like this, but you must see the truth in yourself. Life is too complicated to bring it to such simple terms. Sarah, you demand so much of everyone . . ."

"No more than I demand of myself. It's not my son's life that hangs in balance, it's the lives of every man and woman. God has His own ways. If Father Noyes believes his successor to be Theodore, then Adam must bring Theodore back to faith. It's so clear."

"Forgive me for saying it but it's not clear," said Katherine. "You think Father Noyes is St. Paul and you are the Virgin Mary, and to that you would sacrifice your own son."

Sarah smiled. "What a clear voice you've become after that pallid woman I brought here so few months ago. Don't you see heaven in that? My son is God's right hand and I am God's handmaiden. This is the coming together of earth and heaven. Christ endured his trial, so will Adam. My son is pure in his faith and he will be sustained."

It was snowing in the small graveyard. A blanket of white, soft as feathers, covered every single thing. The grave was open. Already snow covered the raw cut earth. Sarah stood beside Amos, her face carved in ice. As to the others, they had soft faces. No one was sad. Adam was passing over to God. What a good winter day, someone said, to bury Adam.

Only Theodore looked rumpled and ill. And her mother and father. They were outsiders who didn't feel the glory, and they never would.

Deirdre stood alone. Her childhood was over. She'd learned things she was too young to know. She saw the world in all its sharp configurations. She saw the coffin of a boy she should have slept with and loved, and now would never see again.

The cold earth was shoveled in. The grave was filled. She walked to the edge of Adam's grave and took a little of the cold earth and threw it in. She wanted to give him a token. What? She looked around her. Yes, she knew what token. She walked over to where Corinthe stood and took Corinthe by the hand and led Corinthe to the side of the new-filled grave. And there where Adam could feel her or see her, she kissed Corinthe and put an arm around her. Adam thanked her for it.

What she understood of the world now, she understood as a woman. Oh, someday she would lie with other men, but she would never love a man again, not in the way she loved Adam. And if that made her hard, so be it.

ELEVEN

KNOCK ONCE, KNOCK TWICE

The stupendous achievements of mechanical skill with which we are surrounded; the spread of commercial enterprise, mainly impelled by the engrossing pursuit of material prosperity, the marvelous development of physical and psychological science, the open unbelief of hundreds of philosophers and men of science, who feel themselves constrained to deny altogether the existence of the soul, the semi-scepticism prevalent among the people, thousands of whom, absorbed in cares of the world and deceitfulness of riches, having outgrown ancestral creeds and as yet have elaborated no living faith; these circumstances serve to deepen the interest and attraction of such an inquiry.

"Exposition of Views
Respecting the Modern Spirit
Manifestations"
Adin Ballou, 1853

"No doubt about it, Katie. This is the pregnant season. Biggest crop of babies I'm ever likely to see."

Katherine put her feet over the side of Theodore's examining table, holding the sheet up around herself. Of course she'd known it. It was too pure a thing, too pure a device not to be consummated.

"Was it Martin? If he made a *mistake,* Father will want it for his black book of errors.

It wasn't Martin, it was Peter."

Theodore whistled through his teeth. He sat with his hands folded on his ample belly. "Well, this is the place to have a baby. You'll only keep it until it's weaned, and then you can put it in with the other children. Myself, I'm not that fond of babies."

She set the sheet aside and began to dress. This was one benefit she'd take with her, this lack of self-consciousness of the body. "All these pregnant girls, they agreed to the experiment?"

"They signed articles for it. You know how they take up all my father's enthusiasms. Stirpiculture, *stirpes,* race; *culture,* improvement. Race improvement. Did you know he'd sired seven or eight himself? I mean, I'm such a sterling example of his stud powers, he wants to repeat me. How's that for logic?"

"He has an enthusiasm and fifty-three women sign away the right to choose the fathers of their babies. I found that a very odd way of liberating women."

"Sheer madness. I'll never forgive Adam for hauling me back to all this. I hope he does knock on the table tonight. I'll give him a piece of my mind. Katie . . . if you don't mind my asking . . . was this . . . truly an accident?"

She slipped into her shoes. "Peter simply claimed what he thought was his property. So much for Communism."

"Martin's had a criticism. Did you know that?"

"Yes, I knew it."

"And he's slept with other women, he was shamed into it."

"What's the shame? It's Martin's way of life. I'm the intruder."

"And what of you, Katie?"

What of her. She couldn't think. The only thing alive in her was the child in her belly, and she dared not think of that. She loved Martin, she would never love anyone else.

As to Peter . . . all those years languishing away in front of the fire, that was her way of fighting him. She had always fought for possession of her self. He'd never willingly let her go, she knew that. She was one of his possessions, like a chess piece. He played on her, and when he wanted to stop playing, he put her away in a drawer. As he had by bringing her here. Curiously, she wasn't angry with him. Pure and simple, she would not be played.

Nor was she above revenge.

Deirdre was practicing in front of the mirror in the small parlor when Sarah found her. "I want you with us tonight at the seance. Please don't disappoint us."

"Oh, I don't see whatever good I'll do. I don't believe in spirits."

"I don't care whether you believe or not. You loved Adam, it was such a pure kind of love, if he comes back for anyone, it will be for you."

Deirdre couldn't believe what she'd heard. Love *pure?* Love for *her?* And it cost her a night with Amos, and it had cost Adam dearly. Sarah must have been crazy with grief to come to her like this.

"I could have told him to take the ice, you know." Sarah was disarranged, her eyes were wild, like Lady Macbeth. She frightened Deirdre with her eyes.

"He was a grown man," Deirdre said. "It was his choice."

"No, he had no choice. His life was predestined by mine. He respected and loved me. He knew that if he took the ice, he would have made my life a lie. I dream of him at night. He calls me. I must know . . . I have to know if he forgives me."

It was awful to see Sarah like this.

"All my life I've believed in John Noyes, and now he chooses Theodore, who is not worthy. Please, you must sit in with us tonight. Bring Adam back. Bring Theodore back his faith. Adam can't have died for nothing. If the Community falls apart, what will become of the women?"

"Stay another moment in that position, I almost have it."

"I'm a poor excuse for an artist's model," Martin said. He lay naked on the bed, watching her hands. "You're so sure of yourself these days. With the colors I mean. Your hand hovers, like a bird, searching, searching, and then it goes to the mark."

"And who do I thank for that but you?"

"I have a feeling . . . that you're putting me down so you won't forget me."

She stopped sketching, crayon in hand. She didn't look at him but at the sketchpad. "I don't want to have to forget you. I want to be with you, you know that."

"God help me, I brought four women to happiness, every one was you. Do you hate me for it?"

She started to sketch again. Then she asked quickly, while she could get it out. "Was it because I was carrying Peter's baby?"

His face took on an incredulous look. "Knowing me, how could you think that?" He came over to her, he knelt before her, he buried his face in her skirt, into her stomach. "It was as much mine as his."

"I thought . . . after it happened . . . that I'd go away to New York and have Madame Restell take care of it . . . you know . . . do away with it."

"You couldn't do it, it's not in your nature."

"Why can't we simply go away together, you and me?"

He ran a hand slowly down the length of her leg, and then around her belly, feeling the contours. "What would I be outside?"

He'd said that before. "Exactly what you are here."

He stood up, he walked back to the bed and sat defeated. "What will you be once you're home in the city, in your rich clothes, with your servants, waited on, the grand lady. I'd come by, you'd see a gardener, one of the tradesmen who come to the back entrance."

"And knowing me, how could *you* think that?"

He beckoned for her to come to him, she moved to the bed like a sleepwalker. She began to unbutton her tunic, but he wanted to do it. He undid her slowly, looking at her the way she looked at him, memorizing her shoulders and her collarbone, her neck, her ear. "I've been dreaming . . . I'm home in Gramercy Park and I'm alone and I'm waiting for my wounded soldier and suddenly I hear pebbles at my window, and I see him there, and I run down, and he says, *Come away with me,* and I say *yes,* and he says, *What of your family?* And I say I no longer love my husband but that I must have my children . . ."

He stopped her. She wanted him to speak now, it was time for him to speak. He didn't.

Outside a soft snow was falling, the moon was big, it was a white pregnant moon, and the snow fell soft with the moon behind, the snowflakes stuck to the window. Yes, they breathed the same air. Only with him was she whole, and she would have to go home with Peter and Peter's baby and what would *she* be?

They made love to the falling of the snow. When the time came for him to leave her body, she said, "Don't. Stay inside. *Come* inside. I want your seed on his seed. I want it to be your baby too."

He slipped out of her.

She turned away. It was cruel of her to ask. He hadn't Peter's strength. They lay that way, his arm around her, until Sarah knocked.

"Poor dear Fanny, oh, Fanny, where are you, Fanny? Fanny Conant is dead. I went to Boston for her funeral, Emma Hardinge wanted me there. Without Fanny, Emma carries on the war, against false priests, against false spiritualists, against the 'free lovers' who have taken her as a priestess against her will. Now Fanny Conant is a spirit and she will keep up the battle to wrest the true world of spirits from the hands of 'spoilers' and in the end there will be the glorious marriage of Religion and Science."

"Who is Fanny Conant? Who is Emma Hardinge?"

"Shhh."

Ann Hobart closed all the windows tight. "We must not let in the bad spirits of the night."

"Ann is Theo's lover," Deirdre whispered.

"Shhhh," Katherine whispered.

Ann Hobart had seated Theodore on her right and Sarah on her left. And then Katherine, Martin, and Deirdre. "Theo and Sarah will hold my two hands, so Theo shall know that anything that happens comes from the true spirit. Do you trust me, Theodore?"

"More or less."

"Is there any disbeliever here?" asked Ann Hobart.

"I," said Theodore.

"Yes, we know that," said Ann impatiently, "I mean any other." She waited. The room was heavy with silence and burnt wax. Suddenly the table under them wrenched. Deirdre screamed. Katherine clutched at Martin's hand. He put an arm around her shoulders. She could feel his own body shudder. Across the carpet a candle fell over. Ann jumped up and righted it before it caught the carpet. Another fell over. "Let's be calm," said Ann. "We have a poltergeist. A mischievous spirit."

"Is it Adam?" Sarah's voice cracked with emotion.

"Don't be silly. As if Adam would knock things over. It may be the guide. I'll go to sleep now, and if you hear voices, they shall come from me. Make a circle of hands. Hold tight."

"Have you got her other hand, Sarah?" Theodore was highly distressed. "It may be Adam. this is exactly how he'd behave, the idiot."

"Yes," said Sarah, "yes, I have her other hand. Adam, son, are you with us? Knock one for yes and two for no."

The table knocked once. Katherine grasped Martin's arm, they held each other like frightened children.

"Have you come to speak with us?" asked Ann Hobart.

One knock. The table moved. Sarah moaned.

"Do you have her other hand, dammit!" said a frantic Theodore.

"Firmly in my own. It is my son."

"Are you well and happy?" asked Ann Hobart.

One knock.

"Do you have a message?"

One knock. The table slid a little out of their reach, they had to rearrange the chairs.

"Son, do you blame me? Adam, *do you blame me?*"

Knock . . . knock. Sarah began to cry softly.

"And Theodore . . . do you have a message for him?"

The table slid toward Theodore. He jumped up and turned up the gaslight. "I've had enough of this. Let me out."

"Oh, please," Sarah begged, "he'll leave us."

Ann Hobart, who to Katherine's eye had a thin and spiteful face, seemed filled with the light of truth. "The world of the living and the world of the dead are reconciled. Theodore cannot refute it." She took Sarah's hand. "Your son forgives you. You all heard . . ."

"I'm undone," said Theodore as he ran out of the room.

Ann Hobart led Sarah away to spread the good word.

Katherine sat numbly at the table. Martin looked bewildered.

"And you believe it all," said Deirdre. "Only look at Martin's face. He's swallowed it all. You are so simple. It was me."

"*What* was you?" said Katherine.

"All. I did it all. When Ann was being so deceptive, oh, you are all so gullible, I threw paper balls, see one over there, I knocked over the candle, I pushed the table. You were so keen on seeing Ann's hands, nobody thought to watch mine. I was the one who did the knocking."

"But why! Why such a horrible deception? It's too awful! By now the whole family will think . . ."

"What will they think? Ann is trying to deceive Theodore. Everyone knows why. But she does it for the Community. So nobody sees the truth of it. If you must know, I did it for Sarah who was dying of guilt that Adam had killed himself. Well, he did, you know it as well as I. He killed *himself.* And we're to blame, you and I and Poppa. So I lied, and now Sarah is happy and Theo will become father to the Community and maybe I've mended some of the damage we've done."

It was true. Katherine's hand was on Martin's arm. "Oh yes, we have done."

"We brought in the *outside* and you can't mix worlds, any more than you can mix the world of spirits and the world of men. Adam and I could have been happy. We loved each other, we loved music, we could have made a happy marriage. But he lived in a world so different, you brought us together only to keep us apart." She looked with scorn at Katherine and Martin. "And the two of you . . . you love each other so much and what does Martin do? He goes to other women. You can knock on his world as hard as you can, Momma, but you won't get in. Don't you know that? You said I knew so little. It's you who are the children. People deceive you and you take it calmly. Look at what father did to you. Pregnant at your age, and you go right on with your little courtesies and your little philosophies and don't even do a thing about it!"

Deirdre walked out of the room.

Martin hadn't said a word; he looked stunned, more stunned than by any poltergeists. The room was full of spirits, the spirit of his presence, of her love, of his love, of his fears, her confusion.

She and Martin walked the corridors in silence. "We must speak," Katherine said. "What we have between us is stronger than a failed marriage and your groves of trees. I won't lose you the way she lost

Adam. You can't refute what you've found with me and I with you. There must be a way. . . ."

He shook his head, he couldn't speak, not there, not now. He kissed her and left her at her door.

Peter Berger was a survivor. In whatever perilous ocean he found himself, he floundered and then searched for a spar on which to float until he had his solid footing again.

He had learned about the pregnancy from Sarah, not from Katherine. Fate had its own mysterious ways. It had not been his intention to make her pregnant. But he knew he would get her away from here in no other way. What he had learned of loving had rescued him from a life of despair. The agonies of the past could be let go. He had learned that love was a gentle thing between two people. He also knew, after much trial and error, that there was no woman in the Community to touch his own wife and he wanted her back more than anything in his life. They were even now, sin for sin. It was time to begin again.

He'd posted a letter to Bannerman to arrange for the tenants to vacate. He wanted to go home as soon as he could. Even as early as March.

He knocked on Katherine's door. He had to break the ice. Lord, it would take him to March to get through her wall of anger. He'd find her the best nurse in New York. She needn't be tied to a baby. She could go back to her little pictures, he would never deny her that.

She opened the door a crack. He waited to see her angry face, but she wasn't angry. "Katie, I want to talk with you." No, that was too demanding. "Katie, please *let* me talk to you." A more conciliatory tone. She kept a hand on the door and waited. "As things have worked out, I think . . . it's best that we go home in the spring."

Her hand went to her stomach. "As things have worked out, you may be right."

"Then let me come in now." He wanted her in his arms again. There was no harm in lovemaking in the old way now. The horse was out of the barn.

"But until spring," she said, "it's only right that we live the Community life in the best way we can. Don't you think so?"

He pressed against the door, he wanted her. "Of course I do. I mean to do the same. Let me talk to you now."

"In the morning. I have a guest."

Guest. So that was it. She would go home with him in the spring, but for the pregnancy, she would make him pay. Martin was in there with her. He wanted to push into the room and haul that damn cripple out of her bed and thrash him. But reality was reality. It was blow for blow. He had brought her here, she submitted, he'd made her pregnant, she had no voice in that, so she'd make him suffer until spring with Martin in her bed.

In a way he admired her spunk. He would survive until spring, although for the life of him he couldn't understand what she saw in the bastard.

"Good-night, Peter."

His curiosity overwhelmed him. He pushed slightly on the door only to see how a man would behave observed in a wife's bedroom by a husband.

She yielded the door and stood back. Sitting on her bed with the covers drawn up about him was Sewall Newhouse. She closed the door to a crack. "The next time you come without invitation, knock twice. If I don't answer, please assume I'm occupied. As for the rest, we'll discuss it in the spring."

TWELVE

COMPROMISES

If two lie together, then they have heat;
but how can one be warm alone?
Ecclesiastes 4:11

I am an advocate of women's rights, but my ideas of her rights are peculiar perhaps. The grand rights I ask for women is to love the men and to be loved by them. It is but a cold and dismal right, in my opinion, to be allowed to vote, and to acquire and hold property. I want a right of the most intimate partnership with man, not in politics particularly, but in his business, in his studies and his pleasures, and in the occupation of his whole time. I would rather be tyrannized over by him, than to be *independent* of him, and I would rather have no *rights* than be separate.

Oneida Circular
January 23, 1858

Bella couldn't bear the house, now that there was death in it. Just when she'd got it furnished so nice with a maroon velvet sofa and lovely silk lamps and then everything terrible happened, the poor child took consumption and died, just like that, whimpering in her arms. She ran to her parish church for comfort, well, she hadn't been around *there* much because the neighborhood was talking, women being what they were, but God was open to everyone, *let them cast the first stones* and all that, but the bastard priest wouldn't let her bury her innocent child, and she had to go far out in the country with a veil on her face and swear her husband died in Antietam before they'd give a tiny corner under an elm to the poor dead thing and Bella knew that the tree roots would go right through the coffin. She'd bought him a wonderful stone, though, with three angels hovering over his dear head and she wrote the inscription herself: *Here lies Anthony Gluck, who lived a little while and ran out of luck.*

It was her luck had run out. She cried all the night and in the morning when she went to give her poor old mother a cup of tea, there *she* was, lying open-eyed on the bed, her teeth were out, her terrible open mouth gaping.

And that wasn't the worst. She had the house in mourning, black velvet on the mirrors, she was so afraid she'd look in it and see their faces coming out of the *other world,* she cried so much she thought she had no tears left in her.

And then on her doorstep the letter from a sailor's wife, she didn't even remember which one he was, but it was a straw that broke a camel's back.

"I don't know what you call yourself I know what Id call you, I want this letter on your conscense for the rest of your life, my husband came to visit you the night before we got married well

Im not forgiving him for that but Im not blaming him nether men being what they are, but you gave him a disease and he gave it to me on our weding night and my life is runed thanks to you, I don't understand women like you, your dirty life not caring about family and home only your own dirty habits, and I hope you never sleep another night knowing what you done to me and mine. Yours truly."

She read the letter a hundred times, tears of shame and regret, what tears were left in her, and in the end she knew she'd been dealt a mortal blow. Everything that happened since the night she'd slept in that wagon with the butcher's boy had been a punishment on her, all she wanted was a bit of warmth and hugging and now her life was destroyed, even God didn't want her child buried, what more could she say.

It was a ceremony, like. She laid out her best clothes. Her good underwear, her best corset, her new calf-hugger shoes, her silk waist and her velvet skirt with the braid and all the buttons. She'd put a picture of the child in a gold locket around her neck and in her pocket was a note that she was sorry for all the evil she'd done in the world, she put on a velvet evening jacket, it was fearfully cold, and she set out to drown herself in the pond.

Only she realized the pond was frozen over so she caught an omnibus into the city and then headed generally toward the ocean, she would lay her coat on the sand with the note and the locket, she supposed the waves would carry her body all the way to China and she wanted the coat and the locket and the note to be her testament, she caught the bus down into the city and the Fourth Street line down to Madison, it was cold and clear, it was Saturday afternoon and everyone had just got paid, people around her looked happy and excited, ready for a big night and her life was over, she wanted them to see her sad eyes and shed a tear for her, but people being what they were, selfish, cruel and all that, oh the priest who said he was a man of God and turned her little Tony away from the sweet white-fenced church where she could visit him every day and tend his grave, he was probably even now pierced by the roots of that old tree, up and down Third Street she saw those Wall Street types and ladies from up over Fourteenth Street looking for bargains, oh she knew them, with their families and their husbands who came home and handed over the paychecks and brought them flowers, oh oh it wasn't fair the way things happened in life. She got back on a Third Street car and went into the Bowery, she'd have her last little bit of life and then find a place on the sand to make her last good-byes and walk into the cold and permanent sea. The cars were crowded, men hanging on the outside like bees on a hive, and then she saw the grimy mechanics and workmen and shopgirls and the girls from the factories, they looked tired, but at least they had honest money in their pockets, she could have done that, on Saturday if you had ten dollars in your pocket you were rich as Astor weren't you, well he made ten dollars a minute they said and it was the same ten dollars. And for so brief a time she'd had fortunes in her hands and God had taken that away too. She got off at the Bowery stop, at least here there was some life, you wouldn't know it was America from the look of things, all the signs were in German and the paper boys were selling German papers, you could smell the lager, or some of the names were in French, she recognized French because she'd had to learn some words to accommodate the French gentlemen like *foutre* or something like that, she walked along the tenement houses, well some of them lived ten in a room, she'd never had to do that, thank God for it, and now the little house with the velvet sofa, who could get that? she wondered. Squatters probably, putting their dirty oily heads on her antimacassars which she'd made with her own hand, she was that good at handwork, now all the sidewalks were little shops and stands, you could buy anything here, and cheap, the signs said so, books and furniture and hardware, she watched a family of Israelites, she didn't like to call them *Jews* the way some people did, she knew men from the skin and they were all alike, no pot could call a kettle black, not in her business, well they'd made themselves a respectable business hadn't they, and the father and the mother, how they stayed close together, their eyes roaming for pickpockets and thieves well there were enough of those weren't there in this filthy world, as if she didn't want what every woman wanted, a husband to lie beside and children, she read all the sweet stories in *Harper's* about love and passion and nobility, she loved the noble women best, who lost their lovers in the war and then when they had a chance to marry again, they refused and went into service for the returning soldiers and then one day they came across another man, an enemy soldier, and in his pocket was a letter for her from her dead lover and she swore to give her life to service and so she got old in her nobility, the story was called "The Great Price" and Bella had cried over it. The Bowery Theatre was lighting up, they were doing *The Red Robber of the Blue Hills,* she hadn't been to the theater for so long and now she never would again, being caught in her lonely watery grave, there weren't any Bowery Boys around anymore, except once or twice she thought she saw a couple of Chatham Square Comanches from over on Division Street, thank God she'd never had to stoop to taking one of those. She walked past the Tompkins Market where German families were buying their liver and bologna sausage, the stout wives and all the little fat children, she'd never got Anthony to put on that kind of weight, maybe it was the judgment of God because of the way Anthony was made, just a quick in and out before she'd even realized it, she could have laid there with her legs up until it caught proper if she was thinking of babies but she didn't even know then how they were made! To think she could have been one of those wives going home to a lighted house and a warm food-smelling kitchen and a husband to come up behind her and kiss her on the neck, oh oh, she had to have a drink, a glass of wine, she couldn't faint on the sidewalk, she couldn't just die of despair there, they'd just steal her clothes and her locket and there wouldn't be any ritual about it, she walked into the Atlantic Garden which was just filling up with the families out for a night on the town, it was a grand place actually, even for her who was used to Josie Woods's kind of life, the great high-ceilinged room two stories high with pictures on the ceiling and tables on each side and against one carved and paneled wall the platform where the band played, it was smoky and warm with lager smell, she loosened her cloak and took a table by herself, she needed something badly, the German waiter came over eying her because she was without an escort, she wished with all her heart she'd had a husband on her arm, sitting her down and putting in an order for her, she asked for whiskey and he said as if she were crazy *they didn't have no whiskey* just Rhine wine and lager and she wasn't going to stoop to German beer so she ordered a glass of wine and listened to the music. They were singing something patriotic and she wished they'd play a dance tune, and she got so warm from the wine she had to unbutton her collar, and finally a man sat down, he wasn't German he was French, he asked her if she was alone, she didn't want to talk to him this being her last night on earth she wanted to be alone with her thoughts, but the way men were they wouldn't take *no* for an answer.

She had a few glasses of wine, he was just over from a long sea voyage with a terrible captain and she'd just read about Pitcairns Island and the *Mutiny on the Bounty* in the *Harper's* and she was interested in life on a ship like that, and as they were drinking and talking and the music was playing she began to think about things in another light.

It was the butcher boy who did her in, she never knew she was sinning so how was that a sin? And going to Josie's, she had no choice did she, she had to eat and feed her mother, the factory girls didn't earn a living most of them were out in Five Points, thank God she'd never sank that low, and who told the sailor to come to her on his wedding night, the pig, why couldn't he save it up for his wife if he was that good, and the wife, a virgin who got took by her husband on the wedding night, likely story, half the girls in New York had the sickness, she'd probably been glad he had it because it covered up her own problems and she wrote the letter to prove her innocence to her husband and tried to pin it on Bella, who never did a harmful thing in her life but survive.

And she was going to drown herself. Not likely.

She loved life too much.

Poor women, they were trapped, no doubt of it. She didn't want to get married, those fat German women stuck in the kitchen cooking sausages for husbands who probably beat them half the time, but you longed for the sweet touch of a man's hand, you couldn't get along without that, could you, and in her business she could lie so sweetly and take the pleasure of it, some of the time anyway, they had you coming and going, men did, you couldn't live with them, the pigs, and still you couldn't live without them, and when he asked her if he could come home with her, he'd bring a bottle of wine and some cakes from the shops, she couldn't bear to go home alone and he was a good sort, she'd look him over good and make sure he had it himself before she let him do anything, if only he could understand her heart, if only he'd talk the way they talked in *Harper's* stories, *Oh my dearest, let me lie beside you and stroke your hair* or something like that, just the touch of someone to make her night sweet, she didn't care, she'd be with someone at least, and as for tomorrow, well it was almost the new year and who knew what would happen, she'd had her run of bad luck she was due for better, he kissed her cheek and she took his arm and they went out on the cold bright laughing Bowery Streets, well life was a compromise for women, wasn't it?

While they were waiting for the car she tore up the letter of goodbye and dropped it in a burning trash can and he said she was the prettiest thing he'd ever seen, and that was something.

Bitsie felt the groom's hands on her waist as he helped her up onto her horse. He didn't have to keep his hands on her that long but he was taken with her, she knew that, and she felt the thrill of being a woman again. Harry was struggling to get up on the horse himself, he was half frantic trying to talk with her but she'd promised herself a ride in Central Park if the snow cleared, it was clean and cold, she knew that her cheeks were red, she'd been brushing out her hair a hundred strokes at night and the life was coming back into it and her hands and dainty feet, now she stopped to look in every mirror she passed, she couldn't believe it was herself.

"Bitsie, wait for me."

The groom helped her into the saddle, she had on a tight bodice, she wished she didn't have to ride sidesaddle, when she was a girl in Virginia she used to put on boy's pants and take the fences. The groom was so handsome, a dark Italian boy and he got up on his horse to lead her down to the main paths and he leaned over and whispered, *"Is that your father back there?"*

She started to giggle, she hiccuped, she felt her face flush. When Harry had his horse turned around the other way the boy took up her hand and kissed it, he said he wasn't a groom but a starving actor earning a living and he liked older women, especially beautiful ones with good figures and would she have a drink with him some night?

She hit the horse with her crop and took off down the path, she heard Harry behind her begging her to wait for him!

She rode with the wind, the cold sweet air in her face. If Katherine could see her.

She knew enough to put Harry into jail for a hundred years. She knew about the whole scheme to widen Broadway and she knew about the water scheme and she knew what Harry got from it. And she could have the house and the money and the young Italian boy.

On the other hand, she wasn't bohemian like Moira, she liked her parties, even if she didn't eat at them and she liked her clothes; now that she was thin again her closets were stuffed, she'd just bought an evening jacket in Chinese silk, a great loose sack down her back done in the finest embroidery and tassels hanging down and she wanted to go to the opera even though she hated the music and you had to have a husband for that.

She reined in the horse and cantered until old Harry came puffing and panting to her side. "What did that oily wop say to you?"

She noted how the men passing rose up in their stirrups and touched a hat to her. "Nothing, he said I was natural on a horse."

She was pleased to see how worried Harry was, twice he'd tried something with her in bed and twice she said what a migraine she had but since all the fat had melted off her she didn't have migraines.

"Let's get off these damn horses and go to lunch."

She hit the horse with her crop and they galloped ahead, the day was so fine, yes, she wanted to have lunch and let all the gentlemen bow to her on Harry's arm, maybe she'd save Harry after all, so that she could have her dinners and her opera and she might still have the Italian boy, Moira would show her how to do it, well, Katherine could live in that place and peel potatoes and spend her evenings reading Bible chapters and verses with God-this and God-that and still sleep with other men, so why couldn't she?

A woman's life was nothing clear, it was complicated, it was all compromises; as long as you didn't eat you were all right.

On the other hand, she might still tell on Harry and get her picture drawn in all the papers. She still might do that.

Berthe folded Deirdre's letter and laid it on the breakfast tray. Her toast was cold, the egg . . . she couldn't bear food, she couldn't bear anything in fact. Her life was over. (Hector, are you satisfied?) No word from Peter, that was a vain dream, and Deirdre proposing to go to Paris with Moira. Was Katherine mad? They were fighting in Paris, the Germans were in the city, didn't anyone read the papers? And Katherine, the irony of it all. Katherine was living the libertine's life and with God's grace. Perhaps she'd been wrong, perhaps Katherine knew something she didn't. Life here in the city without a husband was nothing. She went out into company with her new widow's face, with her whole new wardrobe, and no men looked her way. Well, she wasn't all that keen on marriage, but in fact she missed a man around the house. Even a man to scold at. Someone. It was a natural thing to have a man's presence. Sometimes, God help her, she turned in the night and reached for Hector. She hadn't slept well, she had the servants keep all the gaslights lit, so that she wouldn't be a specter walking a dark house. She couldn't even dream of Peter anymore, she detested him now. She'd been a fool, not knowing when she was well off. And now she had that pain in her breast, she was going to see Dr. Hammond again, if it was her heart that would be the greatest irony.

She heard the commotion downstairs, the heavy boots on the steps. Dolores came running in to say that Dr. Hammond was there. "What for? I didn't call him to the house." She had Dolores take up the tray and shake out the bedcovers, she combed her hair and spread it against the pillow and pulled up the sheets.

He burst into the room, his face red from the cold. "My dear lady." He was rather upset about something. Dear God, had he learned something about her heart, some condition he was keeping from her? He dropped his bag on a chair, he closed Dolores out. He was a short heavy man, double chins, heavy jowls, his thin hair combed across the shiny top of his head, but he was kindness itself. He was the only one these days who cared whether she lived or died.

"What is it?" she begged him. "What's wrong? Is it my heart, it's had the stitch again, I took the powders but they only gave me gas. Please tell me before I faint."

He sat heavily on the side of her bed, he took her hands in his but his hands were cold, he drew them back, warmed them between his fat calves, blew on them, and then took her hands again. "Dear Berthe, not your heart but mine."

It was a few moments before she came back to herself. The old fool, what was he up to? She lay back in amazement while he disclosed his affection for her, but an affection from afar as long as poor dear departed Hector was alive and now as she came to his office so often, his affection had bloomed to love. She couldn't believe her ears. He was a stout cuddly bear of a man, gentle yes, but for marriage? Not to be considered!

"Dear dear Berthe, hear me out. A woman as lovely as you, it isn't right for her to live alone. All the dangers of a woman by herself, without protection, unescorted, I lie awake thinking of it. Well, you knew my late wife, my Clarinda . . ." And on and on and on. She lay back with a heart of irony, how Hector would have laughed at this. To have left her to another of his sort.

On the other hand, life was full of compromises. Look at what Katherine had done, compromised her life and children and body to make her marriage secure. The thought of another one of these in her bed, it made her queasy. But then she supposed, at his age, he wouldn't be wanting it much. And he had a fine practice, all the women waited months for his appointments, he had a good social standing, and a fine house, by the time he was panting and kissing the backs of her fingers she had figured how they could sell his house and live in hers and invest the money in stocks, they were offering a new issue in first mortgage gold bonds, or the railroad companies connecting New York with the Great Lakes, those canal stocks she'd read about in the *Times,* and she could do worse than to take his name, everyone in New York knew that name, and more than that, she'd have a man about the house again.

She realized he'd stopped and was sweating and waiting for her answer. She'd lost the thread of his discourse, but she could imagine what it had been. She thought with some old tenderness of Katherine, well, Katherine had to make compromises, all women did, you couldn't live with men and you couldn't live without them. "Edmund, you take my breath away. I never dreamed . . . I never imagined."

He tried to get down on his knees but she was afraid he'd split his breeches and she didn't want a ludicrous display, and so she smiled. "I shall consider your kind proposal most seriously."

He was all astonishment. "Then you will give me hope?"

She smiled as coyly as she could under the circumstances. "Well, we shall see."

Later she took her breakfast downstairs in the dining room, she'd need to redecorate the house and get Hector out of it, and she decided to write to Katherine. She couldn't have a wedding without her only living relatives. Over coffee something delicious came to her: Peter was also Edmund's patient. Who in New York society wasn't? Wouldn't it be lovely to have Edmund set up his offices here in the house. And of course being safely married to Edmund of whom Peter was fond, they could all be friends again. She'd be no threat to Peter now. This morning she took a roll and some Damson plum preserves Katie had sent her. How kind fate was, they would soon all be friends again.

She called for writing paper and ink and she dipped in her pen and began: "My dearest sister Katie . . ."

Moira lay back on the pillows, Edgar leaned over to light her small black cigarette. He kissed her hand and settled beside her and went on reading:

> *. . . the smoke of my own breath,*
> *Echoes, ripples, buzz'd whispers, love-root,*
> *silk-thread, crotch and vine,*
> *My respiration and inspiration . . .*

David came in with her cognac and handed one to Edgar and settled down on the other side of her, a pillow under his head. "Crotch and vine . . ."

She watched the smoke curl against the background of the maroon velvet walls, David's apartment was done in the style of the Oriental, with thick Persian carpets and wall hangings, and odalisque things and odors of incense. Very affected, but she was comfortable there. "Crotch and vine," she said. "How many times I read that as if it were a thing outside myself. I have been caught in forms . . ."

"Divine I am inside and out," David continued . . .

> *"and I make holy whatever I touched*
> *or am touch'd from.*
> *The scent of these armpits aroma*
> *finer than prayer . . .*

"Caught in forms," Moira said, "like a prisoner in a mirror, and I can thank Katie that I've broken through . . ."

"In fact," David said, putting down the book of verse, "in *fact,* I've read Noyes's *Berean* and I love it; if they are all angels and wed to one another, where's the objection to sleeping brother and sister together?"

"Surely not," Moira said.

"*Probably* not," Edgar said, "but in theory, yes. If they're all angels, why not father and daughter? They've done a long dissertation on cousins being able to marry, they see no objection to that. I couldn't find a thing written on *pederasts,* however."

She sipped the cognac. "Form. How we do love it in New York. And Katie broke the mirror, what will become of her now coming back to it?"

David closed the book. "Your verse is passable good . . . although not yet Walt Whitman. We'll open the house at Ury . . ."

"Will the Prussians be out of Paris by then, do you think?"

"Ury is outside of Fontainebleau, it's a charming little village, I have a farmhouse and a great garden, the bees from the garden buzz around the dormer windows, you can hear them when the sun hits the windows in the morning. What have we to do with the Prussians? Art transcends war. We'll take the child with us and be her guardians and Moira shall write a novel of passionate freedom."

Moira lay back, the smoke curling, she thought of marbles that children played with, how the curled smoke was trapped in the glass and fixed forever. She'd been smoke trapped in glass, now the glass had shattered. If Walt Whitman could live free, if Katie could live free, then she could. She reached out an arm to Edgar, he kissed her hand. She reached out an arm to David, he kissed her palm. And over her head Edgar and David joined hands.

She was a princess of Babylon.

"I'll start the novel on a ship, I think. A ship pitching and rolling on a turbulent sea."

"*Trite, trite,*" David warned her.

. . . on a pitching and tumultuous sea, and her heroine, wearing only a thin silk shawl about her shoulders, her hair undone in the gale, pitching with the ship. The wind catches the edge of the shawl and drags it down into the churning sea, she sees how the tassels swirl in the foam and then gone. The wind screams out of hell, the tips of the waves reach up like fingers, she droops her head over the rail, she feels the magnetic tug of a cold watery grave . . . no, *watery grave* is inexcusable . . . she feels the magnetic tug of resolution . . . slowly she lets her body move toward the siren calls of the raging water. And then someone touches her arm. The young steward. 'Madame!' She slips down . . . he catches her in his arms . . . she swoons . . .'"

THIRTEEN

*T*IDES

On the admission of any member, all property belonging to him or her, becomes the property of the Association. A record of the estimated amount will be kept, and in case of subsequent withdrawal of the member, the Association, according to its practice heretofore, will refund the property or an equivalent amount. This practice, however, stands on the ground, not of obligation, but of expediency and liberality; and the time and manner of refunding must be trusted to the discretion of the Association. While a person remains a member, his subsistence and education in the Association are held to be just equivalents for his labor; and no accounts are kept between him and the Association, and no claim of wages accrues to him in case of subsequent withdrawal.   Register of the Association

Oneida Community

Think not that I am come to send peace on earth: I
came not to send peace, but a sword. For I am
come to set a man at variance against his father, and
the daughter against her mother . . .
Matthew 10: 34, 35

Ⓘt was an epiphany Katherine was groping for, something as clear and unequivocal as the Community itself. The Mansion House had begun its morning song. Outside on the east lawn the clarinetist was tuning up, the drummer gave two long stirring rolls, calling the family to a bee to turn the vegetable garden just in case winter decided not to return. The first rays of a pale sun shifted shadows and moved them, touching the yellow heads of crocuses. At any moment the tulips might open, given a little encouragement. In the orchard the sap was rising; all the bare stick trees were pregnant.

Why am I leaving to return to the city with a man I don't love?

Behind her eyes Martin blinked at the question.

She had gone over and over her inventory of things she clearly understood to get clutter out of the way.

She knew:

Oneida was a great and marvelous hive; Father Noyes was the king bee. He buzzed; they acted. Even now everything was humming; the feet of children pattered to the dressing rooms; in the kitchen pots were on the boil; bread rose in the great baking ovens; the griddle sizzled waiting for a hundred griddle cakes; in the laundry sheets were folded; in the bag shop bindings were stitched; in the silk room bobbins turned and the rainbow colors turned on their wooden spools; soon the trees would bloom and the peas would bud and flower and the pods would be fat and a bee would be called to shell them. And she would go on that bee with two hundred others of the hive and she'd come back starving for breakfast and she'd have a good laugh watching Sewall Newhouse move in line up to the new revolving table, seeing the pies and the eggs and the cheese move by and then when he found his favorite dish, he'd stop the table with his big thumb; the warm chatter, the easy ways, a kiss from this one, an embrace from that, a gentle flowing energy; the tide came in, the tide went out, so it would be tomorrow and forever.

But in her need for clarity, she had stepped outside that pattern. *The perfect system* was as much a fixed sphere as Gramercy Park, another kind of crystal palace, albeit dedicated to the love of God, not mammon. Exclusive in its own way. The hive hummed *inside,* but she had stepped *outside* and she could never wholly enter that rhythm again.

It was a different pattern she was groping for: the clap of thunder on a dry afternoon, or it could be a tapping at the window, a knock at the door; the thing for which she held her breath. And it would happen and suddenly she'd feel safe again.

All she heard was silence, and out on the quadrangle the clicking of ball against mallet.

And Paulie needed to get back to school. And Deirdre's life needed to be resolved. And she was pregnant.

And she knew something else that she tried to force out of her consciousness, but it kept coming back, like something undigested on the stomach:

Peter had raped her to keep her.

Martin, who loved her, was letting her go.

"As God is my witness," Peter protested, "I have acted with as much honor as I'm capable. I am not the perfect man. I kept back some of my goods from you, yes, because of just such a chance as this. Any prudent man would have done the same. I need something to live on until I rebuild my law practice. But I'm not asking back my full investment. I know well enough what I've gained from being here. I'll thank you all the rest of my life. For the past two months I've pulled together all the legal affairs of the Community, not

only here in Oneida but the Wallingford Community and the Brooklyn branch as well. And my legal services are free to you for the rest of
my life.

"And I swear, moreover, that I won't go back to a life of self-
service. I've decided to fight slavery as a primary evil. I can see what's
happening in the South, all the hard-fought gains, paid in blood, and
now the Klan is hanging and burning our black brothers. I mean to get
involved with the reward given for information about the Klan, I'll
tithe toward it. And in my own field, I know how to use the scalpel of
criticism and I'm going to cut through the sick heart of the law, to
scrape away putrid flesh, I'll bring a name to the law you'll be proud of.
Just tell me I leave with your respect and embrace me this last time."

"So be it," said Amos.

Newhouse sat grim-faced, the same smirk he'd seen on Newhouse's
face when he opened Katherine's door. He swallowed gall and offered
Newhouse a hand. "I have a soft heart. No hard feelings. Let's make a
good parting."

Sewall spat. Not an imaginary spit, a clump of spittle hit the floor.
"I know you," Newhouse said, "I knew you the day you came. You
rich men and your enthusiasms, your love of being topdog. You're
going to fight the system? You're going to make the system honest?
Man, you are the system, you and yours. You game lover! You love to
win, it's all over you. You played at Communism, you took what you
wanted and you're turning tail. What guides you, man? What is your
North Star? I teach poor men how to survive in the wilderness, how to
trap a few pelts and make an honest living. And then I have to teach
them to sell the pelts and deal with the likes of you. And I teach them
they'd better hold onto their hats and balls or they'll lose them both.
You keep yourself above the rest. I know you clear through. I know
you from behind. Well, you can deceive yourself but you don't fool
me." Newhouse got up and walked away.

Only Cunningham stayed behind, holding out to him a warmer
hand. "As God is my witness," said Peter, "I tried."

"Leave God out of it," said Cunningham. "The *witness* is you. The *defendant* is you. The *prosecution* is you. You've sentenced yourself."

"You've seen how much I've tried to throw myself into Community ways. Even if this thing with Katie hadn't happened. Look, it's my responsibility to see that the bills are paid. And suddenly there's no cash to pay them. So I'd go to Noyes, he'd smile me his beatific smile and say, 'God will provide.' And leave me there totally confused with unbalanced books. You can't do business in the clouds like that."

"And did the bills get paid?"

"Well . . . in the last moment . . . it was helter-skelter."

"But to Noyes's eyes God *did* provide. Peter, there's a single issue here and it's not God. It's man. If Darwin is right, if man has evolved, then it's clear he hasn't evolved enough. Give up this competitive spirit, that's what's driving you away. If man can't learn to love his fellow, we might as well give the planet back to the apes."

"I *understand* that, I've *tried* to live it, but I am what has evolved, even with the best intentions. I have desires and angers and jealousies, if a man hurts me I can't turn the other cheek as you do. If I do, he'll come back tomorrow and kill me and mine. This is a little island in the clouds, Arthur, this isn't reality. Reality was that look you saw on Newhouse's face when he spoke to me. It was pure vindictive hate."

"We're Perfection*ists*," said Cunningham, "we're not perfect. Peter, you poor pragmatist. Listen to me. No matter that we're an island, no matter that the enemy is at the battlements and may very well swim the moat and this house come tumbling down. Something has to happen here, now, some change in man's animal nature, and that is the link between ourselves and the *true* survival. If man fights and even if he wins, he goes back to fight another day. Something's happened to me, it can happen to you. Listen to me. Here is a frozen pond. And I tell you from my *experience* that the water under the ice isn't cold, it's warm. Not only warm, but the ultimate warmth the soul hungers for. Trust me and jump in."

"I can't jump in. My eyes *see* ice. I *touch* ice. I *know* what's cold, I have *sensation*. And those are sensations I'll need back out in the world to take care of myself and my family."

"Forget what you perceive. Jump in and live forever or at least begin a new species of man. But you, you skate over the ice, chilled to the bone, you build yourself a little fire and sit hunched over it, warming your hands."

"So I've failed," said Peter. "That's the sentence I'll have to live with. But I'll live with as much honor as I can muster. Can you make them understand that?"

"Them? Do you think because you're turning a back on *them, they'll* turn a back on you? You don't know what manner of men you've been dealing with, you haven't begun to understand. We're in your heart now, run where you will, do what you will, we're working on you. Wait and see. Mark my words. We'll have you back one way or the other."

Cunningham embraced him and called him *brother*.

Paulie sat on the edge of Deirdre's bed, watching her pack some of her old dresses into a traveling bag. "I can't believe we're leaving."

Deirdre could. "I'm only sorry for poor Momma."

"I can't believe how my ideas have changed. My sense of honor, for one thing."

She didn't like any of the dresses anymore. She didn't mind pantaloons, they were so comfortable. But in Paris, well, she'd see what they were wearing, the arty crowd, anyway.

". . . for instance, when I bring fellows home from school and they fall in love with my sister, how will I explain why she's not a virgin?"

Deirdre laughed harder than she'd laughed for months. She threw her arms around Paulie and kissed him. "And when I bring my friends back to New York to visit, how will I explain to them that my handsome brother *is?*"

Katherine packed and repacked her traveling bags because it was a mechanical and mindless thing to do. It kept her from thinking. He had to come. He couldn't allow her to leave his life without a word. Finally the bags were closed and she simply sat, hands in lap, waiting.

Martin opened the door without knocking. "Get your cloak. You're coming with me."

At last. He looked terrible; for the past months he hadn't trimmed his beard, it was blond and soft and scraggly, now he looked more like her monastery monk than ever. "Where are we going?"

He moved ahead of her out of the building, limping as he walked too fast, catching himself on the wall from time to time. "Joppa."

Joppa was the summer cottage on Oneida Lake, a full twelve miles away. Nobody used it in winter. In summer they went on the train. "I've saddled a wagon."

Did he mean to kidnap her?

Thank God, but why had he waited so long? And why Joppa?

He drove like a madman, he careened around sharp turns, once the wheel hit a rock. "Martin, the baby!" She'd never seen him so angry. No, she'd never seen him angry at *all!* Was he bringing her to Joppa to rape her as Peter had done, to claim her in a primitive way? She was ready to go with him, anywhere he wanted to go. It didn't matter where. But with Rebecca. Deirdre was a woman now, Paulie was safe with his father. But she had to have Rebecca.

By the time they reached Joppa they were both wobbly. She waited to be helped down. He didn't. He went to the door and shoved it open. The house had been closed since the first snow. She got down as best she could, she'd been working in the fields, she was no wilting violet.

But she was conscious of the baby. It made her a bit clumsy.

Inside the cottage the rustic furniture was all dust. Martin piled logs on the hearth and set on the kindling. The kindling caught, the fire was set. She drew in a chair to catch the first warmth. He crouched before the fire like some wild creature. "Why are you leaving me?"

"I'm not leaving you, I'm leaving Oneida. That's a different thing."

Still he didn't face her. He looked into the fire. "Do you love me?"

"How can you even ask me the question? You know what we are to each other."

"Then how can you go away?"

"Why have you waited so long to ask? We know each other so well, how is it you haven't understood what I've been saying all winter? I'm not a Communist, and to stay on as if I were, it would be a lie."

"You're a liar now."

She'd never known him like this, using the harsh voice and words of the *outside*. "How am I a liar? You know I'm not."

"You've slept with other men. That was your objection. If you can do that, then you could swallow Communism and stay."

"I only slept with others because you did!"

Now he turned his face up to hers. "It wasn't the *same!*" There was much bitterness in his voice. "I slept with other women because this is my home and it's the custom. You slept with other men out of revenge."

It was true.

"It's not that which hurts me. If only it were revenge against me, but it was revenge against him, against Peter, he was still in your heart. How could you have been with me and still kept so much of him?"

She bent down and took his face in her hands. "And how can you feel such selfish and jealous love and call yourself a Communist? Come away with me. Anywhere. I'm ready to go."

He pulled away from her. "You're lying to me and to yourself. Look in a mirror."

It frightened her to hear him talking that way. "How do I lie?"

"You know that if you stayed, you might find that you didn't love me well enough to make a life of it, and then it would be too late to run back to Peter."

"No! It's the other way! Are you afraid that you might tire of me? Is that why you haven't spoken? If you took me away you'd get bored with me. And you'd be stuck with one wife the rest of your life. *Martin, why haven't you spoken to me before!*" She felt so much anger she could strike him.

He took both her hands and held them. "And if I took you away and you became only a farmer's wife, if you'd begin to long for your servants and your carriages, what then? What would become of me? This has been my home all these years. At least here I know where I am."

She was wild, she was crazy. "Martin, tell me what to do and I'll do it. It's mad for us to separate. I can't make a life here, you know it! I'd never tire of you, never! What do I care for carriages and servants!"

"You say that now because you always knew it was a year and not a life."

The mirror was forced between them, it was an ugly mirror, a circus mirror, distorting and mocking. "Let me go home and put my life in order. Let me show you how little I care for servants and carriages. And then come for me. What will my life be without you, what!"

"Ha, you have a higher opinion of me than I do." He hugged his crooked foot. "I haven't the courage of a fish or I'd have thrown you over my shoulder and escaped with you before now. Once you have the baby, once you're home with him, you'll never leave. To the victor goes the spoils."

It was incredible. "Why are we talking like this? We're talking like married people on the *outside*. We know better, you and I. We know what loving is. How can we be so unkind to each other? Martin, think. What shall we do? And why have you waited *all these months* to talk to me!"

"I thought . . . we didn't need to speak. I thought there was something so magnetic between us . . . I thought we understood without words."

"You were sure I'd stay?"

"Yes . . . I could kill Peter," he muttered.

She couldn't believe this from him. *"Could* you?"

He looked for answers deep in the fire. "No." He picked up a poker and helped himself to his feet, he separated the logs and beat out the fire. "I wish to God I had died on the battlefield. To bring me to heaven and to offer me the only thing in the world I ever wanted and then to take it away."

She threw her arms around him. "I love you! Take me away with you! I swear I'll be constant all my life! You're my life, I'm yours!"

He pulled her arms from around his neck. "I can't, Kate." He said it softly in his own voice. It was in that softness she understood defeat.

They drove back in silence.

She sat dazed, without any life in her. Peter found her that way. He took the cases and stacked them near the door. "Isn't it time the two of us had it out, Katie? Look at me, don't look through me as if I'm transparent. We've both had criticism, we both know enough of what makes honest speech between man and woman."

He was right. *But Martin lived behind her eyes.* "You never intended to divorce me, that was only a lie."

"A gentle kind of lie, for your own good."

"And the baby, that was no accident."

"I don't know. I wanted to keep you, it seemed the only way. Believe me, I've been washed in the blood of the lamb. I've been turned inside out. You'd driven me crazy, sleeping with other men. I never thought you'd open yourself to someone else. The fault was mine as well as yours."

"There is no *fault.* I love Martin. What has fault to do with it?"

"The fault was yours in that," he said. "To lead him on where there was no hope. You're as innocent as Deirdre. To give yourself to a . . . a gardener."

"I can see how you're washed in the blood of the lamb. You still hold yourself above other men. To call him that. You might as well understand that no matter what happens, I love him."

She saw the muscle twitch in his cheek. "I don't expect you to come back all at once. It's all over, Katie. There have been harsh words between us. But you're my wife and have always been. I'm changed now. Full of new energy and hope. Can't you feel that?"

What did she feel? What did she hear? Not her own heart. That was dead.

He took her hands and pressed them to his lips. "Then let's go home."

Paulie bent down to look into the little opening in the rock, it was little more than a rabbit warren. "Rebecca, come out of there!"

"No!" she screamed, "no!"

"We have to go to the train soon. Don't be an ass, Becca!"

"I won't *go* to New York, I *won't*. I want to stay here!"

Paulie scuttled out between scratchy bushes and brushed off his knees. "I guess you'll have to drag her to the train screaming."

"We should have seen what was happening," Katherine said. "The illness, her fever dreams, poor Mathilda, who knows what's going on in the child's head."

Peter pushed his long body through and bent to talk with her. "Rebecca, come out this instant or you're in for a whipping."

"You can whip me blue, I won't go *back!*"

They walked back to the wagon to confer with Sarah. "What a little firebrand," Sarah said. "A will of iron. She'll be a voice for the cause one day, you'll see."

"I'll *firebrand* her backside," Peter said impatiently, checking his pocket watch.

"And what good will that do? A child who could throw her doll into the fire. No, do it another way. She's chosen to stay without you, let her face the consequences of her own actions. Leave her with us."

Peter's face turned dark. "Never."

Sarah looked on him bitterly. "So much for your Communist leanings. No, I meant for a week or two. She's only being sticky because she's trying to make you stay. Once she sees you're gone, she'll face the consequences of her own decision." Sarah looked clearly at Katherine saying that. "And when she does she'll want to go to you. In fact I'll bring her to New York myself. I have business there. Or Katherine can come and get her."

"No," Peter said, "I want it finished cleanly."

"We've been so much caught in our own lives," said Katherine, "we didn't see her battle with God and the devil. She believes the devil is in New York."

Peter was fuming, he got out of the wagon and went back to try another assault.

Katherine was still hanging on to slender threads. "You think she'd be all right for a week or two? I want to go home, to see about Paulie and Deirdre . . . to see . . . I don't know what I expect to see . . . but I want to come back. Martin and I . . . there are unfinished things between us."

"Understand me clearly," Sarah said. "We don't play word games here. We speak right out. I want you to come back. I think you ought to come back to stay. This is the place that made you well and you owe it something. You came for your own designs, Peter and you. You never saw the larger picture. Marriage does not work, not between two people. Society does not work, not between states, not between nations, not the way we have done it up to now. Look at the newspapers. The war is over. Blood spilled and now hooded men come and burn and hang the Negroes. New York City is exploding with corruption. The Germans are fighting the French. Where is peace? Where is love? You can find fault with us, Perfectionism is a goal, not a present state. I know that as well as you. We need you and we need Rebecca. Come back to us."

"There's too much ego in me, Sarah. I want to paint. I have to keep the center of my *self.*"

"And you'll get that by going back to Peter?"

"Not *to* Peter. *With* Peter. I must speak with Martin, we must make plans. . . ."

Sarah set a stern face. "You have in your eyes a picture of yourself as Martin's wife. Give it up. Martin is marrried to me, and to Mary Darcy, and to Corinthe, and to all the other wives. He is one of our husbands. We are one of his wives. We take care of his food and his room and his trousers and his handkerchiefs, we love him and he loves us, we do for him and he does for us. This is our marriage. If you want a part of it, come back, because a *part* is all you're entitled to. Your way, the selfish possessive marriage, leads to everything else. Possess a husband, possess a house, possess a nation, possess a business and starve your workers out. No. Accept it. Rebecca will be all right with us. Take a few weeks. See your life. And then come and take her away, or come and be my sister and my husband's wife."

"Tell him to write to me," Katherine begged. "Only ask him to write. Promise."

Peter returned without Rebecca. "She won't come. Well, let her learn consequences then. I'll come back for her. Or you'll bring her, Sarah. I'll pay your fare and give you a holiday in the city."

"I'm not for hire," Sarah said. She took up the reins and jerked them, the horses pawed the ground, Paulie and Peter jumped up. "But when she's ready, I'll take her home."

The station was all confusion, Peter was concerned about some missing bags and Paulie and Isaac had gone off for a final few words, Corinthe was crying, all Deirdre's singing friends had come to say a tearful good-bye.

Katherine watched the edges of the crowd hoping that Rebecca would come flying to them. No, she wasn't looking for Rebecca, she wanted Rebecca to stay, she wanted to hold onto that last little thread. It was Martin she looked for. She wanted the epiphany now; the afternoon was soft and clear and cloudless; she wanted the clap of thunder, she wanted Martin to run out of the crowd and claim her. Or he would write. Perhaps he had written her already and when Sarah came to embrace her for a last good-bye, the note would be in her hand.

In the distance she heard the whistle of the Midland train, coming from the west. *Where was Martin?* Peter gathered the bags together. Paulie and Isaac embraced. Amos shook Peter's hand. Corinthe gave a flower to Deirdre. Sarah waited for last. The letter would be in Sarah's pocket. She kissed the others good-bye, she waited for Sarah . . . the whistle came closer and clearer. . . .

Mr. McMichaels, the stationmaster, caught Peter aside. "A word, Mr. Berger."

Peter looked nervously toward the slowing train.

"Sir," McMichaels took off his cap and wiped his brow with the back of his sleeve, "sir, I've been thinking hard of joining the Community, I've almost come to it, and now I see a gentleman like yourself pulling out. Is there something I ought to know? Maybe I'm a fool, my family thinks so, but I hoped . . . and then I saw you leaving . . . can you tell me . . ."

Peter clapped him on the shoulder. "A man couldn't do a better thing than join on. I have to leave for family matters. This is heaven on earth. Don't think twice."

McMichaels smiled. He put his cap on and nodded and went to the platform to see that his passengers got safely on. And to say a word to the young conductor on the train. And to get his last taste of capitalistic life.

Sarah came to embrace her. "Come
back to us," Sarah said. Katherine waited for the letter. There was no
letter. A message, then. She waited for a message. Sarah let her go. She
looked to the edges of the crowd. *Martin, don't be a fool!* He wasn't
there. *He was somewhere, longing for her as she longed for him.*

"Tell him he must write . . ." But Katherine said the words to open
air. Sarah had walked away and Peter took her by the elbow and she was
being helped up by Mr. McMichaels, who tipped his hat to her and said
good-bye, she ran to a window seat, the car was crowded, Peter was
putting up the bags and Deirdre had gone forward to take a solitary
seat, Paulie found two seats for him and Peter, Peter leaned over and·
asked if she wanted company, she said *No,* the voice wasn't hers, her
eyes were out the window, *Where was he?* The hiss and screech of the
engine, someone tapped her on the shoulder, a woman, and asked her
had she been visiting *that place* and what was it like?

She didn't see him until the train had pulled almost out of the
station. He was standing beside some boxes piled for shipping. He had
his rake with him, *oh, Martin, you fool,* all the time she had been waiting
for him he was raking leaves to ease the pain, *Martin write to me!* She
half stood at the window, she raised a hand to him but the train had
passed. She tried to see back, it moved too fast, she wanted to pull the
cord and stop the train, *Martin, why?*

Peter came and sat beside her.

"Can I get you something, is your stomach unsettled?"

She sank back. "No, nothing."

"Would you like to have Deirdre sit with you?"

"Yes."

The train was moving away from her life. Deirdre came and sat
beside her but so full of her own thoughts. Katherine would have liked
to hold Deirdre's hand but Deirdre kept her hands to herself, and had
closed her eyes, dreaming.

Moira, help me to see it as a picture, to detach myself from it, or I will perish. A painting mounted on the wall: the solid fortress of God and St. Paul, the twin towers looking out for strangers, strangers beware, here is love and peace, take your hate and jealousy in another place; the soft quadrangle and the trees beginning to leaf and the strollers out for a breath before dinner, or sitting on the benches listening to the click and clack of croquet mallets on balls, the children rolling on the slope pretending that winter was still with them, getting ready to take off their shoes for summer, summer was for bare feet only, and the little foursomes, heads together, planning a picnic at the Cascades at Stockbridge Falls or an overnight to Joppa, on the train to Fish Creek Station and then a laughing walk to the house and a sweet and rustic overnight and then back to the Mansion House in the morning; and the kitchen warm with dinner, all the hot pies and the potatoes baking and in the children's room Rebecca sitting glass-eyed knowing that she'd been left behind; and in the orchard Martin stumbling over his raked cuttings and falling onto the rustic bench where they'd sat the summer out, talking, touching, loving, knowing that she was moving away from him; oh, he needed her . . . he *needed* her . . . She heard Sarah saying: *I am his wife and Mary Darcy and Corinthe and a hundred others and he is my husband and will you have him yours?*

The picture evaporated and the train was a hum of voices and women were looking at her and whispering and nodding their heads. Deirdre went to sit alone and Peter took the seat beside her and held her hand. She was thankful that he didn't speak. She dared not cry, she *dared not.* In any case there would be a letter waiting for her that would mend this terrible tear in her heart, and the sureness that it would be there kept all her life from spilling out. It would be there. He was writing it now. It was easier without Peter there and without all the chaos. He would write to her *Dear Kate, my dear Kate, my only heart, my love.*

FOURTEEN

FOR *Everything* *There is a* *Season*

The winter is past, the rain is over and gone. By night on my bed I sought him whom my soul loveth: I sought him but I found him not. He cometh leaping upon the mountains skipping over the hills. Make haste my beloved, be thou like a roe or to a young hart upon the mountain. Many waters cannot quench love, neither can the floods drown it. His left hand should be under my head and with his right hand he should embrace me.

(from) The Song of Solomon

She had been awake since dawn . . . a city dawn . . . not the sweet country clearness . . . the lowing of cows . . . the clarinet calling her to . . . she wanted . . . she wanted . . .

Katherine lay on her side of the marriage bed. She wasn't free to *want,* nor even to let loose her fantasies. Fantasies were too dangerous now, and so she drifted through an unpeopled world looking for a landscape, half-asleep half-awake through the empty orchards of her mind.

She felt the twitch and shudder of Peter's body. He was dreaming again, making little inarticulate choking cries, his legs pumping for escape. She touched his arm lightly to release him. He jolted awake, bewildered, between nightmare and reality. She saw the appeal in his eyes for her to come to him. She could not. She turned away and pretended to sleep.

And waited for the movement in the house, for the shuffle of feet, for the sounds of horse on cobble, the clink of milk bottles on doorstep, and then, with agony, for the postman's ring.

Peter was still giving himself the luxury of late breakfasts. The thought of Else's heavy sausage and griddle cakes made her stomach turn. She wanted a cup of tea and a good piece of fresh baked bread. She'd been too inactive. As soon as things settled down, she would take herself long striding walks. Her body ached for the woods.

At the ring of the bell she felt a wave of morning sickness. No, it wasn't that. It was Else at the door downstairs taking in the post, and shuffling her little mincing steps into the kitchen to fix Katherine's tea, and the clink of the cup against tray, and Peter's taking the tray on his way back to the bedroom, and opening the door and setting down the tray and taking up the letters carelessly, and dropping them one by one on the bed.

There was one letter still in his hand. He ripped it open. Her heart raced. He sat on the edge of the bed and showed it to her. "Sarah writes that Rebecca has confessed Christ, that she misses us terribly and she thinks the devil has us in New York because we haven't come back for her."

"It's too cruel for her. I can't bear it. I'm going back to bring her home," Katherine said.

He dropped the letter on the bed. It wasn't Rebecca in his eyes. "Sarah will bring her home. It's all over, Katie. Let it go."

He took his morning's clothes and went into his dressing room. She sat up, reading the letter. Was there something between the lines? Some hint, some cipher, some code?

Deirdre stood in the doorway in her morning robe, hairbrush in hand. "Nothing from Martin?"

She lay back defeated in that. "No."

Deirdre sat at the side of the bed to have her hair brushed out. Katherine touched the long silk night-tangled hair and thought: how Adam would have loved that hair, the waste of it.

"So you've forgiven Father. I can't believe you have."

Katherine pulled gently through the strands. "Forgive? I try not to keep a hard heart. I've brought that away, at least."

"I don't believe you," Deirdre said. "It's against nature." She stopped Katherine's hand and held it. "I've tried . . . over and over . . . to see things through Father's eyes. When it . . . happened . . . that night with Amos . . . afterward you came to me with so much compassion. I don't think you understood, but you cared that I'd hurt myself. But Father, when he came back and found out, all he cared about was himself and what others might think."

"You're too hard on him."

"Not hard enough," said Deirdre bitterly. "I've learned to trust my feelings. It wasn't me he *cared* about!"

There was much pain in Deirdre's voice. "But you're wrong. He does care about us both, deeply. But he was caught, you see. We were both caught."

"Caught how?"

How could she answer that? She was still caught. She saw herself running through an orchard untended and unpruned, the fruit rotting on the ground. She caught her hair in the low-hanging branches, she tried to pull free but her hair was tangled in the leaves.

Peter walked into the room, buttoning his shirt. He bent to the cheval mirror, but Katherine could see it wasn't himself he looked at, but them. "Paris is defeated by the Prussians," he said. "Richelieu is paying five thousand francs to the Germans and he's lost half of Lorraine and Alsace to boot. It's all over the papers."

"Father is only saying that for my benefit." Deirdre's pain had gone to petulance. "Mother doesn't give a hoot about the Prussians. The war is over. You promised I could go abroad with Aunt Moira and now you want to go back on it."

Katherine could see how Peter worked to swallow his anger. He was still nervous and tentative with Deirdre. "I said you could go abroad, I didn't say you could walk into an enemy camp."

"Oh bother, what has the war to do with me!"

"The borders have only just been opened." He appealed to Katherine. "Let her wait until things are more settled."

"Edgar's bought a little farmhouse in Ury," Deirdre protested. "Near Fontainebleau. It's miles outside of Paris. It's a quiet country village. I'm aching to get out of the city. All my trunks are packed!"

"Then unpack them. I only asked for you to wait until a less chaotic time. Trust me in this. You have been known to make impetuous decisions."

Deirdre turned to Katherine in appeal. "But I want to leave now!"

"Please don't upset your mother. Remember she's carrying a baby."

"I didn't think she was carrying a goat!" Deirdre turned on him with righteous anger. "She's not fragile, you know. Some women work up to the last moment and deliver babies in the field."

"God save me from daughters," Peter said futilely.

"And how many of *them* did you leave behind?" Deirdre asked.

"What the devil do you mean by that?"

"I mean," she said pointedly, "that gossip has it you made a few mistakes in bed. I guess Father Noyes has you all written down in his book. Everyone talked of it. Mother wasn't the first you left with child."

Peter was livid. "How dare you talk to me like that!"

"What are you so hot about, Father? You brought me to the Community. They taught me to talk frankly about sexual things."

"This is my home! This isn't Oneida!"

"How well I know that," said Deirdre.

Peter floundered for words. He had lost. He took his tie and his coat. He walked out hurt and angered.

Deirdre looked after him almost with regret. She sat contrite beside Katherine and lowered her head for her hair to be brushed, a child again. "I can't stop my mouth anymore. When he brought me to Oneida, he opened a Pandora's Box."

"It's so easy to blame," said Katherine. "Knowing that Moira will be supporting you. But if she wasn't, you'd come running back to Father soon enough for his protection."

"Is that why *you?*" asked Deirdre. "I mean with Martin? Giving up your dreams so soon?"

Katherine felt the baby turn. She couldn't catch her breath, she felt lightheaded. "What have I to dream on?"

"Then come with Moira and me to Paris. Paint in Paris. You'll be yourself again."

"If I knew what *was* myself."

"Well, I mean to be my own master." Deirdre turned and embraced her. "No matter what, I want you to know that I love you, truly love you. Not just out of family, but love and respect you."

Katherine took that embrace, a thing so genuine and lovely, it was pure gold. "And I respect and love you. I suppose we've gone sticky on each other, for a fact."

"Peter, over here!"

Why Bannerman had chosen the Hoffman House Peter couldn't think. Two statues of blackamoors supporting baskets of metallic grapes, and in the Gentlemen's Bar an enormous painting called *Nymphs and Satyr,* Turkish rugs and Oriental sconces. For a man in mourning, it was bizarre. Bannerman half rose and then gave it up and resettled his stomach. "My dear boy, welcome back to civilization. I thought Hoffman's might be a nice change from your period of austerity. From Eden to Sodom, that's the Grand Tour." Bannerman ordered two Manhattan cocktails from a barmaid in a red velvet corset. "Try that, it will wash the holy water out of your mouth. And what's this great problem you're so upset about? You look fit, by God, you look grand. A knight errant about to don armor, climb his white horse and set a lance against vice and corruption."

"The trouble is Harry."

"Harry, like Old Harry or Old Ned, Beelzebub? I thought you'd left the devil behind you wrestling with good Mr. Noyes."

"I mean Harry Bergstrom, Bitsie's husband."

"Oh, *that* Harry! What of him?"

"Harry's been my client for fifteen years and he's in a bit of a mess."

"*Bit,* you say? *Bit?* Harry Bergstrom is Mr. Tweed's Tweedledum. Mr. Tweed is off to Albany to set his water scheme in motion, and Harry Bergstrom is in that little stream dabbling his fingers in the water. And the widening of Broadway, he's up to his ballocks in that one."

"*And* he's begged me to defend him."

"And so? I thought that was what you did for a living?"

"It's Paulie, what am I going to tell him?"

Bannerman took his drink from the barmaid and shoved one over to Peter. "I see the whole dilemma laid out like a panorama, a classic case. You've been filling Paulie with the same rot you've been writing me for two months; you're ready to fight this great battle against evil and suddenly you're engaged to defend the enemy. Delicious. Welcome home."

"Don't joke about it, he was greatly influenced by the goodness of religious life."

"*Goodness,* you say? I have a new case, Peter, it's been written up in the *Times.* Great scandal. Family named Cahen. Mother and her son tried to murder the daughter of the family. Brother held a pillow to his sister's mouth with the purpose of strangling her to death. And what had the girl done? She'd fallen in love with a Christian. And the Cahens were Israelites. Her own brother, a pillow over her face. All over some event that happened two thousand years ago. Will the horrors in the name of religion never cease?" He took a sip of his Manhattan. "Oh, pardon me, you are so recently come from the upper regions. I don't want to offend your ecclesiastical affiliations. A man chooses his God, vows his allegiance and skewers anyone who says *he* has seen another God walking the same heaven. Jesus said, 'I come to bring you not peace but the sword.' St. Matthew. And He's certainly done that. All these Christians pray to the same God, but outside the walls of the Mansion House, Professor Mears and his Presbyterians have been sharpening their knives for years, just waiting for a way into the soft underbelly of Noyes. If Mears had been Hindoo or Muslim, but they both pray to the same Christ! So it has always been, in *spiritu sanctum,* angels battling on heads of pins. Since the dawn of man. Darwin's close to it, to my mind, but even Mr. Darwin hasn't got it straight. He says men were descended from the animal kingdom. Well, he misses the obvious boat if he were any real student of human nature as well as human evolution. There were *two* species of animal from which we descended. One was pastoral and herbivorous, nudging its neighbor and baaing and gamboling on the green hills, nibbling grass. And the other, the snarling predator, flesh-eating, eyes flashing, jaws dripping, just waiting for their pastoral neighbors to drop by for lunch, or they'd take the pastorals on just for the game or the sport, or because they were bored. Your Mr. Noyes claims it's poverty and the ills of capitalism and ungodliness that make men turn against their brothers. That's all bosh. Man can have his bellyful and kill his neighbor for the sport. Men haven't changed, dear boy, since the beginning of civilization. Read the Bible. Read Leviticus. Or Cain and Abel. All the types you see today. Take our own North and South. Your pastoral Southerners who wouldn't harm a hair of a slave and wouldn't keep them if it wasn't the custom, and your predator Southerners who would as soon hang a black as spit. The lines were wrongly drawn. The pastoral South and the pastoral North should have banded together with a big baa-lamb on their escutcheon, and they could have fought the North-South wolves. And your Mr. Noyes has banded together some woolly lambs. Well, I hope the gate is tightly shut or the Noyes-eating Presbyterians will get them. So don't let Paulie go through a cock-eyed view of life without showing him the other. A man needs to teach his son reality. Big bear teaches little bear about the jungle. Save Paulie from a life of lies. Teach him to survive in the jungle for that is where we are. Harry is your client. You're honor-bound to defend him. I rest my case." Bannerman ordered another round of drinks.

"You're in damn fine spirits for a man who's recently bereaved and hopelessly diseased."

Bannerman fished in his breast pocket for two of his Cuban cigars, offered one to Peter, clipped the end of his, lit it, and settled back. "How true. Adelaide, Cleopatra of my life, ah, her infinite variety, she left me. And so did the best little dog in the world. In one fell stroke I was un-Adelaided and dis-Graced. As to the affliction, it's a noble one at least. The pox and the gout. Henry the Eighth and I. Napoleon. And in truth, I had resigned myself to lying about like a vegetable waiting for the maggots to eat out my brain. But life is a marvel, Peter. I found a new interest, dear boy, that has lifted my boots and spirits no end." Peter leaned across the table to hear what Bannerman leaned forward to say. "I think we ought to leave this place and take a little walk in the park. This is a subject that requires . . . a delicate privacy."

"Can you at least give me a hint of it?"

"A hint? I'll call it by its name. Philanthropy."

It was a slow stroll, with poor Bannerman's obesity and the lack of Grace on the leash. He steadied himself on Peter's arm. They walked through the Fifth Avenue gate of

Central Park, down the broad plaza of the Mall to watch the swans in the lake. A small crowd of children had gathered in delight around two little barouches done in gilt and velvet, drawn by goats and guided by two colored boys in livery. Some laughing children climbed a kneeling camel which was in the charge of an Arab from Tipperary in scarlet drawers and a fez.

"Philanthropy," Bannerman began as they sat on a bench to watch the camel rise and take its slow stately walk. "I was at the lowest ebb of my life. I was a pariah to my usual world, without my Adelaide to keep my house for me and order the servants, knowing that the filthiness of my ailment would separate me forever from any sort of female companionship. God help me, I've kept my taste for it. And now that too was being taken away. Un-Adelaided, dis-Graced, and de-fucked. Where was I to go? I took myself to the Bowery, among the low-life who seemed at that moment to be my brothers in suffering and degradation. Night after night I roamed the Bowery streets. And then one prophetic night, I had a thirst on me. I stepped into that monstrosity, the Atlantic Garden, that mob of heavy-jowled Dutchmen drinking their lager beer, the saddest band in the world playing their ooom-pahs and a *rifle* range where these wild predator types could practice shooting at pictures of animal-Turks, you know the kind of low-life out on the town."

"Hardly a place for Bannerman."

"*Exactly!* And if anything might convince me of divine providence, it was that fact! The last place in the world you would find Bannerman, sunk to the low state of a sodden German laborer. And there in the midst of all these heavy breasted, large-assed, fat-cheeked German girls was an angel, a lost angel, sitting alone at a table, being bothered by a sailor. Well, she attracted my attention at first by her beauty, and then by *God* the realization came to me that I had seen her before!"

"In the courts?"

"No, by Jove, in the *bed!* She was the very baggage who had given me the foul disease, the very one to whom you in your own philanthropy had given up your money."

"Bella!"

"The same. Now my first impulse was to hit her over the head with my umbrella. But I looked at the poor child, that a thing of beauty and a joy forever should be wasted on the dregs. And then as I watched her own sad face, I realized that she and I were both victims. It was someone like myself, someone of wealth and talent and the finest breeding who had passed it on to her, she had passed it on to me, and in one stroke un-Bannermaned me and had her thrown out of her business bed. In my own disgrace and despair I still had my money and my servants; what did she have, poor child? When she saw me she tried to run out of the place, but in the end we left and went to a more appropriate establishment and had a good cry. Her poor dear child was dead . . . her child, my wife, her mother, my dog. Don't you see the neatness, the marvelous coincidence of it all, my boy?"

"And after all she did to you, you still gave her money? I'd agree, that was true philanthropy."

"Money? To let her go back to what? No, the child was at the end of her tether. She wanted care and attention. And I could give her that. And in exchange . . . don't you see the beauty of it, Peter? The only two people in the world who could choose no other partners?"

"My God, Bannerman, surely you don't mean . . ."

Bannerman started to laugh, he had to hold his belly, the muscles hurt. He coughed and laughed until the sweat ran down his forehead. "I do indeed. And so I won't be going much out in company."

"Not in your own *home!*"

"You have to see her delight. She runs from room to room not believing her luck. The servants treat her like a princess, which, in her way, she is my boy, she is. And she shows her appreciation in a thousand ways. A *thousand.* If you could try those ways, Peter, you'd know what heaven is."

Now that he saw Bannerman in the light of this truth, he recognized how poorly Bannerman looked. His color, his breathing, he was heavier than ever. A thousand ways of loving with a whore. But Peter thought of Mary Darcy, in whose arms he found the truest kind of love. So he spoke carefully. "If Bella gives you such comfort in these hard times, I'd say indeed she was a princess. But you realize how much you're punishing your health. A thousand ways with Bella? She'll be the death of you."

Bannerman mopped his forehead with a great linen handkerchief. "Exactly, Peter. And that is the ultimate justice. It will be a just and delicious way to end. Adelaide finds it so. I hear her laughing up there and saying, *It's just like you, Bannerman.* Somehow at the end of it all I can almost understand John Humphrey Noyes. Every man has to make himself a taste of heaven in this hell of a world. And who does it harm? All those angels at sword point on the head of a pin. And in the true heavens Jove and Loki, the Trickster having the last laugh, knowing the true way of gods and men on this poor and lonely and disenfranchised planet."

"Ah Bannerman," said Peter bleakly, "how well I understand. I ran to get a taste of heaven. And what have I done? I've lost Deirdre, Rebecca is afraid to come home, and as to my wife . . . I have no wife. Where am I to go from here?"

Moira sat smiling as Katherine hung out the carriage window, getting her fill of the New York streets. The racing madness seemed to be in the city. Four-in-hands, single spans, a light phaeton with a high-hatted groom in the back seat. They took a quick sharp corner, throwing her to the side of the carriage. *She was in a wagon, careening on the road to Joppa.* She felt sick and dizzy.

"Are you all right, Katie?"

"Nothing . . . just something I remembered."

Moira settled back and lit a slim black cigarette. "Remembering can be a dangerous game."

They pulled into the long curved driveway that led to Bitsie's new Greek villa with its marble colonnades and its myriad statues of stone-draped gods and goddesses. "Now wait until you see this," Moira said with amusement.

Bitsie and Harry walked onto the porch, arguing. *"Is* that Bitsie? She's lovely! She's sixteen again!"

"From a distance."

Bitsie was pulling on her gloves, walking with a spritely step. Harry dragged after her, looking pathetic. He appealed to Katherine and Moira to help him with a difficult wife. "She says you're off to Lord and Taylor's to buy bronzes. We've already got a Dedo and some other rot, would you please urge her to curb her appetite to spend money?" He tried to take her hand to help her up, but she took hold and pulled herself in. Poor Harry, he tried to pull her down to kiss her cheek. She pushed him away with her delicate gloved hand. "Now now, Harry."

The driver clucked to the horses, they drove away, leaving an unhappy Harry in the street.

Bitsie sat back self-satisfied and smiling. She took a mirror from her handbag and gave herself a good look-over. Well, Katherine could see she'd never have that milky skin again but she was well made up and her face leaner, all the fat gone, and her eyes, they were the eyes Katherine had known in Virginia. "Bitsie, how well you look."

"Haven't we all come around?" Bitsie took out a pencil and painted a brown beauty spot high on her cheek near her left eye. "I'm going to the races. Bonnie Doon is running against Yankee Dan. Shall I place a bet for anyone?"

"But aren't we lunching?"

Moira smiled wickedly and squeezed Katherine's hand.

Bitsie tapped the driver to stop at the next corner. "Well, marriage isn't so bad as long as it's you who are riding the horse and holding the reins . . . and as long as your figure holds." She kissed Katherine's cheek and waved her little gloved hand to Moira and opened the door and let herself out. Another cab was waiting, the door opened, a hand reached out to help her up.

"Does Harry know?" Katherine asked.

"Let Harry blame himself. He gave one *oink* too many."

In Delmonico's private little room, drinking champagne as they had once before, she told it all out. Day by day. Katherine spun it out like a spider, making a web of it, so that she could see it all *outside* herself. The mornings and the evenings, the great hall after supper, sewing and listening to lessons in geometry, the mushroom hunts, a bee to can the last of the Damson plums, and Martin teaching her to look at things, and the gentle kind of sex, sometimes she came on two or three times. . . .

"The sexual thing, that's what's remarkable."

"When sex is all so available, it takes on less importance, frankly. Poor Peter, he made such a drama out of it. Shall I tell you a private truth? I had as much pleasure in the sexual play with a rough woodsman as I did with Martin. He made love the way he wrestled bears. There's something provocative in the bizarre."

"Oh, don't tell *me*," said Moira.

"No, sex wasn't the issue. Father Noyes understood the human body when it came to sex. But he made one serious mistake."

"A man who can dream up such a paradise is entitled to make one mistake, surely."

"There is something about *one* man and *one* woman. It's more than sexual satisfaction. When the Oneida women were allowed to bear children, they were paired up for the best human stock. But you should have seen their faces when they couldn't be tied in love with the fathers of their children-to-be. Or the men who had fathered the children, they wanted a private connection and that was the forbidden fruit. There are some women who need *one* man. . . ."

"Some need one and get two." Moira raised a finely arched eyebrow. "Are you sure this isn't part of the fantasy?"

"I've been trying to work it out, to see the pattern of what *love* is. You see, I've been thinking in terms of Peter. I want to be fair to him, if he's what I settle for. I don't feel a victim anymore. I'm not *done* to. I have a choice in it. I could have stayed on in the Community, accepting Martin's way of life. I could still go back. This is how I piece it all out. Love isn't just the thing between the legs. Of course every man has the desire for that adventure in all its variations. It was what I felt with Martin. It was the sort of *nurturing* way he looked at me, the way he looked at his trees, the way a mother looks at a child, when she sees that child take its first steps and she laughs because it also gives her pleasure. The way a mother nibbles at a child's fingers, saying . . . *I love you so much, I could eat you up!* A man and a woman with that sort of nurturing love take each other *in.* Does that make sense to you? I was so profoundly comfortable with Martin. So comfortably free that ideas came out of me like stars exploding. There weren't enough hours of the day to see things. It wasn't any longer that sort of romantic love that was exchanged every night in a hundred beds of the Mansion House, it was simply something that was so palpably *there* that I could get *on* with things. It was an . . . *absence* of certain needs, they were simply filled and that was that."

"And you gave that up because you couldn't have the *whole* of it? Oh, Katie, the more fool you. Look at my own life, I've had to tear apart everything I believed, I had to strip my heart naked to understand essences, and in the end I took what I could and I'm grateful for it. How could you have let Martin go?"

"I . . . haven't . . . I only have to stand back to see the pattern."

"Did it ever occur to you"—Moira put out the ash end of her small cigar—"that Martin may also be standing back to see the pattern?"

"No, I don't understand, Father. Uncle Harry is a crook, he's cheated people, he may even have cheated widows and orphans."

"Oh, come on, Paul, he took graft money. Don't sentimentalize it."

"All right, *graft,* then. He was dishonest. How can you even consider defending him?"

"He's a very old friend, he bought you your first rocking horse."

"Then invite him to Christmas dinner and all that. But to defend a man when you know he's guilty as sin!"

"But that's the law, Paul! Every man has a right to be defended!"

"When he's guilty? Then let him get some pettifogger, some *shyster!* You said you were after a new kind of law."

"Listen to me, Paul. You're still a child in many ways. The kind of public morality you're asking for is the kind I want, believe me. But the world is full of compromise. You aim for the stars because you have to settle for less. You know how much I love you, don't let's be divided in this. Say you had a choice. Defend a dear old friend and make a lot of money which can be used for the best of causes and Paul, I *swear* to you that no penny of this fee will go to me, I'll let you choose the charities. Let's say this choice was yours. Are you sure you know what you'd do?"

"Good Lord, Father, I love you too. As for Harry, there is no choice. Either you live by principle or it isn't living. That's the long and the short of it."

Berthe waited to see from Katherine's face how much damage had been done between them. Katherine looked younger, if anything, slimmer, her hair cut like a girl's, awful the way it was cropped, but it made her eyes sharp and those eyes fixed on Berthe, without a smile, but without judgment.

"I couldn't let this silence go on. You understand why I . . . acted as I did. Only my concern for Deirdre." Katherine gave her the oddest kind of look, watching her like a cat. It made her nervous. "Come, let's put this thing aside. You heard I'm going to marry again." She took a handkerchief from her bag and held it to her eyes. "When . . . Hector . . . left me . . . I found life unbearably lonely."

"Spare me the crocodile tears," Katherine said.

Berthe was shocked totally. "How can you say such a thing to me?"

"Why not? Seeing it's the truth."

She folded the handkerchief. "Well, what's happened to my silent Katie?"

"She's gone." Katherine went to stand beside the window looking out. Cool as brass. But pregnant.

"Is it Peter's child?"

Katherine turned, not angry, but laughing. "The way your mind turns, Berthe."

Berthe pulled off the glove of her left hand and casually laid the ringed hand across the back of her chair. The effect of the large stone was lost on Katherine. "Why are you staring at me that way? If I'm not welcome, just say so."

"I'm trying to remember back to Poppa's house. It seems to me you always had that fox look about you, always watching me, as if you were searching me through for vulnerabilities. You'd come into a room where I was reading or sketching, or just sitting and stir up all the air like an angry stream. Why, Berthe? What had I done?"

She might as well not have spent an hour at her mirror. They stood naked to each other. "Because you had it all, you had it when you were born, with your little golden curls, and your simpering ways. That's what men like. You have a charmed life with men. You've gone through hell and you come out without a scar."

"How do you know what scars I wear?"

Berthe was astonished with the force of Katherine's voice. "Well, look at you. More beautiful than ever, pregnant and Peter still adores you. You're like a cat. No matter where you're dropped you land on your feet."

"You always make yourself the victim," Katherine said. "And every time you look at me, you set me a blame. You've got your house and your jewels and your servants and now you've caught yourself another fish. That poor man."

"You *dare* talk to me like that?"

"You ought to learn to take a criticism. Perhaps you'd learn to let your anger go. I'm not to blame for anything that happened in your life. There's nothing I have you want, Berthe, believe me. The little girl in Poppa's house is gone."

She fell back in dismay. She felt such chagrin, well, it wasn't Katherine's fault that Peter had chosen Katherine and not her. "I never meant . . ."

"Let's forget it. Let's be finished with it. I don't have any more energy to deal with it."

Berthe never meant to cry, but she burst into tears. "We shouldn't be estranged . . . when it comes down to the bottom, we're all we have, you and me. Blood is thicker, Momma always said." She forced herself to stop, she wouldn't let Katie see her with puffy eyes. "Once I'm married we can settle down"—she fanned herself with the handkerchief—"like proper sisters. And one Friday dinner you shall come to me and the next I'll come to you. . . ."

Katherine let Peter make long and languid love to her but she couldn't fall into his rhythms. His hands, they were too stiff, his fingers had a life of their own, little probing animals, knowing what they wanted, where they wanted. She needed something . . . she closed her eyes . . . she drifted back to Martin's bed, she felt Martin's loving hands on her body, she drifted to Martin's rhythms, she let her hands move over the familiar back and arms, belly, legs . . . dear God, had she whispered his name?

Peter stopped. He moved off her, and sat up against his pillows, he turned up the gaslight, he lay eyes closed, breathing hard.

"What's wrong?"

"Ask yourself. What do you want of me? I am what I am. No more no less. No matter what complaint you have of me, I've stood by you, steadfast as rock."

"I'm sorry . . . it's just . . ."

"You can't live in two worlds. Live there or live here. And if you live here, come back to me."

She turned away. They both lay like that, back to back.

"I'm a man, not a god. I have a man's faults, but I take care of my own, in the only way I know. I've satisfied women all my life, always other women, why not you?"

"Perhaps I'm the wrong woman for you."

"You're a rock-headed woman. You've got a fantasy in your head, you're worse than Deirdre."

"I've tried, I don't mean to hold back, but we are too unalike."

"How . . . how are we unalike?"

"If you can't sense it, I can't tell you."

"What's missing in me? I look for truth, I try to find a shred of . . . goodness to live by, I've let go of the past, why can't you? And start with me again?"

"You have no idea of who I am," said Katherine.

"And you have no idea of who I am," said Peter. In his voice she heard the kind of desperation she had been hearing in her own. But she had no answer to it.

He got out of bed. It was only dawn. He took his traveling bag out of the closet and began to pack. She sat up against the pillow. "Where are you going?"

"I'm going to bring Rebecca home. I'll catch the early train. I'm bringing my daughter back where she belongs. Now you have a good long think, Katie. If you want to go back to the Community, then come with me and I'll bid you good-bye with as good a heart as I can muster. If you want the divorce, take your little contract and make your plans and be gone when I get back. But if you're here when I return, be my wife. If we go on like this the rest of a lifetime, what does it matter how I've changed in my life? It's still ashes."

"Have you changed?" asked Katherine. "Or is it simply change you demand of me?"

He didn't answer. He packed his case. He dressed and went down.

When it was light, she heard him leave the house. She saw him from the window, signaling to a cab. She heard the snort of the horses, and the clatter of hooves on the cobbles, and he was gone.

She was in the house alone. She threw open the windows of her little study, and dusted out the cupboards and found her paints and set them out. She painted furiously. All the faces she had seen in New York, the eyes, the mouths, she painted Barthe, Else in the kitchen, she wanted to paint the body naked, the spirit naked, she wanted to paint the truth of New York City. And above that, she wanted to work so hard she could push a dream out of her head.

The night was not so easy. With Peter gone, with the house empty of children, she had space to mourn. She took out her Community sketches, she wept over them, she spotted them with tears, even in the empty house she closed the door and locked it, she closed the curtains and took out the sketch of Martin lying on the bed. Her heart was so wrenched, she was frightened for the child.

... going back ... going back ... going back ... Peter averted his eyes from all travelers, no easy conversation, no small talk ... just the anesthetic clicking of the wheels ... *going back* ... into the black maw of his failure, for something he had left behind. No soldier burned out at the end of a battle's bleak season went back with more despair.

By the time he had changed to the inland train, despair had changed to anger. Shapeless and formless, this anger pressed against his heart, squeezing out all other feeling. He had been robbed. And hoist on his own petard of professed belief, he had been powerless to defend himself. He had been cuckolded, humiliated, shorn of his manhood by the gardener. The gardener was a sorcerer who had put those damned romantic visions into Katherine's head, and now she was bewitched, she would lie dreaming all her life in front of that damned fire. A life ruined. Two lives destroyed.

By the time he got off the train at Oneida Castle the anger was bile in his mouth. He walked the long dusty road, trying to release himself from this inchoate desire for revenge, to think how he might get his daughter and escape without letting the anger and despair out of his mouth. He was without control.

The sight of the Mansion House filled him with dread. There was no way he could enter it. His head buzzed, his heart pounded. No. Not yet. He turned down the long dusty path that led to the orchards. The trees held out those skeletal arms, knobbed and budded in green but still in their winter shape. *What drew him this way?* It was the magnet of his anger. He tried to turn back, but he was pulled beyond his ordinary powers to resist. Revenge swirled in him, he was caught in some universal maelstrom of revenge, the current of revenge that came from the animal kingdom, from the days when he swung from trees, when he protected his little tree kingdom from predators, when he was smarter and did not let into his domain the predator beast, and with his blessing say *Take my wife, betray my daughter, let me kiss your hairy cheek.* Kiss your cheek? *My arse.* A man made his hand into a fist and took revenge. Hurt for hurt. Death for death. He saw a little plume of dust where someone raked the ground. And then, the figure he detested. The baggy coat, the wide-brimmed hat, that damned crooked foot, the gardener hopping around like a wounded animal as he scraped the rake against the ground.

Peter was filled with a preternatural excitement. Visions of himself: the hurt child, the man proud and self-absorbed, the aspirant, the true believer, the betrayed, the villain, the bad father, the cold husband, the plaintiff, the defendant, and now the jury and the hangman . . . all one.

He stood clear in the center of the path. "Martin!"

Martin looked up, stared with disbelief, pushed back his hat, leaning on his rake, then taking the hat and throwing it to the ground, wiping at his forehead with the back of his sleeve to clear his vision, to make certain Peter was the reality and not the specter.

"Martin, you bastard! You piss-arse!" Peter clenched his fists against the man who had not only cuckolded him but followed him home, into his own bed.

The still-bare branches were accusing fingers, pointing to them both, dead and gnarled fingers just returned from the winter death with their sap rising into the cuckold's world, with their green buds that lied with false promise. . . .

Martin came limping toward him, holding the rake in his two hands like a weapon, walking unsteadily toward Peter. Peter was back in the jungle he understood. Heaven? Lies, all lies. He saw a shovel lying against a tree trunk. This he picked up and waited as Martin came toward him, animal to animal. His knuckles tightened. Face to face. Claw to claw.

"For what you've done to me," said Martin with deadly bitterness, "I could kill you."

Peter raised the shovel. "Done to you? You lying bastard, she was my wife!"

"Not Kate. I don't *mean* Kate. I hate you, do you understand? I hate you and you've destroyed me."

"Bloody liar. It's you who are destroying my life."

Martin was a slender man, but Peter could see how much he was like his trees, sinewy and tough. Peter had the strength, Martin had the sorcerer's eyes. They were matched. "You destroyed me," said Martin, waving the rake. "You took her and then you took everything else that had meaning in my life."

"I took nothing from you that wasn't mine."

Martin's mouth twisted in his fury. "You took the only thing I had left! You stole that from me, don't you understand what you've done!"

"I took nothing but her! What did I take from you!"

"My faith, don't you understand! My faith! The only thing that belonged to me! The only thing standing between me and despair!"

Martin set down the rake, leaned against the handle, head on arm, rocking there, like the shell of a man moved by an unseen wind.

"What the hell have I to do with your faith! You've spoiled my life. I have Katie and I don't have her. You mesmerized her, you damned magician."

"I swore out there on the battlefield . . . I swore before God to hate no other man. That was my pledge. I came here . . . I made that pledge to my wives and brothers. Then you came, you and Kate. I loved her with the purest kind of love . . . and that you can't understand. My love for her took nothing away from you, it should have enriched you, me, all of us. But not you, you animal, you and yours, up out of the slime, spreading slime on everything with your selfishness and your pride. I taught her to understand love and to know love. And then you took her back. I couldn't come to claim her, I had other wives. I couldn't help her. I knew she'd be tied to you for the rest of her life, languishing . . . languishing. I lie there night after night seeing her in that kind of hell, and hating you . . . don't you understand yet? *Hating* you not only for what you've taken from her, but for what you'd done to me, that you've turned me into what you are, you poor cripple."

The afternoon buzzed around them, in the distance Peter heard cowbells, and a rill of laughter, and the crack of the croquet mallet on ball. His anger was gone. All that was left to him was astonishment. He saw Martin's eyes filled with tears for poor Katie who had known love and did not have it now, for poor Katie who lived with a husband who had failed to understand the ultimate secret; and tears for poor Peter who stood forever on the frozen ice knowing that the water beneath the surface was warm, that it only waited for him, and able to do nothing else than to build himself a superficial fire and warm his hands. To the lowing of the sheep and the whisper of wind over branches, he heard the gardener's words. "I could have loved you both," said Martin. "You bastard."

Peter was dizzy. His head spun. His vision of the world suddenly shimmered and altered. *I could have loved you both.* His perception of Martin changed. Martin stood before him a man so strong and so loving, more whole than Peter had ever been. Peter *was* the cripple, living a shallow half-life. What Peter had always hungered for hung palpable in the air. It was without his volition that his pride cracked, shattered like an ice-encrusted branch touched by the first sun. He let go of his pragmatic life and jumped. The wave of warm love that washed over him overwhelmed him. Tears, warm tears spilled over. There was no way his pragmatic mind could understand that he'd come back not only to take Rebecca home, but to take the gardener in his arms.

They came together like the two lovers they were. Man to man. In defiance of the deepest primordial urge. "Forgive me," said Peter.

"Forgive me," said Martin.

"Help me," Peter said.

Else waked her the next morning with a tray, and the post. A letter from Deirdre. Deirdre was in Ury; they were a million miles away from the tension in the city. The farmhouse had a loft. Deirdre slept there and in the morning the buzzing bees around the climbing passion flower vines woke her. All the young men of the town were captivated by her, but Uncle Edgar and Uncle David were two clucking mother hens. David cooked like a dream and Moira saw to her lessons. Her voice was developing beautifully.

After breakfast Katherine went up to her studio. She pinned her pictures around the wall, Martin, where her eyes could soak him up. It was a gray morning, she set a fire on the grate. She closed the door and took a glass of claret and sat her slippers up to the fender. The wine . . . this was an old drug . . . she let the purple fumes work at her brain, she drifted in the blue and orange points of the fire . . . she moved back into the world of her desire. . . . *She heard Else's knock. Else came in nervously. "Mrs. Berger, we'll be robbed in our sleep, I'm that upset. I wanted to tell Mr. Berger but he's not home. . . ."*

She didn't want to be disturbed. "What is it?"

"It's the carriage, Mrs. Berger, it's been there all morning, I saw it when I went to market. Cook saw it too. It sits out there, someone watches the house, it never leaves . . .

It was a bother. "What carriage? What are you talking about?"

"It watches us all day, to see when we come in or go out. And when they see Mr. Berger isn't coming home, they'll rob us, it's terrible in the city, thieves and murderers . . ."

Her head was lazy with wine, she'd sat too long. She pulled herself out of the chair and went to the window with Else. "There, across the way, near the big tree . . ."

She blinked her eyes to clear them. Something stirred. Like a little breeze on a hot arid plain. A little wind stirred the dust.

The carriage . . . the horse looked resigned; the driver slept on the seat. She opened the window wide and leaned out. The carriage door must have opened on the street side, someone stepped out. She heard the little tinkling of breaking glass. He came around the carriage so she could see him. A little latch in her head clicked. All the little valves and shutters of her body turned and opened. She was all at once wide-awake. He stood below leaning on his cane, so odd in city clothes, looking up at her.

She was still wearing her morning gown and slippers. The gown was silk, it billowed out behind her as she ran, one hand on her belly to hold the baby . . . out the door . . . a carriage passed between them . . . she drew her robe around her . . . a woman in the passing carriage stared . . . she ran across the road.

He looked dreadful, pale and nervous, and he was so badly dressed, wearing an ill-fitting coat from the Community closet. He looked anxiously into her face trying to read it. He was worried to death . . . frightened . . . three days outside her door . . . wondering if she'd already seen him and had decided not to come down, afraid to knock . . .

All she could think to say was, "What on earth took you so long?"

She saw beads of perspiration break out on his lip and on his forehead. She knew how awkward he felt and how out of place. "I would have come sooner but I had to find the right man for the orchards. I couldn't leave the Community without doing that. I had to train him . . . this was the hardest . . . you understand. . . ."

"Where are we going, then?"

He tried to read her eyes. He didn't trust it yet. "Kate, are you sure?"

"I don't know. What's sure? I'm sure I have no life in me as Peter's wife. It's neither his fault nor mine. It's simply what is. I'm sure the moment I'm back with you I can relax again. Don't ask me what it is. It just goes click and there it is. I know that I'll never get back to work until we get this settled and I'm alive again. So, where are we going?"

"My cousin, he has a little piece of land in New Hampshire. The groves are good but very much neglected. They'll need a lot of work. But there's a sturdy house on the land . . ."

"Give me half an hour to pack. Will you come and help me?"

"I couldn't step into his house. Kate, what of Peter?"

Else and cook were hanging out the window. Half the street was watching this. "I told you a long time ago, I don't love my husband. But I must have Rebecca."

"She's waiting for us. I said we'd be back in a few days."

"Is she well?"

"Well enough. I've convinced her that the devil is busy in New York, he never comes to New Hampshire. She asked would Peter come so she could at least have two fathers."

He seemed so tired. He needed looking after. "Come inside."

"It's Peter's house. I can't."

"Poor Peter. I think he loves me as much as he can love any woman. He thought he learned about love, and he never will. He'll find a way to blame me and get revenge by building himself another life. Peter will manage. But what of you and the Community? Can you make your peace with that?"

Finally he took the courage to touch her face. Just the tips of his fingers down her cheek. He wanted to come closer, he couldn't, not like this. "I don't seem to have much choice, frankly. I can live without them, I can live without God if I have to, but not without you."

She nodded. "Whatever there is of love in my life, it comes from you. As much as I understand love in this mad world. I love you, Martin. It comes out so easy to say it."

"Mrs. Berger . . ." Katherine was awakened out of reverie. Dreams within dreams. Fantasies in fantasies. And always the dream and the reality collided. Thus it was and thus it would always be. She heard Rebecca's running steps. Rebecca burst in on her, flew at her, poor lost starling, into her arms. "Oh, dear Rebecca . . . dear dear Becca . . ."

Rebecca held on for life, afraid to let go.

"It's all right now, Poppa brought you home. We have waited for you . . ."

Rebecca buried her face in Katherine's robe. "I was afraid to come."

"Afraid? Of your own house?"

"My house is *Oneidacommunity.* Why didn't you come back?"

She stroked Rebecca's silken hair. "What a terrible thing we did, to bring you to that wonderful place and take you away again."

"I *wanted* you," sobbed Rebecca. "Where's Deirdre?"

"Still in France, but she'll be back."

"Is Paulie far away?"

At school. And Poppa went all that way to bring you home."

"Poppa and Martin did. Martin said it was time to go back."

Her heart stopped. How did you live with a heart that didn't beat? "Poppa and . . ."

". . . Martin. I hate New York. I miss the other children. There'll be tapping in the night. Can I sleep with you? Is it all right to be sticky in New York?"

She looked up to see Peter in the doorway. What was on his face she could not read. But he stepped aside. Martin was there. Her Martin, her heart's Martin . . . looking smaller and thinner than she remembered, in those awful city clothes, his hair badly combed. And she could see how his eyes took in the elegant furnishing of her little room. *Martin, this is not my life! Peter, what have you done!*

Else came to lure Rebecca into the kitchen with fresh pie. "I don't like to eat alone," she said. "I don't like it here anymore." Else half carried her out of the room, with scathing glances for them all, for what they'd done to this angel child.

And Martin walked in, unsteadily, not of the leg alone. He settled himself in a chair. He looked around the walls at all her sketches. At himself. His eyes on her eyes. *My dear Martin* . . . Peter opened his vest and loosed his tie. It must have been a hard journey. He saw the wine and poured out a glass. He offered it to Martin. Martin declined. He drank it himself.

Katherine drew her robe around her and waited for the storm, for the clap of thunder, for the first volley . . .

"So," said Peter, full of civility, "shall I leave you two alone?"

"No, stay," Martin said.

Don't be a fool, let him go, we have so much to say . . .

"This belongs to us three," Martin said.

Peter nodded his agreement, he closed the door and pulled in a chair. They made a circle. Her life was caught between them. *Peter, don't hurt me, let me go.*

There was perspiration on Martin's brow, he mopped it with a handkerchief. One of his wives had kindly pressed it and put it in his pocket. "I love Kate," said Martin. "She knows that. You know that, Peter. Kate will never be a moment out of my thoughts. I love her now and will love her all my life." So, it was said. Now she longed to fly to him and be embraced.

"Kate, I should have written . . . Sarah said you waited for a letter. But I was in hell. To have lost you. You know that I never could have come away. I don't think you ever really understood how committed I was to Community life. I said it again and again, you never heard me. I'd die outside, the way I almost died on the battlefield. *Outside* is a battlefield. When I vowed my life, it was a sacred vow. Whether I truly understood God or not. It was my vow. And the groves, they feed the family. Could I turn my back on that? But the worse loss, Kate"—he put his hands on his knees to steady them—"the loss worse than the pain of losing you was my anger against your husband."

Katherine held her stomach so that the baby would not be hurt by her anguish.

"But Peter came back. He had come to us the first time a proud man and he'd left a proud man. He came back not only for his daughter but for his soul. He came to me, Kate, to *me* just as broken in spirit as I'd been after the war. He came to say he couldn't find his way to you. And that you'd never be free until you were resolved with me. But I was resolved, Kate, the moment you went away. Didn't you under-stand that? And then . . . Peter asked me . . ."

"Don't," Peter begged.

"Peter came to me and asked me to teach him how to love you."

The baby turned, her head began to spin, she held the sides of the chair to keep from fainting.

"When Peter gave his hand to me and I a hand to him, that was a moment. Do you know what that cost him, Kate?"

"I love you!" Katherine cried out.

"And I you. And Peter loves you and Peter loves me, I do believe it, heart and soul, and in a way you love Peter, I understood that when the train pulled away and you were on it. If you hadn't felt the tug of love you would have stayed with me. I saw you leaving, my heart was wrenched. And yet it's all by God's design. Sarah said to tell you . . . she was mistaken. Theodore is not the messenger. But she said you and Peter were."

"No!" She forced her eyes on Peter's face. Was he contriving? No, there was no malice on his face. Only love, and compassion. She was so shaken. *Moira, only you will understand this. What was between Martin and Peter at that moment was a stronger thing than Martin's love for me.* The two men looked at each other, both touched with emotion.

. . . while she sat outside of it. *Moira, life has such a way of turning.*

The moment passed. The men retreated into their manly selves.

Martin pulled himself up out of the chair. He came to where she sat. He bent over the chair and with his back to Peter kissed her full on the mouth. *It was a farewell.* She heard the horses on the cobbles, impatient to be away. But he gave her one last loving look. *We were caught from the first, all of us, caught in dreams of heaven. He came to tell me he was a married man, married to God and St. Paul. That he was a poor man, he had nothing to give me. Peter was his only legacy to me.*

Katherine stood numbly at the window watching the carriage pull away. Martin did not turn and wave. The carriage moved out of sight and earshot. They were gone. It was finished.

Peter never said another word. He spent the whole of the afternoon reading to Rebecca. She could not think or feel. She was in her room when Peter came in. He didn't look at her face. She tried to read his. *Was he dissembling? Was this all another trick?* She saw nothing but astonishment and fear and bewilderment. He seemed undone. And even if it were a trick, why torment himself like this for *her* when she'd given him nothing? It occurred to her then, in that dark place, that she'd come through a kind of mad heaven and had never truly understood what they were about.

That evening Peter left for a long walk in the park. She and Rebecca walked through the house, throwing open all the windows to the fresh air. "I want to go back," Rebecca said.

"Poppa and I, we don't belong."

"When I'm old as Deirdre, can I go back then?"

"Without us?"

Rebecca thought about it, so serious. The child in her had gone, just as Deirdre's childhood had gone. It was too hard.

"Let me buy you another doll. To keep you company in the night. A lovely doll, like Mathilda."

"What silly things dolls are," said Rebecca. "They're not alive."

"We just pretend they are, we can do that."

Rebecca thought for a long while. "Is God pretend?" she asked.

Rebecca fell asleep between them that night. Peter carried her back to her own bed. When he returned, he seemed so numb, he lay on the bed openeyed, a man out of his body, a spirit looking for a body to shelter him.

They lay back to back. She was numb too, the feeling only beginning to return to her.

Moira, how imperfect we all are, all of us striving for love, groping in the dark. I, in all that newborn ego, thinking that Martin was dying of love for me, when it was another kind of love he languished for. And Peter, poor atheist, without even a God to shelter him, had turned his smitten cheek to the enemy. . . .

The bed moved, he was dreaming, giving out little anguished sighs, little child cries. For the first time, she began to recognize this business with the bed. He was such a strong man, so in control of the day world, but nights were lost to him. And so he came to her for safety. And she'd denied him, thinking he wanted her only for his own comfort. But hadn't she come to Martin for that same comfort? Hadn't she singularly expected Martin to give up everything in life he cherished, his very soul, for her? In the oddest way she hadn't lost Martin's love. Perhaps that was why she wasn't grieving now. She had that love forever fixed and clean and absolute, never-changing, not altered by time. What a fantasy. What she also had was a frightened husband who had offered up his soul for her. A stubborn rock-headed single-minded man who asked a simple thing from her. She moved against his night-tortured body, she put an arm around him, she stroked him gently, down the belly, into the tangle where the root was joined, where body and soul were joined. And there she stroked him gently until he came awake. But he didn't move toward her. They lay that way, in a new world she did not yet understand. Nor did he. If he had a new soul, it was very fragile, like a new-hatched egg. He lay that way, finally he took her hand. *Moira, that was the whole of it. We slept that way all of the night.*

The child came two months early. Deirdre was back from France and Paulie home from Harvard for the great occasion of the christening. Poor twisted Dr. Berger, supported by his brown wren of a wife, presided. Peter submitted to that, the old man was barely still alive, and what was the harm now that all the anger had subsided. They named the child Adam. Deirdre rocked him for an hour in a ceremony of her own.

That night Deirdre came to her studio to see what work she was doing. What an air of sophistication, and the way she did her hair. "How queer you both are, you and Poppa. You're not the same at all."

"Have you reconciled with your father, then?"

"Oh, that. What foolishness. He's a little gray at the temples. He's too young for that. But it does give him a worldly air. What's wrong with Becca? She acts like a nun, she's so pious."

"She wants to go back."

"Will she, when she's older?"

"There or carry tracts in the street for women's rights. Poor Rebecca. Shall I tell her that women will never get the vote? I think the thing that must happen with women happens in each heart, not in the marketplace. Freedom is such a personal thing."

She did a study of Deirdre nude.

Deirdre marveled at the sketch. "It's quite the best work you've ever done."

"How odd. I never noticed you'd recognized that I'd worked at all."

"Well, after all, I was such a child. . . ."

One day she asked Peter if she could paint him. "Dressed in my court suit? To hang over the fireplace?"

". . . in the flesh."

"Don't be daft."

"Not I. Never. I have a head on me."

"I suppose you have." Reluctant, he let her paint him. It was then, she supposed, that she saw Peter Berger for the first time. Something of the man she'd seen that first tryst in the open air before they were married. That, and something else. The animal who survived the jungle. She painted them both. When the picture was done, Peter inspected it. "Damn if that isn't good enough to have been painted by a man!" He must have seen her displeasure, he quickly amended: "Well, you know what I mean."

She cleaned off her brushes. "I do not. Tell me what you mean."

He laughed, playing with her a little. "Even Father Noyes would admit that there's a difference between men's strength and women's."

"And you see a mere woman's strength on the canvas, do you?"

"Oh, come, you're an artist, don't make noises like a lawyer."

"You admit I am an artist, then?"

Moira, he is pig-headed. He makes no admissions. But I fancy he admires my work a little.

One day she came into the city and heard him in the court. Pleading for a woman who had almost killed a drunken husband with a skillet by hitting him over the head while he slept. Katherine was amazed to hear how he charmed a jury. That was quite where Deirdre got her voice. "How eloquent you were," she said over lunch.

The small-boy pleasure shone in his face. Who would have thought it?

Moira, that look on his face, it was the first glimmer of a true softness between us. At that moment I began to understand that I had come through the year untouched by the best of what they had to offer. Peter had been wrenched to the roots of his soul, and I had come alive and yet never given back a thing. Sarah said I was the messenger. One little tender thing I said to Peter and his whole hungry heart rose to the surface for more.

When the baby was three months old, Peter sat one evening watching her nurse. "What are you looking at?"

"What splendid breasts you have. It makes me jealous, his suckling at them like that."

"The child sucking makes me quite hot. Is it sinful, do you suppose?"

They gave the baby over to the nurse. He closed the bedroom door. She waited for him. He lay beside her on the bed. She hadn't the patience for watching, she undid his shirt. *I suppose I was beginning to look at Peter as a lover. To see his body from a new perspective. Fancy, married to a man all those years, a man who was still in many ways a stranger. When* he made love to her, Martin was in his hands. *My dear Martin . . .* But that didn't seem to worry her this time. *Life has such a funny way about it.* She fell into a different rhythm, a new rhythm. He was a powerful man, she took that power into her, she didn't find it an adversary now. She used it to her good advantage. His body understood. This communication, it came from the body, it spoke more eloquently than any words. How fond she felt of him suddenly. They were not at war. Finally he came above her, he waited until she reached her full satisfaction, and then he looked down at her in such a way, like a father taking in a child, wanting to eat her up and take her in. She reached down to feel how they were connected. *I suppose that in a way we've always been connected. There are connections and connections.*

When Adam was a year old they began to build their country house. She was glad to get out of city clothes. And Rebecca needed the country life. Rebecca began to sleep well again. Once Katherine went in to her as she was calling out in a dream. Rebecca opened her half-dream eyes. "Croquet," she said.

"Who plays croquet, sweet? The white rabbit?"

She turned back into her pillow and said yes.

Moira, I have got so fond of Peter. I wonder now as Deirdre asked, what the fuss was all about? The Oneidans and their Complex Marriage. How much more complex marriage is outside. The country house is almost finished. Twice we made love in the fields. And how astonished Peter continues to be at my sexual freedom. It was lovely in the open. Brooklyn is such a different world. Peter says they are building a bridge over to New York. I hope it doesn't come to pass. I want Brooklyn as it is forever, a wild country place with bird marshes and splendid rocks. You ask, what of Martin, if he came to my door one afternoon with Peter in the city? And Peter, if he was overtaken with a momentary passion, given the easy way we lived in the Community. Men and women are not monogamous by nature, Father Noyes was right in that way. But marriage is quite another thing. And since you have asked to put it all in your novel, I have tried to sort it out.

Any woman can be happily married to any one of a hundred men. Marriages are not made in heaven. They are hard-wrought. From the goodly number, she chooses one. Someone she can honor. Or someone whose ethic she approves. Or someone whose nose she likes, or whose smile. She fixes on him and she makes her bargain, for that is what marriage is, a domestic arrangement and a pact. That he shall give her heart and body sanctuary and she shall keep him safely through the night. And once accepting that, she does not hold back a dot of her affection. We are all such children after all, needing to be taken in. And so she says to him, you are my heart's desire and he says you are the apple of my eye. And if they have differences and oh, they will have differences, Peter is an argumentative man and I, a stubborn woman, well, what matter? They are no more no less different than any couple. But she opens the floodgates of her affection and he is washed not in the blood of the lamb but in the love of it. And any man surfeited in love, why should he go straying. And then they go on with their work. For a woman must have work, a woman without work is a woman in slavery. Too bad we do not get paid for it. But that will never come around until the Second Coming. Did you know that as well as the country house, I keep a studio in the city? I paint as you write, under a man's name, life being what it is. Sometimes at a showing I stand back and see people staring at my portraits of the naked world. So often shocked and angry. And the effort of it all quite overwhelms me, and I look over the heads of the crowd and I see Pater, he smiles and waves and assures me that he's there, and I think, this man's heart belongs to me and mine to him, not in slavery, as Sarah thought, but two against the world's dark places. This is the marriage bargain. And above all, nothing regretted and no shred of affection held back. For some things one turns the other way and swallows hard. But in the long run, what is this small thing or that when you note the good exchange.

But why am I telling you things you know so well already?